To Aaron Asher and Jason Epstein

MY LIFE AS A MAN

"Simply the best novel I've read in ages . . . the funniest, truest, most horrifying."
　　　　　　　　　—Mary Ellin Barrett, *Cosmopolitan*

"Funnier and more outrageous . . . than *Portnoy's Complaint.*"
　　　　　　　　　—Joyce Carol Oates

"It burns you as you read . . . A scalding, unique addition to the lasting literature about men and women."
　　　　　　　　　—Seymour Krim, *Newsday*

"Virtuoso writing illumined by Roth's meticulous observation, sardonic humor, and what Alfred Kazin has aptly called his psychological 'toughness.' "
　　　　　　　　　—*John Barkham Reviews*

"A very grand work . . . in invention, in perception . . . in coming to grips with the wild inconsistencies of life and art, in the exposure of the most serious and agonizing matters to outright farce."
　　　　　　　　　—Eliot Fremont-Smith, *New York* Magazine

Bantam Books by Philip Roth
Ask your bookseller for the books you have missed

THE BREAST
GOODBYE, COLUMBUS
THE GREAT AMERICAN NOVEL
LETTING GO
MY LIFE AS A MAN
OUR GANG
PORTNOY'S COMPLAINT
WHEN SHE WAS GOOD

My Life As a Man

Philip Roth

This low-priced Bantam Book
has been completely reset in a type face
designed for easy reading, and was printed
from new plates. It contains the complete
text of the original hard-cover edition.
NOT ONE WORD HAS BEEN OMITTED.

MY LIFE AS A MAN
A Bantam Book

PRINTING HISTORY
Holt, Rinehart and Winston edition published June 1974
2nd printing ..... June 1974
3rd printing ..... June 1974
Bantam edition / June 1975

Portions of this book have appeared, in somewhat different form,
in AMERICAN REVIEW *18*, ESQUIRE, MARRIAGE & DIVORCE, MODERN
OCCASIONS, and THE NEW YORK TIMES.

Published simultaneously in the United States and Canada

Bantam Books are published by Bantam Books, Inc. Its trademark, consisting of the words "Bantam Books" and the por-
trayal of a bantam, is registered in the United States Patent
Office and in other countries. Marca Registrada. Bantam
Books, Inc., 666 Fifth Avenue, New York, New York 10019.

PRINTED IN THE UNITED STATES OF AMERICA

A Note to the Reader

The two stories in part I,
"Useful Fictions," and part II,
the autobiographical narrative
"My True Story," are drawn from
the writings of Peter Tarnopol.

I could be his Muse, if only he'd let me.

—*Maureen Johnson Tarnopol,*
from her diary

I

Useful Fictions

Salad Days

First, foremost, the puppyish, protected upbringing above his father's shoe store in Camden. Seventeen years the adored competitor of that striving, hot-headed shoedog (that's all, he liked to say, a lowly shoedog, but just you wait and see), a man who gave him Dale Carnegie to read so as to temper the boy's arrogance, and his own example to inspire and strengthen it. "Keep up that cockiness with people, Natie, and you'll wind up a hermit, a hated person, the enemy of the world—" Meanwhile, downstairs in his store, Polonius displayed nothing but contempt for any employee whose ambition was less fierce than his own. Mr. Z.—as he was called in the store, and at home by his little son when the youngster was feeling his oats—Mr. Z. expected, *demanded,* that by the end of the workday his salesman and his stock boy should each have as stupendous a headache as he did. That the salesmen, upon quitting, invariably announced that they hated his guts, always came to him as a surprise: he expected a young fellow to be grateful to a boss who relentlessly goaded him to increase his commissions. He couldn't understand why anyone would want less when he could have more, simply, as Mr. Z. put it, "by pushing a little." And if they wouldn't push, he would do it for them: "Don't worry," he admitted proudly, "I'm not proud," meaning by that apparently that he had easy access to his wrath when confronted with another's imperfection.

And that went for his own flesh and blood as well as the hired help. For example, there was the time (and

3

the son would never forget it—in part it may even account for what goaded him to be "a writer"), there was the time the father caught a glimpse of his little Nathan's signature across the face of a booklet the child had prepared for school, and nearly blew their house down. The nine-year-old had been feeling self-important and the signature showed it. And the father knew it. "This is the way they teach you to sign your name, Natie? This is supposed to be the signature that somebody on the other end is supposed to read and have respect for? Who the hell can read something that looks like a train wreck! Goddam it, boy, *this is your name.* Sign it *right!*" The self-important child of the self-important shoedog bawled in his room for hours afterward, all the while strangling his pillow with his bare hands until it was dead. Nonetheless, when he emerged in his pajamas at bedtime, he was holding by its topmost corners a sheet of white paper with the letters of his name, round and legible, engraved in black ink at the center. He handed it over to the tyrant: "Is *this* okay?" and in the next instant was lifted aloft into the heaven of his father's bristly evening stubble. "Ah, now *that's* a signature! *That's* something you can hold your head up about! *This* I'm going to tack up over the counter in the store!" And he did just that, and then led the customers (most of whom were Negroes) all the way around behind the register, where they could get a really close look at the little boy's signature. "What do you think of *that!*" he would ask, as though the name were in fact appended to the Emancipation Proclamation.

And so it went with this bewildering dynamo of a protector. Once when they were out fishing at the seashore, and Nathan's Uncle Philly had seen fit to give his nephew a good shake for being careless with his hook, the shoedog had threatened to throw Philly over the side of the boat and into the bay for laying a hand on the child. "The only one who touches him is me, Philly!" "Yeah, that'll be the day . . ." Philly mumbled. "Touch him again, Philly," his father said savagely,

"and you'll be talking to the bluefish, I promise you!
You'll be talking to *eels!*" But then back at the rooming
house where the Zuckermans were spending their two-
week vacation, Nathan, for the first and only time in
his life, was thrashed with a belt for nearly taking his
uncle's eye out while clowning around with that goddam hook. He was astonished that his father's face, like
his own should be wet with tears when the three-stroke
beating was over, and then—more astonishing—he
found himself crushed in the man's embrace. "An *eye,*
Nathan, a person's *eye*—do you know what it would be
like for a grown man to have to go through life without
eyes?"

No, he didn't; any more than he knew what it would
be like to be a small boy without a father, or wanted to
know, for all that his ass felt on fire.

Twice his father had gone bankrupt in the years
between the wars: Mr. Z.'s men's wear in the late
twenties, Mr. Z.'s kiddies' wear in the early thirties; and
yet never had a child of Z.'s gone without three nourish-
ing meals a day, or without prompt medical attention,
or decent clothes, or a clean bed, or a few pennies "al-
lowance" in his pocket. Businesses crumbled, but never
the household, because never the head of the house.
During those bleak years of scarcity and hardship, little
Nathan hadn't the faintest idea that his family was trembling on the brink of anything but perfect contentment,
so convincing was the confidence of that volcanic father.

And the faith of the mother. *She* certainly didn't act
as though she was married to a businessman who'd been
bankrupt and broke two times over. Why, the husband
had only to sing a few bars of "The Donkey Serenade"
while shaving in the bathroom, for the wife to announce
to the children at the breakfast table, "And I thought
it was the radio. For a moment I actually thought it was
Allan Jones." If he whistled while washing the car,
she praised him over the gifted canaries who whistled
popular songs (popular maybe, said Mr. Z., among
other canaries) on WEAF Sunday mornings; dancing
her across the kitchen linoleum (the waltz spirit often-

times seized him after dinner) he was "another Fred Astaire"; joking for the children at the dinner table he was, at least to her way of thinking, funnier than anyone on "Can You Top This"—certainly funnier than that Senator Ford. And when he parked the Studebaker— it never failed—she would look out at the distance between the wheels and the curbstone, and announce—it never failed—"Perfect!" as though he had set a sputtering airliner down into a cornfield. Needless to say, never to criticize where you could praise was a principle of hers; as it happened, with Mr. Z. for a husband, she couldn't have gotten away with anything else had she tried.

Then the just desserts. About the time Sherman, their older son, was coming out of the navy and young Nathan was entering high school, business suddenly began to boom in the Camden store, and by 1949, the year Zuckerman entered college, a brand new "Mr. Z." shoe store had opened out at the two-million-dollar Country Club Hills Shopping Mall. And then at last the one-family house: ranch style, with a flagstone fireplace, on a one-acre lot—the family dream come true just as the family was falling apart.

Zuckerman's mother, happy as a birthday child, telephoned Nathan at college the day the deed was signed to ask what "color scheme" he wanted for his room.

"Pink," Zuckerman answered, "and white. And a canopy over my bed and a skirt for my vanity table. Mother, what is this 'your room' crap?"

"But—but why did Daddy even buy the house, if not for you to have a real boy's room, a room of your own for you and all your things? This is something you've wanted all your life."

"Gee whiz, could I have pine paneling, Mother?"

"Darling, that's what I'm telling you—you can have *anything*."

"And a college pennant over my bed? And a picture on my dresser of my mom and my girl?"

"Nathan, why are you making fun of me like this? I was so looking forward to this day, and all you have for me when I call with such wonderful news is—sarcasm. College sarcasm!"

"Mother, I'm only trying very gently to break it to you—you just cannot delude yourself into thinking there is something called 'Nathan's room' in your new house. What I wanted at the age of ten for all 'my things,' I don't necessarily want any longer."

"Then," she said weakly, "maybe Daddy shouldn't pay your tuition and send you a check for twenty-five dollars a week, if you're that independent now. Maybe it works both ways, if that's the attitude . . ."

He was not much impressed, either by the threat or the tone in which it was delivered. "If you want," said he in the grave, no-nonsense voice one might adopt to address a child who is not acting his age, "to discontinue paying for my education, that is up to you; that is something you and Dad will have to decide between you."

"Oh darling, what's turned you into this cruel person —you, who were always so so sweet and considerate—?"

"Mother," replied the nineteen-year-old, now a major in English language and literature, "try to be precise. I'm not cruel. Only direct."

Ah, the distance he had traveled from her since that day in 1942 when Nathan Zuckerman had fallen in love with Betty Zuckerman the way men seemed to fall in love with women in the movies—yes, smitten by her, as though she weren't his mother but a famous actress who for some incredible reason happened also to cook his meals and keep his room in order. In her capacity as chairwoman of the war bond drive at his school, she had been invited to the assembly hall that morning to address the entire student body on the importance of saving war stamps. She arrived dressed in the clothes she ordinarily wore only when she and her "girl friends" went in to Philadelphia to see the matinee performance of a stage show: her tailored gray suit and a white silk blouse. To top it off, she delivered her talk (without notes) from back of a lectern luxuriantly draped with red, white, and blue bunting. For the rest of Nathan's life, he was to find himself unduly susceptible to a woman in a gray suit and a white blouse, because of the glamor his slender, respectable, well-mannered mother radiated from the stage that day. Indeed, Mr. Loomis, the principal (who may have been somewhat smitten himself), compared her demeanor as chairwoman of the bond drive and president of the PTA to that of Madame Chiang Kai-shek. And in shyly acknowledging his compliment, Mrs. Zuckerman had conceded from the platform that Madame Chiang was in fact one of her idols. So too, she told the assembled students, were Pearl Buck and Emily Post. True enough. Zuckerman's mother had a deep belief in what she called "graciousness," and a reverence, such as is reserved in India for the cow, toward greeting cards and thank you notes. And while they were in love, so did he.

One of the first big surprises of Zuckerman's life was seeing the way his mother carried on when his brother Sherman entered the navy to serve his two-year hitch in 1945. She might have been some young girl whose fiancé was marching off to die in the front lines, while the fact of the matter was that America had won World War Two in August and Sherman was only a hundred miles away, in boot camp in Maryland. Nathan did everything he could possibly think of to cheer her up: helped with the dishes, offered on Saturdays to carry the groceries home, and talked nonstop, even about a subject that ordinarily embarrassed him, his little girl friends. To his father's consternation he invited his mother to come and look over his shoulder at his hand when "the two men" played gin rummy on Sunday nights at the bridge table set up in the living room. "Play the game," his father would warn him, "concentrate on my discards, Natie, and not on your mother. Your mother can take care of herself, but you're the one who's going to get schneidered again." How could the man be so *heartless?* His mother could *not* take care of herself—*something had to be done.* But what?

It was particularly unsettling to Nathan when "Mamselle" was played over the radio, for against this song his mother simply had no defense whatsoever. Along with "The Old Lamplighter," it had been her favorite number in Sherman's entire repertoire of semiclassical and popular songs, and there was nothing she liked better than to sit in the living room after dinner and listen to him play and sing (at her request) his "interpretation." Somehow she could manage with "The Old Lamplighter," which she had always seemed to love equally well, but now when they began to play "Mamselle" on the radio, she would have to get up and leave the room. Nathan, who was not exactly immune to "Mamselle" himself, would follow after her and listen through the door of her bedroom to the muffled sounds of weeping. It nearly killed him.

Knocking softly, he asked, "Mom . . . you all right? You want anything?"

"No, darling, no."

"Do you want me to read you my book report?"

"No, sweetheart."

"Do you want me to turn off the radio? I'm finished listening, really."

"Let it play, Nathan dear, it'll be over in a minute."

How awful her suffering was—also, how odd. After all, for *him* to miss Sherman was one thing—Sherman happened to be *his only older brother*. As a small boy Nathan's attachment to Sherman had been so pronounced and so obvious that the other kids used to make jokes about it—they used to say that if Sherman Zuckerman ever stopped short, his kid brother's nose would go straight up Sherm's ass. Little Nathan could indeed be seen following behind his older brother to school in the morning, to Hebrew school in the afternoon, and to his Boy Scout meetings at night; and when Sherman's five-piece high-school band used to go off to make music for bar mitzvahs and wedding parties, Nathan would travel with them as "a mascot" and sit up in a chair at the corner of the stage and knock two sticks together during the rumbas. That he should feel bereft of his brother and in their room at night grow teary at the sight of the empty twin bed to his right, that was to be *expected*. But what was his mother carrying on like this about? How could she miss Sherman so, when *he* was still around—and being nicer, really, than ever. Nathan was thirteen by this time and already an honor student at the high school, but for all his intelligence and maturity he could not figure that one out.

When Sherman came home on his first liberty after boot camp, he had with him a ditty bag full of dirty photographs to show to Nathan as they walked together around the old neighborhood; he also had a pea jacket and a sailor cap for his younger brother, and stories to tell about whores who sat on his lap in the bars around Bainbridge and let him stick his hand right up their dresses. *And for nothing.* Whores *fifty* and *sixty* years old. Sherman was eighteen then and wanted to be a jazz musician à la Lenny Tristano; he had already been assigned to Special Services because of his musical talent, and was going to be MCing shows at the base, as well as helping the chief petty officer organize the entertainment program. He was also that rarity in show business, a marvelous *comic* tap dancer, and could give an impression of Bojangles Robinson that would cause his younger brother to double over with laughter. Zuckerman, at thirteen, expected great things from a brother who could do all this. Sherman told him about pro kits and VD films and let him read the mimeographed stories that the sailors circulated among themselves during the nights they stood guard duty. Staggering. It seemed to the adolescent boy that his older brother had found access to a daring and manly life.

And when, upon being discharged, Sherman made directly for New York and found a job playing piano in a bar in Greenwich Village, young Zuckerman was ecstatic; not so, the rest of the family. Sherman told them that his ambition was to play with the Stan Kenton band, and his father, if he had had a gun, would probably have pulled it out and shot him. Nathan, in the meantime, confided to his high-school friends stories about his brother's life "in the Village." They asked (those bumpkins), "What village?" He explained, scornfully; he told them about the San Remo bar on Mac-Dougal Street, which he himself had never seen, but could imagine. Then one night Sherman went to a party after work (*which was four in the morning*) and met June Christie, Kenton's blonde vocalist. June Christie. *That* opened up a fantasy or two in the younger brother's head. Yes, it began to sound as though the possibilities for someone as game and adventurous as Sherman Zuckerman (or Sonny Zachary, as he called himself in the cocktail lounge) were going to be just about endless.

And then Sherman was going to Temple University, taking pre-dent. And then he was married, not to June Christie but to *some girl,* some skinny Jewish girl from Bala-Cynwyd who talked in baby talk and worked as a dental technician somewhere. Nathan couldn't believe it. Say it ain't so, Sherm! He remembered those cantaloupes hanging from the leering women in the dirty pictures Sherman had brought home from the navy, and then he thought of flat-chested Sheila, the dental technician with whom Sherman would now be going to bed every night for the rest of his life, and he couldn't figure the thing out. What had happened to his glamorous brother? "He saw the light, that's what," Mr. Z. explained to relatives and friends, but *particularly* to young Nathan, "he saw the handwriting on the wall and came to his goddam senses."

Seventeen years then of family life and love such as he imagined everyone enjoyed, more or less—and then his four years at Bass College, according to Zuckerman an educational institution distinguished largely for its lovely pastoral setting in a valley in western Vermont. The sense of superiority that his father had hoped to temper in his son with Dale Carnegie's book on winning friends and influencing people flourished in the Vermont countryside like a jungle fungus. The apple-cheeked students in their white buck shoes, the *Bastion* pleading weekly in its editorial column for "more school spirit," the compulsory Wednesday morning chapel sermons with visiting clergy from around the state, and the Monday evening dormitory "bull sessions" with notables like the dean of men—the ivy on the library walls, the dean told the new freshmen boys, could be heard on certain moonlit nights to whisper the word "tradition"—none of this did much to convince Zuckerman that he ought to become more of a pal to his fellow man. On the other hand, it was the pictures in the Bass catalogue of the apple-cheeked boys in white bucks crossing the sunlit New England quadrangle in the company of the apple-cheeked girls in white bucks that had in part drawn Zuckerman to Bass in the first place. To him, and to his parents, beautiful Bass seemed to partake of everything with which the word "collegiate" is so richly resonant for those who have not been beyond the twelfth grade. Moreover, when the family rode up in the spring, his mother found the dean of men—who three years later was to tell Zuckerman that he ought to be driven from the campus with a pitchfork for the so-called parody he had written in his literary magazine about the homecoming queen, a girl who happened to be an orphan from Rutland—this same dean of men, with briar pipe and football shoulders swathed in tweed, had seemed to Mrs. Zuckerman "a perfectly gracious man," and that about sewed things up—that and the fact that there was, according to the dean, "a top-drawer Jewish fraternity" on the campus, as well as a sorority for the college's thirty "outstanding" Jewish girls, or "gals," as the dean called them.

Who knew, who in the Zuckerman family knew, that the very month he was to leave for his freshman year of college, Nathan would read a book called *Of Time and the River* that was to change not only his attitude toward Bass, but toward Life Itself?

After Bass he was drafted. Had he continued into advanced ROTC he would have entered the service as a second lieutenant in the Transportation Corps, but almost alone among the Bass undergraduates, he disapproved of the skills of warfare being taught and practiced at a private educational institution, and so after

two compulsory years of marching around the quadrangle once a week with a rifle on his shoulder, he had
declined an invitation from the colonel in charge to
proceed further with his military training. This decision
had infuriated his father, particularly as there was another war on. Once again, in the cause of democracy,
American young men were leaving this world for
oblivion, this time at a rate of one every sixty minutes,
and twice as many each hour were losing parts of themselves in the snowdrifts and mudfields of Korea. "Are
you crazy, are you *nuts* to turn your back on a deal in
the Transportation Corps that could mean life or death?
You want to get your ass shot off in the infantry, instead? Oh, you are looking for trouble, my son, and
you are going to find it, too! The shit is going to hit the
fan, buddy, and you ain't going to like it one bit! Especially if you are dead!" But nothing the elder Zuckerman could think to shout at him could change his
stubborn son's mind on this matter of principle. With
somewhat less intensity (but no less befuddlement) Mr.
Zuckerman had responded to his son's announcement in
his freshman year that he intended to drop out of the
Jewish fraternity to which he had begun to pledge only
the month before. "Tell me, Nathan, how do you quit
something you don't even belong to yet? How can you be
so goddam superior to something when you don't even
know what it's like to *belong* to the thing yet? Is this
what I've got for a son all of a sudden—a *quitter?*"

"Of some things, yes," was the undergraduate's reply,
spoken in that tone of cool condescension that entered
into his father's nervous system like an iron spike.
Sometimes when his father began to seethe, Zuckerman
would hold the telephone out at arm's distance and just
look at it with a poker face, a tactic he had seen people
resort to, of course, only in the movies and for comic
effect. Having counted to fifty, he would then try again
to address the entrepreneur: "It's beneath my dignity,
yes, that's correct." Or: "No, I am not against things to
be against them, I am against them on matters of principle." "In other words," said—seethed—Mr. Zucker-

man, "you are right, if I'm getting the idea, and the rest of the world is wrong. Is that it, Nathan, you are the new god around here, and the rest of the world can just go to hell!" Coolly, coolly, so coolly that the most sensitive seismograph hooked into their long-distance connection would not have recorded the tiniest quaver in his voice: "Dad, you so broaden the terms of our discussion with a statement like that—" and so on, temperate, logical, eminently "reasonable," just what it took to bring on the volcano in New Jersey.

"Darling," his mother would plead softly into the phone, "did you talk to Sherman? At least did you think to talk this over with him first?"

"Why should I want to talk it over with 'him'?"

"Because he's your brother!" his father reminded him.

"And he loves you," his mother said. "He watched over you like a piece of precious china, darling, you remember that—he brought you that pea jacket that you wore till it was rags you loved it so, oh Nathan, *please,* your father is right, if you won't listen to us, listen to him, because, when he came out of the navy, Sherman went through an independent stage exactly like the one you're going through now. To the T."

"Well, it didn't do him very much good, Mother, did it?"

"WHAT!" Mr. Zuckerman, flabbergasted yet again. "What kind of way is that to talk about your brother, damn it? Who *aren't* you better than—please just tell me one name, for the record book at least. Mahatma Gandhi maybe? Yehudi? Oh, do you need some humility knocked into you! Do you need a good stiff course in Dale Carnegie! Your brother happens to be a practicing orthodontist with a wonderful practice and also *he is your brother.*"

"Dad, brothers can have mixed feelings about one another. I believe you have mixed feelings about your own."

"But the issue is *not* my brothers, the issue is *yours,* don't confuse the issue, which is your KNOW-IT-ALL

ARROGANCE ABOUT LIFE THAT DOESN'T
KNOW A GODDAM THING!"

Then Fort Dix: midnights on the firing range, sit-ups
in the rain, mounds of mashed potatoes and Del Monte
fruit cup for "dinner"—and again, with powdered eggs,
at dawn—and before even four of the eight weeks of
basic infantry training were over, a graduate of Seton
Hall College in his regiment dead of meningitis. Could
his father have been *right? Had* his position on ROTC
been nothing short of insane, given the realities of army
life and the fact of the Korean War? Could he, a summa
cum laude, have made such a ghastly and irreversible
mistake? Oh God, suppose he were to come down now
with spinal meningitis from having to defecate each
morning with a mob of fifty! What a price to pay for
having principles about ROTC! Suppose he were to
contract the disease while scrubbing out the company's
hundred stinking garbage cans—the job that seemed
always to fall to him on his marathon stints of KP.
ROTC (as his father had prophesied) would get on
very nice without him, ROTC would *flourish,* but what
about the man of principle, would he keel over in a
garbage pail, dead before he'd even reached the front
lines?

But like Dilsey (of whom Zuckerman alone knew,
in his platoon of Puerto Ricans), he endured. Basic
training was no small trial, however, particularly coming
as quickly as it did upon that last triumphant year at
Bass, when his only course but one, taken for nine
hours' credit, was the English honors seminar conducted
by Caroline Benson. Along with Bass's two other most
displaced Jews, Zuckerman was the intellectual power-
house of "The Seminar," which assembled every
Wednesday from three in the afternoon until after six
—dusk in the autumn and spring, nightfall in the winter
—on Queen Anne dining chairs pulled around the worn
Oriental rug in the living room of Miss Benson's cozy
house of books and fireplaces. The seven Christian
critics in The Seminar would hardly dare to speak when
the three dark Jews (all refugees from the top-drawer

Jewish fraternity and founders together of Bass's first literary magazine since—ah, how he loved to say it—the end of the nineteenth century), when these three Jews got to shouting and gesticulating at one another over *Sir Gawain and the Green Knight*. A spinster (who, unlike his mother, happened not to look half her age), Caroline Benson had been born, like all her American forebears, over in Manchester, then educated at Wellesley and "in England." As he would learn midway through his college career, "Caroline Benson and her New York Jew" was very much a local tradition, as much a part of Bass as the "hello spirit" the dean of men was so high on, or the football rivalry with the University of Vermont that annually brought the ordinarily respectable campus to a pitch of religious intensity only rarely to be seen in this century beyond the Australian bush. The wittier New Englanders on the faculty spoke of "Caroline's day-vah Jew experience, it always feels like something that's happened to her in a previous semester . . ." Yes, he was, as it turned out, one of a line—and didn't care. Who was Nathan Zuckerman of Camden, New Jersey, to turn his untutored back on the wisdom of a Caroline Benson, educated in England? Why, she had taught him, within the very first hour she had found him in her freshman literature class, to pronounce the *g* in "length"; by Christmas vacation he had learned to aspirate the *h* in "whale"; and before the year was out he had put the word "guy" out of his vocabulary for good. Rather *she* had. Simple to do, too.

"There are no 'guys,' Mr. Zuckerman, in *Pride and Prejudice*."

Well, he was glad to learn that, delighted to, in fact. She could singe him to scarlet with a line like that, delivered in that clipped Vermont way of hers, but vain as he was he took it without so much as a whimper—every criticism and correction, no matter how minute, he took unto himself with the exaltation of a martyred saint.

"I think I should learn to get along better with people," he explained to Miss Benson one day, when she came upon him in the corridor of the literature building

and asked what he was doing wearing a fraternity
pledge pin (wearing it on the chest of the new V-neck
pullover in which his mother said he looked so collegiate). Miss Benson's response to his proposed scheme
for self-improvement was at once so profound and so
simply put that Zuckerman went around for days repeating the simple interrogative sentence to himself;
like *Of Time and the River,* it verified something he had
known in his bones all along, but in which he could
not place his faith until it had been articulated by someone of indisputable moral prestige and purity: "Why,"
Caroline Benson asked the seventeen-year-old boy,
"should you want to learn a thing like that?"

The afternoon in May of his senior year when he
was invited—not Osterwald who had been invited, not
Fischbach, but Zuckerman, the chosen of the Chosen—
to take tea with Caroline Benson in the "English"
garden back of her house, had been, without question,
the most civilized four hours of his life. He had been
directed by Miss Benson to bring along with him the
senior honors paper he had just completed, and there
in a jacket and tie, amid the hundreds of varieties of
flowers, none of whose names he knew (except for the
rose), sipping as little tea as he could politely get away
with (he was unable as yet to dissociate hot tea with
lemon from the childhood sickbed) and munching on
watercress sandwiches (which he had never even heard
of before that afternoon—and wouldn't miss, if he
didn't hear of them again), he read aloud to Miss
Benson his thirty-page paper entitled, "Subdued Hysteria: A Study of the Undercurrent of Agony in Some
Novels of Virginia Woolf." The paper was replete with
all those words that now held such fascination for him,
but which he had hardly, if ever, uttered back in the
living room in Camden: "irony" and "values" and
"fate," "will" and "vision" and "authenticity," and, of
course, "human," for which he had a particular addiction. He had to be cautioned repeatedly in marginal
notes about his relentless use of that word. "Unnecessary," Miss Benson would write. "Redundant." "Man-

nered." Well, maybe unnecessary to her, but not to the
novice himself: human character, human possibility,
human error, human anguish, human tragedy. Suffering
and failure, the theme of so many of the novels that
"moved" him, were "human conditions" about which
he could speak with an astonishing lucidity and even
gravity by the time he was a senior honors student—
astonishing in that he was, after all, someone whose
own sufferings had by and large been confined up till
then to the dentist's chair.

They discussed first the paper, then the future. Miss
Benson expected him after the army to continue his
literary studies at either Oxford or Cambridge. She
thought it would be a good idea for Nathan to spend a
summer bicycling around England to see the great
cathedrals. That sounded all right to him. They did not
embrace at the end of that perfect afternoon, but only
because of Miss Benson's age, position, and character.
Zuckerman had been ready and willing, the urge in him
to embrace and be embraced all but overpowering.

His eight unhappy weeks of basic infantry training
were followed by eight equally unhappy weeks of military police training with a herd of city roughnecks and
southern hillbillies under the equatorial sun at Fort
Benning, Georgia. In Georgia he learned to direct traffic so that it flowed "through the hips" (as the handbook
had it) and to break a man's larynx, if he should
wish to, with a swat of the billy club. Zuckerman was as
alert and attentive at these army schools as he had been
earning his summa cum laude degree from Bass. He
did not like the environment, his comrades, or "the
system," but he did not wish to die in Asia either, and
so applied himself to every detail of his training as if
his life depended upon it—as it would. He did not pretend, as did some of the other college graduates in his
training company, to be offended or amused by the
bayonet drill. One thing to be contemptuous of soldierly
skills while an undergraduate at Bass, another when you
were a member of an army at war. "KILL!" he
screamed, "KILL!" just as "aggressively" as he was in-

structed to, and drove the bayonet deep into the bowels of the sandbag; he would have spat upon the dying dummy too if he had been told that that was standing operating procedure. He knew when to be superior and when not to be—or was beginning at least to find out. "What are you?" Sergeant Vinnie Bono snarled at them from the instructor's platform (a jockey before Korea, Sergeant Bono was reputed to have slain a whole North Korean platoon with nothing but an entrenching tool)—"What are you with your stiff steel pricks, you troopers—pussycats or lions?" "LIONS!" roared Zuckerman, because he did not wish to die in Asia, or anywhere for that matter, ever.

But he would, and, he feared, sooner rather than later. At those Georgia reveille formations, the captain, a difficult man to please, would be giving the troopers their first dressing down of the long day—"I guaran-fuckintee you gentlemen, not one swingin' dick will be leavin' this fiddlefuckin' area to so much as chew on a nanny goat's tittie—" and Zuckerman, ordinarily a cheery, a dynamic morning riser, would suddenly have a vision of himself falling beneath the weight of some drunken redneck in an alley back of a whorehouse in Seoul. He would expertly crack the offending soldier in the larynx, in the groin, on the patella, in all the places where he had crippled the dummy in the drill, but the man facedown in the mud would be Zuckerman, crushed beneath the drunken lawbreaker's brute strength —and then from nowhere, his end would come, by way of the knife or the razor blade. Schools and dummies were one thing—the world and the flesh something else: How would Zuckerman find the wherewithal to crack his club against a real human patella, when he had never been able to do so much as punch somebody's face with his fist in a schoolyard fight? And yet he had his father's short fuse, didn't he? And the seething self-righteousness to go with it. Nor was he wholly without physical courage. After all, as a boy he had never been much more than skin and bones beneath his shoulder pads and helmet, and yet in the sandlot football games he played in weekly every fall, he had not flinched or cried aloud when the stampede had come sweeping around his end of the line; he was fast, he was shifty—"wiry" was the word with which he preferred to describe himself at that time, "Wiry Nate Zuckerman" —and he was "smart," and could fake and twist and fight his way through a pack of thirteen-year-old boys built like hippos, for all that he was a boy built like a giraffe. He had in fact been pretty fearless on the football field, *so long as everybody played according to the rules and within the spirit of the game.* But when (to his surprise) that era of good fellowship came to an end, Wiry Nate Zuckerman retired. To be smashed to the ground because he was the left end streaking for the goal line with the ball had always been all right with him; indeed he rather liked the precarious drama of plucking a spiral from the air one moment, and then in the next, tasting dirt, as the pounds piled up above him. However, on a Saturday morning in the fall of 1947, when one of the Irish kids on the Mount Holly Hurricanes came flying onto the pileup (at the bottom of which lay Zuckerman, with the ball) screaming, "Cream that Yid!" he knew that his football career was over. Henceforth football was no longer to be a game played by the rules, but a battle in which each of the combatants would try to get away with as much as he could, for whatever "reasons" he had. And Zuckerman could get away with nothing—he could not even hit back when attacked. He could use what strength he had to try to restrain somebody else from going at him, he would struggle like hell to prevent damage or disfigurement to himself, but when it came to bringing his own knuckles or knees into violent contact with another, he just could not make it happen. Had never been up to it on the neighborhood playground, would be paralyzed for sure on the mainland of Asia. An attentive and highly motivated student, he had earned the esteem of a trained killer for the manner in which he disemboweled the sandbag in basic training—"That's it, Slim," Sergeant Bono would megaphone down to his favorite college graduate, "that's grabbin' that gook by his gizzard, that's cuttin' off the Commie bastard's cock!"—but face to face with a real live enemy, he might just as well be carrying a parasol and wearing a bustle for all the good his training as a warrior was going to do himself or the Free World.

So, it looked as though he would not be taking that prilgrimage to Canterbury Cathedral after all, nor would he get to see the Poets' Corner in Westminster Abbey, or the churches where John Donne had preached, or the Lake District, or Bath, the setting of *Persuasion* (Miss Benson's favorite novel), or the Abbey Theatre, or the River Liffey, nor would he live to be a professor of literature some day, with a D. Litt. from Oxford or Cambridge and a house of his own cozy with fireplaces and walled with books; he would never see Miss Benson again, or her garden, or those fortunate 4Fs, Fischbach and Osterwald—and worse, no one, ever again, would see him.

It was enough to make him cry; so he did, invariably after being heroically lighthearted on the telephone with his worried mother and father in New Jersey. Yes, outside the phone booth, within hearing distance of the PX jukebox—"Oh, the red we want is the red we got in th' old red, white, and blue"—he would find himself at the age of twenty-one as tearful and panic-stricken as he had been at four when he had finally had to learn to sleep with all the lights off in his room. And no less desperate for his mommy's arms and the feel of his daddy's unshaven cheek.

Telephoning Sharon, being brave with her, would also reduce him to tears afterward. He could hold up all right during the conversations, while *she* cried, but when it came time to give up the phone to the soldier standing next in the line, when he left the phone booth where he had been so good at cheering her up and started back through the dark across that alien post— "Yes, the red we want is the red we got in th' old red, white, and blue"—he had all he could do not to scream out against the horrible injustice of his impending doom. No more Sharon. *No more Sharon!* NO MORE SHARON! What proportions the loss of Sharon Shatzky assumed in young Zuckerman's mind. And who was she? Who was Sharon Shatzky that the thought of leaving her forever would cause him to clap a hand over his mouth to prevent himself from howling at the moon?

Sharon was the seventeen-year-old daughter of Al "the Zipper King" Shatzky. With her family she had recently moved into Country Club Hills, the development of expensive ranch-type houses where his own parents now lived, on the outskirts of Camden, in a landscape as flat and treeless as the Dakota badlands. Zuckerman had met her in the four weeks between his graduation from Bass and his induction into the army in July. Before their meeting his mother had described Sharon as "a perfect little lady," and his father had said she was "a lovely lovely child," with the result that Zuckerman was not at all prepared for the rangy Amazon, red-headed and green-eyed, who arrived in short shorts that night, trailing sullenly behind Al and Minna. All four parents present fell over themselves treating her like a baby, as though that might convince the college graduate to keep his eyes from the powerful curve of haunch beneath the girl's skimpy summer outfit. Mrs. Shatzky had just that day taken Sharon shopping in Philadelphia for her "college wardrobe." "Mother, *please*," Sharon said, when Minna began to describe how "adorable" Sharon looked in each of her new outfits. Al said (proudly) that Sharon Shatzky here now owned more pairs of shoes than he owned undershorts. *"Daddy,"* moaned Sharon, closing her jungle eyes in exasperation. Zuckerman's father said that if Sharon had any questions about college life she should ask his son, who had been editor up at Bass of "the school paper." It had been the literary magazine that Zuckerman had edited, but he was by now accustomed to the inaccuracies that accompanied his parents' public celebration of his achievements. Indeed, of late, his tolerance for their failings was growing by leaps and

bounds. Where only the year before he might have
been incensed by some line of his mother's that he
knew came straight out of *McCall's* (or by the fact that
she did not know what an "objective correlative" was
or in what century Dryden had lived), now he was
hardly perturbed. He had also given up trying to edu-
cate his father about the ins and outs of the syllogism;
to be sure, the man simply could not get it through his
head that an argument in which the middle term was
not distributed at least once was invalid—but what
difference did that make to Zuckerman any more? He
could afford to be generous to parents who loved him
the way they did (illogical and uneducated though they
were). Besides, if the truth be known, in the past four
years he had become more Miss Benson's student than
their offspring . . . So he was kind and charitable to
all that night, albeit "amused" by much of what he saw
and heard; he answered the Shatzkys' questions about
"college life" without a trace of sarcasm or snobbishness
(none, at any rate, that he could hear), and all the
while (without success) tried to keep his eyes from
their daughter's perky breasts beneath her shrunken
polo shirt, and the tempting cage of her torso rising from
that slender, mobile waist, and the panthery way she
moved across the wall-to-wall carpet on the balls of
her bare feet . . . After all: what business did a student of English letters who had taken tea and watercress sandwiches only a few weeks earlier in the garden
of Caroline Benson have with the pampered middle-
class daughter of Al "the Zipper King" Shatzky?

By the time Zuckerman was about to graduate (third
in his class, same rank as at Bass) from MP school,
Sharon was a freshman at Juliana Junior College, near
Providence. Every night she wrote him scandalous letters on the monogrammed pink stationery with the
scalloped edges that Zuckerman's mother had given the
perfect young lady for a going-away present: "dearest
dearest all i could think about while playing tennis in
gym class was getting down on my hands and knees
and crawling across the room toward your prick and

then pressing your prick against my face i love it with your prick in my face just pressing your prick against my cheeks my lips my tongue my nose my eyes my ears wrapping your gorgeous prick in my hair—" and so on. The word, which (among others) he had taught her and encouraged her to use during the sex act and also, for titillation's sake, on the phone and through the mails— had a strong hold over the young girl locked up in the dormitory room in Rhode Island: "every time the ball came over the net," wrote Sharon, "i saw your wonderful prick on top of it." This last, of course, he didn't believe. If Sharon had a fault as a student of carnality, it was a tendency to try a little too hard, with the result that her prose (to which Zuckerman, trained by Miss Benson in her brand of the New Criticism, was particularly attuned) often offended him by a too facile hyperbole. Instead of acting upon him as an aphrodisiac, her style frequently jarred him by its banal insistence, reminding him less of Lawrence than of those mimeographed stories his brother used to smuggle home to him from the navy. In particular her use of "cunt" (modified by "hot") and "prick" (modified by "big" or "gorgeous" or both) could be as mannered and incantatory, in a word, as sentimental, as his own use, or misuse, in college of the adjective "human." Nor was he pleased by her refusal to abide by the simple rules of grammar; the absence of punctuation and capitalization in her obscene letters was not exactly an original gesture of defiance (or an interesting one either, to Zuckerman's mind, whether the iconoclast was Shatzky or cummings), and as a device to communicate the unbridled flow of passion, it seemed to him, a votary not only of *Mrs. Dalloway* and *To the Lighthouse*, but also of *Madame Bovary* and *The Ambassadors* (he really could not read Thomas Wolfe any more), to have been conceived at a rather primitive level of imagination.

However, as for the passion itself, he had no criticism to make.

Practically overnight (correction: overnight), the virgin whose blood had stained his thighs and matted his pubic hair when he had laid her on a blanket in the back seat of his father's new Cadillac, had developed into the most licentious creature he'd ever known. Nobody like Sharon had been in attendance at Bass, at least nobody he had ever undressed, and he had traveled with the college's half dozen bohemians. Even Barbara Cudney, leading lady of the Bass Drama Society and Zuckerman's companion during his final year of success and celebrity at college, a girl who had thrown herself all over the stage in *Medea* and was now studying at the Yale Drama School, had nothing like Sharon's sensual adventurousness or theatricality, nor had it ever occurred to Zuckerman to ask of Barbara, free and uninhibited spirit that she was, such favors as Sharon virtually begged to bestow upon him. Actually the teacher was not so far out in front of his pupil as he led her to think he was, though of course his surprise at her willingness to satisfy his every whim and farfetched desire was something he kept to himself. In the beginning it exceeded all understanding, this bestiality he had awakened in her simply by penetration, and recalled to mind those other startling and baffling metamorphoses he had witnessed—his mother's transformation into the Maiden Bereft when Sherman left home for the navy, and the descent of Sherman himself from glamor boy to orthodontist. With Sharon, he had only to *allude* to some sexual antic or other, give the slightest *hint* of an interest—for *he* was not without inhibitions —for her to fall into the appropriate posture or turn up with the necessary equipment. "Tell me what you want me to say, Nathan, tell me what you want me to do—" As Zuckerman was a highly imaginative boy, and Sharon so anxious to please, there was, that June, very nearly something new and exciting to do every night.

The sense of adventure that surrounded their lovemaking (if such is the term that applies here) was heightened further by the presence often of the four parents in some other part of the house, or out on the back terrace, drinking iced tea and gabbing. While buggering Sharon on the floor beneath the ping-pong table in the basement of her parents' house, Zuckerman would call out from time to time, "Nice shot," or "Nice return, Sharon"—even as the feverish young girl whispered up from the canine position, "Oh it's so strange. It hurts, but it doesn't hurt. Oh Nathan, it's *so strange*."

Very spicy stuff; more reckless than made him comfortable (Al Shatzky hadn't risen to the top of the zipper industry by being a gentle or forgiving fellow), but irresistible. At the suggestion of the adults, they would go off to the kitchen late at night and there like good little children eat oversized syrup-covered portions of ice cream out of soup bowls. Out on the terrace the adults would laugh about the appetite on those two kids—yes, those were his father's very words—while beneath the table where they sat, Zuckerman would be bringing Sharon to orgasm with his big toe.

Best of all were "the shows." For Zuckerman's pleasure and at his instigation, Sharon would stand in the bathroom with the door open and the overhead light on, performing for him as though she were on a stage, while he would be seated in the dark living room at the other end of the corridor, seemingly looking in the direction of the television set. A "show" consisted of Sharon unfastening her clothes (very slowly, deftly, very much the teasing pro) and then, with the little underthings at her feet, introducing various objects into herself. Transfixed (by the Phillies game, it would appear), Zuckerman would stare down the hallway at the nude girl writhing, just as he had directed her to, upon the plastic handle of her hairbrush, or her vaginal jelly applicator, or once, upon a zucchini purchased for that purpose earlier in the day. The sight of that long green gourd (uncooked, of course) entering into and emerging from her body, the sight of the Zipper King's daughter sitting on the edge of the bathtub with her legs flung apart, wantonly surrendering all five feet nine inches of herself to a vegetable, was as mysterious and compelling a vision as any Zuckerman had ever seen in his (admittedly) secular life. Almost as stirring as when she crawled to him across the length of her parents' living room that night, her eyes leveled on his exposed member and her tongue out and moving. "I want to be your whore," she whispered to him (without prompting too), while on the back terrace her mother told his mother how adorable Sharon looked in the winter coat they'd bought for her that afternoon.

It was not, it turned out, a complicated sort of rebellion Sharon was engaged in, but then she wasn't a complicated girl. If her behavior continued to exceed understanding it was now because it seemed so pathetically *transparent*. Sharon hated her father. One reason she hated him—so she said—was because of that ugly name of theirs *which he refused to do anything about.* Years and years ago, when she was still an infant in the crib, all five brothers on the Shatzky side had gotten together to decide to change the family name, "for business reasons." They had decided on Shadley. Only her father, of the five, refused to make the improvement. "I ain't ashamed," he told the other four—and went on from there, he informed his daughter, to become the biggest success of them all. As if, Sharon protested to Zuckerman, that proved anything! What about the sheer *ugliness* of that *name?* What about the way it *sounded* to people? Especially for a girl! Her cousin Cindy was Cindy Shadley, her cousin Ruthie was Ruthie Shadley —she alone of the girls in the family was still Shatzky! "Come on, will you please—I'm a trademark," her father told her, "I'm known nationwide. What am I supposed to become all of a sudden, Al 'the Zipper King' *Shadley*? Who's *he,* honey?" Well, the truth was that by the time she was fifteen she couldn't bear that he called himself "the Zipper King" either. "The Zipper King" was as awful as Shatzky—in ways it was worse. She wanted a father with a name that wasn't either a joke or an outright lie; she wanted *a real name;* and she warned him, some day when she was old enough, she would hire a lawyer and go down to the county courthouse and get one. "You'll get one, all right —and you know how? The way all the other nice girls do. You'll get married, and why I'll cry at the wedding

is out of happiness that I won't have to hear any more
of this *name* business—" and so on, in this vein, for
five tedious years of Sharon's adolescence. Which wasn't
quite over yet. "What is Shatzky," she cried sorrowfully
to Zuckerman, "but the past tense of Shitzky? Oh why
won't he change it! How stubborn can a person *be!*"

In her denunciations of the family name, Sharon was
as witty as she would ever be—not that the wit was intentional. The truth was that when she was not putting
on a three-ring circus for him, Sharon was pretty much
of a bore to Zuckerman. She didn't know anything about
anything. She did not pronounce the *g* in "length," nor
did she aspirate the *h* in "when" or "why," nor would
she have in "whale" had the conversation ever turned to
Melville. And she had *the* most Cockney Philadelphia *o*
he had ever heard on anyone other than a cabdriver. If
and when she did get a joke of his, she would sigh and
roll her eyes toward heaven, as though his subtleties
were on a par with her father's—Zuckerman, who had
been the H. L. Mencken of Bass College! whose edito-
rials (on the shortcomings of the administration and the
student body) Miss Benson had likened in their savage
wit to Jonathan Swift! How could he ever take Sharon
up to Bass with him to visit Miss Benson? What if she
started telling Miss Benson those pointless and intermi-
nable anecdotes about herself and her high-school
friends? Oh, when she started talking, she could bury
you in boredom! Rarely in conversation did Sharon finish a sentence, but rather, to Zuckerman's digust, glued
her words together by a gummy mixture of "you knows"
and "I means," and with such expressions of enthusiasm
as "really great," "really terrific," and "really neat" . . .
the last usually to describe the gang of kids she had
traveled with at Atlantic City when she was fifteen,
which, to be sure, had only been the summer before last.

Coarse, childish, ignorant, utterly lacking in that ex-
quisiteness of feeling and refinement of spirit that he had
come to admire so in the novels—in the person—of
Virginia Woolf, whose photograph had been tacked
above his desk during his last semester at Bass. He en-

tered the army after their feverish, daredevil month together secretly relieved at having left behind him
(seemingly as he had found her) Al and Minna's five-
foot nine-inch baby girl; she was a tantalizing slave and
an extraordinary lay, but hardly a soul mate for someone who felt as he did about great writers and great
books. Or so it seemed, until that day they issued him
his M1 rifle, and he found he needed everyone he had.

"I love your prick," the girl wept into the phone. "I
miss your prick *so much*. Oh, Nathan, I'm touching my
cunt, I'm touching my cunt and making believe it's you.
Oh, Nathan, should I make myself come on the phone?
Nathan—?"

In tears, in terror, he went reeling from the phone
booth: think of it, both he and his genitals would shortly
be extinct! Oh what if just the genitals went, and *he*
lived on—suppose a land mine were to explode beneath his boots, and he was returned to a girl like
Sharon Shatzky, a blank between the legs. "No!" he told
himself. "Stop having such thoughts! Lay off! Use your
brains! That is only irrational guilt over Sharon and the
zucchini—it is only fear of punishment for buggering the
daughter right under the father's nose! Casebook fantasies of retribution! *No such thing can happen!*" To
him, was what he meant, because of course in warfare
such things do happen, they happen every day.

And then, after the eight weeks of infantry training
followed by eight more at MP school, he was assigned as
a clerk-typist to a quartermaster unit at Fort Campbell,
in the southwestern corner of Kentucky, sixty miles east
of Paducah, eight thousand east of the land mines. Lucky
Zuckerman! Beneficiary of one of those administrative
errors by which doomed men are suddenly pardoned,
and the happy-go-lucky are, overnight, earmarked for
death. These things also happen every day.

Zuckerman could type only with his index fingers,
and he knew nothing about filing or making out forms,
but fortunately for him, the captain in charge of the
supply room to which he was assigned was so pleased
to have a Jew around to bait—and that too has been

known to happen—that he was willing to make do with an inept assistant. He did not—as the inept assistant continuously feared he would—report the error in classification that had sent Zuckerman to Fort Campbell instead of to his bloody demise in the mud behind a brothel in Seoul, nor did he request a replacement for him from personnel. Instead, each afternoon before departing for the links over by the air base, Captain Clark would tune up for his game by driving cotton golf balls out of his office in the direction of the cubicle occupied by the clerk-typist manqué. Zuckerman did his best to look unperturbed when the golf balls glanced off his shirt. "On target, sir," said he with a smile. "Not kwat," replied his superior, all concentration, "not kwat . . ." and would continue to swat them out through the open door of his office until at last he'd found the mark. "Ah, they we go, Zuckuhmun, rat on the nose."

Sadistic bully! Southern bigot! Zuckerman left the supply room at the end of each day bound for the office of the adjutant general, where he intended to bring charges against Captain Clark (who, for all he knew, held secret membership in the KKK). But since actually Zuckerman was not even supposed to *be* in Kentucky, but had been allocated for destruction in Korea (and might wind up there yet, if he gave Clark any trouble), he invariably saw fit to suppress his indignation and proceed on over to the mess hall for dinner, and then on to the post library, to continue to read his way through the Bloomsbury group, with time out every hour or so for another look at the day's bawdy letter from the teen-age debauchee he hadn't been able to bring himself to relinquish quite yet. But, oh Christ, was he mad! His human dignity! His human rights! His *religion!* Oh, each time a golf ball caromed softly off his flesh, how he seethed with indignation . . . which isn't, however (as Private Zuckerman well knew), the same as running with blood. Nor is it what is meant in literature, or even in life for that matter, by suffering or pain.

Though pain would come to Zuckerman in time—in the form of estrangement, mortification, fierce and unremitting opposition, antagonists who were not respectable deans or loving fathers or dim-witted officers in the Army Quartermaster Corps; oh yes, pain would enter his life soon enough, and not entirely without invitation. As the loving father had warned him, looking for trouble, he would find it—and what a surprise that would be. For in severity and duration, in sheer *painfulness,* it would be like nothing he had known at home, in school, or in the service, nor would it be like anything he had imagined while contemplating the harrowed, soulful face of Virginia Woolf, or while writing his A + honors paper on the undercurrent of agony in her novels. Only a short time after having been shipped by providential error—his last big dose, as it turned out, of beginner's luck—to the rural American southland instead of the Korean slaughter, adversity was to catch up with the young conquistador. He would begin to pay . . . for the vanity and the ignorance, to be sure, but above all for the contradictions: the stinging tongue and the tender hide, the spiritual aspirations and the lewd disires, the softly boyish needs and the manly, the *magisterial* ambitions. Yes, over the next decade of his life he was to learn all that his father might have wished Dale Carnegie to teach him about humility, and then some. And then some more.

But that is another story, and one whose luridness makes the small-time southern Jew-baiter lofting cotton golf balls toward his nose, makes even seventeen-year-old Sharon Shatzky, performing for him on a gourd like a Pigalle whore at an exhibition, seem as much a part of his idyllic and innocent youth as that afternoon he once spent sipping tea and eating watercress in Caroline Benson's garden. The story of Zuckerman's suffering calls for an approach far more *serious* than that which seems appropriate to the tale of his easeful salad days. To narrate with fidelity the misfortunes of Zuckerman's twenties would require deeper dredging, a darker sense of irony, a grave and pensive voice to replace the amused, Olympian point of view . . . or maybe what that story requires is neither gravity nor complexity, but just another author, someone who would see it too for the simple five-thousand-word comedy that it very well may have been. Unfortunately, the author of this story, having himself experienced a similar misfortune at about the same age, does not have it in him, even yet, midway through his thirties, to tell it briefly or to find it funny. "Unfortunate" because he wonders if that isn't more the measure of the man than of the misfortune.

Courting Disaster
(or, Serious in the Fifties)

No, I did not marry for conventional reasons; no one can accuse me of that. It was not for fear of loneliness that I chose my wife, or to have "a helpmate," or a cook, or a companion in my old age, and it certainly was not out of lust. No matter what they may say about me now, sexual desire had nothing to do with it. To the contrary: though she was a pretty enough woman—square, strong Nordic head; resolute blue eyes that I thought of admiringly as "wintry"; straight wheat-colored hair worn in bangs; a handsome smile; an appealing, openhearted laugh—her short, heavy-legged body struck me as very nearly dwarfish in its proportions and was, from first to last, unremittingly distasteful. Her gait in particular displeased me: mannish, awkward, it took on a kind of rolling quality when she tried to move quickly, and in my mind associated with images of cowhands and merchant seamen. Watching her run to meet me on some Chicago street—after we had become lovers—I would positively recoil, even at a distance, at the prospect of holding that body against me, at the idea that voluntarily I had made her *mine*.

Lydia Ketterer was a divorced woman, five years my senior, and mother of a ten-year-old girl who lived with Lydia's former husband and his second wife in a new suburban housing development south of Chicago. During their marriage, whenever Lydia dared to criticize or question her husband's judgment he would lift her from the floor—a massive man twice her weight and a foot taller—and heave her against the nearest wall; in the months following the divorce he abused her through her child, who was then six and in Lydia's custody; and when Lydia broke down, Ketterer took the child to live with him, and subsequently, after Lydia had been released from the hospital and was back in her apartment, refused to return the little girl.

He was the second man nearly to destroy her; the first, Lydia's father, had seduced her when she was twelve. The mother had been bedridden since Lydia's birth, a victim it would seem of nothing more than lumbago, but perpetually weak unto dying. After the father fled, Lydia had been taken to be raised in the home of two spinster aunts in Skokie; until she ran off with Ketterer at the age of eighteen, she and her mother shared a room at the rear of this haven whose heroes were the aviator Lindbergh, the senator Bilbo, the cleric Coughlin, and the patriot Gerald L. K. Smith. It had been a life of little but punishment, humiliation, betrayal, and defeat, and it was to this that I was drawn, against all my misgivings.

Of course, the contrast to my own background of familial devotion and solidarity was overwhelming: whereas Lydia remembered a thousand and one nights of rubbing Sloan's liniment into her mother's back, I could not remember a single hour of my childhood when my mother was incapable of performing the rites of her office. If indeed she ever had been indisposed, it seemed not even to interfere with her famous whistling, that continuous medley of "show tunes" she chirped melodiously away at through her day of housework and family chores. The sickly one in our home was me: suffocating diphtheria, subsequent annual respiratory infections, debilitating glandular fevers, mysterious visitations of "allergies." Until puberty, I spent as much time at home in my bed or under a blanket on a sofa in the living room as I did in my seat in the classroom, all of which makes the disposition of my mother, the whistler—"Mrs. Zuckerbird" the postman called her—even more impressive. My father, though not so sunny in his indestructibility, and constitutionally a much more solemn person than my peppy peasant of a mother, was no less equal to the hardships our family endured; specifically, the Depression, my ailments, and my older sister Sonia's inexplicable marriages, *twice* to the sons of Sicilians: the first an embezzler and in the end a suicide; the second, honest in his business but otherwise "common as dirt"—in the Yiddish word, which alone seemed to carry the weight of our heartbreak and contempt, *prust*.

We ourselves were not elegant, but surely we were not coarse. Dignity, I was to understand, had nothing to do with one's social station: character, conduct, was everything. My mother used to laugh and make cracks about the ladies around who had secret dreams of mink coats and Miami Beach vacations. "To her," she would say disparagingly of some silly neighbor, "the be-all and end-all is to put on a silver fox and go gallivanting with the hoi polloi." Not until I got to college and misused the word myself did I learn that what my mother took to mean the elite—perhaps because "hoi polloi" sounded like another of her disdainful expressions for people who put on airs, "the hoity-toity"—actually referred to the masses.

So much for the class struggle as a burning issue in my house, or social resentment or ambitiousness as a motive for action. A strong character, not a big bankroll, was to them the evidence of one's worth. Good, sensible people. Why their two offspring should have wasted themselves as they did, why both children should have wed themselves to disaster, is difficult to understand. That my sister's first husband and my only wife should both have taken their own lives would seem to suggest something about our common upbringing. But what? I have no theories. If ever a mother and father were not responsible for the foolishness of their children, it was mine.

My father was a bookkeeper. Because of his excellent memory and his quickness with figures, he was considered the local savant in our neighborhood of hardworking first-generation Jews and was the man most frequently consulted by people in trouble. A thin, austere, and humorless person, always meticulous in a white shirt and a tie, he communicated his love for me in a precise, colorless fashion that makes me ache with tenderness for him, especially now that he is the bed-ridden one, and I live in self-exile thousands of miles from his bed.

When *I* was the sickly, feverish patient, I felt something more like mystification, as though he were a kind of talking electrical toy come to play with me promptly each evening at six. His idea of amusing me was to teach me to solve the sort of arithmetical puzzles at which he himself was a whiz. " 'Marking Down,' " he would say, not unlike a recitation student announcing the title of a poem. "A clothing dealer, trying to dispose of an overcoat cut in last year's style, marked it down from its original price of thirty dollars to twenty-four. Failing to make a sale, he reduced the price still further to nineteen dollars and twenty cents. Again he found no takers, so he tried another price reduction and this time sold it." Here he would pause; if I wished I might ask him to repeat any or all of the details. If not, he proceeded. "All right, Nathan; what was the selling price, if the last markdown was consistent with the others?" Or: " 'Making a Chain.' A lumberjack has six sections of chain, each consisting of four links. If the cost of cutting open a link—" and so on. The next day, while my mother whistled Gershwin and laundered my father's shirts, I would daydream in my bed about the clothing dealer and the lumberjack. To whom had the haberdasher finally sold the overcoat? Did the man who bought it realize it was cut in last year's style? If he wore it to a restaurant, would people laugh? And what did "last year's style" look like anyway? " 'Again he found no takers,' " I would say aloud, finding much to feel melancholy about in that idea. I still remember how charged for me was that word "takers." Could it have been the lumberjack with the six sections of chain who, in his rustic innocence, had bought the overcoat cut in last year's style? And why suddenly did he need an overcoat? Invited to a fancy ball? By whom? My mother thought the questions I raised about these puzzles were "cute" and was glad they gave me something to think about when she was occupied with housework and could not take the time to play go fish or checkers; my father, on the other hand, was disheartened to find me intrigued by fantastic and irrelevant details of geography and personality and intention instead of the simple beauty of the arithmetical solution. He did not think that was intelligent of me, and he was right.

I have no nostalgia for that childhood of illness, none at all. In early adolescence, I underwent daily school-yard humiliation (at the time, it seemed to me there could be none worse) because of my physical timidity and hopelessness at all sports. Also, I was continually enraged by the attention my parents insisted upon paying to my health, even after I had emerged, at the age of sixteen, into a beefy, broad-shouldered boy who, to compensate for his uncoordinated, ludicrous performances in right field or on the foul line, took to shooting craps in the fetid washroom of the corner candy store and rode out on Saturday nights in a car full of "smoking wise guys"—my father's phrase—to search in vain for that whorehouse that was rumored to be located somewhere in the state of New Jersey. The dread *I* felt was of course even greater than my parents': surely I would awaken one morning with a murmuring heart, or gasping for air, or with one of my fevers of a hundred and four . . . These fears caused my assault upon them to be particularly heartless, even for a teenager, and left them dazed and frightened of me for years thereafter. Had my worst enemy said, "I hope you die, Zuckerman," I could not have been any more provoked than I was when my well-meaning father asked if I had remembered to take my vitamin capsule, or when my mother, to see if a cold had made me feverish, did so under the guise of giving my forehead a lingering kiss at the dinner table. How all that tenderness enraged me! I remember that it was actually a relief to me when my sister's first husband got caught with his fist in the till of his uncle's heating-oil firm, and Sonia became the focus of their concern. And of my concern. She would sometimes come back to the house to cry on my seventeen-year-old shoulder, after having been to visit Billy in jail where he was serving a year and a day; and how good it felt, how uplifting it was, not to be on the receiving end of the solicitude, as was the case when Sonia and I were children and she would entertain the little shut-in by the hour, and without complaint.

A few years later, when I was away at Rutgers, Billy did my parents the favor of hanging himself by a cord from the drapery rod in their bedroom. I doubt that he expected it would hold him; knowing Billy, I guess he wanted the rod to give under his weight so that he might be found, still breathing, in a heap on the floor when my parents came back from their shopping. The sight of a son-in-law with a sprained ankle and a rope around his neck was supposed to move my father to volunteer to pay Billy's five-thousand-dollar debt to his bookie. But the rod turned out to be stronger than Billy had thought, and he was strangled to death. Good riddance, one would think. But no; the next year Sunny married (in my father's phrase) "another one." Same wavy black hair, same "manly" cleft in his chin, same repellent background. Johnny's weakness was not horses but hookers. The marriage has flourished, nonetheless. Each time my brother-in-law gets caught, he falls to his knees and begs Sunny's forgiveness; this gesture seems to go a long way with my sister —not so with our father: "Kisses her shoes," he would say, closing his eyes in disgust; "actually kisses *shoes,* as though that were a sign of love, of respect—of anything!" There are four handsome wavy-haired children, or were when last I saw them all in 1962: Donna, Louis, John Jr., and Marie (that name the unkindest cut of all). John Sr. builds swimming pools and brings in enough each week to be able to spend a hundred dollars on a New York call girl without feeling a thing, financially speaking. When last I saw it, their summer house in the Italian Catskills had even more pink "harem" pillows in the living room than the one in Scotch Plains,

and an even grander pepper mill; in both "homes," the
silver, the linens, and the towels are monogrammed
SZR, my sister's initials.

How come? I used to be plagued by that question.
How could it be that the sister of mine who had re-
hearsed for hours on end in our living room, over and
over again singing to me the songs from *Song of Norway* and *The Student Prince* until I wished I were Nor-
wegian or nobility; the sister who took "voice" from Dr.
Bresslenstein in his studio in North Philadelphia and at
fifteen was already singing "Because" for money at weddings; a sister who had the voluptuous, haughty airs of
a prima donna when the other little girls were still
fretting over boys and acne—how could *she* wind up
in a house with a harem "motif," mothering children
taught by nuns, and playing "Jerry Vale Sings Italian
Hits" on the stereo to entertain our silent parents when
they come for a Sunday visit? *How? Why?*

I used to wonder, when Sonia married for the second
time, if perhaps she were involved in a secret and
mysterious religious rite: if she had not deliberately set
out to mortify herself, so as to sound to the depths her
spiritual being. I would imagine her in bed at night
(yes, in bed), her pretty-boy slob of a husband asleep
beside her, and Sonia exultant in the dark with the
knowledge that unbeknownst to everyone—everyone
being the bewildered parents and incredulous college-
boy brother—she continued to be the very same person
who used to enchant us from the stage of the Y with
what Bresslenstein (a poor refugee from Palestine, but
according to himself formerly the famous impresario of
Munich) described to my mother as "a beautiful beautiful coloratura quality—the beginnings of another Lily
Pons." I could imagine her one evening at dinnertime
knocking on the back door to our apartment, her black
hair to her shoulders again, and wearing the same long
embroidered dress in which she had appeared in *The
Student Prince*—my graceful and vivacious sister, whose
appearance on a stage would cause tears of pride to
spring to my eyes, our Lily Pons, our Galli-Curci, re-

turning to us, as bewitching as ever *and uncorrupted:* "I had to do it," she explains, when we three rush as one to embrace her, "otherwise it meant nothing."

In brief: I could not easily make peace with the fact that I had a sister in the suburbs, whose pastimes and adornments—vulgar to a snobbish college sophomore, an elitist already reading Allen Tate on the sublime and Dr. Leavis on Matthew Arnold with his breakfast cereal —more or less resembled those of millions upon millions of American families. Instead I imagined Sonia Zuckerman Ruggieri in Purgatorio.

Lydia Jorgenson Ketterer I imagined in Hell. But who wouldn't have, to hear those stories out of her lurid past? Beside hers, my own childhood, frailty, fevers, and all, seemed a version of paradise; for where I had been the child served, she had been the child servant, the child slave, round-the-clock nurse to a hypochondriacal mother and fair game to a benighted father.

The story of incest, as Lydia told it, was simple enough, so simple that it staggered me. It was simply inconceivable to me at the time that an act I associated wholly with a great work of classical drama could actually have taken place, without messengers and choruses and oracles, between a Chicago milkman in his Bloomfield Farms coveralls and his sleepy little blue-eyed daughter before she went off to school. Yet it had. "Once upon a time," as Lydia liked to begin the story, early on a winter morning, as he was about to set off to fetch his delivery truck, her father came into her room and lay down beside her in the bed, dressed for work. He was trembling and in tears. "You're all I have, Lydia, you're all Daddy has. I'm married to a corpse." Then he lowered his coveralls to his ankles, all because he was married to a corpse. "Simple as that," said Lydia. Lydia the child, like Lydia the adult, did not scream out, nor did she reach up and sink her teeth into his neck once he was over her. The thought of biting into his Adam's apple occurred to her, but she was afraid that his screams would awaken her mother, who needed her sleep. *She was afraid that his screams would awaken her mother.* And, moreover, she did not want to hurt him: he was her father. Mr. Jorgenson showed up for work that morning, but his truck was found abandoned later in the day in the Forest Preserve. "And where he went," said Lydia, in mild storybook fashion, "nobody knew," neither the invalid wife whom he had left penniless nor their horrified little child. Something at first made Lydia believe that he had run away "to the North Pole," though simultaneously she was convinced that he was lurking in the neighborhood, ready to crush her skull with a rock if she should tell any of her little friends the thing he had done to her before disappearing. For years afterward— even as a grown woman, even after her breakdown— whenever she went to the Loop at Christmastime, she would wonder if he might not be one of the Santa Clauses standing outside the department stores ringing a little bell at the shoppers. In fact, having decided in the December of her eighteenth year to run away from Skokie with Ketterer, she had approached the Santa Claus outside Goldblatt's and said to him, "I'm getting married. I don't care about you any more. I'm marrying a man who stands six feet two inches tall and weighs two hundred and twenty-five pounds and if you ever so much as follow me again he'll break every bone in your body."

"I still don't know which was more deranged," said Lydia, "pretending that that poor bewildered Santa Claus was my father, or imagining that the oaf I was about to marry was a man."

Incest, the violent marriage, then what she called her "flirtation" with madness. A month after Lydia had divorced Ketterer on grounds of physical cruelty, her mother finally managed to have the stroke she had been readying herself for all her life. During the week the woman lay under the oxygen tent in the hospital, Lydia refused to visit her. "I told my aunts that I had put in all the hours I owed to the cause. If she were dying, what help could I be in preventing it? And if she were faking again, I refused to participate." And when the mother did expire at long last, Lydia's grief, or relief, or delight, or guilt, took the form of torpor. Nothing seemed worth bothering to do. She fed and clothed Monica, her six-year-old daughter, but that was as far as she went. She did not change her own clothes, make the bed, or wash the dishes; when she opened a can to eat something she invariably discovered that she was eating the cat's tinned food. Then she began to write on the walls with her lipstick. The Sunday after the funeral, when Ketterer came to take Monica away for the day, he found the child in a chair, all dressed and ready to go, and the walls of the apartment covered with questions, printed in big block letters with a lipstick: WHY NOT? YOU TOO? WHY SHOULD THEY? SAYS WHO? WE WILL? Lydia was still at her breakfast, which consisted that morning of a bowl full of kitty litter, covered with urine and a sliced candle.

"Oh, how he loved that," Lydia told me. "You could just see his mind, or whatever you'd call what he's got in there, turning over. He couldn't bear, you see, that I had divorced him, he couldn't bear that a judge in a courtroom had heard what a brute he was. He couldn't bear losing his little punching bag. 'You think you're so smart, you go to art museums and you think that gives you a right to boss your husband around—' and then he'd pick me up and throw me at the wall. He was always telling me how I ought to be down on my knees for saving me from the houseful of old biddies, how I ought to *worship* him for taking somebody who was practically an orphan and giving her a nice home and a baby and money to spend going to art museums. Once, you see, during the seven years, I had gone off to the Art Institute with my cousin Bob, the bachelor high-school teacher. He took me to the art museum and when we were all alone in one of the empty rooms, he exposed himself to me. He said he just wanted me to look at him, that was all. He said he didn't want me to touch it. So I didn't; I didn't do anything. Just like with my father—I felt sorry for *him*. There I was, married to an ape, and here was Cousin Bob, the one my father used to call 'the little grind.' Quite a distinguished family I come from. *Anyway:* Ketterer broke down the door, saw the handwriting on the wall was mine, and couldn't have been happier. Especially when he noticed what I was pretending to be eating for my breakfast. Because it was all pretense, you see. I knew exactly what I was doing. I had no intention of drinking my own urine, or eating a candle and kitty litter. I knew he was coming to call, that was the reason I did it. You should have heard how solicitous he was: 'You need a doctor, Lydia, you need a doctor real bad.' But what he called was a city ambulance. I had to smile when two men came into my apartment actually wearing white coats. I didn't have to smile, that is, but I did. I said: 'Won't you gentlemen have some kitty litter?' I knew that was the kind of thing you were supposed to say if you were mad. Or at least that's what everybody else thought. What I really say when I'm insane are things like 'Today is Tuesday,' or 'I'll have a pound of chopped meat, please.' Oh, that's just cleverness. Strike that. I don't know *what* I say if I'm mad, or if I've even *been* mad. Truly, it was just a mild flirtation."

But that was the end of motherhood, nonetheless. Upon her release from the hospital five weeks later, Ketterer announced that he was remarrying. He hadn't planned on "popping the question" so soon, but now that Lydia had proved herself in public to be the nut he had had to endure in private for seven miserable years, he felt duty bound to provide the child with a proper home and a proper mother. And if she wanted to contest his decision in court, well, just let her try. It seemed he had taken photographs of the walls she had defaced and had lined up neighbors who would testify to what she had looked like and *smelled* like in the week before "you flipped your Lydia, kid," as it pleased Ketterer to describe what had happened to her. He did not care how much it would cost him in legal fees; he would spend every dime he had to save Monica from a crazy woman who ate her own filth. "And also," said Lydia, "to get out of paying support money in the bargain."

"I ran around frantically for days, begging the neighbors not to testify against me. They knew how much Monica loved me, they knew that I loved her—they knew it was only because my mother had died, because I was exhausted, and so on and so forth. I'm sure I terrified them, telling them all they 'knew' that they didn't begin to know about my life. I'm sure I *wanted* to terrify them. I even hired a lawyer. I sat in his office and wept, and he assured me that I was within my rights to demand the child back, and that it was going to be a little harder for Mr. Ketterer than he thought, and so on and so forth, very encouraging, very sympathetic, very optimistic. So I left his office and walked to the bus station and took a bus to Canada. I went to Winnipeg to look for an employment agency—I wanted to be a cook in a logging camp. The farther north the better. I wanted to be a cook for a hundred strong, hungry men. All the way to Winnipeg in the bus I had visions of myself in the kitchen of a big mess hall up in the freezing wilds, cooking bacon and eggs and biscuits and pots and pots of coffee for the morning meal, cooking their breakfast while it was still dark—the only one awake in the logging camp, me. And then the long sunny mornings, cleaning up and beginning preparations for the evening meal, when they'd all come in tired from the heavy work in the forest. It was the simplest and most girlish little daydream you can imagine. *I* could imagine. I would be a servant to a hundred strong men, and they in return would protect me from harm. I would be the only woman in the entire camp, and because there was only one of me, no one would ever dare to take advantage of my situation. I stayed in Winnipeg three days. Going to movies. I was afraid to go to a logging camp and say I wanted work there—I was sure they would think I was a prostitute. Oh, how banal to be crazy. Or maybe just banal being me. What could be more banal then having been seduced by your own father and then going around being 'scarred' by it forever? You see, I kept thinking all the while, 'There's no need for me to be behaving in this way. There is no need to be acting crazy—and there never was. There is no need to be running away to the North Pole. I'm just pretending. All I have to do to stop is *to stop*.' I would remember my aunts telling me, if I so much as uttered a whimper in objection to anything: 'Pull yourself together, Lydia, mind over matter.' Well, it couldn't be that I was going to waste my life defying *those* two, could it? Because making myself their victim was sillier even than continuing to allow myself to be my father's. There I sat in the movies in Canada, with all these expressions I used to hate so, going through my head, *but making perfect sense*. Pull yourself together, Lydia. Mind over matter, Lydia. You can't cry over spilled milk, Lydia. If you don't succeed, Lydia— and you don't—try, try again. Nothing could have been clearer to me than that sitting in the movies in Winnipeg was as senseless as anything I could do if I ever hoped to save Monica from her father. I could only conclude that I didn't want to save her from him. Dr. Rutherford now tells me that that was exactly the case. Not that it requires a trained therapist to see through somebody like me. How did I get back to Chicago? According to Dr. Rutherford, by accomplishing what I set out to do. I was staying in a two-dollar-a-night hotel on what turned out to be Winnipeg's skid row. As if Lydia didn't know, says Dr. Rutherford. The third morning that I came down to pay for the room, the desk clerk asked me if I wanted to pick up some easy cash. I could make a lot of money posing for pictures, especially if I was blonde all over. I began to howl. He called a policeman, and the policeman called a doctor, and eventually somehow they got me home. And that's how I managed to rid myself of my daughter. You would have thought it would have been simpler to drown her in the bathtub."

To say that I was drawn to her story because it was so lurid is only the half of it: there was the way the tale was told. Lydia's easy, familiar, even cozy manner with misery, her droll acceptance of her own madness, greatly increased the story's appeal—or, to put it another way, did much to calm whatever fears one might expect an inexperienced young man of a conventional background to have about a woman bearing such a ravaged past. Who would call "crazy" a woman who spoke with such detachment of her history of craziness? Who could find evidence of impulses toward suicide and homicide in a rhetorical style so untainted by rage or vengeful wrath? No, no, this was someone who had *experienced* her experience, who had been *deepened* by all that misery. A decidedly ordinary looking person, a pretty little American blonde with a face like a million others, she had, without benefit of books or teachers, mobilized every ounce of her intelligence to produce a kind of *wisdom* about herself. For surely it required wisdom to recite, calmly and with a mild, even forgiving irony, such a ghastly narrative of ill luck and injustice. You had to be as cruelly simpleminded as Ketterer himself, I thought, not to appreciate the moral triumph this represented—or else you just had to be someone other than me.

I met the woman with whom I was to ruin my life only a few months after arriving back in Chicago in the fall of 1956, following a premature discharge from the army. I was just short of twenty-four, held a master's degree in literature, and prior to my induction into the service had been invited to return to the College after my discharge as an instructor in the English composition program. Under any circumstances my parents would have been thrilled by what they took to be the eminence of that position; as it was, they looked upon this "honor" as something like divine compensation for the fate that had befallen their daughter. Their letters were addressed, without irony, to "Professor Nathan Zuckerman"; I'm sure many of them, containing no more than a line or two about the weather in New Jersey, were mailed solely for the sake of addressing them.

I was pleased myself, though not so awestruck. In fact, the example of my own tireless and resolute parents had so instilled in me the habits that make for success that I had hardly any understanding at all of failure. Why *did* people fail? In college, *I* had looked with awe upon those fellows who came to class *un*prepared for examinations and who did *not* submit their assignments on time. Now why should they want to do it that way, I wondered. Why would anyone prefer the ignobility of defeat to the genuine pleasures of achievement? Especially as the latter was so easy to effectuate: all you had to be was attentive, methodical, thorough, punctual, and persevering; all you had to be was orderly, patient, self-disciplined, undiscourageable, and industrious—and, of course, intelligent. And that was it. What could be simpler?

What confidence I had in those days! What will-power and energy! And what a devourer of schedules and routines! I rose every weekday at six forty-five to don an old knit swimsuit and do thirty minutes of push-ups, sit-ups, deep knee bends, and half a dozen other exercises illustrated in a physical-fitness guide that I had owned since adolescence and which still served its purpose; of World War Two vintage, it was titled *How To Be Tough as a Marine.* By eight I would have bicycled the mile to my office overlooking the Midway. There I would make a quick review of the day's lesson in the composition syllabus, which was divided into sections, each illustrating one of a variety of rhetorical techniques; the selections were brief—the better to scrutinize meticulously—and drawn mostly from the work of Olympians: Aristotle, Hobbes, Mill, Gibbon, Pater, Shaw, Swift, Sir Thomas Browne, etc. My three classes of freshman composition each met for one hour, five days a week. I began at eight thirty and finished at eleven thirty, three consecutive hours of hearing more or less the same student discussion and offering more or

less the same observations myself—and yet never with
any real flagging of enthusiasm. Much of my pleasure, in
fact, derived from trying to make each hour appear to be
the first of the day. Also there was a young man's satisfaction in authority, especially as that authority did not
require that I wear any badge other than my intelligence,
my industriousness, a tie, and a jacket. Then of course
I enjoyed, as I previously had as a student, the courtesy
and good-humored seriousness of the pedagogical exchange, nearly as much as I enjoyed the sound of the
word "pedagogical." It was not uncommon at the university for faculty and students eventually to call one
another by their given names, at least outside the classroom. I myself never considered this a possibility, however, any more than my father could have imagined
being familiar in their offices with the businessmen who
had hired him to keep their books; like him, I preferred
to be thought somewhat stiff, rather than introduce considerations extraneous to the job to be done, and which
might tempt either party to the transaction to hold himself
less accountable than was "proper." Especially for one
so close to his students in age, there was a danger in trying to appear to be "a good guy" or "one of the boys"—
as of course there was equally the danger of assuming
an attitude of superiority that was not only in excess of
my credentials, but distasteful in itself.

That I should have to be alert to every fine point of
conduct may seem to suggest that I was unnatural in my
role, when actually it was an expression of the enthusiasm
with which I took to my new vocation and of the passion
I had in those days to judge myself by the strictest
standard in every detail.

By noon I would have returned to my small quiet
apartment, eaten a sandwich I had prepared for myself,
and already have begun work on my own fiction. Three
short stories I had written during the evenings when I
was in the army had all been accepted for publication
in a venerable literary quarterly; they were, however,
no more than skillful impersonations of the sort of
stories I had been taught to admire most in college—

stories of "The Garden Party" variety—and their publication aroused in me more curiosity than pride. I owed it to myself, I thought, to find out if I might have a talent that was my own. "To owe it to oneself," by the way, was a notion entirely characteristic of a man like my father, whose influence upon my thinking was more pervasive than might have been apparent to anyone—myself included—who had listened to me, in the classroom, discussing the development of a theory in Aristotle or a metaphor in Sir Thomas Browne.

At six P.M., following five hours of working at my fiction and an hour brushing up on my French—I planned to travel to Europe during the summer vacation—I bicycled back to the university to eat dinner in the Commons, where I had formerly taken my meals as a graduate student. The dark wood tones of the paneled hall, and the portraits of the university's distinguished dead hanging above the refectory tables, satisfied a strong taste in me for institutional dignity. In such an environment I felt perfectly content to eat alone; indeed, I would not have considered myself unblessed to have been told that I would be dining off a tray in this hall, eating these stews and salisbury steaks, for the rest of my days. Before returning to my apartment to mark one seventh of my weekly stack of sixty-odd freshman essays (as many as I could take in a sitting) and to prepare the next day's lesson, I would browse for half an hour or so in the secondhand bookstores in the neighborhood. Owning my own "library" was my only materialistic ambition; in fact, trying to decide which two of these thousands of books to buy that week, I would frequently get so excited that by the time the purchase was accomplished I had to make use of the bookseller's toilet facilities. I don't believe that either microbe or laxative has ever affected me so strongly as the discovery that I was all at once the owner of a slightly soiled copy of Empson's *Seven Types of Ambiguity* in the original English edition.

At ten o'clock, having completed my classroom preparation, I would go off to a local graduate-student hangout, where generally I ran into somebody I knew and had a glass of beer—one beer, one game of pinball soccer, and then home, for before I went to sleep, there were still fifty pages to be underlined and annotated in some major work of European literature that either I hadn't yet read or had misread the first time around. I called this "filling in the gaps." Reading—and noting—fifty pages a night, I could average three books a month, or thirty-six a year. I also knew approximately how many short stories I might expect to complete in a year, if I put in thirty hours at it a week; and approximately how many students' essays I could mark in an hour; and how large my "library" would be in a decade, if I were to continue to be able to make purchases in accordance with my present budget. And I liked knowing all these things, and to this day like myself for having known them.

I seemed to myself as rich as a young man could be in spiritual goods; as for worldly goods, what could I possibly need that I didn't have? I owned a bicycle to get around the neighborhood and provide me with exercise, a Remington portable (my parents' gift for my graduation from high school), a briefcase (their gift for my grade-school graduation), a Bulova watch (their gift for my bar mitzvah); I had still from my undergraduate days a favorite well-worn tweed jacket to teach my classes in, complete with leather elbow patches, my army khakis to wear while writing and drinking my beer, a new brown glen plaid suit for dressing up, a pair of tennis sneakers, a pair of cordovan shoes, a ten-year-old pair of slippers, a V-neck sweater, some shirts and socks, two striped ties, and the kind of jockey shorts and ribbed undershirts that I had been wearing since I had graduated from diapers, Fruit of the Loom. Why change brands? They made me happy enough. All I wanted to be happier still were more books to inscribe my name in. And to travel to Europe for two months to see the famous cultural monuments and literary landmarks. Two times each month I would be surprised to find in my mailbox a check from the university for one hundred and twenty-five dollars. Why on earth were they sending me money? It was I, surely, who should be paying them for the privilege of leading such a full, independent, and honorable life.

In the midst of my contentment there was one difficulty: my headaches. While a soldier I had developed such severe migraines that I had finally to be separated with a medical discharge after serving only eleven months of my two-year term. Of course, I didn't miss the tedium and boredom of peacetime army life; from the day I was drafted I had been marking off the time until I could return to a life no less regimented and disciplined than a soldier's, but overseen by me and for the sake of serious literary studies. However, to have been released back into a studious vocation because of physical incapacity was disconcerting to one who had spent nearly ten years building himself, by way of exercise and diet, into a brawny young man who looked as though he could take care of himself out in the harsh world. How doggedly I had worked to bury the frail child who used to lie in his bed musing over his father's puzzles, while the other little children were out on the streets learning to be agile and fearless! I had even been pleased, in a way, when I had found myself assigned by the army to military police school in Georgia: they did not make sissy invalids into MPs, that was for sure. I was to become a man with a pistol on his hip and starch in the knifelike creases of his khakis: a humanist with a swagger, an English teacher with a billy club. The collected stories of Isaac Babel had not appeared yet in the famous paperback edition, but when I read them five years later, I recognized in Babel's experience as a bespectacled Jew with the Red cavalry something like a highly charged version of what I had experienced during my brief tour of duty as an MP in the state of Georgia. An MP, until those headaches knocked me off my spit-shined boots . . . and I lay mummified on

my bed for twenty-four hours at a stretch, the most
ordinary little sound outside the barracks window—a
soldier scratching at the grass with a rake, some pass-
erby whistling a tune between his teeth—as unbearable
as a spike being driven in my brain; even a beam of
sunlight, filtering through the worn spot in the drawn
green shade back of my bunk, a sunbeam no larger
than the head of a pin, would be, in those circumstances, intolerable.

My "buddies," most of them without a twelfth-grade
education, assumed that the college genius (and Jew-
boy) was malingering, especially when I discovered
that I could tell *the day before* that one of my disabling
headaches was on its way. It was my contention that if
only I were allowed to retire to my bed prior to the on-
set of the headache, and to remain there in the dark and
quiet for five hours or so, I could ward off an otherwise
inevitable attack. "Look, I think you could too," said
the wise sergeant, while denying me permission to do
so, "I have often thought the same thing about myself.
You can't beat a day in the sack for making you feel
good all over." Nor was the doctor on sick call much
more sympathetic; I convinced no one, not even myself. The "floating" or "ghostly" sensation, the aura of
malaise that served as my warning system was, in
truth, so unsubstantial, so faint, that I too had to
wonder if I wasn't imagining it; and then subsequently
"imagining" the headache to justify the premonition.

Eventually, when headaches began to flatten me regularly every ten or twelve days, I was admitted to the
post hospital for "observation," which meant that, except if I was actually in pain, I was to walk around in a
pair of blue army pajamas pushing a dry mop. To be
sure, when the aura of a headache came upon me, I
could now retire immediately to my bed; but that, as it
turned out, worked only to forestall the headache for
another twelve hours or so; on the other hand, if I were
to remain *continually* in bed . . . But I couldn't; in
the words of Bartleby the Scrivener (words that were
with me frequently in the hospital, though I had not

read the story for several years), I preferred not to. I preferred instead to push my mop from one ward to another and wait for the blow to fall.

Rather quickly I came to understand that my daily work routine had been devised as a combination punishment and cure by the hospital authorities. I had been assigned my mop so as to be brought into contact with those who were truly ill, irreversibly and horribly so. Each day, for instance, I went off to mop between the beds of patients in "the burn ward," young men so badly disfigured by fire that in the beginning either I had to turn away at the sight of them or else could not withdraw my gaze at all. Then there were amputees who had lost limbs in training accidents, in automobile collisions, in operations undertaken to arrest the spread of malignancies. The idea seemed to be that I would somehow be shamed out of my alleged illness by the daily contact that I made on my rounds with these doomed mortals, most of them no older than myself. Only after I was called before a medical board and awarded a discharge did I learn that no such subtle or sadistic therapy had been ordered in my case. My internment in the hospital had been a bureaucratic necessity and not some sly form of purifying and healing imprisonment. The "cure" had been wholly of my own devising, my housecleaning duties having been somewhat less extensive than I had imagined. The nurse in charge of my section, an easygoing and genial woman, was amused to learn from me, on the day of my discharge, that I had been wandering through the hospital from nine to five every day, cleaning the floors of all the open wards, when the instructions she had given me had been only to clean up each morning around my own bed. After that I was to have considered myself free to come and go as I wished, so long as I did not leave the hospital. "Didn't anyone ever stop you?" she asked. "Yes," I said, "in the beginning. But I told them I'd been ordered to do it." I pretended to be as amused as she was by the "misunderstanding," but wondered if bad conscience was not leading her to lie now about the instructions she had given me on the day I had become her patient.

In Chicago, a civilian again, I was examined by a neurologist at Billings Hospital who could offer no explanation for the headaches, except to say that my pattern was typical enough. He prescribed the same drugs that the army had, none of which did me any good, and told me that migraines ordinarily diminish in intensity and frequency with time, generally dying out around the age of fifty. I had vaguely expected that mine would die out as soon as I was my own man again and back at the university; along with my sergeant and my envious colleagues, I continued to believe that I had induced this condition in myself in order to provide me with grounds for discharge from an army that was wasting my valuable time. That the pain not only continued to plague me, but in the months following my discharge began to spread until it had encompassed both halves of my skull, served to bolster, in a grim way, a faltering sense of my own probity.

Unless, of course, I was covering my tracks, "allowing" the headaches a somewhat longer lease on my life than might be physically desirable, for the sake of my moral well-being. For who could accuse me of falling ill as a means of cutting short my tour of army duty when it was clear that the rewarding academic life I had been so anxious to return to continued to be as marred by this affliction as my purposeless military existence had been? Each time I had emerged from another twenty-four-hour session of pain, I would think to myself, "How many more, before I've met my obligation?" I wondered if it was not perhaps the "plan" of these headaches to visit themselves upon me until such time as I would have been discharged from the service under ordinary conditions. Did I, as it were, *owe* the army a migraine for each month of service I had escaped, or was it for each week, or each day, or each hour? Even to believe that they might die out by the time I was fifty was hardly consolation to an ambitious twenty-four-year-old with as strong a distaste for the sickbed as I had developed in my childhood; also to one made buoyant by fulfilling the exacting demands of schedules and routines, the prospect of being dead to the world and to my work for twenty-four hours every ten days for the next thirty-six years, the thought of all *that* waste, was as distressing as the anticipation of the pain itself. Three times a month, for God only knew how long, I was to be sealed into a coffin (so I described it to myself, admittedly in the clutch of self-pity) and buried alive. Why?

I had already considered (and dismissed) the idea of taking myself to a psychoanalyst, even before the neurologist at Billings informed me that a study in psychosomatic medicine was about to be initiated at a North Shore clinic, under the direction of an eminent Freudian analyst. He thought it was more than likely that I might be taken on as a patient at a modest fee, especially as they were said to be interested particularly in the ailments that manifested themselves in "intellectuals" and "creative types." The neurologist was not suggesting that migraines were necessarily symptomatic of a neurotic personality disturbance; rather he was responding, he said, to what he took to be "a Freudian orientation" in the questions I asked him and in the manner in which I had gone about presenting the history of the disorder.

I did not know that it was a Freudian orientation so much as a literary habit of mind which the neurologist was not accustomed to: that is to say, I could not resist reflecting upon my migraines in the same supramedical way that I might consider the illnesses of Milly Theale or Hans Castorp or the Reverend Arthur Dimmesdale, or ruminate upon the transformation of Gregor Samsa into a cockroach, or search out the "meaning" in Gogol's short story of Collegiate Assessor Kovalev's temporary loss of his nose. Whereas an ordinary man might complain, "I get these damn headaches" (and have been content to leave it at that), I tended, like a student of high literature or a savage who paints his body blue, to see the migraines as *standing for some-*

thing, as a disclosure or "epiphany," isolated or acci-
dental or inexplicable only to one who was blind to the
design of a life or a book. What did my migraines
signify?

The possibilities I came up with did not satisfy a
student as "sophisticated" as myself; compared with
The Magic Mountain or even "The Nose," the texture
of my own story was thin to the point of transparency.
It was disappointing, for instance, to find myself as-
sociating the disability that had come over me when I
had begun to wear a pistol on my hip with either my
adolescent terror of the physical life or some traditional
Jewish abhorrence of violence—such an explanation
seemed too conventional and simplistic, too "easy." A
more attractive, if in the end no less obvious, idea had
to do with a kind of psychological civil war that had
broken out between the dreamy, needy, and helpless
child I had been, and the independent, robust, manly
adult I wanted to be. At the time I recalled it, Bartleby's
passive but defiant formula, "I would prefer not to,"
had struck me as the voice of the man in me defying
the child and his temptation to helplessness; but couldn't
it just as well be the voice of the frail and sickly little
boy answering the call to perform the duties of a man?
Or of a *police*man? No, no, much too pat—my life surely
must be more complex and subtle than that; *The Wings
of the Dove* was. No, I could not imagine myself *writing*
a story so tidy and facile in its psychology, let alone
living one.

The stories I *was* writing—the fact of the writing
itself—did not escape my scrutiny. It was to keep open
the lines to my sanity and intelligence, to engage in a
solitary, thoughtful activity at the end of those mindless
days of directing traffic and checking passes at the gate
into town, that I had taken up writing for three hours
each evening at a table in the corner of the post library.
After only a few nights, however, I had put aside my
notes for the critical article I had planned on some
novels of Virginia Woolf (for an issue of *Modern Fiction
Studies* to be devoted entirely to her work) to begin

what was to turn out to be my first published short story. Shortly thereafter, when the migraines began, and the search for a cause, a reason, a meaning, I thought I saw in the unexpected alteration the course of my writing had taken something analogous to that shift in my attention that used to disconcert my father when he presented the little boy in the sickbed with those neat arithmetical puzzles of his—the movement from intellectual or logical analysis to seemingly irrelevant speculation of an imaginary nature. And in the hospital, where in six weeks' time I had written my second and third stories, I could not help wondering if for me illness was not a necessary catalyst to activate the imagination. I understood that this was not an original hypothesis, but if that made it more or less applicable to my situation I couldn't tell; nor did I know what to do with the fact that the illness itself was the one that had regularly afflicted Virginia Woolf and to some degree contributed to the debilitation that led to suicide. I knew about Virginia Woolf's migraines from having read her posthumous book, *A Writer's Diary,* edited by her husband and published in my senior year of college. I even had the book with me in my footlocker, for the essay I had been going to write on her work. What was I to think then? No more than a coincidence? Or was I imitating the agony of this admirable writer, as in my stories I was imitating the techniques and simulating the sensibilities of still other writers I admired?

Following my examination by the neurologist, I decided to stop worrying about the "significance" of my condition and to try to consider myself, as the neurologist obviously did, to be one hundred and eighty pounds of living tissue subject to the pathology of the species, rather than a character in a novel whose disease the reader may be encouraged to diagnose by way of moral, psychological, or metaphysical hypotheses. As I was unable to endow my predicament with sufficient density or originality to satisfy my own literary tastes —unable to do "for" migraines what Mann had done in

The Magic Mountain for TB or in *Death in Venice* for cholera——I had decided that the only sensible thing was to have my migraine and then forget about it till the next time. To look for meaning was fruitless as well as pretentious. Though I wondered: Couldn't the migraines themselves be diagnosed as "pretentious" in origin?

I also withstood the temptation to take myself for an interview to the North Shore clinic where the study of psychosomatic ailments was getting under way. Not that I was out of sympathy with the theories or techniques of psychotherapy as I had grasped them through my reading. It was, rather, that aside from these headaches, I was as vigorous in the execution of my duties, and as thrilled with the circumstances of my life, as I could ever have dreamed of being. To be sure, to try to teach sixty-five freshmen to write an English sentence that was clear, logical, and precise was not always an enchanting experience; yet, even when teaching was most tedious, I maintained my missionary spirit and with it the conviction that with every clichéd expression or mindless argument I exposed in the margins of my students' essays, I was waging a kind of guerrilla war against the army of slobs, philistines, and barbarians who seemed to me to control the national mind, either through the media or the government. The presidential press conference provided me with material for any number of classroom sessions; I would have samples of the Eisenhower porridge mimeographed for distribution and then leave him to the students to correct and grade. I would submit for their analysis a sermon by Norman Vincent Peale, the president's religious adviser; or an ad for General Motors; or a "cover story" from *Time*. What with television quiz shows, advertising agencies, and the Cold War all flourishing, it was a period in which a composition teacher did not necessarily have to possess the credentials or doctrines of a clergyman to consider himself engaged in the business of saving souls.

If the classroom caused me to imagine myself to be something of a priest, the university neighborhood

seemed to me something like my parish—and of course
something of a Bloomsbury—a community of the faithful, observing the sacraments of literacy, benevolence,
good taste, and social concern. My own street of low,
soot-stained brick apartment buildings was on the grim
side, and the next one over, run-down only the year
before, was already in rubble—leveled as though by
blockbusters for an urban renewal project; also, in the
year I had been away, there had been a marked increase of random nighttime violence in the neighborhood. Nonetheless, within an hour of my return, I felt
as comfortable and at home as someone whose family
had dwelled in the same small town for generations.
Simultaneously I could never forget that it was not in
such a paradise of true believers that I had been born
and raised; and even if I should live in the Hyde Park
neighborhood for the next fifty years—and why should
I ever want to live elsewhere?—the city itself, with
streets named for the prairie and the Wabash, with
railroad trains marked "Illinois Central" and a lake
bearing the name "Michigan," would always have the
flavor of the faraway for one whose fantasies of adventure had been nurtured in a sickbed in Camden, New
Jersey, over an aeon of lonely afternoons. How could
I be in "Chicago"? The question, coming at me while
shopping in the Loop, or watching a movie at the Hyde
Park Theatre, or simply opening a can of sardines for
lunch at my apartment on Drexel, seemed to me un-
answerable. I suppose my wonderment and my joy were
akin to my parents', when they would address those
envelopes to me in care of Faculty Exchange. How
could *he* be a professor, who could barely breathe with
that bronchitis?

All this by way of explaining why I did not betake
myself to that clinic for the study of psychosomatic ailments and offer up my carcass and unconscious for
investigation. I was too happy. Everything that was a
part of getting older seemed to me to be a pleasure:
the independence and authority, of course, but no less
so the refinement and strengthening of one's moral

nature—to be magnanimous where one had been selfish and carping, to be forgiving where one had been resentful, to be patient where one had been impetuous, to be generous and helpful where one had previously been needful . . . It seemed to me at twenty-four as natural to be solicitous of my sixty-year-old parents as to be decisive and in command with my eighteen- and nineteen-year-old students. Toward the young girls in my classes, some as lovely and tempting as the junior at Pembroke College with whom I had just concluded a love affair, I behaved as I was expected to; it went without saying that as their teacher I must not allow myself to take a sexual interest in them or to exploit my authority for personal gratification. No difficulty I encountered seemed beyond my powers, whether it was concluding a love affair, or teaching the principles of logic to my dullest composition students, or rising with a dry mouth to address the Senate of the Faculty, or writing a short story four times over to get it "right" . . . How could I turn myself over to a psychoanalyst as "a case"? All the evidence of my life (exclusive of the migraines) argued too strongly against that, certainly to one to whom it meant so much never to be classified as a patient again. Furthermore, in the immediate aftermath of a headache, I would experience such elation just from the *absence* of pain that I would almost believe that whatever had laid that dose of suffering upon me had been driven from my body for good—that the powerful enemy (yes, more feeble interpretation, or superstition) who had unleashed upon me all his violence, who had dragged me to the very end of my endurance, had been proved unable in the end to do me in. The worse the headache the more certain I was when it was over that I had defeated the affliction once and for all. *And was a better man for it.* (And no, my body was not painted blue in these years, nor did I otherwise believe in angels, demons, or deities.) Often I vomited during the attacks, and afterward, not quite daring to move (for fear of breaking), I lay on the bathroom floor with my chin on the toilet bowl and a hand mirror to my face, in a parody perhaps of Narcissus. I wanted to see what I looked like having suffered so and survived; in that feeble and euphoric state, it would not have frightened me—might even have thrilled me—to have observed black vapors, something like cannon smoke, rolling out of my ears and nostrils. I would talk to my eyes, reassuring them as though they were somebody else's: "That's it, the end, no more pain." But in point of fact there would be plenty more; the experiment which has not ended was only beginning.

In the second semester of that—no other word will do; if it smacks of soap opera, that is not unintentional— of that fateful year, I was asked if I should like to teach, in addition to my regular program, the night course in "Creative Writing" in the downtown division of the university, a single session each Monday night running for three consecutive hours, at a salary of two hundred and fifty dollars for the semester. Another windfall it seemed to me—my round-trip tourist-class fare on the *Rotterdam*. As for the students, they were barely versed in the rules of syntax and spelling, and so, I discovered, hardly able to make head or tail of the heady introductory lecture that, with characteristic thoroughness, I had prepared over a period of a week for delivery at our first meeting. Entitled "The Strategies and Intentions of Fiction," it was replete with lengthy (and I had thought) "salient" quotations from Aristotle's *Poetics,* Flaubert's correspondence, Dostoevsky's diaries, and James's critical prefaces—I quoted only from masters, pointed only to monuments: *Moby Dick, Anna Karenina, Crime and Punishment, The Ambassadors, Madame Bovary, Portrait of the Artist as a Young Man, The Sound and the Fury.* " 'What seems to me the highest and most difficult achievement of Art is not to make us laugh or cry, or to rouse our lust or our anger, but to do as nature does—that is, fill us with wonderment. The most beautiful works have indeed this quality. They are serene in aspect, incomprehensible . . . *pitiless.*' " Flaubert, in a letter to Louise Colet ("1853," I told them, in responsible scholarly fashion, "a year into the writing of *Madame Bovary*"). " 'The house of fiction has in short not one window but a million . . . every one of which is pierced, or is still pierceable, in its vast front, by the need of the individual vision and by the pressure of the individual will. . . .' " James, the preface to *The Portrait of a Lady*. I concluded with a lengthy reading from Conrad's inspirational introduction to *The Nigger of the "Narcissus"* (1897): " '. . . the artist descends within himself, and in that lonely region of stress and strife, if he be deserving and fortunate, he finds the terms of his appeal. His appeal is made to our less obvious capacities: to that part of our nature which, because of the warlike conditions of existence, is necessarily kept out of sight within the more resisting and hard qualities —like the vulnerable body within a steel armor. His appeal is less loud, more profound, less distinct, more stirring—and sooner forgotten. Yet its effect endures forever. The changing wisdom of successive generations discards ideas, questions facts, demolishes theories. But the artist appeals to that part of our being which is not dependent on wisdom: to that in us which is a gift and not an acquisition—and, therefore, more permanently enduring. He speaks to our capacity for delight and wonder, to the sense of mystery surrounding our lives; to our sense of pity, and beauty, and pain; to the latent feeling of fellowship with all creation—to the subtle but invincible conviction of solidarity that knits together the loneliness of innumerable hearts, to the solidarity in dreams, in joy, in sorrow, in aspirations, in illusions, in hope, in fear, which binds men to each other, which binds together all humanity—the dead to the living and the living to the unborn. . . .' "

When I finished reading my twenty-five pages and asked for questions, there was to my surprise and disappointment, just one; as it was the only Negro in the class who had her hand raised, I wondered if it could be that after all I had said she was going to tell me she was offended by the title of Conrad's novel. I was already preparing an explanation that might turn her touchiness into a discussion of frankness in fiction—fiction as the secret and the taboo disclosed—when she rose to stand at respectful attention, a thin middle-aged woman in a neat dark suit and a pillbox hat: "Professor, I know that if you're writing a friendly letter to a little boy, you write on the envelope 'Master.' But what if you're writing a friendly letter to a little girl? Do you still say 'Miss'—or just what *do* you say?"

The class, having endured nearly two hours of a kind of talk none of them had probably ever heard before outside of a church, took the occasion of her seemingly ludicrous question to laugh uproariously—she was the kid who had farted following the principal's lecture on discipline and decorum. Their laughter was *pointedly* directed at student, not teacher; nonetheless, I flushed with shame and remained red all the while Mrs. Corbett, dogged and unperturbed in the face of the class's amusement, pursued the knowledge she was there for.

Lydia Ketterer turned out to be by far the most gifted writer in the class and, though older than I, still the youngest of my students—not so young, however, as she looked in the bleak heart of a Chicago winter, dressed in galoshes, knee stockings, tartan skirt, "reindeer" sweater, and the tassled red wool hat, from which a straight curtain of wheat-colored hair dropped down at either side of her face. Outfitted for the ice and cold, she seemed, amid all those tired night-school faces, a junior-high-school girl—in fact, she was twenty-nine and mother of a lanky ten-year-old already budding breasts more enticing than her own. She lived not far from me in Hyde Park, having moved to the university neighborhood four years earlier, following her breakdown—and in the hope of changing her luck. And indeed when we met in my classroom, she probably was living through what were to be the luckiest months of her life: she had a job she liked as an interviewer with a university-sponsored social science research project at two dollars an hour, she had a few older graduate students (connected to the project) as friends, she had

a small bank account and a pleasant little apartment
with a fireplace from which she could see across the
Midway to the Gothic façades of the university. Also at
that time she was the willing and grateful patient of a
lay psychoanalyst, a woman named Rutherford, for
whom she dressed up (in the most girlish dress-up
clothes I'd seen since grade school, puffed sleeves,
crinolines, etc.) and whom she visited every Saturday
morning in her office on Hyde Park Boulevard. The
stories she wrote were inspired mostly by the childhood
recollections she delivered forth to Dr. Rutherford on
these Saturdays and dealt almost exclusively with the
period after her father had raped her and run, when
she and her mother had been taken on as guests—her
mother as guest, Lydia as Cinderella—by the two aunts
in their maidenly little prison house in Skokie.

It was the accumulation of small details that gave
Lydia's stories such distinction as they had. With pains-
taking diligence she chronicled the habits and attitudes
of her aunts, as though with each precise detail she was
hurling a small stone back through her past at those
pinch-faced little persecutors. From the fiction it appeared that the favorite subject in that household was,
oddly enough, "the body." "The body surely does not
require that much milk on a bowl of puffed oats, my
dear." "The body will take only so much abuse, and
then it will *balk*." And so on. Unfortunately, small details, accurately observed and flatly rendered, did not
much interest the rest of the class unless the detail was
"symbolic" or sensational. Those who most hated
Lydia's stories were Agniashvily, an elderly Russian
émigré who wrote original "Ribald Classics" (in Geor-
gian, and translated into English for the class by his
stepson, a restaurateur by trade) aimed at the *Playboy*
"market"; Todd, a cop who could not go two hundred
words into a narrative without a little something running in the gutter (blood, urine, "Sergeant Darling's
dinner") and was a devotee (I was not—we clashed)
of the O. Henry ending; the Negro woman, Mrs. Corbett, who was a file clerk with the Prudential during the

day and at night wrote the most transparent and pathetic pipe dreams about a collie dog romping around a dairy farm in snow-covered Minnesota; Shaw, an "ex-newspaperman" with an adjectival addiction, who was always quoting to us something that "Max" Perkins had said to "Tom" Wolfe, seemingly in Shaw's presence; and a fastidious male nurse named Wertz, who from his corner seat in the last row had with his teacher what is called "a love-hate" relationship. Lydia's most ardent admirers, aside from myself, were two "ladies," one who ran a religious bookshop in Highland Park and rather magnified the moral lessons to be drawn from Lydia's fiction, and the other, Mrs. Slater, an angular, striking housewife from Flossmoor, who wore heather-colored suits to class and wrote "bittersweet" stories which concluded usually with two characters "inadvertently touching." Mrs. Slater's remarkable legs were generally directly under my nose, crossing and uncrossing, and making that whishing sound of nylon moving against nylon that I could hear even over the earnestness of my own voice. Her eyes were gray and eloquent: "I am forty years old, all I do is shop and pick up the children. I live for this class. I live for our conferences. Touch me, advertently or inadvertently. I won't say no or tell my husband."

In all there were eighteen of them and, with the exception of my religionist, not one who seemed to smoke less than a pack a night. They wrote on the backs of order forms and office stationery; they wrote in pencil and in multicolored inks; they forgot to number pages or to put them in order (less frequently, however, than I thought). Oftentimes the first sheet of a story would be stained with food spots, or several of the pages would be stuck together, in Mrs. Slater's case with glue spilled by a child, in the case of Mr. Wertz, the male nurse, with what I took to be semen spilled by himself.

When the class got into a debate as to whether a story was "universal" in its implications or a character was "sympathetic," there was often no way, short of gassing them, of getting them off the subject for the rest of the night. They judged the people in one another's fiction not as though each was a collection of attributes (a mustache, a limp, a southern drawl) to which the author had arbitrarily assigned a Christian name, but as though they were discussing human souls about to be consigned to Hades or elevated to sainthood —depending upon which the class decided. It was the most vociferous among them who had the least taste or interest in the low-keyed or the familiar, and my admiration for Lydia's stories would practically drive them crazy; invariably I raised *somebody's* hackles, when I read aloud, as an example they might follow, something like Lydia's simple description of the way in which her two aunts each had laid out on a doily in the bedroom her hairbrush, comb, hairpins, toothbrush, dish of Lifebuoy, and tin of dental powder. I would read a passage like this: "Aunt Helda, while listening to Father Coughlin reasoning with the twenty thousand Christians gathered in Briggs Stadium, would continually be clearing her throat, as though it were she who was to be called upon to speak next." Such sentences were undoubtedly not so rich and supple as to deserve the sort of extensive, praiseful exegesis I would wind up giving them, but by comparison with most of the prose I read that semester, Mrs. Ketterer's line describing Aunt Helda listening to the radio in the 1940s might have been lifted from *Mansfield Park*.

I wanted to hang a sign over my desk saying ANYONE IN THIS CLASS CAUGHT USING HIS IMAGINATION WILL BE SHOT. I would put it more gently when, in the parental sense, I lectured them. "You just cannot deliver up fantasies and call that 'fiction.' Ground your stories in what you know. Stick to that. Otherwise you tend, some of you, toward the pipe dream and the nightmare, toward the grandiose and the romantic—and that's no good. Try to be precise, accurate, measured . . ." "Yeah? What about Tom Wolfe," asked the lyrical ex-newspaperman Shaw, "would you call that measured, Zuckerman?" (No Mister or Professor from him to a kid half his age.)

"What about prose-poetry, you against that too?" Or Agniashvily, in his barrel-deep Russian brogue, would berate me with Spillane—"And so how come he's got ten million in prrrint, Prrrofessor?" Or Mrs. Slater would ask, in conference, inadvertently touching my sleeve, "But *you* wear a tweed jacket, Mr. Zuckerman. Why is it 'dreamy'—I don't understand—if Craig in my *story* wears—" I couldn't listen. "And the pipe, Mrs. Slater: now why do you think you have him continually puffing on that pipe?" "But men *smoke* pipes." "Dreamy, Mrs. Slater, too damn dreamy." "But—" "Look, write a story about shopping at Carson's, Mrs. Slater! Write about your afternoon at Saks!" "Yes?" "Yes! Yes! Yes!"

Oh, yes, when it came to grandiosity and dreaminess, to all manifestations of self-inflating romance, I had no reservations about giving them a taste of the Zuckerman lash. Those were the only times I lost my temper, and of course losing it was always calculated and deliberate: scrupulous.

Pent-up rage, by the way—that was the meaning the army psychiatrist had assigned to my migraines. He had asked whether I liked my father better than my mother, how I felt about heights and crowds, and what I planned to do when I was returned to civilian life, and concluded from my answers that I was a vessel of *pent-up rage.* Another poet, this one in uniform, bearing the rank of captain.

My friends (my only real enemy is dead now, though my censurers are plentiful)—my friends, I earned those two hundred and fifty dollars teaching "Creative Writing" in a night school, every penny of it. For whatever it may or may not "mean," I didn't once that semester get a migraine on a Monday, not that I wasn't tempted to take a crack at it when a tough-guy story by Patrolman Todd or a bittersweet one by Mrs. Slater was on the block for the evening . . . No, to be frank, I counted it a blessing of sorts when the headaches happened to fall on the weekend, on my time off. My superiors in the college and downtown were sympathetic and assured me that I wasn't about to lose my job because I had to be out ill "from time to time," and up to a point I believed them; still, to be disabled on a Saturday or a Sunday was to me far less spiritually debilitating than to have to ask the indulgence of either my colleagues or students.

Whatever erotic curiosity had been aroused in me by Lydia's pretty, girlish, Scandinavian block of a head—and odd as it will sound to some, by the exoticism of the blighted middle western Protestant background she wrote about and had managed to survive in one piece—was decidedly outweighed by my conviction that I would be betraying my vocation, and doing damage to my self-esteem, if I were to take one of my students to bed. As I have said, suppressing feelings and desires extraneous to the purpose that had brought us together seemed to me crucial to the success of the transaction—as I must have called it then, the pedagogical transaction—allowing each of us to be as teacherly or as studently as was within his power, without wasting time and spirit being provocative, charming, duplicitous, touchy, jealous, scheming, etc. You could do all that out in the street; only in the classroom, as far as I knew, was it possible to approach one another with the intensity ordinarily associated with love, yet cleansed of emotional extremism and free of base motives having to do with profit and power. To be sure, on more than a few occasions, my night class was as perplexing as a Kafka courtroom, and my composition classes as wearisome as any assembly line, but that our effort was characterized at bottom by modesty and mutual trust, and conducted as ingenuously as dignity would permit, was indisputable. Whether it was Mrs. Corbett's innocent and ardent question about how to address a friendly letter to a little girl or my own no less innocent and ardent introductory lecture to which she was responding, what we said to one another was not uttered in the name of anything vile or even mundane. At twenty-four, dressed up like a man in a clean white shirt and a tie, and bearing chalk powder on the tails of my worn tweed jacket, that seemed to me a truth to be held self-evident. Oh, how I wanted a soul that was pure and spotless!

In Lydia's case, professorial discretion was helped along some, or I should have thought it would be, by that rolling, mannish gait of hers. The first time she entered my class I actually wondered if she could be some kind of gymnast or acrobat, perhaps a member of a women's track and field association; I was reminded of those photographs in the popular magazines of the strong blue-eyed women athletes who win medals at the Olympic games for the Soviet Union. Yet her shoulders were as touchingly narrow as a child's, and her skin pale and almost luminously soft. Only from the waist to the floor did she seem to be moving on the body of my sex rather than her own.

Within the month I had seduced her, as much against her inclination and principles as my own. It was standard enough procedure, pretty much what Mrs. Slater must have had in mind: a conference alone together in my office, a train ride side by side on the IC back to Hyde Park, an invitation to a beer at my local tavern, the flirtatious walk to her apartment, the request by me for coffee, if she would make me some. She begged me to think twice about what I was doing, even after she had returned from the bathroom where she had inserted her diaphragm and I had removed her underpants for the second time and was hunched, unclothed, over her small, ill-proportioned body, preparatory to entering her. She was distressed, she was amused, she was frightened, she was mystified.

"There are so many beautiful young girls around, why pick on me? Why choose me, when you could have the cream of the crop?"

I didn't bother to answer. As though she were the one being coy or foolish, I smiled.

She said: "Look, look at me."

"I'm doing that."

"Are you? I'm five years older than you. My breasts sag, not that they ever amounted to much to begin with.

Look, I have stretch marks. My behind's too big, I'm hamstrung—'Professor,' listen to me, I don't have orgasms. I want you to know that beforehand. I never have."

When we later sat down for the coffee, Lydia, wrapped in a robe, said this: "I'll never know why you wanted to do that. Why not Mrs. Slater, who's *begging* you for it? Why should anyone like you want me?"

Of course I didn't "want" her, not then or ever. We lived together for almost six years, the first eighteen months as lovers, and the four years following, until her suicide, as husband and wife, and in all that time her flesh was never any less distasteful to me than she had insistently advertised it to be. Utterly without lust, I seduced her on that first night, the next morning, and hundreds of times thereafter. As for Mrs. Slater, I seduced her probably no more than ten times in all, and never anywhere but in my imagination.

It was another month before I met Monica, Lydia's ten-year-old daughter, so it will not do to say that, like Nabokov's designing rogue, I endured the uninviting mother in order to have access to the seductive and seducible young daughter. That came later. In the beginning Monica was without any attraction whatsoever, repellent to me in character as well as appearance: lanky, stringy-haired, undernourished, doltish, without a trace of curiosity or charm, and so illiterate that at ten she was still unable to tell the time. In her dungarees and faded polo shirts she had the look of some mountain child, the offspring of poverty and deprivation. Worse, when she was dressed to kill in her white dress and round white hat, wearing her little Mary Jane shoes and carrying a white handbag and a Bible (white too), she seemed to me a replica of those overdressed little Gentile children who used to pass our house every Sunday on their way to church, and toward whom I used to feel an emotion almost as strong as my own grandparents' aversion. Secretly, and despite myself, I came close to despising the stupid and stubborn child when she would appear in that little white church-going

outfit—and so too did Lydia, who was reminded by
Monica's costume of the clothes in which she had had
to array herself each Sunday in Skokie, before being led
off to Lutheran services with her aunts Helda and
Jessie. (As the story had it: "It did a growing body
good to sit once a week in a nice starched dress, and
without squirming.")

I was drawn to Lydia, not out of a passion for
Monica—not yet—but because she had suffered so and
because she was so brave. Not only that she had survived, but *what* she had survived, gave her enormous
moral stature, or glamor, in my eyes: on the one hand,
the puritan austerity, the prudery, the blandness, the
xenophobia of the women of her clan; on the other, the
criminality of the men. Of course, I did not equate
being raped by one's father with being raised on the
wisdom of the *Chicago Tribune;* what made her seem
to me so valiant was that she had been subjected to
every brand of barbarity, from the banal to the wicked,
had been exploited, beaten, and betrayed by every last
one of her keepers, had finally been driven crazy—
and in the end had proved indestructible: she lived
now in a neat little apartment within earshot of the bell
in the clock tower of the university whose atheists,
Communists, and Jews her people had loathed, and at
the kitchen table of that apartment wrote ten pages for
me every week in which she managed, heroically I
thought, to recall the details of that brutal life in the
style of one a very long way from rage and madness.
When I told the class that what I admired most in Mrs.
Ketterer's fiction was her "control," I meant something
more than those strangers could know.

Given all there was to move me about her character,
it seemed to me curious that I should be *so* repelled
by her flesh as I was that first night. I was able myself
to achieve an orgasm, but afterward felt terrible for
the "achievement" it had had to be. Earlier, caressing
her body, I had been made uneasy by the unexpected
texture of her genitals. To the touch, the fold of skin
between her legs felt abnormally thick, and when I

looked, as though to take pleasure in the sight of her nakedness, the vaginal lips appeared withered and discolored in a way that was alarming to me. I could even imagine myself to be staring down at the sexual parts of one of Lydia's maiden aunts, rather than at a physically healthy young woman not yet into her thirties. I was tempted to imagine some connection here to the childhood victimization by her father, but of course that was too literary, too poetic an idea to swallow—this was no stigma, however apprehensive it might make me.

The reader may by now be able to imagine for himself how the twenty-four-year-old I was responded to his alarm: in the morning, without very much ado, I performed cunnilingus upon her.

"Don't," said Lydia. "Don't do that."

"Why not?" I expected the answer: *Because I'm so ugly there.*

"I told you. I won't reach a climax. It doesn't matter what you do."

Like a sage who'd seen everything and been everywhere, I said, "You make too much of that."

Her thighs were not as long as my forearm (about the length, I thought, of one of Mrs. Slater's Pappagallos) and her legs were open only so far as I had been able to spread them with my two hands. But where she was dry, brownish, weatherworn, I pressed my open mouth. I took no pleasure in the act, she gave no sign that she did; but at least I had done what I had been frightened of doing, put my tongue to where she had been brutalized, as though—it was tempting to put it this way—that would redeem us both.

As though that would redeem us both. A notion as inflated as it was shallow, growing, I am certain, out of "serious literary studies." Where Emma Bovary had read too many romances of her period, it would seem that I had read too much of the criticism of mine. That I was, by "eating" her, taking some sort of sacrament was a most attractive idea—though one that I rejected after the initial momentary infatuation. Yes, I continued to resist as best I could all these high-flown, prestigious interpretations, whether of my migraines or my sexual relations with Lydia; and yet it surely did seem to me that my life was coming to resemble one of those texts upon which certain literary critics of that era used to enjoy venting their ingenuity. I could have done a clever job on it myself for my senior honors thesis in college: "Christian Temptations in a Jewish Life: A Study in the Ironies of 'Courting Disaster.' "

So: as often during a week as I could manage it, I "took the sacrament," conquering neither my fearful repugnance nor the shame I felt at being repelled, and neither believing nor disbelieving the somber reverberations.

During the first months of my love affair with Lydia, I continued to receive letters and, on occasion, telephone calls from Sharon Shatzky, the junior at Pembroke with whom I had concluded a passionate romance prior to my return to Chicago. Sharon was a tall, handsome, auburn-haired girl, studious, enthusiastic, and lively, an honor student in literature, and the daughter of a successful zipper manufacturer with country-club affiliations and a hundred-thousand-dollar suburban home who had been impressed with my credentials and entirely hospitable to me, until I began to suffer from migraines. Then Mr. Shatzky grew fearful that if he did not intervene, his daughter might one day find herself married to a man she would have to nurse and support for the rest of her life. Sharon was enraged by her father's "lack of compassion." "He thinks of my life," she said, angrily, "as a business investment." It enraged her even more when I came to her father's defense. I said that it was as much his paternal duty to make clear to a young daughter what might be the long-range consequences of my ailment as it had been years before to see that she was inoculated against smallpox; he did not want her to suffer for no reason. "But I love you," Sharon said, "that's my 'reason.' I want to be with you if you're ill. I don't want to run out on you then, I want to take care of you." "But he's saying that you don't know all that 'taking care of' could entail." "But I'm telling you—I *love* you."

Had I wanted to marry Sharon (or her family's money) as much as her father assumed I did, I might not have been so tolerant of his opposition. But as I was just into my twenties then, the prospect of marriage, even to a lovely young woman toward whom I had so strong an erotic attachment, did not speak to the range of my ambitions. I should say, *particularly* because of this strong erotic attachment was I suspicious of an enduring union. For without that admittedly powerful bond, what was there of consequence, of *importance*, between Sharon and myself? Only three years my junior, Sharon seemed to me vastly younger, and to stand too much in my shadow, with few attitudes or interests that were her own; she read the books I recommended to her, devouring them by the dozen the summer we met, and repeated to her friends and teachers, as hers, judgments she had borrowed from me; she had even switched from a government to a literature major under my influence, a satisfaction to me at first, in the fatherly stage of my infatuation, but afterward a sign, among others, of what seemed to me an excess of submissiveness and malleability.

It did not, at that time, occur to me to find evidence of character, intelligence, and imagination in the bounteousness of her sexuality or in the balance she managed to maintain between a bold and vivacious animality and a tender, compliant nature. Nor did I begin to understand that it was in that tension, rather than in the sexuality alone, that her appeal resided. Rather, I would think, with something like despair, "That's all we really have," as though unselfconsciously fervent lovemaking, sustained over a period of several years, was a commonplace phenomenon.

One night, when Lydia and I were already asleep in my apartment, Sharon telephoned to speak with me. She was in tears and didn't try to hide it. She could not bear any longer the *stupidity* of my decision. Surely

I could not hold her accountable for her father's cold-blooded behavior, if that was the explanation for what I was doing. What *was* I doing anyway? And *how* was I doing? Was I well? Was I ill? How was my writing, my teaching—I *had* to let her fly to Chicago . . . But I told her she must stay where she was. I remained throughout calm and firm. No, I did not hold her accountable for anybody's behavior but her own, which was exemplary. I reminded her that it was not I who had judged her father "cold-blooded." When she continued to appeal to me to come to "my senses," I said that it was she who had better face facts, especially as they were not so unpleasant as she was making them out to be: she was a beautiful, intelligent, passionate young woman, and if she would stop this theatrical grieving and make herself available to life once again—

"But if I'm all those things, then why are you throwing me away like this? Please, I don't understand—make it clear to me! If I'm so exemplary, why don't *you* want me? Oh, Nathan," she said, now openly weeping again, "you know what I think? That underneath all that scrupulousness and fairness and reasonableness, you're a madman! Sometimes I think that underneath all that 'maturity' you're just a crazy little boy!"

When I returned from the kitchen phone to the living room, Lydia was sitting up in my sofa bed. "It was that girl, wasn't it?" But without a trace of jealousy, though I knew she hated her, if only abstractly. "You want to go back to her, don't you?"

"*No.*"

"But you know you're sorry you ever started up with me. *I* know it. Only now you can't figure how to get out of it. You're afraid you'll disappoint me, or hurt me, and so you let the weeks go by—and I can't stand the suspense, Nathan, or the confusion. If you're going to leave me, please do it now, tonight, this minute. Send me packing, please, I beg of you—because I don't want to be endured, or pitied, or rescued, or whatever it is that's going on here! What *are* you doing with me—what am *I* doing with someone like *you!* You've got success writ-

ten all over—it's in every breath you take! So what is
this all about? You know you'd rather sleep with that
girl than with me—so stop pretending otherwise, and
go back to her, and do it!"

Now *she* cried, as hopeless and bewildered as Sharon.
I kissed her, I tried to comfort her. I told her that nothing she was saying was so, when of course it was
true in every detail: I loathed making love to her, I
wished to be rid of her, I couldn't bear the thought
of hurting her, and following the phone call, I did indeed want more than ever to go back to the one Lydia
referred to always as "that girl." Yet I refused to confess
to such feelings or act upon them.

"She's sexy, young, Jewish, *rich*—"

"Lydia, you're only torturing yourself—"

"But I'm so *hideous*. I have *nothing*."

No, if anyone was "hideous," it was I, yearning for
Sharon's sweet lewdness, her playful and brazen sensu-
ality, for what I used to think of as her *perfect pitch*,
that unfailingly precise responsiveness to whatever our
erotic mood—wanting, remembering, envisioning all
this, even as I labored over Lydia's flesh, with its
contrasting memories of physical misery. What was "hideous" was to be so queasy and finicky about the imperfections of a woman's body, to find oneself an adherent
of the most Hollywoodish, *cold-blooded* notions of
what is desirable and what is not; what was "hideous"
—alarming, shameful, astonishing—was the significance that a young man of my pretensions should attach
to his lust.

And there was more which, if it did not cause me to
feel so peculiarly desolated as I did by what I took to
be my callow sexual reflexes, gave me still other good
reasons to distrust myself. There were, for instance,
Monica's Sunday visits—how brutal they were! And
how I recoiled from what I saw! Especially when I
remembered—with the luxurious sense of having been
blessed—the Sundays of my own childhood, the daylong
round of visits, first to my two widowed grandmothers
in the slum where my parents had been born, and then

around Camden to the households of half a dozen
aunts and uncles. During the war, when gasoline was
rationed, we would have to walk to visit the grandmothers, traversing on foot five miles of city streets in
all—a fair measure of our devotion to those two queenly
and prideful workhorses, who lived very similarly in
small apartments redolent of freshly ironed linen and
stale coal gas, amid an accumulation of antimacassars,
bar mitzvah photos, and potted plants, most of them
taller and sturdier than I ever was. Peeling wallpaper,
cracked linoleum, ancient faded curtains, this nonetheless was my Araby, and I their little sultan . . . what
is more, a sickly sultan whose need was all the greater
for his Sunday sweets and sauces. Oh how I was fed
and comforted, washerwoman breasts for my pillows,
deep grandmotherly laps, my throne!

Of course, when I was ill or the weather was bad, I
would have to stay at home, looked after by my sister,
while my father and mother made the devotional safari
alone, in galoshes and under umbrellas. But that was
not so unpleasant either, for Sonia would read aloud
to me, in a very actressy way, from a book she owned
entitled *Two Hundred Opera Plots;* intermittently she
would break into song. " 'The action takes place in
India,' " she read, " 'and opens in the sacred grounds of
the Hindoo priest, Nilakantha, who has an inveterate
hatred for the English. During his absence, however, a
party of English officers and ladies enter, out of curiosity, and are charmed with the lovely garden. They
soon depart, with the exception of the officer, Gerald,
who remains to make a sketch, in spite of the warning
of his friend, Frederick. Presently the priest's lovely
daughter, Lakmé, enters, having come by the river.
. . .' " The phrase "having come by the river," the
spelling of Hindu in Sunny's book with those final twin
o's (like a pair of astonished eyes; like the middle
vowels in "hoot" and "moon" and "poor"; like a distil-
lation of everything and anything I found mysterious),
appealed strongly to this invalid child, as did her performing so wholeheartedly for an audience of one . . .

Lakmé is taken by her father, both of them disguised as beggars, to the city market: " 'He forces Lakmé to sing, hoping thus to attract the attention of her lover, should he be amongst the party of English who are buying in the bazaars.' " I am still barely recovered from the word "bazaars" and its pair of *a*'s (the sound of "odd," the sound of a sigh), when Sunny introduces "The Bell Song," the aria *"De la fille du paria,"* says my sister in Bresslenstein's French accent: the ballad of the pariah's daughter who saves a stranger in the forest from the wild beasts by the enchantment of her magic bell. After struggling with the soaring aria, my sister, flushed and winded from the effort, returns to her highly dramatic reading of the plot: " 'And this cunning plan succeeds, for Gerald instantly recognizes the thrilling voice of the fair Hindoo maiden—' " And is stabbed in the back by Lakmé's father; and is nursed back to health by her " 'in a beautiful jungle' "; only there the fellow " 'remembers with remorse the fair English girl to whom he is betrothed' "; and so decides to leave my sister, who kills herself with poisonous herbs, " 'the deadly juices of which she drinks.' " I could not decide whom to hate more, Gerald, with his remorse for "the fair English girl," or Lakmé's crazy father, who would not let his daughter love a white man. Had I been "in India" instead of at home on a rainy Sunday, and had I weighed something more than sixty pounds, I would have saved her from them both, I thought.

Later, at the back landing, my mother and father shake the water off themselves like dogs—our loyal Dalmatians, our lifesaving Saint Bernards. They leave their umbrellas open in the bathtub to dry. They have carried home to me—two and a half miles through a storm, and with a war on—a jar of my grandmother Zuckerman's stuffed cabbage, a shoe box containing my grandmother Ackerman's strudel: food for a starving Nathan, to enrich his blood and bring him health and happiness. Later still, my exhibitionistic sister will stand exactly in the center of the living-room rug, on the "oriental" medallion, practicing her scales, while my father reads the battlefront news in the *Sunday Inquirer* and my mother gauges the temperature of my forehead with her lips, each hourly reading ending in a kiss. And I, all the while, an Ingres odalisque languid on the sofa. Was there ever anything like it, since the day of rest began?

How those rituals of love out of my own antiquity (no nostalgia for me!) return in every poignant nostalgic detail when I watch the unfolding of another horrific Ketterer Sunday. As orthodox as we had been in performing the ceremonies of familial devotion, so the Ketterers were in the perpetuation of their barren and wretched lovelessness. To watch the cycle of disaster repeating itself was as chilling as watching an electrocution—yes, a slow electrocution, the burning up of Monica Ketterer's life, seemed to me to be taking place before my eyes Sunday after Sunday. Stupid, broken, illiterate child, she did not know her right hand from her left, could not read the clock, could not even read a slogan off a billboard or a cereal box without someone helping her over each syllable as though it were an alp. Monica. Lydia. Ketterer. I thought: "What am I doing with these people?" And thinking that, could see no choice for myself but to stay.

Sundays Monica was delivered to the door by Eugene Ketterer, just as unattractive a man as the reader, who has gotten the drift of my story, would expect to find entering the drama at this point. Another nail in Nathan's coffin. If only Lydia had been exaggerating, if only I could have said to her, as it isn't always impossible to say to the divorced of their former spouses, "Come on now, he isn't nearly so bad as all that." If only, even in a joking way, I could have teased her by saying, "Why, I rather like him." But I hated him.

The only surprise was to discover him to be physically uglier than Lydia had even suggested. As if that character of his wasn't enough. Bad teeth, a large smashed nose, hair brilliantined back for church, and, in his dress, entirely the urban yokel . . . Now how

could a girl with a pretty face and so much native refinement and intelligence have married a type like this
to begin with? Simple: he was the first to ask her. Here
was the knight who had rescued Lydia from that prison
house in Skokie.

To the reader who has not just "gotten the drift," but
begun to balk at the uniformly dismal situation that I
have presented here, to the reader who finds himself
unable to suspend his disbelief in a protagonist who
voluntarily sustains an affair with a woman sexless to
him and so disaster-ridden, I should say that in retrospect I find him nearly impossible to believe in myself.
Why should a young man otherwise reasonable, far-
sighted, watchful, judicious, and self-concerned, a man
meticulously precise in the bread-and-butter concerns
of life, and the model of husbandry with his endowment, why should he pursue, in this obviously weighty
encounter, a course so *defiantly* not in his interest? For
the sake of defiance? Does that convince *you?* Surely
some protective, life-sustaining instinct—call it common
sense, horse sense, a kind of basic biological alarm
system—should have awakened him to the inevitable
consequences, even as a glass of cold water thrown in
his face will bring the most far-gone sleepwalker back
from the world of stairwells without depth and boule-
vards without traffic. I look in vain for anything resembling a genuine sense of religious mission—that
which sends missionaries off to convert the savages or
to minister to lepers—or for the psychological abnor-
mality pronounced enough to account for this preposterous behavior. To make *some* sort of accounting, the
writer emphasizes Lydia's "moral glamor" and develops,
probably with more thoroughness than is engrossing,
the idea of Zuckerman's "seriousness," even going so
far, in the subtitle, as to describe that seriousness as
something of a social phenomenon; but to be frank, it
does not seem, even to the author, that he has, sugges-
tive subtitle and all, answered the objection of im-
plausibility, any more than the young man Zuckerman's
own prestigious interpretations of his migraines seemed

to him consonant with the pain itself. And to bring
words like "enigmatic" and "mysterious" into the discussion not only goes against my grain, but hardly
seems to make things any less inconceivable.

To be sure, it would probably help some if I were at
least to mention in passing the pleasant Saturday strolls
that Lydia and Nathan used to take together down by
the lake, their picnics, their bicycle rides, their visits to
the zoo, the aquarium, the Art Institute, to the theater
when the Bristol Old Vic and Marcel Marceau came to
town; I could write about the friendships they made
with other university couples, the graduate-student parties they occasionally went to on weekends, the lectures
by famous poets and critics they attended at Mandel
Hall, the evenings they spent together reading by the
fire in Lydia's apartment. But to call up such memories
in order to make the affair more credible would actually
be to mislead the reader about the young man Nathan
Zuckerman was; pleasures and comforts of the ordinary
social variety were to him inconsequential, for they
seemed *without moral content*. It wasn't because they
both enjoyed eating Chinese food on Sixty-third Street
or even because both admired Chekhov's short stories
that he married Lydia; he could have married Sharon
Shatzky for that, and for more. Incredible as it may
seem to some—and I am one of them—it was *precisely*
"the uniformly dismal situation" that did more for
Lydia's cause than all the companionable meals and
walks and museum visits and the cozy fireside conversations in which he corrected her taste in books.

To the reader who "believes" in Zuckerman's predicament as I describe it, but is unwilling to take such a
person as seriously as I do, let me say that I am tempted
to make fun of him myself. To treat this story as a
species of comedy would not require more than a slight
alteration in tone and attitude. In graduate school, for a
course titled "Advanced Shakespeare," I once wrote a
paper on *Othello* proposing just such a shift in emphasis.
I imagined, in detail, several unlikely productions, including one in which Othello and Iago addressed each

other as "Mr. Interlocutor" and "Mr. Bones," and another, somewhat more extreme, in which the racial situation was entirely reversed, with Othello acted by a white man and the rest of the cast portrayed by blacks, thus shedding another kind of light (I concluded) on the "motiveless malignity."

In the story at hand, it would seem to me that from the perspective of this decade particularly, there is much that could be ridiculed having to do with the worship of ordeal and forbearance and the suppression of the sexual man. It would not require too much ingenuity on my part to convert the protagonist here into an insufferable prig to be laughed at, a character out of a farce. Or if not the protagonist, then the narrator. To some, the funniest thing of all, or perhaps the strangest, may not be how I conducted myself back then, but the literary mode in which I have chosen to narrate my story today: the decorousness, the orderliness, the underlying sobriety, that "responsible" manner that I continue to affect. For not only have literary manners changed drastically since all this happened ten years ago, back in the middle fifties, but I myself am hardly who I was or wanted to be: no longer am I a member in good standing of that eminently decent and humane university community, no longer am I the son my parents proudly used to address by mail as "professor." By my own standards, my private life is a failure and a disgrace, neither decorous, nor sober, and surely not "responsible." Or so it seems to me: I am full of shame and believe myself to be a scandalous figure. I can't imagine that I shall ever have the courage to return to live in Chicago, or anywhere in America.

Presently we reside in one of the larger Italian cities; "we" are myself and Monica, or Moonie, as I eventually came to call her in our intimacy. The two of us have been alone together now since Lydia gouged open her wrists with the metal tip of a can opener and bled to death in the bathtub of our ground-floor apartment on Woodlawn, where the three of us were living as a family. Lydia was thirty-five when she died, I was just thirty, and Moonie sixteen. After Ketterer's second divorce, I had gone to court, in Lydia's behalf, and sued to regain custody of her daughter—and I won. How could I lose? I was a respectable academic and promising author whose stories appeared in serious literary quarterlies; Ketterer was a wife beater, two times over. That was how Moonie came to be living with us in Hyde Park—and how Lydia came to suffer her final torment. For she could not have been any more excluded from their lives by the aunts in Skokie, or more relegated to the position of an unloved Cinderella, than she was by what grew up between Moonie and myself and constituted during those years my only sexual yearning. Lydia used to awaken me in the middle of the night by pounding on my chest with her fists. And nothing Dr. Rutherford might do or say could stop her. "If you ever lay a finger on my daughter," she would cry, "I'll drive a knife into your heart!". But I never did sleep with Moonie, not so long as her mother was alive. Under the guise of father and daughter, we touched and fondled one another's flesh; as the months went by we more and more frequently barged in upon one another—unknowingly, inadvertently—in the midst of dressing or unclothed in the bathtub; raking leaves in the yard or out swimming off the Point we were playful and high-spirited, as a man and his young mistress might be expected to be . . . but in the end, as though she were my own offspring or my own sister, I honored the incest taboo. It was not easy.

Then we found Lydia in the tub. Probably none of our friends or my colleagues assumed that Lydia had killed herself because I had been sleeping with her daughter—until I fled with Moonie to Italy. I did not know what else to do, after the night we finally did make love. She was sixteen years old—her mother a suicide, her father a sadistic ignoramus, and she herself, because of her reading difficulties, still only a freshman in high school: given all that, how could I desert her? But how ever could we be lovers together in Hyde Park?

So I at last got to make the trip to Europe that I had been planning when Lydia and I first met, only it wasn't to see the cultural monuments and literary landmarks that I came here.

I do not think that Moonie is as unhappy in Italy as Anna Karenina was with Vronsky, nor, since our first year here, have I been anything like so bewildered and disabled as was Aschenbach because of his passion for Tadzio. I had expected more agony; with my self-dramatizing literary turn of mind, I had even thought that Moonie might go mad. But the fact is that to our Italian friends we are simply another American writer and his pretty young girl friend, a tall, quiet, somber kid, whose only distinction, outside of her good looks, appears to them to be her total devotion to me; they tell me they are unused to seeing such deference for her man in a long-legged American blonde. They rather like her for this. The only friend I have who is anything like an intimate says that whenever I go out of a room, leaving her behind, Moonie seems almost to cease to exist. He wonders why. It isn't any longer because she doesn't know the language; happily, she became fluent in Italian as quickly as I did and, with this language, suffers none of those reading difficulties that used to make her nightly homework assignments such hell for the three of us back in Chicago. She is no longer stupid; or stubborn; though she is too often morose.

When she was twenty-one, and legally speaking no longer my "ward," I decided to marry Moonie. The very worst of it was over by then, and I mean by that, voracious, frenzied lust as well as paralyzing fear. I thought marriage might carry us beyond this tedious second stage, wherein she tended to be silent and gloomy, and I, in a muted sort of way, to be continually anxious, as though waiting in a hospital bed to be wheeled down to the operating room for surgery. Either I must marry her or leave her, take her upon me forever or end it entirely. So, on her twenty-first birthday, having firmly decided which was the choice for me, I proposed. But Moonie said no, she didn't ever want to be a wife. I lost my temper, I began to speak angrily in English—in the restaurant people looked our way. "You mean, *my* wife!" *"E di chi altro potrei essere?"* she replied. *Whose could I ever be anyway?*

That was that, the last time I attempted to make things "right." Consequently, we live on together in this unmarried state, and I continue to be stunned at the thought of whom my dutiful companion is and was and how she came to be with me. You would think I would have gotten over that by now, but I seem unable, or unwilling, to do so. So long as no one here knows our story, I am able to control the remorse and the shame.

However, to stifle the sense I have that I am living *someone else's life* is beyond me. I was supposed to be elsewhere and otherwise. This is not the life I worked and planned for! Was made for! Outwardly, to be sure, I am as respectable in my dress and manner as I was when I began adult life as an earnest young academic in Chicago in the fifties. I certainly *appear* to have no traffic with the unlikely or the unusual. Under a pseudonym, I write and publish short stories, somewhat more my own by now than Katherine Mansfield's, but still strongly marked by irony and indirection. To my surprise, reading through the magazines at the USIS library one afternoon recently, I came upon an article in an American literary journal, in which "I" am mentioned in the same breath with some rather famous writers as one whose literary and social concerns are currently out of date. I had not realized I had ever become so well known as now to be irrelevant. How can I be certain of anything from here, either the state of my pseudonymous reputation or my real one? I also teach English and American literature at a university in the city, to students more docile and respectful than any I have ever had to face. The U. of C. was never like this. I pick up a little extra cash, very little, by reading American novels for an Italian publishing house and telling them what I think; in this way I have been able to keep abreast of the latest developments in fiction.

And I don't have migraines any more. I outgrew them some twenty years before the neurologist said I might— make of that what you wish . . . On the other hand, I need only contemplate a visit to my aging and ailing father in New Jersey, I have only to pass the American airline offices on the Via ——, for my heart to go galloping off on its own and the strength to flow out of my limbs. A minute's serious thought to being reunited with those who used to love me, or simply knew me, and I am panic-stricken . . . The panic of the escaped convict who imagines the authorities have picked up his scent—only I am the authority as well as the escapee. *For I do want to go home.* If only I had the wherewithal to extradite myself! The longer I remain in hiding like this, the more I allow the legend of my villainy to harden. And how do I even know from here that such a legend exists any longer outside my imagination? Or that it ever did? The America I glimpse on the TV and read about once a month in the periodicals at the USIS library does not strike me as a place where people worry very much any more about who is sleeping with whom. Who cares any longer that this twenty-four-year-old woman was once my own stepdaughter? Who cares that I took her virginity at sixteen and "inadvertently" fondled her at twelve? Who back there even remembers the late Lydia Zuckerman or the circumstances surrounding her suicide and my departure in 1962? From what I read it would appear that in post-Oswald America a man with my sort of record can go about his business without attracting very much attention. Even Ketterer could cause us no harm, I would think, now that his daughter is no longer a minor; not that after we ran off he felt much of anything anyway, except perhaps relief at no longer having to fork over the twenty-five bucks a week that the court had ordered him to pay us for Moonie's support.

I know then what I must do. I know what must be done. I do know! Either I must bring myself to leave Moonie (and by this action, rid myself of all the confusion that her nearness keeps alive in me); either I must leave her, making it clear to her beforehand that there is another man somewhere in this world with whom she not only could survive, but with whom she might be a gayer, more lighthearted person—I must convince her that when I go she will not be left to dwindle away, but will have (as she will) half a hundred suitors within the year, as many serious men to court a sweet and statuesque young woman like herself as there are frivolous ones who follow after her here in the streets, hissing and kissing at the air, Italians imagining she is Scandinavian and wild—either I must leave Moonie, and *now* (even if for the time being it is only to move across the river, and from there to look after her like a father who dwells in the same city, instead of the lover who lies beside her in bed and to whose body she clings in her sleep), either that, or return with her to America, where we will live, we two lovers, like anybody else—like *everybody* else, if I am to believe what they write about "the sexual revolution" in the newsmagazines of my native land.

But I am too humiliated to do either. The country may have changed, I have not. I did not know such depths of humiliation were possible, even for me. A reader of Conrad's *Lord Jim* and Mauriac's *Thérèse* and Kafka's "Letter to His Father," of Hawthorne and Strindberg and Sophocles—of Freud!—and still I did not know that humiliation could do such a job on a man. It seems either that literature too strongly influences my ideas about life, or that I am able to make no connection at all between its wisdom and my existence. For I cannot fully believe in the hopelessness of my predicament, and yet the line that concludes *The Trial* is as familiar to me as my own face: "it was as if the shame of it must outlive him"! Only I am not a character in a book, certainly not *that* book. I am real. And my humiliation is equally *real*. God, how I thought I was suffering in adolescence when fly balls used to fall through my hands in the schoolyard, and the born athletes on my team would smack their foreheads in despair. What I would give now to be living again back in that state of disgrace. What I would give to be living back in Chicago, teaching the principles of composition to my lively freshmen all morning long, taking my simple dinner off a tray at the Commons at night, reading from the European masters in my bachelor bed before sleep, fifty monumental pages annotated and underlined, Mann, Tolstoy, Gogol, Proust, in bed with all that genius—oh to have that sense of worthiness again, and migraines too if need be! How I wanted a dignified life! And how confident I was!

To conclude, in a traditional narrative mode, the story of that Zuckerman in that Chicago. I leave it to those writers who live in the flamboyant American present, and whose extravagant fictions I sample from afar, to treat the implausible, the preposterous, and the bizarre in something other than a straightforward and recognizable manner.

In my presence Eugene Ketterer did his best to appear easygoing, unruffled, and nonviolent, just a regular guy. I called him Mr. Ketterer, he called me Nathan, Nate, and Natie. The later he was in delivering Monica to her mother, the more offhand and, to me, galling was his behavior; to Lydia it was infuriating, and in the face of it she revealed a weakness for vitriolic rage which I'd seen no evidence of before, not at home or in class or in her fiction. It did not help any to caution her against allowing him to provoke her; in fact, several times she accused me—afterward, tearfully asking forgiveness—of taking Ketterer's side, when my only concern had been to prevent her from losing her head in front of Monica. She responded to Ketterer's taunting like some animal in a cage being poked with a stick, and I knew, the second Sunday that I was on hand to witness his cruelty and her response, that I would shortly have to make it clear to "Gene" that I was not just some disinterested bystander, that enough of his sadism was enough.

In the beginning, before Ketterer and I finally had

it out, if Lydia demanded an explanation from him for showing up at two P.M. (when he had been due to arrive with Monica at ten thirty in the morning) he would look at *me* and say, fraternally, "Women." If Lydia were to reply, "That's idiotic! That's meaningless! What would a thug like you know about 'women,' or men, or children! Why are you late with her, Eugene?" he would just shrug and mumble, "Got held up." "That will not do—!" "Have to, Lyd. 'Fraid that's the way the cookie crumbles." Or without even bothering to give her an answer, he would say, again to me, "Live 'n' learn, Natie." A similarly unpleasant scene would occur in the evening, when he arrived to pick Monica up either much too early or too late. "Look, I ain't a clock. Never claimed to be." "You never claimed to be anything—because you're *not* anything!" "Yeah, I know, I'm a brute and a slob and a real bad thug, and you, you're Lady Godiva. Yeah, I know all that." "You're a tormentor, that's what you are! That you torture me is not even the point any more—but how can you be so cruel and heartless as to torture your own little child! How can you play with us like this, Sunday after Sunday, year after year—you caveman! you hollow ignoramus!" "Let's go, Harmonica"—*his* nickname for the child—"time to go home with the Big Bad Wolf."

Usually Monica spent the day at Lydia's watching TV and wearing her hat. Ready to go at a moment's notice.

"Monica," Lydia would say, "you really can't sit all day watching TV."

Uncomprehending: "Uh-huh."

"Monica, do you hear me? It's three o'clock. Maybe that's enough TV for one day—do you think? Didn't you bring your homework?"

Completely in the dark: "My *what?*"

"Did you bring your homework this week, so we can go over it?"

A mutter: "Forgot."

"But I told you I'd help you. You *need* help, you know that."

Outrage: "Today's *Sunday.*"

"And?"

Law of Nature: "Sundays I don't *do* no homework."

"Don't talk like that, please. You never even spoke like that when you were a little six-year-old girl. You know better than that."

Cantankerous: "What?"

"Using double negatives. Saying I don't do *no*—the way your father does. And please don't sit like that."

Incredulous: *"What?"*

"You're sitting like a boy. Change into your dungarees if you want to sit like that. Otherwise sit like a girl your age."

Defiant: "I am."

"Monica, listen to me: I think we should practice your subtraction. We'll have to do it without the book, since you didn't bring it."

Pleading: "But today's *Sunday*."

"But you need help in subtraction. That's what you need, not church, but help with your math. Monica, take that hat off! Take that silly hat off this minute! It's three o'clock in the afternoon and you just can't wear it all day long!"

Determined. Wrathful: "It's my hat—I can too!"

"But you're in my house! And I'm your mother! And I'm telling you to take it off! Why do you insist on behaving in this silly way! I *am* your mother, you know that! Monica, I love you and you love me—don't you remember when you were a little girl, don't you remember how we used to play? Take that hat off *before I tear it off your head!*"

Ultimate Weapon: "Touch my head and I'll tell my dad on you!"

"And don't call him 'Dad'! I cannot stand when you call that man who tortures the two of us 'Dad'! And sit like a girl! Do as I tell you! Close your legs!"

Sinister: "They're closed."

"They're *open* and you're showing your underpants and stop it! You're too big for that—you go on buses, you go to school, if you're wearing a dress then behave as though you're wearing one! You cannot sit like this watching television Sunday after Sunday—not when you cannot even add two and two."

Philosophical: "Who cares."

"I care! *Can* you add two and two? I want to know! Look at me—I'm perfectly serious. I have to know what you know and what you don't know, and where to begin. How much is two and two? *Answer me.*"

Dumpish: "Dunno."

"You *do* know. And pronounce your syllables. And answer me!"

Savage: "I don't know! Leave me alone, you!"

"Monica, how much is eleven minus one? Eleven take away one. If you had eleven cents and someone took away one of them, how many would you have left? Dear, please, what number comes before eleven? You must know *this.*"

Hysterical: *"I don't know it!"*

"You do!"

Exploding: "Twelve!"

"How can it be *twelve?* Twelve is *more* than eleven. I'm asking you what's *less* than eleven. Eleven take away one—is how much?"

Pause. Reflection. Decision: "One."

"No! You *have* eleven and you take *away* one."

Illumination: "Oh, take *away.*"

"Yes. Yes."

Straight-faced: "We never had take-aways."

"You *did.* You *had* to."

Steely: "I'm telling you the truth, *we don't have take-aways in James Madison School.*"

"Monica, this is *subtraction*—they have it everywhere in every school, and you have to know it. Oh darling, I don't care about that hat—I don't even care about him, that's *over.* I care about *you* and what's going to happen to *you.* Because you cannot be a little girl who knows nothing. If you are you'll get into trouble and your life will be awful. You're a girl and you're growing up, and you have to know how to make change of a dollar and what comes before eleven, which is how old you'll be *next year,* and you have to know how to sit— please, please don't sit like that, Monica, please don't go on buses and sit like that in public even if you insist on doing it here in order to frustrate me. Please. Promise me you won't."

Sulky, bewildered: "I don't understand you."

"Monica, you're a developing girl, even if they do dress you up like a kewpie doll on Sundays."

Righteous indignation: "This is for *church.*"

"But church is beside the *point* for you. It's reading and writing—oh, I swear to you, Monica, every word I say is only because I love you and I don't want anything awful to happen to you, ever. I do love you— *you must know that!* What they have told you about me *is not so.* I am not a crazy woman, I am not a lunatic. You mustn't be afraid of me, or hate me—I was sick, and now I'm well, and I want to strangle myself every time I think that I gave you up to him, that I thought he could begin to provide you with a mother and a home and everything I wanted you to have. And now you don't have a mother—you have this person, this woman, this ninny who dresses you up in this ridiculous costume and gives you a Bible to carry around that you can't even *read!* And for a father you have that man. Of all the fathers in the world, *him!*"

Here Monica screamed, so piercingly that I came running from the kitchen where I had been sitting alone over a cup of cold coffee, not even knowing what to think.

In the living room all Lydia had done was to take Monica's hand in her own; yet the child was screaming as though she were about to be murdered.

"But," wept Lydia, "I only want to hold you—"

As though my appearance signaled that the *real* violence was about to begin, Monica began to froth at the mouth, screaming all the while, *"Don't! Don't! Two and two is four! Don't beat up on me! It's four!"*

Scenes as awful as this could be played out two and

three times over in the course of a single Sunday afternoon—amalgams, they seemed to me, of soap opera
(that genre again), Dostoevsky, and the legends of
Gentile family life that I used to hear as a child, usually
from my immigrant grandmothers, who had never forgotten what life had been like amid the Polish peasantry.
As in the struggles of soap opera, the emotional ferocity
of the argument exceeded by light-years the substantive
issue, which was itself, more often than not, amenable
to a little logic, or humor, or a dose of common sense.
Yet, as in the scenes of family warfare in Dostoevsky,
there was murder in the air on those Sundays, and it
could not be laughed or reasoned away: an animosity
so deep ran between those two females of the same
blood that though they were only having that standard
American feud over a child's schoolwork (the subject
not of *The Possessed* or *The Brothers Karamazov* but
of Henry Aldrich and Andy Hardy) it was not impossible
(from another room) to imagine them going about it
with firebrand, pistol, hanging rope, and hatchet. Actually, the child's cunning and her destructive stubborn-
ness were nothing like so distressing to me as Lydia's
persistence. I could easily envision, and understand,
Monica's pulling a gun—bang bang, you're dead, no
more take-aways—but it was imagining Lydia trying
to *bludgeon* the screaming child into a better life that
shocked and terrified me.

Ketterer was the one who brought to mind those
cautionary tales about Gentile barbarity that, by my
late adolescence, I had rejected as irrelevant to the
kind of life that I intended to lead. Exciting and
gripping as they were to a helpless child—hair-raising
tales of "their" alcoholism, "their" violence, "their" im-
perishable hatred of us, stories of criminal oppressors
and innocent victims that could not but hold a powerful
negative attraction for any Jewish child, and particularly
to one whose very body was that of the underdog—
when I came of age and began the work of throwing
off the psychology and physique of my invalid childhood,

I reacted against these tales with all the intensity my mission required. I did not doubt that they were accurate descriptions of what Jews had suffered; against the background of the concentration camps I hardly would dare to say, even in my teenage righteousness, that these stories were exaggerated. Nonetheless (I informed my family), as I happened to have been born a Jew not in twentieth-century Nuremberg, or nineteenth-century Lemberg, or fifteenth-century Madrid, but in the state of New Jersey in the same year that Franklin Roosevelt took office, et cetera, et cetera. By now that diatribe of second-generation American children is familiar enough. The vehemence with which I advanced my position forced me into some ludicrous positions: when my sister, for instance, married her first husband, a man who was worthless by most anyone's standards (and certainly repulsive to me at fifteen, with his white shirt cuffs rolled back twice, his white calfskin loafers, his gold pinkie ring, and the way he had with his well-tanned hands of touching everything, his cigarette case, his hair, my sister's cheek, as though it were silk—the whole effeminate side of hooliganism), I nonetheless berated my parents for opposing Sunny's choice of a mate on the grounds that if she wished to marry a Catholic that was her right. In the anguish of the moment they missed my point, as I, with my high-minded permissiveness, missed theirs; in the end it was they of course who turned out to be prophetic, and with a vengeance. Only a few years later, at last a free agent myself, I was able to admit that what was so dismal and ridiculous about my sister's marriages wasn't her penchant for Italian boys from South Philly, but that both times out she chose precisely the two who confirmed, in nearly every detail, my family's prejudice against them.

Dim-witted as it may seem in retrospect—as much does, in my case—it was not until Ketterer and Monica came into my life that I began to wonder if I was being any less perverse than my sister; more so, because

unlike Sunny, I was at least alert to what I might
be up to. Not that I had ever been unaware of all
there was in Lydia's background to lend support to
my grandmothers' observations about Gentile disorder
and corruption. As a child, no one of course had mentioned incest to me, but it went without saying that if
either of these unworldly immigrants had been alive to
hear the whole of Lydia's horror story, they would not
have been so shocked as was I, their college-professor
grandson, by the grisliest detail of all. But even without
a case of incest in the family, there was more than
enough there for a Jewish boy to break himself upon:
the unmotherly mother, the unfatherly father, the love-
less bigoted aunts—my grandmothers could not themselves have invented a shiksa with a more ominous
and, to their way of thinking, representative dossier
than the one their fragile Nathan had chosen. To be
sure, Dr. Goebbels or Air Marshal Goering might have
a daughter wandering around somewhere in the world,
but as a fine example of the species, Lydia would do
nicely. I knew this; but then the Lydia I had chosen,
unlike Sunny's elect, *detested this inheritance herself*.
In part what was so stirring about her (to me, to me)
was the price she had paid to disown it—it had driven
her crazy, this background; and yet she had lived to
tell the tale, to *write* the tale, and to write it for *me*.

But Ketterer and his daughter Monica, who as it
were came *with* Lydia, in the same deal, were neither
of them detached chroniclers or interpreters or enemies
of their world. Rather, they were the embodiment of
what my grandparents, and great-grandparents, and
great-great-grandparents, had loathed and feared:
shagitz thuggery, shiksa wiliness. They were to me like
figures out of the folk legend of the Jewish past—only
they were real, just like my sister's Sicilians.

Of course I could not stand around too long being
mesmerized by this fact. Something had to be done.
In the beginning this consisted mostly of comforting
Lydia in the aftermath of one of her tutorial disasters;

then I tried to get her to leave Monica alone, to forget about saving her on Sundays and just try to make her as happy as she could for the few hours they had together. This was the same sort of commonsense advice that she received from Dr. Rutherford, but not even the two of us together, with the considerable influence we had over her, could prevent her from collapsing into frantic instruction before the day was out and bombarding Monica with a crash course in math, grammar, and the feminine graces before Ketterer arrived to spirit her back to his cave in the Chicago suburb of Homewood.

What followed, followed. I became the child's Sunday schoolteacher, unless I was down with a migraine. And she began to learn, or to try to. I taught her simple take-aways, I taught her simple sums, I taught her the names of the states bordering Illinois, I taught her to distinguish between the Atlantic and the Pacific, Washington and Lincoln, a period and a comma, a sentence and a paragraph, the little hand and the big hand. This last I accomplished by standing her on her feet and having her pretend hers were the arms of the clock. I taught her the poem I had composed when I was five and in bed with one of my fevers, my earliest literary achievement, according to my family: "Tick tock, Nathan is a clock." "Tick tock," she said, "Monica is a clock," and thrust her arms into the nine fifteen position, so that her white church dress, getting tighter on her by the month, pulled across the little bubbles of her breasts. Ketterer came to hate me, Monica to fall in love with me, and Lydia to accept me at last as her means of salvation. She saw the way out of her life's misery, and I, in the service of Perversity or Chivalry or Morality or Misogyny or Saintliness or Folly or Pent-up Rage or Psychic Illness or Sheer Lunacy or Innocence or Ignorance or Experience or Heroism or Judaism or Masochism or Self-Hatred or Defiance or Soap Opera or Romantic Opera or the Art of Fiction perhaps, or none of the above, or maybe all of the above and more—I found the way into mine.

I would not have had it in me at that time to wander out after dinner at the Commons and spend a hundred dollars on the secondhand books that I wanted to fulfill my dream of a "library" as easily and simply as I squandered my manhood.

II

My True Story

Peter Tarnopol was born in Yonkers, New York, thirty-four years ago. He was educated in public schools there, and was graduated summa cum laude from Brown University in 1954. He briefly attended graduate school, and then served for two years as an MP with the U.S. Army in Frankfurt, Germany, the setting for A Jewish Father, *the first novel for which in 1960 he received the Prix de Rome of the American Academy of Arts and Letters as well as a Guggenheim Fellowship.*

Since then he has published only a handful of stories, devoting himself almost exclusively in the intervening years to his nightmarish marriage to the former Maureen Johnson of Elmira, New York. In her lifetime, Mrs. Tarnopol was a barmaid, an abstract painter, a sculptress, a waitress, an actress (and what an actress!), a short-story writer, a liar, and a psychopath. Married in 1959, the Tarnopols were legally separated in 1962, at which time Mrs. Tarnopol accused the author, before Judge Milton Rosenzweig of the Supreme Court of the County of New York, of being "a well-known seducer of college girls." (Mr. Tarnopol has taught literature and creative writing at the University of Wisconsin and lately at Hofstra College on Long Island.) The marriage was dissolved in 1966 by Mrs. Tarnopol's violent death. At the time of her demise she was unemployed and a patient in group therapy in Manhattan; she was receiving one hundred dollars a week in alimony.

From 1963 to 1966, Mr. Tarnopol conducted a love affair with Susan Seabury McCall, herself a young widow residing in Manhattan; upon the conclusion of the affair, Mrs. McCall attempted unsuccessfully to kill herself and is currently living unhappily in Princeton,

*New Jersey, with a mother she cannot abide. Like Mr.
Tarnopol, Mrs. McCall has no children, but would
very much like to before time runs out, sired preferably
by Mr. Tarnopol. Mr. Tarnopol is frightened of remarrying, among other things.*

*From 1962 until 1967, Mr. Tarnopol was the patient
of the psychoanalyst Dr. Otto Spielvogel of New York
City, whose articles on creativity and neurosis have
appeared in numerous journals, most notably the
American Forum for Psychoanalytic Studies, of which
he is a contributing editor. Mr. Tarnopol is considered
by Dr. Spielvogel to be among the nation's top young
narcissists in the arts. Six months ago Mr. Tarnopol
terminated his analysis with Dr. Spielvogel and went on
leave from the university in order to take up temporary
residence at the Quahsay Colony, a foundation-
supported retreat for writers, painters, sculptors, and
composers in rural Vermont. There Mr. Tarnopol keeps
mostly to himself, devoting nights as well as days to
considering what has become of his life. He is confused
and incredulous much of the time, and on the subject
of the late Mrs. Tarnopol, he continues to be a man
possessed.*

*Presently Mr. Tarnopol is preparing to forsake the
art of fiction for a while and embark upon an autobiographical narrative, an endeavor which he ap-
proaches warily, uncertain as to both its advisability
and usefulness. Not only would the publication of such
a personal document raise serious legal and ethical
problems, but there is no reason to believe that by
keeping his imagination at bay and rigorously adhering
to the facts, Mr. Tarnopol will have exorcised his obsession once and for all. It remains to be seen whether
his candor, such as it is, can serve any better than his
art (or Dr. Spielvogel's therapeutic devices) to de-
mystify the past and mitigate his admittedly uncom-
mendable sense of defeat.*

*P. T.
Quahsay, Vt.
September 1967*

1. PEPPY

Has anything changed?

I ask, recognizing that on the surface (which is not to be disparaged—I live there too) there is no comparing the thirty-four-year-old man able today to manage his misfortunes without collapse, to the twenty-nine-year-old boy who back in the summer of 1962 actually contemplated, however fleetingly, killing himself. On the June afternoon that I first stepped into Dr. Spielvogel's office, I don't think a minute elapsed before I had given up all pretense of being an "integrated" personality and begun to weep into my hands, grieving for the loss of my strength, my confidence, and my future. I was then (miraculously, I am no longer) married to a woman I loathed, but from whom I was unable to separate myself, subjugated not simply by her extremely professional brand of moral blackmail—by that mix of luridness and corn that made our life together resemble something serialized on afternoon TV or in the *National Enquirer*—but by my own childish availability to it. Just two months back I had learned of the ingenious strategy by which she had deceived me into marrying her three years earlier; instead of serving me as the weapon with which finally to beat my way out of our bedlam, what she had confessed (in the midst of her semiannual suicide attempt) seemed to have stripped me of my remaining defenses and illusions. My mortification was complete. Neither leaving nor staying meant anything to me any more.

When I came East that June from Wisconsin, ostensibly to participate as a staff member in a two-week writing workshop at Brooklyn College, I was as bereft of will as a zombie—except, as I discovered, the will to be done with my life. Waiting in the subway station for an approaching train, I suddenly found it advisable to wrap one hand around the links of a chain that anchored a battered penny weighing machine to the iron pillar beside me. Until the train had passed in and out of view, I squeezed that chain with all my strength. "I am dangling over a ravine," I told myself. "I am being hoisted from the waves by a helicopter. *Hang on!*" Afterward I scanned the tracks, to be certain that I had in fact succeeded in stifling this wholly original urge for Peter Tarnopol to be transformed into a mangled corpse; amazed, terrified, I had also, as they say, to laugh: "Commit suicide? Are you kidding? You can't even walk out the door." I still don't know how near I may actually have come that day to springing across the platform and, in lieu of taking my wife head-on, taking on that incoming IRT train. It could be that I didn't have to *cling* to anything, that too could have been so much infantile posturing; then again I may owe my survival to the fact that when I heard blessed oblivion hurtling my way, my right hand fortunately found something impressively durable to hang on to.

At Brooklyn College over a hundred students were present in the auditorium for the opening session; each member of the workshop staff of four was to give a fifteen-minute address on "the art of fiction." My turn came, I rose—and couldn't speak. I stood at the lectern, notes before me—*audience* before me—without air in my lungs or saliva in my mouth. The audience, as I remember it, seemed to me to begin to *hum*. And all I wanted was to go to sleep. Somehow I didn't close my eyes and give it a try. Neither was I entirely there. I was nothing but heartbeat, just that drum. Eventually I turned and left the stage . . . and the job . . . Once, in Wisconsin, after a weekend of quarreling with my wife (she maintained, over my objections, that I had talked too long to a pretty graduate student at a party on Friday night; much discussion on the relativity of time), she had presented herself at the door of the classroom where I taught my undergraduate fiction seminar from seven to nine on Monday evenings. Our quarrel had ended at breakfast that morning with Maureen tearing at my hands with her fingernails; I had not been back to our apartment since. "It's an emergency!" Maureen informed me—and the seminar. The ten middle western undergraduates looked first at her, standing so determinedly there in the doorway, and then with comprehension at my hands, marked with mercurochrome—"The cat," I had explained to them earlier, with a forgiving smile for that imaginary beast. I rushed out into the corridor before Maureen had a chance to say more. There my sovereign delivered herself of that day's manifesto: "You better come home tonight, Peter! You better not go back to some room somewhere with one of those little blondes!" (This was the semester before I went ahead and did just that.) "Get out of here!" I whispered. "Go, Maureen, or I'll throw you down those fucking stairs! Go, *before I murder you!*" My tone must have impressed her—she took hold of the banister and retreated a step. I turned back to the seminar room to find that in my haste to confront Maureen and send her packing, I had neglected to shut the door behind me. A big shy farm girl from Appleton, who had spoken maybe one sentence all semester, was staring fixedly at the woman in the corridor behind me; the rest of the class stared into the pages of *Death in Venice*—no book had ever been so riveting. "All right," said the quavering voice that entered the room —an arm had violently flung the door shut in Maureen's face, I'm not wholly sure it was mine—"why does Mann send Aschenbach to Venice, rather than Paris, or Rome, or Chicago?" Here the girl from Appleton dissolved into tears, and the others, usually not that lively, began answering the question all at once . . . I did not recall every last detail of this scene as I stood yearning for sleep before my expectant audience at Brooklyn College, but it accounts, I think, for the vision that I had as I stepped to the lectern to deliver my prepared address: I saw Maureen, projected like a bullet through the rear door of the auditorium, and shouting at the top of her lungs whatever revelation about me had just rolled off the presses. Yes, to that workshop audience that took me to be an emerging literary figure, a first novelist whose ideas about writing were worth paying tuition to hear, Maureen would reveal (without charge) that I was not at all as I would present myself. To whatever words, banal or otherwise, that I spoke from the platform, she would cry, "Lies! Filthy, self-serving lies!" I could (as I intended to) quote Conrad, Flaubert, Henry James, she would scream all the louder, "Fraud!" But I spoke not a syllable, and in my flight from the stage, seemed to be only what I was—terrified, nothing any longer but my fears.

My writing by this time was wholly at the mercy of our marital confusion. Five and six hours a day, seven days a week, I went off to my office at the university and ran paper through the roller of my typewriter; the fiction that emerged was either amateurishly transparent—I might have been drawing up an IOU or writing the instructions for the back of a detergent box for all the imagination I displayed—or, alternately, so disjointed and opaque that on rereading, I was myself in the dark, and manuscript in hand, would drag myself around the little room, like some burdened figure broken loose from Rodin's "Bourgeois of Calais," crying aloud, "Where was *I* when this was written?" And I asked because I didn't know.

These pounds and pounds of pages that I accumulated during the marriage had the marriage itself as the subject and constituted the major part of the daily effort to understand how I had fallen into this trap and why I couldn't get out. Over the three years I had tried easily a hundred different ways to penetrate that mystery; every other week the whole course of the novel would change in midsentence, and within any one month the surface of my desk would disappear beneath dozens of equally dissatisfying variants of the single unfinished chapter that was driving me mad. Periodically I would take all these pages—"take" is putting it mildly—and consign them to the liquor carton filling up with false starts at the bottom of my closet, and then I would begin again, often with the very first sentence of the book. How I struggled for a description. (And, alas, struggle still.) But from one version to the next nothing of consequence ever happened: locales shifted, peripheral characters (parents, old flames, comforters, enemies, and allies) came and went, and with about as much hope for success as a man attacking the polar ice cap with his own warm breath, I would attempt to release a flow of invention in me by changing the color of her eyes or my hair. Of course, to give up the obsession would surely have made the most sense; only, obsessed, I was as incapable of not writing about what was killing me as I was of altering or understanding it.

So: hopeless at my work and miserable in my marriage, with all the solid achievements of my early twenties gone up in smoke, I walked off the stage, too stupefied even for shame, and headed like a sleepwalker for the subway station. Fortunately there was a train already there receiving passengers; it received me— rather than riding over me—and within the hour I was deposited at the Columbia campus stop only a few blocks from my brother Morris's apartment.

My nephew Abner, surprised and pleased to see me in New York, offered me a bottle of soda and half of his salami sandwich. "I've got a cold," he explained, when I asked in a breaking voice what he was doing home from school. He showed me that he was reading *Invisible Man* with his lunch. "Do you really know Ralph Ellison, Uncle Peppy?" "I met him once," I said, and then I was bawling, or barking; tears streamed from my eyes, but the noises that I made were novel even to me. "Hey, Uncle Pep, what's the matter?" "Get your father." "He's teaching." *"Get him, Abbie."* So the boy called the university—"This is an emergency; his brother is very sick!"—and Morris was out of class and home in minutes. I was in the bathroom by this time; Moe pushed right on in, and then, big two-hundred pounder though he is, kneeled down in that tiny tiled room beside the toilet, where I was sitting on the seat, watery feces running from me, sweating and simultaneously trembling as though I were packed in ice; every few minutes my head rolled to the side and I retched in the direction of the sink. Still, Morris pressed his bulk against my legs and held my two limp hands in his; with a rough, rubbery cheek he wiped the perspiration from my brow. "Peppy, ah, Peppy," he groaned, calling me by my childhood nickname and kissing my face. "Hang on, Pep, I'm here now."

A word about my brother and sister, very different creatures from myself.

I am the youngest of three, always "the baby" in everyone's eyes, right down to today. Joan, the middle child, is five years my senior and has lived most of her adult life in California with her husband Alvin, a land developer, and their four handsome children. Says Morris of our sister: "You would think she'd been born in a Boeing jet instead of over the store in the Bronx." Alvin Rosen, my brother-in-law, is six foot two and intimidatingly handsome, particularly now that his thick curls have turned silvery ("My father thinks he *dyes* it that color," Abner once told me in disgust) and his face has begun to crease like a cowboy's; from all the evidence he seems pretty much at one with his life as Californian, yachtsman, skier, and real estate tycoon, and utterly content with his wife and his children. He and my trim stylish sister travel each year to places slightly off the main tourist route (or just on the brink of being "discovered"); only recently my parents received postcards from their granddaughter, Melissa Rosen, Joannie's ten-year-old, postmarked Africa (a photo safari with the family) and Brazil (a small boat had carried friends and family on a week-long journey up the Amazon, a famous Stanford naturalist serving as their guide). They throw open their house for an annual benefit costume party each year in behalf of *Bridges,* the West Coast literary magazine whose masthead lists Joan as one of a dozen advisory editors—frequently they are called upon to bail the magazine out of financial trouble with a timely donation from the Joan and Alvin Rosen Foundation; they are also generous contributors to hospitals and libraries in the Bay Area and among the leading sponsors of an annual fund drive for

California's migrant workers ("Capitalists," says Morris, "in search of a conscience. Aristocrats in overalls. Fragonard should paint 'em."); and they are good parents, if the buoyancy and beauty of their children are any indication. To dismiss them (as Morris tends to) as vapid and frivolous would be easier if their pursuit of comfort, luxury, beauty, and glamor (they number a politically active movie star among their intimates) weren't conducted with such openness and zest, with a sense that they had discovered *the* reason for being. My sister, after all, was not always so fun loving and attractive or adept at enjoying life. In 1945, as valedictorian of Yonkers High, she was a hairy, hawk-nosed, undernourished-looking little "grind" whose braininess and sallow homeliness had made her just about the least popular girl in her class; the consensus then was that she would be lucky to find a husband, let alone the rich, lanky, Lincolnesque Wharton School graduate, Alvin Rosen, whom she carried away from the University of Pennsylvania along with her A.B. in English. But she did it—not without concentrated effort, to be sure. Electrolysis on the upper lip and along the jawbone, plastic surgery on the nose and chin, and the various powders and paints available at the drugstore have transformed her into a sleek, sensual type, still Semitic, but rather more the daughter of a shah than a shopkeeper. Driving around San Francisco in her Morgan, disguised as a rider off the pampas one day and a Bulgarian peasant the next, has gained her in her middle years something more than mere popularity—according to the society page of the San Francisco paper (also sent on to my mother by little Melissa) Joan is "the most daring and creative tastemaker" alive out there. The photograph of her, with Alvin in velvet on one bare arm and the conductor of the San Francisco Symphony on the other (captioned, by Melissa, "Mom at a party"), is simply staggering to one who remembers still that eight-by-ten glossy of the '45 senior prom crowd at Billy Rose's Diamond Horseshoe in New York—there sits Joan, all nose and shoulder blades, adrift in a taffeta "strapless" into which it appears she will momentarily sink out of sight, her head of coarse dark hair (since straightened and shined so that she glows like Black Beauty) mockingly framed by the Amazonian gams of the chorus girl up on the stage behind her; as I remember it, sitting beside her, at their "ringside" table, was her date, the butcher's large shy son, bemusedly looking down into a glass with a Tom Collins in it . . . And this woman today is the gregarious glamor girl of America's most glamorous city. To me it is awesome: that she should be on such good terms with pleasure, such a success at satisfaction, should derive so much strength and confidence from how she looks, and where she travels, and what she eats and with whom . . . well, that is no small thing, or so it seems to her brother from the confines of his hermit's cell.

Joan has recently written inviting me to leave Quahsay and come out to California to stay with her and her family for as long as I like. "We won't even bother you with our goatish ways, if you should just want to sit around the pool polishing your halo. If it pleases you, we will do everything we can to prevent you from having even a *fairly* good time. But reliable sources in the East tell me that you are still very gifted at that yourself. My dearest Alyosha, between 1939, when I taught you to spell 'antidisestablishmentarianism,' and now, you've changed. Or perhaps not—maybe what sent you into ecstasy over that word was how difficult it was. Truly, Pep, if your appetite for the disagreeable should ever slacken, I am here and so is the house. Your fallen sister, J."

For the record, my reply:

Dear Joan: What's disagreeable isn't being where I am or living as I do right now. This is the best place for me, probably for some time to come. I can't stay on indefinitely of course, but there are approximations to this sort of life. When Maureen and I lived in New Milford, and I had that twelve-by-twelve shack in the woods behind the house—and a bolt to throw on the door—I could be content for hours on end. I haven't changed much since 1939: I still like more than anything to sit alone in a room spelling things out as best I can with a pencil and paper. When I first got to New York in '62, and my personal life was a shambles, I used to dream out loud in my analyst's office about becoming again that confident and triumphant college kid I was at twenty; now I find the idea of going back beyond that even more appealing. Up here I sometimes imagine that I am ten—and treat myself accordingly. To start the day I eat a bowl of hot cereal in the dining room as I did each morning in our kitchen at home; then I head out here to my cabin, at just about the time I used to go off to school. I'm at work by eight forty-five, when "the first bell" used to ring. Instead of arithmetic, social studies, etc., I write on the typewriter till noon. (Just like my boyhood idol, Ernie Pyle; actually I may have grown up to become the war correspondent I dreamed of being in 1943—except that the front-line battles I report on aren't the kind I'd had in mind.) Lunch out of a lunch pail provided by the dining hall here: a sandwich, some carrot sticks, an oatmeal cookie, an apple, a thermos of milk. More than enough for this growing boy. After lunch I resume writing until three thirty, when "the last bell" used to ring at school. I straighten up my desk and carry my empty lunch pail back to the dining hall, where the evening's soup is cooking. The smell of dill, mother's perfume. Manchester is three miles from the Colony by way of a country road that curves down through the hills. There is a women's junior college at the edge of town, and the girls are down there by the time I arrive. I see them inside the laundromat and at the post office and buying shampoo in the pharmacy—reminding me of the playground "after school," aswarm with long-haired little girls a ten-year-old boy could only admire from afar and with wonder. I admire them from afar and with wonder in the local luncheonette, where I go for a cup of coffee. I have been asked by one of the English professors at the college to speak to his writing class. I declined. I don't want them any more accessible than they would be if I were back in the fifth grade. After my coffee I walk down the street to the town library and sit for a while leafing through the magazines and watching the schoolkids at the long tables copying their book reports off the jacket flaps. Then I go out and hitch a ride back up to the Colony; I couldn't feel any more trusting and innocent than when I hop out of the car and say to the driver, "Thanks for the ride—s'long!"

I sleep in a room on the second floor of the big three-story farmhouse that houses the guests; on the main floor are the kitchen, dining hall, and the living room (magazines, record player, and piano); there's a ping-pong table on a side porch, and that's just about it. On the floor of my room, in my undershorts, I do half an hour of calisthenics at the end of each afternoon. In the last six months, through dint of exercise and very little appetite, I have become just about as skinny as I was when you used to pretend to play the xylophone on my ribs. After "gym" I shave and shower. My windows are brushed by the needles of an enormous spruce; that's the only sound I hear while shaving, outside of the water running into the sink. Not a noise I can't account for. I try each evening to give myself a "perfect" shave, as a shaving ten-year-old might. I *concentrate:* hot water, soap, hot water, coat of Rise, with the grain, coat of Rise, against the grain, hot water, cold water, thorough investigation of all surfaces . . . perfect. The vodka martini that I mix for myself at six, I sip alone while listening to the news on my portable radio. (I am on my bed in my bathrobe: face ivory smooth, underarms deodorized, feet powdered, hair combed—clean as a bridegroom in a marriage manual.) The martini was of course not my habit at ten, but something like Dad's when he came home with his headache (and the day's receipts) from the store: looking as though he were drinking turpentine, he would toss down his shot of Schenley's, and then listen in "his" chair to "Lyle Van and the News." Dinner is eaten at six thirty here, in the company of the fifteen or so guests in residence at the moment, mostly novelists and poets, a few painters, one composer. Conversation is pleasant, or annoying, or dull; in all, no more or less taxing than eating night after night with one's family, though the family that comes to mind isn't ours so much as the one Chekhov assembled in *Uncle Vanya*. A young poetess recently arrived here mired in astrology; whenever she gets going on some-body's horoscope I want to jump up from the table and get a pistol and blow her brains out. But as we are none of us bound by blood, law, or desire (as far as I can tell), forbearance generally holds sway. We drift after dinner into the living room, to chat and scratch the resident dog; the composer plays Chopin nocturnes; the *New York Times* passes from hand to hand . . . generally within the hour we have all drifted off without a word. My understanding is that with only five exceptions, all those in residence right now happen to be in flight, or in hiding, or in recovery—from bad marriages, divorces, and affairs. I have overheard tag ends of conversation issuing from the phone booth down in the kitchen to support this rumor. Two teacher-poets in their thirties who have just been through the process of divesting themselves of wives and children and worldly goods (in exchange for student admirers) have struck up a friendship and compare poems they're writing about the ordeal of giving up little sons and daughters. On the weekends when their dazzling student girl friends come to visit, they disappear into the bedsheets at the local motel for forty-eight hours at a clip. I recently began to play ping-pong again for the first time in twenty years, two or three fierce games after dinner with an Idaho woman, a stocky painter in her fifties who has been married five times; one night last week (only ten days after her arrival) she drank everything she could find on the premises, including the vanilla extract in the cook's pantry, and had to be taken away the next morning in a station wagon by the mortician who runs the local AA. We all left our typewriters to stand glumly out on the steps and wave goodbye. "Ah, don't worry," she called to us out the car window, "if it wasn't for my mistakes I'd still be back on the front porch in Boise." She was our only "character" and far and away the most robust and spirited of the survivors hereabouts. One night six of us went down into Manchester for a beer and she told us about her first two marriages. After she finished, the astrologist wanted to know her sign: the rest of us were trying to figure out how come she wasn't dead. "Why the hell do you keep getting married, Mary?" I asked her. She chucked me on the chin and said, "Because I don't want to die shriveled up." But she's gone now (probably to marry the mortician), and except for the muffled cries rising from the phone booth at night, it's as quiet here as a hospital zone. Perfect for homework.

After dinner and the *Times*, I walk back out to my studio, one of twenty cabins scattered along a dirt road that winds through the two hundred acres of open fields and evergreen woods. In the cabin there's a writing desk, a cot, a Franklin stove, a couple of straight-backed chairs painted yellow, a bookcase painted white, and the wobbly wicker table where I eat lunch at noon. I read over what I've written that day. Trying to read anything else is useless; my mind wanders back to my own pages. I think about that or nothing.

Walking back to the main house at midnight I have only a flashlight to help me make my way along the path that runs between the trees. Under a black sky by myself, I am no more courageous at thirty-four than I was as a boy: there is the urge to run. But as a matter of fact invariably I will turn the flashlight off and stand out there in the midnight woods, until either fear subsides or I have achieved something like a Mexican standoff between me and it. What frightens me? At ten it was only oblivion. I used to pass the "haunted" Victorian houses on Hawthorne Avenue on my way home from Cub Scout meetings, reminding myself, *There are no ghosts, the dead are dead,* which was, of course, the most terrifying thought of all. Today it's the thought that the dead *aren't* that turns my knees to water. I think: the funeral was another trick—she's alive! Somehow or other, she will reappear! Down in town in the late afternoon, I half expect to look into the laundromat and see her stuffing a machine with a bag of wash. At the luncheonette where I go for my cup of coffee, I sometimes sit at the counter waiting for Maureen to come charging through the door, with finger pointed—"What are you doing in here! You said you'd meet me by the bank at four!" "By the bank? Four? You?" And we're at it. "You're dead," I tell her, "you cannot meet anyone by any bank if you are, *as you are,* dead!" But still, you will have observed, I keep my distance from the pretty young students buying shampoo to wash their long hair. Who ever accused a shy ten-year-old of being "a well-known seducer of college girls"? Or, for that matter, heard of a plaintiff who was ashes? "She's dead," I remind myself, "and it is over." But how can that be? Defies credulity. If in a work of realistic fiction the hero was saved by something as fortuitous as the sudden death of his worst enemy, what intelligent reader would suspend his disbelief? Facile, he would grumble, and fantastic. Fictional wish fulfillment, fiction in the service of one's dreams. Not True to Life. And I would agree. Maureen's death is not True to Life. Such things simply do not happen, except when they do. (And as time passes and I get older, I find that they do with increasing frequency.)

I'm sending along Xerox copies of two stories I've written up here, both more or less on the Subject. They'll give you an idea as to why I'm here and what I'm doing. So far no one has read the stories but my editor. He had encouraging things to say about both of them, but of course what he would like to see is that novel for which my publisher advanced twenty thousand dollars back when I was a boy wonder. I know how much he would like to see it because he so scrupulously and kindly avoided mentioning it. He gave the game away, however, by inquiring whether "Courting Disaster" (one of the two stories enclosed) was going "to develop into a longer work about a guilt-ridden Zuckerman and his beautiful stepdaughter in Italy—a kind of post-Freudian meditation on themes out of *Anna Karenina* and *Death in Venice*. Is that what you're up to, or are you planning to continue to write Zuckerman variations until you have constructed a kind of full-length fictional fugue?" Good ideas all right, but what I am doing, I had to tell the man standing there holding my IOU, is more like trying to punch my way out of a paper bag. "Courting Disaster" is a post-cataclysmic fictional meditation on nothing more than my marriage: what if Maureen's personal mythology had been biographical truth? Suppose that, and suppose a good deal more— and you get "C.D." From a Spielvogelian perspective, it may even be read as a legend composed at the behest and under the influence of the superego, my adventures as seen through its eyes—as "Salad Days" is something like a comic idyll honoring a Pannish (and as yet unpunished) id. It remains for the ego to come forward then and present *its* defense, for all parties to the conspiracy-to-abscond-with-my-life to have had their day in court. I realize now, as I entertain this idea, that the nonfiction narrative that I'm currently working on might be considered just that: the "I" owning up to its role as ringleader of the plot. If so, then after all testimony has been heard and a guilty verdict swiftly rendered, the conspirators will be consigned to the appropriate correctional institution. You suggest your pool. Warden Spielvogel, my former analyst (whose job, you see, I am now doing on the side), would suggest that the band of desperados be handed back over to him for treatment in the cell block at Eighty-ninth and Park. The injured plaintiff in this action does not really care where it happens, or how, so long as the convicted learn their lesson and NEVER DO IT AGAIN. Which isn't likely: we are dealing with a treacherous bunch here, and that this trio has been entrusted with my well-being is a source of continuous and grave concern. Having been around the track with them once already, I would as soon consign my fate to the Marx Brothers or the Three Stooges; buffoons, but they at least *like* one another. P.S. Don't take personally the brother of "Salad Days" or the sister of "Courting Disaster." Imaginary siblings serving the design of the fiction. If I ever felt superior to you and your way of life, I don't any longer. Besides, it's to you that I may owe my literary career. Trying on a recent afternoon walk to figure out how I got into this line of work, I remembered myself at age six and you at age eleven, waiting in the back seat of the car for Mother and Dad to finish their Saturday night shopping. You kept using a word that struck me as the funniest thing I'd ever heard, and once you saw how much it tickled me, you wouldn't stop, though I begged you to from the floor of the car where I was curled up in a knot from pure hilarity. I believe the word was "noodle," used as a synonym for "head." You were merciless, somehow you managed to stick it somewhere into every sentence you uttered, and eventually I wet my pants. When Mother and Dad returned to the car I was outraged with you and in tears. "Joannie did it," I cried, whereupon Dad informed me that it was a human impossibility for one person to pee in another person's pants. Little he knew about the power of art.

Joan's prompt reply:

Thanks for the long letter and the two new stories, three artful documents springing from the same hole in

your head. When that one drilled she really struck pay
dirt. Is there no bottom to your guilty conscience? Is
there no other source available for your art? A few observations on literature and life—1. You have no reason to hide in the woods like a fugitive from justice. 2.
You did not kill her, in any way, shape or form. Unless
there is something I don't know. 3. To have asked a
pretty girl to have intercourse with a zucchini in your
presence is morally inconsequential. Everybody has his
whims. You probably made her day (if that was you).
You announce it in your "Salad Days" story with all
the bravado of a naughty boy who knows he has done
wrong and now awaits with bated breath his punishment.
Wrong, Peppy, is an ice pick, not a garden vegetable;
wrong is by force or with children. 4. You do disap-
prove of me, as compared with Morris certainly; but
that, as they say, is your problem, baby. (And brother
Moe's. And whoever else's. Illustrative anecdote: About
six weeks ago, immediately after the Sunday supplement
here ran a photo story on our new ski house at Squaw
Valley, I got a midnight phone call from a mysterious
admirer. A lady. "Joan Rosen?" "Yes." "I'm going to
expose you to the world for what you are." "Yes? What
is that?" "A Jewish girl from the Bronx! Why do you
try to hide it, Joan? It's written all over you, you phony
bitch!") So then, I don't take either of those make-
believe siblings for myself. I know you can't write about
me—you can't make pleasure credible. And a working
marriage that works is about as congenial to your talent
and interests as the subject of outer space. You know I
admire your work (and I do like these two stories, when
I can ignore what they imply about your state of mind),
but the fact is that you couldn't create a Kitty and a
Levin if your life depended on it. Your imagination
(hand in hand with your life) moves in the other direction. 5. Reservation ("Courting Disaster"): I never
heard of anyone killing herself with a can opener. Awfully gruesome and oddly arbitrary, unless I am missing
something. 6. Idle curiosity: was *Maureen* seduced by
her father? She never struck me as broken in that way.
7. After the "nonfiction narrative" on the Subject, what
next? A saga in heroic couplets? Suggestion: Why don't
you plug up the well and drill for inspiration elsewhere?
Do yourself a favor (if those words mean anything to

you) and FORGET IT. Move on! Come West, young
man! P.S. Two enclosures are for your edification (and
taken together, right up your fictional alley—if you want
to see unhappiness, you ought to see this marriage in
action). Enclosed note #1 is to me from Lane Coutell,
Bridges' new, twenty-four-year-old associate editor
(good-looking and arrogant and, in a way, brilliant;
more so right now than is necessary), who was here
with his wife for supper and read the stories. He and the
magazine would (his "reservations" notwithstanding)
give anything (except money, of which there's none) to
publish them, though I made it clear that he'd have to
contact you about that. I just wanted to know what
someone intelligent who didn't know your true story
would make of what you've made out of it here. Enclosed note #2 is from Frances Coutell, his wife, who
runs *Bridges'* office now. A delicate, washed-out beauty
of twenty-three, bristling with spiritual needs; also a
romantic masochist who, as you will surmise, has developed a crush on you, not least because she doesn't
like you that much. Fiction does different things to different people, much like matrimony.

#1

Dear Joan: As you know I wasn't one of those who was
taken by your brother's celebrated first novel. I found it
much too proper a book, properly decorous and constrained on the formal side, and properly momentous
(and much too pointed) in presenting its Serious Jewish
Moral Issue. Obviously it was mature for a first novel—
too obviously: the work of a gifted literature student
straitjacketed by the idea that fiction is the means for
proving righteousness and displaying intelligence; the
book seems to me very much a relic of the fifties. The
Abraham and Isaac motif, rich with Kierkegaardian
overtones, reeks (if I may say so) of those English de-
partments located in the upper reaches of the Himalayas.
What I like about the new stories, and why to my mind
they represent a tremendous advance over the novel, is
that they seem to me a deliberate and largely conscious
two-pronged attack upon the prematurely grave and
high-minded author of *A Jewish Father.* As I read it, in
"Salad Days" the attack is frontal, head-on, and ac-

complished by means of social satire, and, more notably, what I'd call tender pornography, a very different thing, say, from the pornography of a Sade or a Terry Southern. For the author of that solemn first novel, a story like "Salad Days" is nothing less than blasphemous. He is to be congratulated heartily for triumphing (at least here) over all that repressive piety and fashionable Jewish angst. "Courting Disaster" is a more complicated case (and as a result not so successful, in a purely literary sense). As I would *like* to read it, the story is actually a disguised critical essay by Tarnopol on his own overrated first book, a commentary and a judgment on all that *principledness* that is *A Jewish Father*'s subject and its downfall. Whether Tarnopol intended it or not, I see in Zuckerman's devotion to Lydia (its joylessness, its sexlessness, its scrupulosity, its madly ethical motive) a kind of allegory of Tarnopol and his Muse. To the degree that this is so, to the degree that the character of Zuckerman embodies and represents the misguided and morbid "moral" imagination that produced *A Jewish Father,* it is fascinating; to the degree that Tarnopol is back on the angst kick, with all that implies about "moving" the reader, I think the story is retrograde, dull, and boring, and suggests that the conventional (rabbinical) side of this writer still has a stranglehold on what is reckless and intriguing in his talent. But whatever my reservations, "Courting Disaster" is well worth publishing, certainly in tandem with "Salad Days," a story that seems to me the work of a brand new Tarnopol, who, having objectified the high-minded moralist in him (and, hopefully, banished him to Europe forevermore, there to dwell in noble sadness with all the other "cultural monuments and literary landmarks"), has begun at last to flirt with the playful, the perverse, and the disreputable in himself. If Sharon Shatzky is your brother's new Muse, and a zucchini her magic wand, we may be in for something more valuable than still more fiction that is "moving." Lane.

#2

Joan: My two cents worth, only because the story L. admires most seems to me smug and vicious and infuriating, all the more so for being so *clever* and *win-*

ning. It is pure sadistic trash and I pray (actually) that
Bridges doesn't print it. Art is long, but the life of a little
magazine is short, and much too short for *this.* I hate
what he does with that suburban college girl—and I
don't even mean what Zuckerman (the predictable prod-
igal son who *majors* in English) does but what the
author does, which is just to twist her arm around behind her back and say, "You are not my equal, you can
never be my equal—*understand?*" Who does he think
he is, anyway? And why would he want to be such a
thing? How could the man who wrote "Courting Disaster" want to write a heartless little story like that? And
vice versa? Because the long story is absolutely heart-
rending and I think (contrary to L.'s cold-blooded
analysis) that *this* is why it works utterly. I was moved
to tears by it (but then I didn't perform brain surgery
on it) and moved to the most aching admiration for the
man who could just *conceive* such a story. The wife, the
daughter, the husband are painfully true (I'm sure because he made me sure), and I shall never forget them.
And Zuckerman *here* is completely true too, sympathetic, interesting, a believable observer and center of
feeling, all the things he has to be. In a strange way they
were all sympathetic to me, even the awful ones. Life is
awful. Yours, Franny. P.S. I apologize for saying that
something your brother wrote is hateful. I don't know
him. And I don't think I want to. There are enough
Jekyll and Hydes around here as it is. You're an older
woman, tell me something. What's the matter with
men? What do they *want?*

My brother Morris, to whom copies of my latest stories
were also sent in response to a letter inquiring about
my welfare, had his own trenchant comments to make
on "Courting Disaster"—comments not so unlike Joan's.

What is it with you Jewish writers? Madeleine Herzog,
Deborah Rojack, the cutie-pie castrator in *After the
Fall,* and isn't the desirable shiksa of *A New Life* a
kvetch and titless in the bargain? And now, for the
further delight of the rabbis and the reading public,
Lydia Zuckerman, that Gentile tomato. Chicken soup in
every pot, and a Grushenka in every garage. With all
the Dark Ladies to choose from, you luftmenschen can

really pick 'em. Peppy, why are you still wasting your talent on that Dead End Kid? Leave her to Heaven, okay? I'm speaking at Boston University at the end of the month, not that far from you. If you're still up on the mountain, come down and stay at the Commander with me. My subject is "Rationality, Planning, and Gratification Deferral." You could stand hearing about *a* and *b;* as for *c,* would you, a leading contender for the title in the highly competitive Jewish Novelist Division, agree to give a black belt demonstration in same to the assembled students of social behavior? Peppy, *enough with her already!*

Back in 1960, following a public lecture *I* had delivered (my first) at Berkeley, Joan and Alvin gave a party for me at the house they had then up on a ridge in Palo Alto. Maureen and I had just returned to the U.S. from our year at the American Academy in Rome, and I had accepted a two-year appointment as "writer-in-residence" at the University of Wisconsin. In the previous twelve months I had become (according to an article in the Sunday *Times* book section) "the golden boy of American literature"; for *A Jewish Father,* my first novel, I had received the Prix de Rome of the American Academy of Arts and Letters, a Guggenheim grant of thirty-eight hundred dollars, and then my invitation to teach at Wisconsin. I myself had expected no less, back then; it was not my good fortune that surprised me at the age of twenty-seven.

Some sixty or seventy of their friends had been invited by Joan and Alvin to meet me; Maureen and I lost sight of one another only a few minutes after our arrival, and when she turned up at my side some time later I was talking rather self-consciously to an extremely seductive looking young beauty of about my own age, self-conscious precisely for fear of the scene of jealous rage that proximity to such a sexpot would inevitably provoke.

Maureen pretended at first that I was talking to no one; she wanted to go, she announced, all these "phonies" were more than she could take. I decided to ignore the remark—I did not know what else to do. Draw a sword and cut her head off? I didn't carry a sword at the time. I carried a stone face. The beautiful girl—from her décolletage it would have appeared that she was something of a daring tastemaker herself; I was too ill at ease, however, to make inquiries of a personal nature—the girl was asking me who my editor was. I told her his name; I said he happened also to be a good poet. "Oh, how could you!" whispered Maureen, and, her eyes all at once flooded with tears; instantly she turned and disappeared into a bathroom. I found Joan within a few minutes and told her that Maureen and I had to go—it had been a long day and Maureen wasn't feeling well. "Pep," said Joan, taking my hand in hers, "why are you doing this to yourself?" "Doing what?" "Her," she said. I pretended not to know what she was talking about. Just presented her with my stone face. In the taxi to the hotel, Maureen wept like a child, repeatedly hammering at her knees (and mine) with her little fists. "How could you embarrass me like that—how could you say that, with me right there at your side!" "Say *what?*" "You know damn well, Peter! Say that *Walter* is your editor!" "But he *is.*" "What about *me?*" she cried. "You?" "I'm your editor—you know very well I am! Only you refuse to admit it! I read every word you write, Peter. I make suggestions. I correct your spelling." "Those are typos, Maureen." "*But I correct them!* And then some rich bitch sticks her tits in your face and asks who your editor is and you say *Walter!* Why must you demean me like this—oh, why did you do that in front of that empty-headed girl? Just because she was all over you with those tits of hers? Mine are as big as hers—touch them some day and you'll see!" "Maureen, not this, not again—!" "Yes, again! And again and again! Because *you will not change!*" "But she meant my editor *at my publishing house!*" "But I'm your editor!" "You're not!" "I suppose I'm not your wife either! Why are you so ashamed of me! In front of those phonies, no less! People who wouldn't look twice at you if you weren't this month's cover boy! Oh, you baby! You infant! You hopeless egomaniac! Must you always be at the center of *everything?*" The next morning, before we left for the airport, Joan telephoned to the hotel to say goodbye. "We're always here," she told me. "I know." "If you want to come out and stay." "Well, thank you," I said, as formally as if I were acknowledging an offer from a perfect stranger, "maybe we'll take you up on it sometime." "I'm talking about you. Just you. You don't have to suffer like this, Peppy. You're proving nothing by being miserable, nothing at all." As soon as I hung up, Maureen said, "Oh, you could really have all the beautiful girls, couldn't you, Peter —with your sister out procuring for you. Oh, she would really enjoy that, I'm sure." "What the hell are you talking about *now?*" "That deprived little look on your face—'Oh, if I wasn't saddled with this witch, couldn't I have a time of it, screwing away to my heart's content at all the vapid twittering ingenues!' " "Again, Maureen? *Again?* Can't you at least let twenty-four hours go by?" "Well, what about that girl last night who wanted to know who your *editor* was? Oh, she really cared about that, I'm sure. Well, be honest, Peter, didn't you want to fuck her? You couldn't take your *eyes* off those tits of hers." "I suppose I noticed them." "Oh, I suppose you did." "Though apparently not so much as you, Maureen." "Oh, don't use your sardonic wit on me! Admit it! You *did* want to fuck her. You were *dying* to fuck her." "The fact of it is, I was close to catatonic in her presence." "Yes, *suppressing all that goddam lust!* How hard you have to work to suppress it—with everybody but me! Oh, admit it, tell the truth for *once*—if you had been alone, you know damn well you would have had her back here in this hotel! On this very bed! And *she* at least would have gotten laid last night! Which is more than I can say for me! Oh, why do you punish me like this—why do you lust after every woman in this whole wide world, *except your own wife.*"

My family . . . In marked contrast to Joan and

Alvin and their children Mab, Melissa, Kim, and An-
thony, are my elder brother Morris, his wife Lenore,
and the twins, Abner and Davey. In their home the
dominant social concern is not with the accumulation
of goods, but the means by which society can facilitate
their equitable distribution. Morris is an authority on
underdeveloped nations; *his* trips to Africa and the
Caribbean are conducted under the auspices of the
UN Commission for Economic Rehabilitation, one of
several international bodies to which Moe serves as a
consultant. He is a man who worries over everything,
but nothing (excluding his family), nothing so much
as social and economic inequality; what is now famous
as "the culture of poverty" has been a heartbreaking
obsession with him since the days he used to come
home cursing with frustration from his job with the
Jewish Welfare Board in the Bronx—during the late
thirties, he worked there days while going to school
nights at N.Y.U. After the war he married an adoring
student, today a kindly, devoted, nervous, quiet woman,
who some years ago, when the twins went off to kindergarten, enrolled at the School of Library Service at
Columbia to take a master's degree. She is now a
librarian for the city of New York. The twins are
fifteen; last year both refused to leave the local upper
West Side public school to become students at Horace
Mann. On two consecutive days they were roughed up
and robbed of their pennies by a Puerto Rican gang
that has come to terrorize the corridors, lavatories, and
basketball courts back of their school—nonetheless, they
have refused to become "private school hypocrites,"
which is how they describe their neighborhood friends,
the sons and daughters of Columbia faculty who have
been removed from the local schools by their parents.
To Morris, who worries continuously for their safety,
the children shout indignantly, "How can you, of all
people, suggest Horace Mann! How can you betray
your own ideals! You're just as bad as Uncle Alvin!
Worse!"

Moe has, as he says, only himself to congratulate for

their moral heroics; ever since they could understand an English sentence, he has been sharing with them his disappointment with the way this rich country is run. The history of the postwar years, with particular emphasis upon continuing social injustice and growing political repression, has been the stuff of their bedtime stories: instead of Snow White and the Seven Dwarfs, the strange adventures of Martin Dies and the House Un-American Activities Committee; instead of Pinocchio, Joe McCarthy; instead of Uncle Remus, tales of Paul Robeson and Martin Luther King. I can't remember once eating dinner at Moe's, that he was not conducting a seminar in left-wing politics for the two little boys wolfing down their pot roast and kasha—the Rosenbergs, Henry Wallace, Leon Trotsky, Eugene Debs, Norman Thomas, Dwight Macdonald, George Orwell, Harry Bridges, Samuel Gompers, just a few whose names are apt to be mentioned between appetizer and dessert—and, simultaneously, looking to see that everybody is eating what is best for him, pushing green vegetables, cautioning against soda pop gulped too quickly, and always checking the serving bowls to be sure there is Enough. "Sit!" he cries to his wife, who has been on her feet all day herself, and like an enormous lineman going after a loose fumble, rushes into the kitchen to get another quarter pound of butter from the refrigerator. "A glass of ice water, Pop!" calls Abner. "Who else for ice water? Peppy? You want another beer? I'll bring it anyway." His big paws full, he returns to the table, distributes the goods, waving for the boys to go on with what they were saying—intently he listens to them both, the one little boy arguing that Alger Hiss *must* have been a Communist spy, while the other (in a voice even louder than his brother's) tries to come to grips with the fact that Roy Cohn is a Jew.

It was to this household that I went to collapse. Moe, at my request, telephoned Maureen the first night after the Brooklyn College episode to say that I had been taken ill and was resting in bed at his apartment. She asked to speak to me; when Moe said, "He just can't talk now," she replied that she was getting on the next plane and coming East. Moe said, "Look, Maureen, he can't see anybody right now. He's in no condition to." "I'm his wife!" she reminded him. "But he cannot see *anybody*." "What is going on there, Morris, behind my back? He is not a baby, no matter how *you* people think of him. Are you listening to me? I demand to speak to my husband! I will not be put off by somebody who wants to play big brother to a man who has won the Prix de Rome!" But he was not intimidated, my big brother, and hung up.

At the end of two days of hiding behind his bulk, I told Moe I was "myself" again; I was going back to the Midwest. We had rented a cabin for the summer in the upper peninsula of Michigan, and I was anxious to get out of the apartment in Madison and up to the woods. I said I had to get back to my novel. "And to your beloved," he reminded me.

Moe made no secret ever of how much he disliked her; Maureen maintained that it was because, unlike his own wife, she, one, was a Gentile, and, two, had a mind of her own. I tried to give him the same stone face that I had given my sister when she had criticized my marriage and my mate. I hadn't yet told Moe, or anyone, what I had learned from Maureen two months earlier about the circumstances under which we had married—or about my affair with an undergraduate that Maureen had discovered. I just said, "She's my wife." "So you spoke to her today." "She's my *wife*, what do you expect me to do!" "She telephoned and so you picked it up and talked to her." "We talked, right." "Ah, you jerk-off! And do me a favor, will you, Peppy? Stop telling me she's your 'wife.' The word does not impress me to the extent it does you two. She's ruining you, Peppy! You're a wreck! You had a nervous breakdown here only *two* mornings ago! I don't want my kid brother cracking up—*do you understand that?*" "But I'm fine now." "Is that what your 'wife' told you when you were on the phone?" "Moe, lay off. I'm not a frail flower." "But you are a frail flower, putz. You are a frail flower if I ever saw one! Look, Peppy—you were a very gifted boy. That should be obvious. You stepped out into the world like a big, complicated, hypersensitive million-dollar radar system, and along came Maureen, flying her four-ninety-eight model airplane right smack into the middle of it, and the whole thing went on the fritz. And its still on the fritz from all I can see!" "I'm twenty-nine now, Moey." "But you're still worse than my fifteen-year-old kids! *They're* at least going to get killed in behalf of a noble ideal! But you I don't understand—trying to be a hero with a bitch who means *nothing*. *Why*, Peppy? Why are you destroying your young life for *her?* The world is full of kind and thoughtful and pretty young girls who would be *delighted* to keep a boy with your bella figura company. Peppy, you used to take them out by the dozens!"

I thought (not for the first time that week) of the kind and thoughtful and pretty young girl, my twenty-year-old student Karen Oakes, whose mistake it had been to involve herself with a Bluebeard like me. Maureen had just that afternoon—during the course of our *fifth* phone conversation of the hour; if I hung up, she just called back, and I felt duty bound to answer—Maureen had threatened once again to create a scandal at school for Karen—"that sweet young thing, with her bicycle and her braids, blowing her creative writing teacher!"—if I did not get on a plane and come home "instantly." But it wasn't to prevent the worst from happening that I was returning; no, whatever reckless act of revenge I thought I might forestall by doing as I was told and coming home, I was not so deluded as to believe that life with Maureen would ever get better. I was returning to find out what it would be like when it got even worse. How would it all end? Could I imagine the grand finale? Oh, I could, indeed. In the woods of Michigan she would raise her voice about Karen, and I would split her crazy head open with an ax—if, that is, she did not stab me in my sleep or poison my food, first. But one way or another,

I would be vindicated. Yes, that was how I envisioned it. I had by then no more sense of reasonable alternatives than a character in a melodrama or a dream. As if I ever had, with her.

I never made it to Wisconsin. Over my protests, Moe went down in the elevator with me, got in the taxi with me, and rode with me all the way out to LaGuardia Airport; he stood directly behind me in the Northwest ticket line, and when his turn came, bought a seat on the same plane I was to take back to Madison. "You going to sleep in bed with us too?" I asked, in anger. "I don't know if I'll sleep," he said, "but I'll get in there if I have to."

Whereupon I collapsed for the second time. In the taxi back to Manhattan I told him, through my tearful blubbering, about the deception that Maureen had employed to get me to marry her. "Good Christ," he moaned, "you were really up against a pro, kiddo." "Was I? Was I?" I had my face pressed into his chest, and he was holding me in his two arms. "And you were still going back to her," he said, now with a groan. "I was going to kill her, Moey!" "You? *You* were?" "Yes! With an ax! With my bare hands!" "Oh, I'll bet. Oh, you poor, pussywhipped bastard, I'll just bet you would have." "I would have," I croaked through my tears. "Look, you're just the same as when you were a kid. You can give it, but you can't take it. Only now, on top of that, you can't give it either." "Oh, why is that? *What happened?*" "The world didn't turn out to be the sixth-grade classroom at P.S. 3, that's what happened. With gribben on a fat slice of rye bread waiting for you when you got home from a day of wowing the teachers. You weren't exactly trained to take punishment, Peppy." Still weeping, but bitterly now, I asked him, "Is anybody?" "Well, from the look of things, your 'wife' got very good instruction in it—and I think she was planning to pass the torch on to you. She sounds to me just from our phone conversation like one of the great professors in the subject." "Yes?" You see, driving back from the airport that day I felt like somebody being filled in on what had transpired on earth during the sabbatical year he had just spent on Mars; I could have just stepped off a space ship, or out of steerage— I felt so green and strange and lost and dumb.

By late afternoon I was in Dr. Spielvogel's office; out in the waiting room Moe sat like a bouncer with his arms folded and his feet planted solidly on the floor, watching to be sure I did not slip off by myself to the airport. By nightfall Maureen was on her way East. Within two days I had notified the chairman of my department that I would be unable to return to my job in the fall. By the end of the week Maureen—having failed in several attempts to get past the door to Moe's apartment—had returned to Madison, cleared our stuff out of our apartment, and come East a second time; she moved into a hotel for transients on lower Broadway, and there she intended to remain, she said, until I had let go of my brother's apron strings and returned to our life together. Failing that, she said, she would do what I was "forcing" her to do through the courts. She told me on the phone (when it rang, I picked it up, Moe's instructions to the contrary notwithstanding) that my brother was a "woman hater" and my new analyst a "fraud." "He's not even licensed, Peter," she said of Spielvogel. "I looked him up. He's a European quack—practicing here without any credentials at all. He's not attached to a single psychoanalytic institute— no *wonder* he tells you to leave your wife!" "You're lying again, Maureen—you just made that up! You'll say anything!" "But *you're* the liar! You're the betrayer! You're the one who deceived me with that little student of yours! Carried on with her for months behind my back! While I cooked your dinner and washed your socks!" "And what did you do to get me to marry you in the first place! Just *what!*" "Oh, I *knew* I should never have told you that—I knew you would use that against me some day, to excuse yourself and your rotten philandering! Oh, how can you allow two such people to turn you against your own wife—when you were the guilty one, you were the one who was screwing

those students left and right!" "I was *not* screwing
students left and right—" "Peter, I caught you red-
handed with that girl with the braids!" *"That is not left
and right, Maureen!* And you are the one who turned
me against you, with your crazy fucking paranoia!"
"When? When did I do that, I'd like to know?" "From
the *beginning!* Before we were even married!" "Then
why on earth did you marry me, if I was so hateful to
you even then? Just to punish me like this?" "I married
you because you *tricked* me into marrying you! Why
else!" "But that didn't mean you *had* to—you still
could decide on your own! And you did, you liar!
Don't you even remember what *happened?* You *asked*
me to be your wife. You *proposed.*" "Because among
other things *you threatened to kill yourself if I didn't!*"
"And you mean to say you *believed* me?" *"What?"*
"You actually believed that I would kill myself over
you? Oh, you terrible narcissist! You selfish egomaniacal maniac! You actually do think that you are the be-
all and end-all of human existence!" "No, no, it's *you*
who think I am! Why else won't you leave me *alone!*"
"Oh, Jesus," she moaned, "oh Jesus—haven't you ever
heard of *love?*"

2. SUSAN: 1963—1966

It is now nearly a year since I decided that I would not
marry Susan McCall and ended our long love affair.
Until last year marrying Susan had been legally impossible because Maureen continued to refuse to grant
me a divorce under the existing New York State matrimonial laws or to consent to a Mexican or out-of-state
divorce. But then one sunny morning (only one short
year ago), Maureen was dead, and I was a *widower,*
free at last of the wife I had taken, entirely against my
inclinations but in accordance with my principles, back
in 1959. Free to take a new one, if I so desired.
Susan's own absurd marriage to the right Princeton

boy had also ended with the death of her mate. It had been briefer even than my own, and also childless, and she wanted now to have a family before it was "too late." She was into her thirties and frightened of giving birth to a mongoloid child; I hadn't known how frightened until I happened by accident to come upon a secret stockpile of biology books that apparently had been picked up in a secondhand bookstore on Fourth Avenue. They were stuffed in a splitting carton on the floor of the pantry where I had gone in search of a fresh can of coffee one morning while Susan was off at her analyst's. I assumed at first that they were books she had accumulated years ago at school; then I noticed that two of them, *The Basic Facts of Human Heredity* by Amram Scheinfeld and *Human Heredity* by Ashley Montagu, hadn't been published until she was already living alone and widowed in her New York apartment.

Chapter Six of the Montagu book, "The Effects of Environment Upon the Developing Human Being in the Womb," was heavily marked with a black crayon, whether by Susan, or by whoever had owned the book before her, I had no sure way of knowing. "Studies of the reproductive development of the female show that from every point of view the best period during which the female may undertake the process of reproduction extends on the average from the age of twenty-one to about twenty-six years of age. . . . From the age of thirty-five years onward there is a sudden jump in the number of defective children that are born, especially of the type known as *mongoloids*. . . . In mongolism we have the tragic example of what may be an adequately sound genetic system being provided with an inadequate environment with resulting disordered development in the embryo." If it was not Susan who had done the heavy underlining, it was she who had copied out into the margin, in her round, neat schoolgirlish hand, the words "an inadequate environment."

A single paragraph describing mongoloid children was the only one on the page that had not been framed and scored with the black crayon; in its own simple and arresting way, however, it gave evidence of having been read no less desperately. The seven words that I italicize here had, in the book, been underlined by a yellow felt-tipped pen, the kind that Susan liked to use to encourage correspondents to believe that she was in the highest of spirits. "Mongoloid children may or may not have the fold of skin over the inner angle of the eye (epicanthic fold) or the flat root of the nose that goes with this, but they do have smallish heads, fissured tongues, a transverse palmar crease, with extreme intellectual retardation. Their I.Q. ranges between 15 and 29 points, from idiocy to the upper limit of about seven years. *Mongoloids are cheerful and very friendly personalities,* with often remarkable capacities for imitation and memories for music and complex situations which far outrank their other abilities. The expectation of life at birth is about nine years."

After almost an hour with these books on the pantry floor, I returned them to the carton, and when I saw Susan again that evening said nothing about them. Nothing to her, but thereafter I was as haunted by the image of Susan buying and reading her biology books as she was of giving birth to a monstrosity.

But I did not marry her. I had no doubt that she would be a loving and devoted mother and wife, but having been unable ever to extricate myself by legal means from a marriage into which I'd been coerced in the first place, I had deep misgivings about winding up imprisoned once again. During the four years that Maureen and I had been separated, her lawyer had three times subpoenaed me to appear in court in an attempt to get Maureen's alimony payments raised and my "hidden" bank accounts with their hidden millions revealed to the world. On each occasion I appeared, as summoned, with my packet of canceled checks, my bank statements, and my income tax returns to be grilled about my earnings and my expenses, and each time I came away from those proceedings swearing that I would never again put authority over my personal life into the hands of some pious disapproving householder known as a New York municipal judge. Never again would I be so stupid and reckless as to allow some burgher in black robes to tell me that I ought to "switch" to writing movies so as to make sufficient money to support the wife I had "abandoned." Henceforth *I* would decide with whom I would live, whom I would support, and for how long, and not the state of New York, whose matrimonial laws, as I had experienced them, seemed designed to keep a childless woman who refused to hold a job off the public dole, while teaching a lesson to the husband (me!) assumed to have "abandoned" his innocent and helpless wife for no other reason than to writhe in the fleshpots of Sodom. At those prices, would that it were so!

As my tone suggests, I had found myself as humiliated and compromised, and nearly as disfigured, by my unsuccessful effort to get unmarried as I had ever been by the marriage itself: over the four years of separation I had been followed to dinner by detectives, served with subpoenas in the dentist's chair, maligned in affidavits subsequently quoted in the press, labeled for what seemed like all eternity "a defendant," and judged by a man with whom I would not eat my dinner—and I did not know if I could undergo these indignities again, and the accompanying homicidal rage, without a stroke finishing me off on the witness stand. Once I even took a swing at Maureen's dapper (and, let it be known, elderly) lawyer in the corridor of the courthouse, when I learned that it was he who had invited the reporter from the *Daily News* to attend the hearing at which Maureen (for the occasion, in Peter Pan collar and tears) testified that I was "a well-known seducer of college girls." But that story of my swashbuckling in its turn. My point is that I had not responded with much equanimity to the role in which I was cast by the authorities and did not want to be tested by their system of sexual justice ever again.

But there were other, graver reasons not to marry,

aside from my fear of divorce. Though I had never taken lightly Susan's history of emotional breakdown, the fact is that as her lover it had not weighed upon me as I expected it would if I were to become her husband and her offspring's father. In the years before we met, Susan had gone completely to pieces on three occasions: first, in her freshman (and only) year at Wellesley; then after her husband had been killed in a plane crash eleven months into their marriage; and most recently, when her father, whom she had doted upon, had died in great pain of bone cancer. Each time she fell into a kind of waking coma and retired to a corner (or a closet) to sit mutely with her hands folded in her lap until someone saw fit to lift her onto a stretcher and carry her away. Under ordinary circumstances she managed to put down what she called her "everyday run-of-the-mill terror" with pills: she had through the years discovered a pill for just about every phobia that overcame her in the course of a day, and had been living on them, or not-living on them, since she had left home for college. There was a pill for the classroom, a pill for "dates," a pill for buying clothes, a pill for *returning* clothes, and needless to say, pills for getting started in the morning and dropping into oblivion at night. And a whole mixed bag of pills which she took like M&Ms when she had to converse, even on the phone, with her formidable mother.

After her father's death she had spent a month in Payne Whitney, where she'd become the patient of a Dr. Golding, reputedly a specialist with broken china. He had been her analyst for two years by the time I came along and had by then gotten her off everything except Ovaltine, her favorite childhood narcotic; in fact, he had encouraged the drinking of Ovaltine at bedtime and during the day when she was feeling distressed. Actually during the course of our affair Susan did not take so much as an aspirin for a headache, a perfect record, and one that might have served to assure me that *that* past was past. But then so had her record been "perfect" when she had enrolled at Wellesley at the age of eighteen, an A student from Princeton's Miss Fine's School for Young Ladies, and immediately developed such a fear of her German professor, a caustic young European refugee with a taste for leggy American girls, that instead of going off to his class she took a seat in the closet of her room every Monday, Wednesday, and Friday at ten A.M., and until the hour was over, hid out there, coasting along on the belladonna that she regularly obtained from Student Health for her menstrual cramps. By chance one day (and a merciful day it was) a dormitory chambermaid opened the closet door during Susan's German hour, and her mother was summoned from Princeton to take her out from behind her winter coats and away from Wellesley for good.

The possibility of such episodes recurring in the future alarmed me. I believe my sister and brother would argue that Susan's history of breakdowns was largely what had *intrigued* me and *attracted* me, and that my apprehension over what might happen to her, given the inevitable tensions and pressures of marriage, was the first sign I had displayed, since coming of age, that I had a modicum of common sense in matters pertaining to women. My own attitude toward my apprehensiveness is not so unambiguously approving; I still do not know from day to day whether it is cause for relief or remorse.

Then there is the painful matter of the elusive orgasm: no matter how she struggled to reach a climax, "it" never happened. And of course the harder she worked at it, the more like labor and the less like pleasure erotic life became. On the other hand, the intensity of her effort was as moving as anything about her—for in the beginning, she had been altogether content just to open her legs a little way and lie there, a well to pump if anyone should want to, and she herself couldn't imagine why anyone would, lovely and well formed as she was. It took much encouragement and, at the outset, much berating, to get her to be something more than a piece of meat on a spit that you turned this way and that until you were finished; *she* was never finished, but then she had never really begun.

What a thing it was to watch the appetite awaken in this shy and timid creature! And the daring—for if only she dared to, she might actually have what she wanted! I can see her still, teetering on the very edge of success. The pulse beats erratically in her throat, the jaw strains upward, the gray eyes *yearn*—just a yard, a foot, an inch to the tape, and victory over the self-denying past! Oh yes, I remember us well at our honest toil—pelvises grinding as though to grind down bone, fingers clutching at one another's buttocks, skin slick with sweat from forehead to feet, and our flushed cheeks (as we near total collapse) pressing so forcefully into one another that afterward her face is blotchy and bruised and my own is tender to the touch when I shave the following morning. Truly, I thought more than once that I might die of heart failure. "Though in a good cause," I whisper, when Susan had signaled at last a desire to throw in the towel for the night; drawing a finger over the cheekbone and across the bridge of the nose, I would check for tears—rather, *the* tear; she would rarely allow more than one to be shed, this touching hybrid of courage and fragility. "Oh," she whispers, "I was almost almost almost . . ." "Yes?" Then that tear. "Always," she says, "almost." "It'll happen." "It won't. You know it won't. What I consider almost is probably where everybody else begins." "I doubt it." "You don't . . . Peter, next time—what you were doing . . . do it—harder." So I did it, whatever it was, harder, or softer, or faster, or slower, or deeper, or shallower, or higher, or lower, as directed. Oh, how Mrs. Susan Seabury McCall of Princeton and Park Avenue tried to be bold, to be greedy, to be *low* ("Put it . . ." "Yes, say it, Suzie—" "Oh, in me from behind, but don't hurt—!")—not of course that living on bennies in a Wellesley dormitory in 1951 hadn't constituted an act of boldness for a society-bred, mother-disciplined, father-pampered young heiress from a distinguished New Jersey family, replete on the father's side with a U.S. senator and an ambassador to England, and on the mother's, with nineteenth-century industrial barons. But that diversion had been devised to annihilate temptation; now she *wanted* to want . . . Exhilarating to behold, but over the long haul utterly exhausting, and the truth was that by the third year of our affair both of us were the worse for wear and came to bed like workers doing overtime night after night in a defense plant: in a good cause, for good wages, but Christ how we wished the war was over and won and we could rest and be happy.

I have of course to wonder now if Susan wouldn't have been better off if I had deferred to her and simply left her alone about coming. "I don't care about that," she had told me, when I first broached the distressing subject. I suggested that perhaps she *should* care. "Why don't you just worry about your own fun . . ." said she. I told her that I was not worrying about "fun." "Oh, don't be pretentious," she dared to mumble— then, *begging:* "Please, what difference does it make to you anyway?" The difference, I said, would be to her. "Oh, stop trying to sound like the Good Sex Samaritan, will you? I'm just not a nymphomaniac and I never was. I am what I am, and if it's been good enough for everyone else—" "Has it?" "No!" and out came the tear. So the resistance began to crumble, and the struggle, which I initiated and to which I was accomplice and accessory, began.

I should point out here that the distressing subject had been a source of trouble between Maureen and myself as well: she too was unable to reach a climax, but maintained that what stood in her way was my "selfishness." Characteristically she had confused the issue somewhat by leading me to believe for the longest while that she and orgasms were on the very *best* of terms—that I, in fact, had as much chance of holding her back as a picket fence has of obstructing an avalanche. Well into the first year of our marriage, I continued to look on in wonder at the crescendo of passion

that would culminate in her sustained outcry of ecstasy
when *I* began to ejaculate; you might even say that my
ejaculations sort of faded off into nothing beside her
clamorous writhings. It came as a surprise then (to
coin a phrase appropriate to these adventures) to learn
that she had actually been pretending, faking those
operatic orgasms, she explained, so as to protect me
from the knowledge of just how inadequate a lover I
was. But how long could she keep up that pretense in
order to bolster my sense of manliness? What about
her, she wanted to know. Thereafter I was to hear
repeatedly how even Mezik, the brute who was her
first husband, even *Walker,* the homosexual who was
her second, knew more about how to satisfy a woman
than the selfish, inept, questionable heterosexual who
was I.

Oh, you crazy bitch (if the widower may take a moment out to address the ghost of his wife), death is too
good for you, really. Why isn't there a hell, with fire and
brimstone? Why isn't there a devil and damnation? Why
isn't there *sin* any more? Oh, if I were Dante, Maureen,
I'd go about writing this another way!

At any rate: in that Maureen's accusations, no matter
how patently bizarre, had a way of eating into my
conscience, it very well might be that what Susan de-
rided as my sexual good samaritanism was in part an
attempt by me to disprove the allegations brought
against me by a monumentally dissatisfied wife. I don't
really know. I believe I meant well, though at the time
I came to Susan there is no denying how dismayed I
was by my record as a pleasure-giving man.

Obviously what drew me to Susan to begin with—
only a year into my separation and still reeling—was
that in temperament and social bearing she was as
unlike Maureen as a woman could be. There was no
confusing Maureen's recklessness, her instinct for scenes
of wild accusation, her whole style of moral overkill,
with Susan's sedate and mannerly masochism. To Susan
McCall, speaking aloud and at length of disappointment, even to one's lover, was like putting an elbow

on the dinner table, something One Just Didn't Do. She told herself that by making her heartache her business and nobody else's, she was being decorous and tactful, sparing another the inconsequential bellyaching of "a poor little rich girl," though of course the person she was sparing (and deluding) by being so absurdly taciturn and stoically blind about her life was herself. She was the one who didn't want to hear about it, or think about it, or do anything about it, even as she continued to suffer it in her own resigned and baffled way. The two women were wholly antithetical in their response to deprivation, one like a dumb, frightened kid in a street fight who knows no way to save his hide but to charge into the melee, head down and skinny arms windmilling before him, the other docile and done in, resigned to being banged around or trampled over. Even when Susan came to realize that she needn't settle any longer for a diet of bread and water, that it wasn't simply "okay" with me (and the rest of mankind) that she exhibit a more robust appetite, but that it made her decidedly more attractive and appealing, there was the lifelong style of forbearance, abstemiousness in all things but pharmaceuticals, there was the fadeaway voice, the shy averted glance, the auburn hair drawn austerely back in a knot at the back of the slender neck, there was the bottomless patience, the ethereal silence, that single tear, to mark her clearly as a member of another tribe, if not another sex, from Maureen.

It need hardly be pointed out that to me hers was a far more poignant struggle to witness (and be a party to) than that one in which Maureen had been so ferociously engaged—for where Maureen generally seemed to want to have something largely because someone else was able to have it (if I had been impotent, there is no doubt she would have been content to be frigid), Susan now wanted what she wanted in order to rid herself of the woman she had been. Her rival, the enemy whom she hoped to dispossess and drive into exile, if not extinction, was her own constrained and terrified self.

Poignant, moving, admirable, endearing—in the end,

too much for me. I couldn't marry her. I couldn't do
it. If and when I was ever to marry again, it would
have to be someone in whose wholeness I had abounding faith and trust. And if no one drawing breath was
that whole—admittedly I wasn't, my own capacity for
faith and trust, among other things, in a state of serious
disrepair—maybe that meant I would never remarry.
So be it. Worse things had happened, one of them, I
believed, to me.

So: freed from Maureen by her death, it seemed to
me that I had either to go ahead and make Susan a
wife and mother at thirty-four, or leave her so that
she might find a man who would do just that before
she became, in Dr. Montagu's words, a totally "inadequate environment" for procreation. Having been to
battle for nearly all of my adult life, first with Maureen
and then with the divorce laws of the state of New York
—laws so rigid and punitive they came to seem to me
the very codification of Maureen's "morality," the work
of her hand—I no longer had the daring, or the heart,
or the confidence to marry again. Susan would have to
find some man who was braver, or stronger, or wiser,
or maybe just more foolish and deluded—

Enough. I still don't know how to describe my decision to leave her, nor have I stopped trying to. As I
asked at the outset: Has anything changed?

Susan tried to kill herself six months after I had pronounced the affair over. I was here in Vermont. After
I left her, my days in New York, till then so bound up
with hers, had become pointless and empty. I had my
work, I had Dr. Spielvogel, but I had become used to
something more, this woman. As it turned out, I was
no less lonely for her here in my cabin, but at least I
knew that the chances were greatly reduced that she
would show up in the Vermont woods at midnight, as
she did at my apartment on West Twelfth Street, where
she could call into the intercom, "It's me, I miss you."
And what do you do at that hour, *not* let her in? "You

could," Dr. Spielvogel advised me, "take her home in a taxi, yes." "I did—at two." "Try it at midnight." So I did, came downstairs in my coat, to escort her out of the building and back to Park and Seventy-ninth. Sunday the buzzer went off in the morning. "Who is it?" "I brought you the *Times*. It's Sunday." "I know it's Sunday." "Well, I miss you like mad. How can we be apart on Sunday?" I released the lock on the downstairs door ("Take her home in a taxi; there are taxis on Sunday"—"But I miss *her!*") and she came on up the stairs, beaming, and invariably, Sunday after Sunday, we wound up making love in our earnest and strenuous way. "See," says Susan. "What?" "You do want me. Why are you acting as though you don't?" "You want to be married. You want to have children. And if that's what you want you should have it. But I myself don't, can't, and won't!" "But I'm not *her*. I'm *me*. I'm not out to torture you or coerce you into anything. Have I ever? Could I possibly? I only want to make you happy." "I can't do it. *I don't want to.*" "Then don't. You're the one who brought up marriage. I didn't say a word about it. You just said I can't do it and I have to go—and you went! But this is intolerable. Not living with you doesn't make sense. Not even seeing each other—it's just too bizarre." "I don't want to stand between you and a family, Susan." "Oh, Peter, you sound like some dope on a soap opera when you say that. If I have to choose between you and a family, I choose *you*." "But you want to be married, and if you want to be married, and if you want to have children, then you should have them. *But I don't, can't, and won't.*" "It's because I don't come, isn't it? And never will. Not even if you put it in my ear. Well, isn't it?" "No." "It's because I'm a junkie." "You are hardly a junkie." "But it is that, it's those pills I pop. You're afraid of having somebody like me on your hands forever—you want somebody better, somebody who comes like the postman, through rain and snow and gloom of night, and doesn't sit in closets and can live without her Ovaltine at the age of thirty-four—and why shouldn't you? I would too, if were you. I mean that. I understand completely. You're *right* about me." And out rolled the tear, and so I held her and told her no-no-it-isn't-so (what else, Dr. Spielvogel, is there to say at that moment—yes, you're absolutely correct?). "Oh, I don't blame you," said Susan, "I'm not even a person, really." "Oh, what are you then?" "I haven't been a person since I was sweet sixteen. I'm just symptoms. A collection of symptoms, instead of a human being."

These surprise visits continued sporadically over a period of four months and would have gone on indefinitely, I thought, if I just stayed on there in New York. Certainly, I could refuse to respond to the doorbell, pretend when she came by that I wasn't at home, but as I reminded Dr. Spielvogel when he suggested somewhat facetiously that I "marshal" my strength and forget about the bell—"it'll stop soon enough"—this was Susan I was dealing with, not Maureen. Eventually I packed a bag and, marshaling my strength, came up here.

Just before I left my apartment, however, I spent several hours writing Susan notes telling her where I was going—and then tearing them up. But what if she "needed" me? How could I just pick up and *disappear?* I ended up finally telling a couple who were our friends where I would be hiding out, assuming that the wife would pass this confidence on to Susan before my bus had even passed over the New York State line.

I did not hear a word from Susan for six weeks. Because she had been told where I was or because she hadn't?

Then one morning I was summoned from breakfast to the phone here at the Colony—it was our friends informing me that Susan had been found unconscious in her apartment and rushed by ambulance to the hospital. It seemed that the previous night she had finally accepted an invitation to dinner with a man; he had left her at her door around eleven, and she had come back into the apartment and swallowed all the

Seconal and Tuinal and Placidyl that she had been secreting under her lingerie over the years. The cleaning lady had found her in the morning, befouled and in a heap on the bathroom floor, surrounded by empty vials and envelopes.

I got an afternoon flight from Rutland and was at the hospital by the evening visiting hours. When I arrived at the psychiatric ward, I was told she had just been transferred and was directed to a regular private room. The door was slightly ajar and I peered in—she was sitting up in bed, gaunt and scraggly looking and still very obviously dazed and disoriented, like a prisoner, I thought, who has just been returned from an all-night session with her interrogators. When she saw that it was me rapping on the door, out came the tear, and despite the presence of the formidable mother, who coolly took my measure from the bedside, she said, "I love you, that's why I did it."

After ten days in the hospital getting her strength back—and assuring Dr. Golding when he came around to visit each morning, that she would never again lay in a secret cache of sleeping pills—she was released in the care of her mother and went back home to New Jersey, where her father had been a professor of classics at Princeton until his death. Mrs. Seabury, according to Susan, was a veritable Calpurnia; in grace, in beauty, in carriage, in icy grandeur (and, said Susan, "in her own estimation") very much a Caesar's wife—and to top it off, Susan added hopelessly, she happened also to be *smart*. Yes, top marks, it turned out, from the very college where Susan hadn't been able to make it through her freshman year. I had always suspected that Susan might be exaggerating somewhat her mother's majesty—it was, after all, *her* mother—but at the hospital, when by chance our daily visits overlapped, I found myself not a little awed by the patrician confidence radiated by this woman from whom Susan had obviously inherited her own striking good looks, though not a Calpurnian presence. Mrs. Seabury and I had next to nothing to say to one another. She looked at me in fact (or so I imagined it, in those circumstances) as though she did not see there much opposition to be brooked. Only further evidence of her daughter's prodigality. "Of course," her silence seemed to me to say, "of course it would be over the loss of a hysterical Jewish 'poet.'" In the corridors outside the hospital room of my suicidal mistress, it was difficult to rise to my own defense.

When I came down to Princeton to visit Susan, we two sat in the garden back of the brick house on Mercer Street, next door to where Einstein had lived (legend had it that as a little red-headed charmer, back in the years before she was just "symptoms," Susan used to give him candy to do her arithmetic homework); Madame Seabury, wearing pearls, sat with a book just inside the terrace door, no more than ten yards away— it was not *A Jewish Father* she was reading, I was sure. I had taken the train to Princeton to tell Susan that now that she was being looked after by her mother, I would be going back to Vermont. So long as she had been in the hospital, I had, at Dr. Golding's suggestion, been deliberately vague about my plans. "You don't have to tell her anything, one way or another." "What if she asks?" "I don't think she will," Golding said; "for the time being she's content that she got you down here. She won't push her luck." "Not yet. But what about when she gets out? What if she tries it again?" "I'll take care of that," said Golding, with a businesslike smile meant to close off conversation. I wanted to say: "You didn't take such marvelous care of 'that' last time!" But who was the runaway lover to blame the devoted doctor for the castoff mistress's suicide attempt?

It was a warmish March day, and Susan was wearing a clinging yellow jersey dress, looking very slinky for a young woman who generally preferred to keep her alluring body inconspicuous. Her hair, unknotted for the occasion, was a thick mane down her back; a narrow band of girlish freckles faintly showed across the bridge of her nose and her cheekbones. She had been out in the sun every afternoon—in her bikini, she let me know—and looked gorgeous. She could not keep her hands from her hair, and continuously, throughout our conversation, took it from behind her neck and pulled it like a thick, auburn rope over either shoulder; then, raising her chin just a touch, she would push the mass of hair back behind her neck with two open palms. The wide mouth and slightly protrusive jaw that gave a decisive and womanly quality to her delicate beauty, struck me suddenly as *prehistoric,* the sign of what was still raw and forceful in this bridled daughter of propriety and wealth. I had always found her beauty stirring, but never before had it seemed so thoroughly dominated by the sensuous. That was new. Where was Susan the interrogated prisoner? Susan the mousy widow? Susan the awesome mother's downtrodden Cinderella? All gone! Was it having toyed with suicide and gotten away with it that gave her the courage to be so blatantly tempting? Was it the proximity of the disapproving mother that was goading her on? Or was this her calculated last-ditch effort to arouse and lure back the fugitive from matrimony?

Whatever, I was aroused.

With her legs thrown over the filigreed arm of the white wrought-iron chaise, Susan's yellow dress rode high on her tanned thigh—I thought it must be the way she used to sit at age eight with Einstein, before she had begun to be educated by her fears. When she shifted in the chaise, or simply raised her arms to fool with her hair, the edge of her pale underpants came into view.

"Coming on very shameless," I said. "For my benefit or your mother's?"

"Both. Neither."

"I don't think she thinks the world of me to begin with."

"Nor of me."

"Then that won't help any, will it?"

"Please, *you're* 'coming on' like somebody's nanny."

Silence, while I watch that hair fan out in her two hands. One of her tanned legs is swinging to the slowest of beats over the arm of the garden chaise. This is not at all the scenario that I had constructed on the train coming down. I had not counted on a temptress, or an erection.

"She always thought I had the makings of a whore anyway," says Susan, frowning like any victimized adolescent.

"I doubt that."

"Oh, are you siding with my mother these days? It's a regular phalanx. Only you're the one who turned me against her."

"That tack won't work," I said flatly.

"What will then? Living here in my old room like the crazy daughter? Having college boys ask me for dates over the card catalogue in the library? Watching the eleven o'clock news, with my Ovaltine and my mom? What ever *has* worked?"

I didn't answer.

"I ruin everything," she announced.

"You want to tell me that I do?"

"I want to tell you that Maureen does—still! Now why did she have to go and get killed? What are all these people trying to do anyway, dying off on me this way? Everything was really just fine, until *she* upped and departed this life. But out of her clutches, Peter, you're even more haywire than you were *in*. Leaving me like that was *crazy*."

"I'm not haywire, I'm not crazy, and everything was not 'just fine.' You were biding your time. You want to be married and a mother. You dream about it."

"You're the one who dreams about it. You're the one who's obsessed with marriage. I told you I was willing to go ahead without—"

"But I don't want you going ahead 'without'! I don't want to be responsible for denying you *what you want*."

"But that's my worry, not yours. And I don't want it any more, I told you that. If I can't, I won't."

"Yes?—then what am I to make of all those books, Susan?"

"Which *books*?"

"Your volumes on human heredity."

She winced. "Oh." But the mildness of what she said next, the faint air of self-mockery, surprised me. And relieved me too, for in my impatience with what I took to be rather self-deluded assertions about living "without," I had gone further than I'd meant to. "Are *they* still around?" she asked, as though it was a teddy bear that I'd uncovered from a secret hiding place.

"Well, *I* didn't move them."

"I was going through a stage . . . as they say."

"What stage?"

"Pathetic. Morbid. Blue. That stage . . . When did you find them?"

"One morning. Only about a year ago."

"I see . . . Well—" All at once she seemed crushed by my discovery; I thought that she might scream. "Well," she said, inhaling deeply, "what next? What else have you found out about me?"

I shook my head.

"You should know—" she stopped.

I said nothing. But what should I know? *What should I know?*

"A Princeton hippie," said Susan, slyly smiling, "is taking me to a movie tonight. You should know that."

"Very nice," I said. "A new life."

"He picked me up at the library. Want to know what I'm reading these days?"

"Sure. What?"

"Everything about matricide I can get my hands on," she told me, through her teeth.

"Well, reading about matricide in a college library never killed anybody."

"Oh, I just went there because I was bored."

"In that dress?"

"Yes, in this dress. Why not? It's just a little dress to wear around the stacks, you know."

"I can see that."

"I'm thinking of marrying him, by the way."

"Who?"

"My hippie. He'd probably 'dig' a two-headed baby. And a decrepit 'old lady.' "

"That thigh staring me and your mother in the face doesn't look too decrepit."

"Oh," said Susan, "it won't kill you to look at it."

"Oh, it's not killing me," I said, and suppressed an urge to reach out and up and stroke what I saw.

"Okay," she said abruptly—"you can tell me what you came to tell me, Peter, I'm 'ready.' To use a serviceable phrase of my mother's, I've come to grips with reality. Shoot. You're never going to see me again."

"I don't see what's changed," I answered.

"You don't—I know you don't. You still think I'm Maureen. You still think I'm that terrible person."

"Hardly, Susan."

"But how can you go around never trusting anyone ever again just because of a screwball like that! *I* don't lie, Peter. *I* don't deceive. I'm *me. And don't give me that look.*"

"What look?"

"Oh, let's go up to my bedroom. The hell with Mother. I want to make love to you, terribly."

"What look?"

She closed her eyes. "Stop," she whispered. "Don't be furious with me. I swear to you, I didn't mean it that way. It was not blackmail, truly. I just could not bear any longer Being Brave."

"Then why didn't you call your doctor—instead of taking Maureen's favorite home remedy!"

"Because I didn't want him—I wanted *you.* But I didn't pursue you, did I? For six weeks you were up there in Vermont, and I didn't write, and I didn't phone, and I didn't get on an airplane—did I? Instead I went around day after day Being Brave, and not in Vermont either, but in the apartment where I used to eat and sleep with *you.* Finally I even came to grips with reality and accepted an invitation for dinner—and that was my biggest mistake. I tried to Start My Life Again, just like Dr. Golding told me to, and this very upright man that I went out with went ahead and gave me a lecture on how I oughtn't to depend upon people who were 'lacking in integrity.' He told me that he heard from a reliable source in publishing that you were lacking in integrity. Oh, he made me furious, Peter, and I told him I was going home, and so he got up and left with me, and when I got home I wanted to call you so, I wanted to speak to you so badly, and the only way I couldn't do it was to take the pills. I know it makes no sense, it was so utterly stupid, and I would never ever do it again. You don't know how sorry I am. And you may tell yourself that I did it out of anger with you, or to try to blackmail you, or to punish you, or because I actually took what that man said about you to heart—but it was none of that. It was just that I was so worn down from going around for six weeks Being Brave! Oh, let's go somewhere, to a motel room or *somewhere*. I want terribly to be fucked. That's all I've been thinking about down here for days. I feel like—a *fiend*. Oh, please, I'm going to scream, living with this mother of mine!"

Here that mother of hers was out through the terrace doors, across the patio, and into the garden before Susan could even brush away the tear or I could respond to her appeal. And what response would I have made? Her explanation did seem to me at that moment truthful and sufficient. Of course she did not lie or deceive, of course she was not Maureen. If I didn't want Susan, I realized then, it was not because I didn't want her to sacrifice for me her dream of a marriage and a family; it was because I didn't want Susan any more, under any conditions. Nor did I want anyone else. I wanted only to be placed in sexual quarantine, to be weaned from the other sex forever.

Yet everything she said was so convincing.

Mrs. Seabury asked if I could come inside with her a moment.

"I take it," she said, when we were standing together just inside the terrace doors, "that you told her you don't plan to see her again."

"That's right."

"Then perhaps the best thing now would be to go."

"I think she's expecting me to take her to lunch."

"She has no such expectation that I know of. I can see to her lunch. And her welfare generally."

Outside Susan was now standing up beside the chaise. Both Mrs. Seabury and I were looking her way when she pulled the yellow jersey dress up over her head and let it fall to the lawn. It wasn't pale underpants I'd seen earlier beneath the skimpy dress, but a white bikini. She adjusted the back rest of the chaise until it was level with the seat and the foot rest, and then stretched herself out on it, face down. An arm hung limply over either side.

Mrs. Seabury said, "Staying any longer will only make it more difficult for her. It was very good of you," she said in her cool and unruffled way, "to visit her at the hospital every day. Dr. Golding agreed. That was the best thing to do in the situation, and we appreciate it. But now she must really make an effort to come to grips with reality. She must not be allowed to continue to act in ways that are not in her own interest. You must not let her work on your sympathies with her helplessness. She has been wooing people that way all her life. I tell you this for your own good—you must not imagine yourself in any way responsible for Susan's predicament. She has always been all too willing to collapse in other people's arms. We have tried to be kind and intelligent about this behavior always—she is what she is —but one must also be firm. And I don't think it would be kind, intelligent, or firm for you to forestall the inevitable any longer. She must begin to forget you, and the sooner the better. I am going to ask you to go now, Mr. Tarnopol, before my daughter once again does something that she will regret. She cannot afford much more remorse or humiliation. She hasn't the stamina for it."

Out in the garden, Susan had turned over and was lying now on her back, her legs as well as her arms dangling over the sides of the chaise—four limbs seemingly without strength.

I said to Mrs. Seabury, "I'll go out and say goodbye. I'll tell her I'm going."

"I could as easily tell her you've gone. She knows how to be weak but she also knows something about how to be strong. It's a matter of continually making it clear to her that people are not going to be manipulated by the childish ploys of a thirty-four-year-old woman."

"I'll just say goodbye."

"All right. I won't make an issue over a few more minutes," she said, though it was altogether clear how little she liked being crossed by a hysterical Jewish poet. "She has been carrying on in that swimsuit for a week now. She greets the mailman in it every morning. Now she is exhibiting herself in it for you. Given that less than two weeks ago she tried to take her life, I would hope that you could summon up as much self-control as our mailman does and ignore the rather transparent display of teenage vampirism."

"That is not what I am responding to. I lived with Susan for over three years."

"I don't wish to hear about that. I was never delighted by that arrangement. I deplored it, in fact."

"I was only explaining to you why I'd prefer not to leave without at least telling her that I'm going."

She said, "It is not possible for you to leave because she is lying on her back with her legs spread apart and—"

"And," I replied, my face ablaze, "suppose that were the reason?"

"Is that all you people can think about?"

"Which 'people' are you referring to?"

"People like yourself and my daughter, experimenting with one another's genitals, up there in New York. When do you stop being adolescent transgressors and grow up? You know you never had the slightest intention of making Susan your wife. You are too much of a 'swinger' for that. Such people used to be called 'bohemians.' They don't believe in marriage, with its risks and its trials and its difficulties—only in sex, till it bores them. Well, that is your business—and your prerogative, I am sure, as an artist. But you should not be so reckless as to foist your elitist values upon someone like Susan, who happens to come from a different background and was raised according to more traditional standards of conduct. Look at her out there, trying so hard to be a sexpot for your benefit. How could you have wanted to put such a ridiculous idea in that girl's head? Of all the things to encourage a person like Susan to become! Why on earth couldn't you have left such an unlikely candidate alone? Must she be driven crazy with sex too? Must every last woman in the world be 'turned on' by you modern Don Juans? To what end, Mr. Tarnopol, other than to quench your unquenchable sexual vanity? Wasn't she confused and broken enough—without *this?*"

"I don't know where to begin to tell you that you're wrong."

I walked out into the garden and looked down at a body as familiar to me as my own.

"I'm going now," I said.

She opened her eyes against the sun, and she laughed, a small, rather surprisingly cynical laugh; then after a moment's contemplation, she raised the hand nearest to me from where it dangled to the ground and placed it between the legs of my trousers, directly on my penis. And she held me like that, her face now stolid and expressionless in the strong light. I did nothing but stand there, being held. From where she had stepped out onto the patio, Mrs. Seabury looked on.

This all couldn't have lasted as long as a minute.

She lowered her hand to her own bare stomach. "Go ahead," Susan whispered. *"Go."* But just before I moved away she raised her body and pressed her cheek to my trousers.

"And I was 'wrong,' " said Mrs. Seabury, her voice harsh at last, as I passed through the living room to the street.

At the time we met, Susan was just thirty and had been living for eleven years in the co-op apartment at Park and Seventy-ninth that had become hers (along with the eighteenth-century English marquetry furniture, the heavy velvet draperies, the Aubusson carpets, and two million dollars' worth of securities in McCall and Mc-Gee Industries) when the company plane bearing her young husband to a board meeting crashed into a mountainside in upstate New York eleven months into the marriage. In that marrying the young heir had been considered by everyone (excepting her father, who, characteristically, had remained silent) a fantastic stroke of luck for a girl who hadn't enough on the ball to survive two semesters at college, Susan (who eventually confided to me that she really hadn't liked Mc-Call that much) took his death very hard. Believing that her chances were all used up at twenty, she retired to her bed and lay there, mute and motionless, every single day during the month of mourning. As a result she wound up doing woodwork for six months at a fashionable "health farm" down in Bucks County known as the Institute for Better Living. Her father would have preferred that she return to the house on Mercer Street after she had completed her convalescence, but Susan's "counselor" at the Institute had long talks with her about maturity and by the end of her stay had convinced her to return to the apartment at Park and Seventy-ninth and "give it a try on her own." To be sure, she too would have preferred to return to Princeton and the father she adored—doing "research" for him in the library, lunching with him at Lahiere's, hiking with him on weekends along the canal—if only living with her father didn't entail living under the gaze of her mother, that gaze that frightened her largely because it said, "You must grow up and you must go away."

In Manhattan, the rich and busy ladies in her building who "adopted" her made it their business to keep Susan occupied—running their errands for them during the week, and on Saturdays, Sundays, and holidays accompanying schoolchildren around town to be sure they didn't lose their mufflers and were home in time for supper (to which Susan, having sung her servile little lungs out for it, would sometimes be invited). That was what she did *for eleven years*—and, of course, she "fixed up" the apartment that she and this ghost named "Jamey" had never really "finished." Every few years she enrolled in a course at the night division at Columbia. Always she would take copious notes and diligently do all the reading, until such time as she began to fear that the professor was going to call upon her to speak. She would disappear then from the class, for a time, however, keeping up with the reading at home—even giving herself tests of her own devising. Men made some use of her over these eleven years, mostly after charity dinners and dances, which she attended on the arm of a bachelor nephew or some young cousin of the chairwoman, a rising something or other in the world. That was easy enough, and after a while did not even require eight hundred milligrams of Miltown for her to be able to "cope": she just opened her legs a little way, and he who was rising in the world did what little remained to be done. Sometimes the cousins and nephews (or maybe it was just the thoughtful chairwomen) sent her flowers the next day: she saved the cards in a folder in the file cabinet that contained her lecture notes and self-administered, ungraded examinations. "Will call. Great night. Love, A." or B. or C.

Early each summer there would generally be a knock on her apartment door: a man to ask if she would have dinner with him while his wife was away in the country. These were the husbands of the women in the building for whom she went around town all day picking up swatches of fabrics and straightening out errors in charge accounts. Their wives had told them what a lovely young person Susan was, and then they would themselves have caught sight of the five foot nine inch redhead when she was getting in and out of taxis in front of the building, her arms loaded with other people's Bergdorf boxes and her dress shimmying up her slender legs. One of these men, a handsome and charming investment banker ("like a father to me," the

thirty-year-old widow told me, without blinking an eye),
gave her a new electric range for a present when fall
came and he wanted to be sure she kept her mouth
shut; she didn't need a new range (not even to keep
her mouth shut), but because she did not want to hurt
his feelings, she had the one she and Jamey and the
decorator had bought ripped out and the new one
installed. And not one of these hot-weather paramours
of hers, afflicted as he might be with middle-age wife-
weariness, ever wanted to run off with the rich and
beautiful young woman and start a new life—and that
to Susan was as damning a fact as any in the prose-
cution's case against her self-esteem.

I didn't want to run off with her either. Yet I came
back, night after night, returned to her apartment to
eat and read and sleep, which was not what young
A., B., C., D., or E. had ever done. And for good
reason: they obviously had too much going for them,
too much confidence and vitality and hope for the
future, to settle for more than a night with the likes of
Susan the Submissive. I, on the other hand, at the age
of thirty, with my prizes and my publication behind
me, had had it. I sat at dinner in Jamey's baronial
chair, Susan serving me like a geisha. I shaved in Jamey's
lacquered brothel of a bathroom, my towels warming
on the electrical heating stand while I discovered the
luxury of his Rolls razor. I read in his gargantuan club
chair, my feet up on the ottoman covered in Jamey's
mother's favorite flame stitch, a gift for his twenty-
second (and last) birthday. I drank those rare vintages
of Jamey's wine that Susan had kept at the proper
temperature in an air-conditioned pantry all these years,
as though she expected that he might rise from the
grave one day and ask to taste his Richebourg. When
my shoes got wet in a rainstorm, I stuffed them with his
wooden shoe trees and padded around in his velvet
slippers from Tripler's. I borrowed stays from his shirts.
I weighed myself on his scale. And was generally bored
by his wife. *But she did not make a single demand.*

All Susan said to me about our arrangement was

this, and being Susan, she didn't even say it aloud: "I'm yours. I'll do anything. Come and go as you like. Let me feed you. Let me sit with you at night and watch you read. You can do anything you want to my body. I'll do anything you say. Just have dinner with me sometimes and use some of these things. And I'll never utter a peep. I'll be good as gold. I won't ask what you do when you go away. You don't have to take me anywhere. Just stay here sometimes and make use of whatever you want, including me. You see, I have all these thick bath-sized towels and Belgian lace table-cloths, all this lovely crockery, three bathrooms, two televisions, and two million dollars of Jamey's money with more of my own to come, I have these breasts and this vagina, these limbs, this skin—and no life. Give me just a little bit of that, and in return whenever you want to you can come here and recover from your wife. Any hour of the day or night. You don't even have to call beforehand."

It's a deal, I said. The broken shall succor the broken.

Of course, Susan was not the first young woman that I had met in New York since I'd come East seeking asylum in June of '62. She was just the first one I'd settled in with. According to the custom of that era—it is depressing to think that it may be the custom still—I had been to parties, befriended girls (which is to say, stood exchanging ironic quips with them in the corner of someone's crowded West Side apartment), and then had gone to bed with them, either before or after taking them out to dinner a couple of times. Some were un-doubtedly nice people, but I didn't have the staying power or the confidence really to find out. Oftentimes during my first year in New York I discovered that I did not really want to take off my clothes or those of my new-found acquaintance, once we had gotten back to one or another of our apartments, and so I would fall into silent fits of melancholy that must have made me seem rather freakish—or at least affected. One young knockout, I remember, took it very personally and became incensed that I should suddenly have turned lugubrious on her after having been "so ferociously charming" with my back against the wall of one of those crowded living rooms; she asked if it was true that I was trying to kick being queer, and I, dim-witted as can be, began to struggle to remove her pantyhose, an act which turned out to consume such passion as I had. She took her leave shortly thereafter, and the following morning, going down for the paper and my seeded roll, I found wedged into the frame of the door an index card that had penciled on it, "Abandon Hope, All Ye Who Enter Here." Those parties I went to, with their ongoing intersexual competition in self-defense, bred a lot of this sort of scuffling, or maybe a little bit went a long way with me then; eventually invitations from editors and writers to parties where there would be "a lot of girls" I mostly turned down; when I didn't, I generally regretted it afterward.

Only months after my arrival, it became clear to me —depressingly so—that New York City was probably the worst possible place, outside of the Vatican, for a man in my predicament to try to put an end to his old life and begin a new one. As I was discovering at these parties, I was in no shape to get much pleasure out of my status as a "single" man; and, as I discovered in my lawyer's office, the state of New York was hardly about to grant that status *de jure* recognition. Indeed, now that the Peter Tarnopols were New York residents, it looked as though they would be husband and wife forever. Too late I learned that had we gotten separated back in Wisconsin, we could, according to the law there, have been divorced after having voluntarily lived separate and apart for five years. (Of course, had I returned to Wisconsin in June of '62, rather than staying on at Morris's apartment and from there launching into my career as Spielvogel's patient, it is doubtful that I ever could have managed to set myself up in Madison separate and apart from Maureen.) But, as things turned out, in the sanctuary that I had taken New York to be, the only grounds for divorce was adultery, and since Maureen did not want to divorce me on any grounds, and I had no way of knowing whether she was an adulteress, or proving it even if I knew, it looked in all likelihood as though I would be celebrating my golden wedding anniversary on the steps of the State House in Albany. Moreover, because my lawyer had been unable to get Maureen and her attorney to agree to a legal separation or to any kind of financial settlement (let alone to a Mexican or Nevada divorce that would have required mutual consent to be incontestable), my official marital status in New York very shortly came to be that of the guilty party in a separation action brought by a wife against a husband who had "abandoned" her. Though we had lived together as husband and wife for only three years, I was ordered by the New York court to provide maintenance for my abandoned wife to the tune of one hundred dollars a week, and to provide it until death did us part. And in New York State what else could part us?

I could, of course, have moved and taken up residence in some state with a less restrictive divorce law, and for a while, with the aid of *The Complete Guide to Divorce* by Samuel G. Kling—the book that became my bedside Bible in that first bewildering phase of my life as a New York resident—I seriously investigated the possibilities. Reading Kling I found out that in some eleven states "separation without cohabitation and without reasonable expectation of reconciliation" was grounds for divorce, after anywhere from eighteen months to three years. One night I got out of bed at four A.M. and sat down and wrote letters to the state universities in each of the eleven states and asked if there might be a job open for me in their department of English; within the month I had received offers from the universities of Florida, Delaware, and Wyoming. According to Kling, in the first two states "voluntary three-year separation" provided grounds for divorce; in Wyoming, only two years' separation was necessary. My lawyer was quick to advise me of the various means by which Maureen might attempt to contest such a divorce; he also let me know that upon granting me a divorce the out-of-state judge would in all probability order me to continue to pay the alimony set by the New York court in the separation judgment; furthermore (to answer my next question), if I refused after the divorce to make the alimony payments, I could be (and with Maureen as my antagonist, no doubt would be) hauled into court under state reciprocity agreements and held in contempt by the Florida or Delaware or Wyoming judge for failing to support my former spouse in New York. A divorce, my lawyer said, I might be able to pull off—but escape the alimony? never. Nonetheless, I went ahead and accepted a job teaching American literature and creative writing the following September in Laramie, Wyoming. I went immediately to the library and took out books on the West. I went up to the Museum of Natural History and walked among the Indian artifacts and the tableau of the American bison. I decided I would try to learn to ride a horse, at least a little, before I got out there. And I thought of the money I would not be paying to Dr. Spielvogel.

Some ten weeks later I wrote to tell the chairman of the English department in Laramie that because of unforeseen circumstances I would be unable to take the job. The unforeseen circumstance was the hopelessness I had begun to feel at the prospect of a two-year exile in Wyoming. After which I might be able to ride a horse, but I would *still* have to pay through the nose. *If* the divorce even went uncontested! And would Florida be any better? Less remote, but a year longer to qualify for the divorce, and the end result just as uncertain. It was about this time that I decided that the only way out was to leave America and its marital laws and reciprocal state agreements and begin my life anew as a stranger in a foreign country. Since I understood that Maureen could always attach future royalties if they were to come through a New York publishing house, I would have to sell world rights to my next book to my English publisher and receive all payment through him. Or why not start from scratch—grow a

beard and change my name? . . . And who was to
say there would ever be a next book?

I spent the following few months deciding whether to
return to Italy, where I still had a few friends, or to
try Norway, where chances were slim that anybody
would ever find me (unless of course they went looking).
How about Finland? I read all about Finland in the
Encyclopaedia Britannica. High rate of literacy, long
winters, and many trees. I imagined myself in Helsinki,
and, while I was at it, Istanbul, Marrakesh, Lisbon,
Aberdeen, and the Shetland Islands. Very good place
to disappear, the Shetland Islands. Pop. 19,343, and not
that far, really, from the North Pole. Principal industries, sheep farming and fishing. Also raise famous
ponies. No mention in *Britannica* of treaty agreement
with New York State for extradition of marital crimi-
nals . . .

But, oh, if I was outraged in New York over all
I had lost in that marriage, imagine how I would feel
when I woke up bearded in my cottage on the moors
in Scalloway to discover I had lost my country as well.
What "freedom" would I have won then, speaking
American to the ponies? What "justice" would I have
made, an ironical Jewish novelist with a crook and
a pack of sheep? And what's worse, suppose she found
me out and followed me there, for all that my name
is now Long Tom Dumphy? Not at all unlikely, given
that I couldn't shake her in this, a country of two
hundred million. Oh, imagine what that would be like,
me with me stick and Maureen with her rage in the
middle of the roarin' North Sea, and only 19,343 others
to hold us apart?

So, unhappily (and not at all, really) I accepted my
fate as a male resident of the state of New York of the
republic of America who no longer cared to live with
a wife whose preference it was to continue to live with
(and off) him. I began, as they say, to try to make
the best of it. Indeed, by the time I met Susan I was
actually beginning to pass out of the first stages of
shell shock (or was it fallout sickness?) and had even

found myself rather taken with (as opposed to "taken by," very much a preoccupation at the time) a bright and engaging girl named Nancy Miles, fresh out of college and working as a "checker" for the *New Yorker*. Nancy Miles was eventually to go off to Paris to marry an American journalist stationed there, and subsequently to publish a book of autobiographical short stories, most of them based upon her childhood as a U.S. Navy commander's daughter in postwar Japan. However, the year I met her she was free as a bird, and soaring like one, too. I hadn't been so drawn to anyone since the Wisconsin debacle, when I had thrown myself at the feet of my nineteen-year-old student Karen (for whom I intermittently continued to pine, by the way; I imagined her sometimes with me and the sheep in Scalloway), but after three consecutive evenings together of nonstop dinner conversation, the last culminating in lovemaking as impassioned as anything I'd known since those illicit trysts between classes in Karen's room, I decided not to call Nancy again. Two weeks passed, and she sent me this letter:

Mr. Peter Tarnopol
Institute for Unpredictable Behavior
62 West 12th Street
New York, N.Y.

Dear Mr. Tarnopol:
  With reference to our meeting of 5/6/63:
  1. What happened?
  2. Where are we?
  While I fully recognize that numerous demands of this nature must strain the limits of your patience, I nonetheless make bold to request that you fill out the above questionnaire and return it to the address below as soon as it is convenient.

I remain,
yours,
Perplexed

Perplexed perhaps, but not broken. That was the last I heard from Nancy. I chose Susan.

It goes without saying that those seeking sanctuary have ordinarily to settle for something less than a seven-room apartment on the Upper East Side of Manhattan in which to take refuge from the wolves or the cops or the cold. I for one had never lived in anything approaching Susan's place for size or grandeur. Nor had I ever eaten so well in my life. Maureen's cooking wasn't that bad, but generally dinnertime was the hour reserved at our house for settling scores with me and my sex—unsettled scores that some evenings seemed to me to have been piling up ever since the first nucleic acid molecule went ahead and reproduced itself several billion years ago; consequently, even when the food was hot and tasty, the ambience was wrong. And in the years before I took to dining in each night on Maureen's gall, there had been army chow or university cafeteria stew. But Susan was a pro, trained by masters at what she had not learned at Calpurnia's knee: during the year she had been waiting for her fiancé to be graduated from Princeton and their life of beauty and abundance to begin, she had commuted up to New York to learn how to cook French, Italian, and Chinese specialties. The course in each cuisine lasted six weeks, and Susan stayed on (as she hadn't at Wellesley) triumphantly to complete all three. To her great glee she discovered she could now at least *outcook* her mother. Oh, what a wonderful wife (she hoped and prayed) she was going to make for this fantastic stroke of luck named James McCall the Third!

During her widowhood Susan had only rarely had the opportunity to feed anyone other than herself, and so it was that I became the first dinner guest ever to appreciate in full a culinary expertise that spanned the continents. I had never tasted food so delicious. And not even my own dutiful mother had waited on me the way this upper-crust waitress did. I was under standing instructions to proceed to eat without her, so that she could scamper freely back and forth into the kitchen getting the next dish going in her wok. Good enough. We had little outside of the food to talk about anyway. I asked about her family, I asked about her analysis, I asked about Jamey and the McCalls. I asked why she had left Wellesley in her first year. She shrugged and she flushed and she averted her eyes. She replied, oh they're very nice, and he's very nice, and she's such a sweet and thoughtful person, and "Why did I leave Wellesley? Oh, I just left." For weeks I got no more information or animation than I had the night we met, when I was seated next to her at the dinner party I was invited to annually at my publisher's town house: unswerving agreeableness, boundless timidity—a frail and terrified beauty. And in the beginning that was just fine with me. Bring on the blanquette de veau.

Each morning I headed back to the desk in my West Twelfth Street sublet, off to school to practice the three Rs—reading, writing, and angrily toting up yet again the alimony and legal bills. In the elevator, as I descended from 9D, I met up with the schoolchildren a third my age whom Susan took on weekends to the Planetarium and the puppet shows, and the successful business executives whose August recreation she had sometimes been. And what am *I* doing here, I would ask myself. With *her!* Just how debilitated can I be! My brother's recent warning would frequently come back to me as I exited past the doorman, who always courteously raised his cap to Mrs. McCall's gentleman caller, but had surmised enough about my bankroll not to make a move to hail a cab. Moe had telephoned me about Susan the night after I had come around with her to have dinner at his and Lenore's invitation. He laid it right on the line. "Another Maureen, Pep?" "She's hardly a Maureen." "The gray eyes and the 'fine' bones have got you fooled, kiddo. Another fucked-up shiksa. First the lumpenproletariat, now the aristocracy. What are you, the Malinowski of Manhattan? Enough erotic anthropology. Get rid of her, Pep. You're sticking your plug in the same socket." "Moe, hold the advice, okay?" "Not this time. I don't care to come home a year from

now, Peppy, to find you shitting into your socks." "But
I'm all right." "Oh, Christ, here we go again." "Moey, I
happen to know what I'm doing." "With a woman you
know what you're doing? Look, what the hell is Spielvogel's attitude toward this budding catastrophe—what
is *he* doing to earn his twenty bucks an hour, anything?"
"Moe, she is *not* Maureen!" "You're letting the legs
fool you, kid, the legs and the ass." "I tell you I'm not in
it for that." "If not that, what? Her deep intelligence?
Her quick wit? You mean on top of being tongue-tied,
the ice cube can't screw right either? Jesus! A pretty
face must go an awful long way with you—that, plus a
good strong dose of psychoneurosis, and a girl is in
business with my little brother. You come over here tonight for dinner, Peppy, you come eat with *us* every
night—I've got to talk some sense into you." But each
evening I turned up at Susan's, not Moe's, carrying with
me my book to be read later by the fire, envisioning, as
I stepped through the door, my blanquette, my bath,
and my bed.

So the first months passed. Then one night I said,
"Why don't you go back to college?" "Oh, I couldn't do
that." "Why couldn't you?" "I have too much to do already." "You have nothing to do." "Are you *kidding?*"
"Why don't you go back to college, Susan?" "I'm too
busy, really. Did you say you *did* want kirsch on your
fruit?"

Some weeks later. "Look, a suggestion." "Yes?"
"Why don't you move in bed?" "Haven't you enough
room?" "I mean move. Underneath me." "Oh, that. I
just don't, that's all." "Well, try it. It might liven things
up." "I'm happy as I am, thank you. Don't you like the
spinach salad?' "*Listen* to me: why don't you move
your body when I fuck you, Susan?" "Oh, please, let's
just finish dinner." "I want you to move when I fuck
you." "I told you, I'm happy as I am." "You're miserable as you are." "I'm not, and it's none of your
business." "Do you know how to move?" "Oh, why are
you torturing me like this?" "Do you want me to show
you what I mean by 'move'?" "*Stop this.* I am not going

to talk about it! I don't have to be shown anything, certainly not by you! Your life isn't such a model of order, you know." "What about college? Why don't you go back to college?" "Peter, *stop*. Please! Why are you *doing* this to me?" "Because the way you live is awful." "It is *not*." "It's crazy, really." "If it's so crazy then what are you doing here every night? I don't force you to spend the night. I don't ask anything of you at all." "You don't ask anything of anyone, so that's neither here nor there." "That's none of your business either." "It is my business." *"Why? Why yours?"* "Because I *am* here—because I *do* spend the night." "Oh, please, you must stop right now. Don't make me argue, please. I hate arguments and I refuse to participate in one. If you want to argue with somebody, go argue with your wife. I thought you come here *not* to fight."

She had a point, *the* point—here I need contend with *nothing*—but it stopped me only for a while. Eventually one night some two months later she jumped up from the table and, popping her one tear, said, "I can't go back to school, and leave me alone about it—I'm too old and I'm too stupid! What school would even take me!"

It turned out to be C.C.N.Y. They gave her credit for one semester's work at Wellesley. "This is just too silly. I'm practically thirty-one. People will laugh." "Which people are those?" "People. I'm not going to do it. By the time I graduated I'd be fifty." "What are you going to do instead till you're fifty, shop?" "I help my friends." "Those friends can hire fellows pulling rickshaws to help them the way you do." "That's just being cynical about people you don't like. I have a huge apartment to take care of, besides." "What are you so frightened of?" "That's not the issue." "What is then?" "That you won't just let me do things the way I want to. Everything I do is wrong in your eyes. You're just like my mother. She never thinks I can do anything right either." "Well, I think you can." "Only because you're embarrassed by my stupidity. It doesn't do for your 'self-image' to be seen with such a sap—so the upshot is

that in order to save *your* face, *I* have to go to college!
And move in bed! I don't even know where C.C.N.Y.
is—on a map! What if I'm the only person there who's
white?" "Well, you may be the only person there quite
so white—" "Don't joke—not now!" "You're going to
be fine." "Oh, Peter," she moaned, and clinging to her
napkin crawled into my lap to be rocked like a child—
"what if I have to talk in class? What if they call on
me?" Through my shirt I could feel *ice* packs on my
back—her two hands. "What do I do *then?*" she
pleaded. "Speak." "But if I *can't.* Oh, why are you
putting me through this misery?" "You told me why.
My self-image. So I can fuck you with a clear conscience." "Oh, you, you couldn't fuck anybody with a
clear conscience—dumb, smart, or in between. And be
serious. I'm so terrified I feel *faint*." Though not too
terrified to utter aloud, for the first time in her life, that
most dangerous of American words. The next afternoon I had one of those mock headlines printed up in a
Times Square amusement palace and presented it to
her at dinner, a phony tabloid with a black three-inch
banner reading: SUSAN SAYS IT!

In the kitchen one night a year later I sat on a stool
near the stove sipping a glass of the last of Jamey's
Mouton-Rothschild, while Susan prepared ratatouille
and practiced a talk she had to give the next morning in
her introductory philosophy class, a five-minute dis-
course on the Skeptics. "I can't remember what comes
next—*I can't do it*." "Concentrate." "But I'm *cooking*
something." "It will cook itself." "Nothing cooks itself
that tastes any good." "Then stop a minute and let's
hear what you're going to say." "But I don't care about
the Skeptics. And *you* don't, Peter. And nobody in my
class cares, I can assure you of that. And what if I just
can't talk? What if I open my mouth and nothing comes
out? That's what happened to me at Wellesley." And to
me at Brooklyn College, but I didn't tell her, not on
that occasion. "Something," I said confidently, "will
come out." "Yes? *What?*" "Words. Concentrate on the
words the way you concentrate on the eggplant there—"

"Would you come with me? On the subway? Just till I get up there?" "I'll even come to the class with you." "No! You mustn't! I'd be *paralyzed* if you were there." "But I'm here." "This is a kitchen," she said, smiling, but not all that happy. And then, with some further prodding, she went ahead and delivered her philosophy report, though more to the ratatouille than to me. "Perfect." "Yes?" "Yes." "Then why," asked Susan, who was turning out to be a wittier young widow than any of us had imagined, "then why do I have to do it again tomorrow? Why can't this count?" "Because it's a kitchen." "Shit," said Susan, "that's not fair."

Am I describing two people falling in love? If so, I didn't recognize it for that at the time. Even after a year, Susan's still seemed to me my hideout, my sanctuary from Maureen, her lawyer, and the courts of the state of New York, all of whom had designated me a *defendant*. But at Susan's I needed no more defense than a king upon his throne. Where else could I go to be so revered? The answer, friends, is nowhere; it had been a long time between salaams. The least I could do in exchange was to tell her how to live right. Admittedly, A Lot I Knew, but then it did not take much to know that it is better to be a full-time student at City College than a matriculated customer at Bergdorf's and Bonwit's from nine to five, and better, I believed, to be alive and panting during the sex act than in a state of petrifaction, if you are going to bother to perform that act at all. So I, ironically enough, coached my student in remedial copulation and public speaking, and she nursed me with the tenderest tenderness and the sweetest regard. A new experience all around. So was the falling in love, if that's what our mutual education and convalescence added up to. When she made the dean's list I was as proud as any papa, bought her a bracelet and dinner; and when she tried and failed to come, I was crushed and disbelieving, like a high-school teacher whose brilliant, impoverished student has somehow been turned down for the scholarship to Harvard. How could it be, after all those study sessions we had put in together? All that dedication and hard work! Where had we gone wrong? I have suggested how unnerving it was for me to be accomplice to that defeat—the fact is that somewhere along the way Susan's effort to reach an orgasm came to stand in my mind for the full recovery of us both. And maybe this, as much as anything, helped to make it unattainable, the responsibility for my salvation as well as her own being far too burdensome for her to bear. . . You see, I am not claiming here that I went about conducting this affair in the manner of a reclamation engineer—nor was I seeking to unseat Dr. Golding, who was paid to cure the sick and heal the wounded, and whose own theory, as it sifted through to me, seemed to be that the more paternal or patriarchal my influence upon Susan, the more remote the prospect of the orgasm. I thought one could make as good an argument against this line of speculation as for it, but I didn't try. I was neither theoretician nor diagnostician, nor for that matter much of a "father figure" in my own estimation. It would have seemed to me that you hadn't to penetrate very far beneath the surface of our affair to see that I was just another patient looking for the cure himself.

In fact, it required my doctor to get me to continue to take my medicine named Susan, when, along the way, I repeatedly complained that I'd had enough, that the medicine was exacerbating the ailment more than it might be curing it. Dr. Spielvogel did not take my brother Moe's view of Susan—no, with Spielvogel *I* did. "She's hopeless," I would tell him, "a frightened little sparrow." "You would prefer another vulture?" "Surely there must be something in between," thinking, as I spoke, of Nancy Miles, that soaring creature, and the letter I'd never answered. "But you don't have something in between. You have this." "But all that timidity, all that fear. . . The woman is a slave, Doctor, and not just to me—to everyone." "You prefer contentiousness? You miss the scenes of high drama, do you? With Maureen, so you told me, it was the *Götterdämmerung* at breakfast, lunch, and dinner.

What's wrong with a little peace and quiet with your meals?" "But there are times when she is a *mouse*." "Good enough," said Spielvogel, "who ever heard of a little mouse doing a grown man any serious harm?" "But what happens when the mouse wants to be married—and to me?" "How can she marry you? You are married already." "But when I'm no longer married." "There will be time to worry about that then, don't you think?" "No. I don't think that at all. What if when I should want to leave her, she tries to do herself in? She is not stable, Doctor, she is not strong—you must understand that." "Which are you talking about now, Maureen or Susan?" "I can tell them apart, I assure you. But that doesn't mean that it isn't beyond Susan, just because it happens also to be a specialty of Maureen's." "Has she threatened you with suicide if you should ever leave her?" "She wouldn't threaten me with anything. That isn't her way." "But you are certain that she would do it, if at some future date, when the issue arose, you chose not to marry her. That is the reason you want to give her up now." "I don't particularly 'want' to. I'm telling you I ought to." "But you are enjoying yourself somewhat, am I right?" "Somewhat, yes. More than somewhat. But I don't want to lead her on. She is not up to it. Neither am I." "But is it leading her on, to have an affair, two young people?" "Not in your eyes, perhaps." "In whose then? Your own?" "In Susan's, Doctor, in Susan's! Look, what if after the affair is no more, she cannot accept the fact and commits suicide? Answer that, will you?" "Over the loss of you she commits suicide?" "Yes!" "You think every woman in the world is going to kill herself over you?" "Oh, please, don't distort the point I'm making. Not 'every woman'—just the two I've wound up with." "Is this why you wind up with them?" "Is it? I'll think about it. Maybe so. But then that is yet another reason to dissolve this affair right *now*. Why continue if there is anything like a chance of that coming to pass? Why would you want to encourage me to do a thing like that?" "Was I encouraging 'that'? I was only encouraging you to find some pleasure and comfort in her compliant nature. I tell you, many a man would envy you. Not everybody would be so distressed as you by a mistress who is beautiful and submissive and rich, and a Cordon Bleu cook into the bargain." "And, conceivably, a suicide." "That remains to be seen. Many things are conceivable that have little basis in reality." "I'm afraid in my position I can't afford to be so cavalier about it." "Not cavalier. Only no more convinced than is warranted, in the circumstances. And no more terrified." "Look, I am not up to any more desperate stunts. I've got a right to be terrified. I was married to Maureen. I still am!" "Well then, if you feel so strongly, if you've been burned once and don't want to take the chance—" "I am saying, to repeat, that it may not be such a 'chance'—and I don't feel I have a right to take it. It's her life that is endangered, not mine." " 'Endangered'? What a narcissistic melodrama you are writing here, Mr. Tarnopol. If I may offer a literary opinion." "Yes? Is that what it is?" "Isn't it?" "I don't always know, Doctor, exactly what you mean by 'narcissism.' What I think I am talking about is responsibility. You are the one who is talking about the pleasure and comforts in staying. You are the one who is talking about what is in it for me. You are the one who is telling me not to worry about Susan's expectations or vulnerability. It would seem to me that it's *you* who are inviting *me* to take the narcissistic line." "All right, if that's what you think, then leave her before it goes any further. You have this sense of responsibility to the woman—then act upon it." "But just a second ago you were suggesting that my sense of responsibility was *misplaced*. That my fears were *delusional*. Or weren't you?" "I think they are excessive, yes."

Right now I get no advice about Susan from anyone. I am here to be free of advisers—and temptation. Susan a temptation? Susan a temptress? What a word to describe her! Yet I have never ached for anyone like

this before. As the saying goes, we'd been through a
lot together, and not in the way that Maureen and I
had been "through it." With Maureen it was the relentless *sameness* of the struggle that nearly drove me
mad; no matter how much reason or intelligence or
even brute force I tried to bring to bear upon our
predicament, I could not change a thing—everything
I did was futile, including of course doing nothing.
With Susan there was struggle all right, but then there
were rewards. Things changed. *We* changed. There
was progress, development, marvelous and touching
transformations all around. Surely the last thing you
could say was that ours was a comfortable, settled
arrangement that came to an end because our pleasures
had become tiresome and stale. No, the progress *was*
the pleasure, the transformations what gave me most
delight—which is what has made her attempt at suicide
so crushing . . . what makes my yearning for her all
the more bewildering. Because now it looks as though
nothing has changed, and we are back where we began.
I have to wonder if the letters I begin to write to her
and leave unfinished, if the phone calls I break off dialing before the last digit, if that isn't me beginning to
give way to the siren song of The Woman Who Cannot Live Without You, She Who Would Rather Be
Dead Than Unwed—if this isn't me on the brink again
of making My Mistake, contriving to continue, after a
brief intermission, what Spielvogel would call my narcissistic melodrama. . . . But then it is no less distressing for me to think that out of fear of My Mistake,
I am making another even worse: relinquishing for no
good reason the generous, gentle, good-hearted, *un-*
Maureenish woman with whom I have actually come
to be in love. I think to myself, "Take this yearning
seriously. You *want* her," and I rush to the phone to
call down to Princeton—and then at the phone I ask
myself if "love" has very much to do with it, if it
isn't the vulnerability and brokenness, the *neediness,*
to which I am being drawn. Suppose it is really nothing
more than a helpless beauty in a bikini bathing suit

taking hold of my cock as though it were a lifeline, suppose it is only that that inspires this longing. Such things have been known to happen. "Sexual vanity," as Mrs. Seabury says. "Rescue fantasies," says Dr. Spielvogel, "boyish dreams of Oedipal glory." "Fucked-up shiksas," my brother says, "you can't resist them, Pep."

Meanwhile Susan remains under the care of her mother in Princeton, and I remain up here, under my own.

3. MARRIAGE A LA MODE

Rapunzel, Rapunzel,
Let down your hair.

—from the Grimms' fairy tale

For those young men who reached their maturity in the fifties, and who aspired to be grown-up during that decade, when as one participant has written, everyone *wanted* to be thirty, there was considerable moral prestige in taking a wife, and hardly because a wife was going to be one's maidservant or "sexual object." Decency and Maturity, a young man's "seriousness," were at issue precisely because it was thought to be the other way around: in that the great world was so obviously a man's, it was only within marriage that an ordinary woman could hope to find equality and dignity. Indeed, we were led to believe by the defenders of womankind of our era that we were exploiting and degrading the women we *didn't* marry, rather than the ones we did. Unattached and on her own, a woman was supposedly not even able to go to the movies or out to a restaurant by herself, let alone perform an appendectomy or drive a truck. It was up to us then to give them the value and the purpose that society at large withheld—by marrying them. If we didn't marry women, who would? Ours, alas, was the only sex available for the job: the draft was on.

No wonder then that a young college-educated bourgeois male of my generation who scoffed at the idea of marriage for himself, who would just as soon eat out of cans or in cafeterias, sweep his own floor, make his own bed, and come and go with no binding legal attachments, finding female friendship and sexual adventure where and when he could and for no longer than he liked, laid himself open to the charge of "immaturity," if not "latent" or blatant "homosexuality." Or he was just plain "selfish." Or he was "frightened of responsibility." Or he could not "commit himself" (nice institutional phrase, that) to "a permanent relationship." Worst of all, most shameful of all, the chances were that this person who thought he was perfectly able to take care of himself on his own was in actuality "unable to love."

An awful lot of worrying was done in the fifties about whether people were able to love or not—I venture to say, much of it by young women in behalf of the young men who didn't particularly *want* them to wash their socks and cook their meals and bear their children and then tend them for the rest of their natural days. "But aren't you capable of loving anyone? Can't you think of anyone but yourself?" when translated from desperate fifties-feminese into plain English, generally meant "I want to get married and I want you to get married to."

Now I am sure that many of the young women of that period who set themselves up as specialists in loving hadn't a very clear idea of how strong a charge their emotions got from the instinct for survival—or how much those emotions arose out of the yearning to own and be owned, rather than from a reservoir of pure and selfless love that was the special property of themselves and their gender. After all, how lovable *are* men? Particularly men "unable to love"? No, there was more to all that talk about "commitment" and "permanent relationships" than many young women (and their chosen mates) were able to talk about or able at that time fully to understand: the more was the fact of female dependence, defenselessness, and vulnerability.

This hard fact of life was of course experienced and dealt with by women in accordance with personal endowments of intelligence and sanity and character. One imagines that there were brave and genuinely self-sacrificing decisions made by women who refused to accede to those profoundest of self-delusions, the ones that come cloaked in the guise of love; likewise, there was much misery in store for those who were never able to surrender their romantic illusions about the arrangement they had made in behalf of their helplessness, until they reached the lawyer's office, and he threw their way that buoy known as alimony. It has been said that those ferocious alimony battles that have raged in the courtrooms of this country during the last few decades, the way religious wars raged throughout Europe in the seventeenth century, were really "symbolic" in nature. My guess is that rather than serving as a symbol around which to organize other grievances and heartaches, the alimony battle frequently tended to clarify what was generally obscured by the metaphors with which marital arrangements were camouflaged by the partners themselves. The extent of the panic and rage aroused by the issue of alimony, the ferocity displayed by people who were otherwise sane and civilized enough, testifies, I think, to the shocking —and humiliating—realization that came to couples in the courtroom about the fundamental role that each may actually have played in the other's life. "So, it has descended to this," the enraged contestants might say, glaring in hatred at one another—but even that was only an attempt to continue to hide from the most humiliating fact of all: that it really *was* this, all along.

Now I realize that it is possible to dismiss these generalizations as a manifestation of my bitterness and cynicism, an unfortunate consequence of my own horrific marriage and of the affair that recently ended so unhappily. Furthermore, it can be said that, having chosen women like Maureen and Susan (or, if you prefer, having had them chosen for me by my own aberrant, if not pathological, nature), I for one should not generalize, even loosely, about what men want (and get) from women, or what women want and get out of men. Well, I grant that I do not find myself feeling very "typical" at this moment, nor am I telling this story in order to argue that my life is representative of anything; nonetheless, I am naturally interested in looking around to see how much of my experience with women has been special to me and—if you must have it that way—my pathology, and how much is symptomatic of a more extensive social malaise. And looking around, I conclude this: in Maureen and Susan I came in contact with two of the more virulent strains of a virus to which only a few women among us are immune.

Outwardly, of course, Maureen and Susan couldn't have been more dissimilar, nor could either have had a stronger antipathy for the "type" she took the other to be. However, what drew them together as women—which is to say, what drew me to them, for that is the subject here—was that in her own extreme and vivid way, each of these antipathetic originals demonstrated that sense of defenselessness and vulnerability that has come to be a mark of their sex and is often at the core of their relations with men. That I came to be bound to Maureen by *my* helplessness does not mean that either of us ever really stopped envisioning *her* as the helpless victim and myself as the victimizer who had only to desist in his brutishness for everything to be put right and sexual justice to be done. So strong was the myth of male inviolability, of male dominance and potency, not only in Maureen's mind but in mine, that even when I went so far as to dress myself in a woman's clothes and thus concede that as a man I surrendered, even *then* I could never fully assent to the idea that in our household conventional assumptions about the strong and the weak did not adequately describe the situation. Right down to the end, I still saw Maureen, and she saw herself, as the damsel in distress; and in point of fact, beneath all that tough exterior, all those claims to being "in business for herself" and nobody's patsy, Maureen was actually more of a Susan than Susan was, *and to herself no less than to me.*

There is a growing body of opinion which maintains that by and large marriages, affairs, and sexual arrangements generally are made by masters in search of slaves: there are the dominant and the submissive, the brutish and the compliant, the exploiters and the exploited. What this formula fails to explain, among a million other things, is why so many of the "masters" appear themselves to be in bondage, oftentimes to their "slaves." I do not contend—to make the point yet again —that my story furnishes anything like an explanation or a paradigm; it is only an instance, a postchivalric instance to be sure, of what might be described as the Prince Charming phenomenon. In this version of the fairy tale the part of the maiden locked in the tower is played consecutively by Maureen Johnson Tarnopol and Susan Seabury McCall. I of course play the prince. My performance, as described here, may give rise to the sardonic suggestion that I should have played his horse. But, you see, it was not as an animal that I wished to be a star—it was decidedly *not* horsiness, goatishness, foxiness, lionliness, or beastliness in any form that I aspired to. I wanted to be humanish: manly, a man.

At the time when all this began, I would never even have thought it necessary to announce that as an aspiration—I was too confident at twenty-five that success was all but at hand—nor did I foresee a career in which being married and then trying to get unmarried would become my predominant activity and obsession. I would have laughed had anyone suggested that struggling with a woman over a marriage would come to occupy me in the way that exploring the South Pole had occupied Admiral Byrd—or writing *Madame Bovary* had occupied Flaubert. Clearly the last thing I could have imagined was myself, a dissident and skeptical member of my generation, succumbing to all that moralizing rhetoric about "permanent relationships." And, in truth, it did take something more than the rhetoric to do me in. It took a Maureen, wielding it. Yet the humbling fact remains: when the dissident and skeptical member of his generation was done in, it was on the same grounds as just about everyone else.

I was fooled by appearances, largely my own.

As a young writer already publishing stories in literary quarterlies, as one who resided in a Lower East Side basement apartment between Second Avenue and the Bowery, living on army savings and a twelve-hundred-dollar publisher's advance that I doled out to myself at thirty dollars a week, I did not think of myself as an ordinary or conventional university graduate of those times. My college acquaintances were all off becoming lawyers and doctors; a few who had been friends on the Brown literary magazine were working on advanced degrees in literature—prior to my induction into the army, I had myself served a year and a half in the Ph.D. program at the University of Chicago, before falling by the wayside, a casualty of "Bibliography" and "Anglo-Saxon"; the rest—the fraternity boys, the athletes, the business majors, those with whom I'd had little association at school—were by now already married and holding down nine-to-five jobs. Of course I dressed in blue button-down oxford shirts and wore my hair clipped short, but what else was I to wear, a serape? long curls? This was 1958. Besides, there were other ways in which it seemed to me I was distinguishable from the mass of my contemporaries: I read books and I wanted to write them. My master was not Mammon or Fun or Propriety, but Art, and Art of the earnest moral variety. I was by then already well into writing a novel about a retired Jewish haberdasher from the Bronx who on a trip to Europe with his wife nearly strangles to death a rude German housewife in his rage over "the six million." The haberdasher was modeled upon my own kindly, excitable, hard-working Jewish father who had had a

similar urge on a trip he and my mother had taken to
visit me in the army; the haberdasher's GI son was
modeled upon myself, and his experiences closely par-
alleled mine in Germany during my fourteen months
as a corporal in Frankfurt. I had had a German girl
friend, a student nurse, large and blonde as a Valkyrie,
but sweet to the core, and all the confusion that she
had aroused in my parents, and in me, was to be at
the heart of the novel that eventually became *A Jewish Father*.

Over my desk I did not have a photograph of a sail-
boat or a dream house or a diapered child or a travel
poster from a distant land, but words from Flaubert,
advice to a young writer that I had copied out of one
of his letters: "Be regular and orderly in your life like
a bourgeois, so that you may be violent and original in
your work." I appreciated the wisdom in this, and
coming from Flaubert, the wit, but at twenty-five, for
all my dedication to the art of fiction, for all the discipline and seriousness (and *awe*) with which I approached the Flaubertian vocation, I still wanted my
life to be *somewhat* original, and if not violent, at least
interesting, when the day's work was done. After all,
hadn't Flaubert himself, before he settled down at his
round table to become the tormented anchorite of modern literature, gone off as a gentleman-vagabond to the
Nile, to climb the pyramids and sow his oats with dusky
dancing girls?

So: Maureen Johnson, though not exactly Egyptian,
struck me as someone who might add a little outside
interest to my dedicated writer's life. Did she! Eventually she *displaced* the writing, she was so interesting.
To begin with, she was twenty-nine years of age, that
temptingly unknown creature of a young man's eroto-
heroic imaginings, *an older woman*. Moreover, she had
the hash marks to prove it. Not one but two divorces:
first from the husband in Rochester, a Yugoslav saloon-
keeper named Mezik, whose sixteen-year-old barmaid
she had been; she claimed that Mezik, a heavy drinker
with a strong right hook, had once "forced" her to go

down on a friend of his, the manager of an upholstery
factory—later she changed the story somewhat and said
that the three of them had been drunk at the time, and
that the men had drawn straws to see which of them
young Maureen would go off with to the bedroom; she
had decided to blow Mezik's buddy, rather than have intercourse with him, because it had seemed to her, in the
circumstances and in her innocence, less demeaning. "It
wasn't," she added. Then the marriage and divorce from
Walker, a handsome young actor with a resonant voice
and a marvelous profile who turned out to be a homosexual—that is to say, he'd "promised" Maureen he'd get
over it after the wedding, but only got worse. Twice
then she had been "betrayed" by men—nonetheless
there was plenty of the scrapper in her when we met.
And plenty of tough wit. "I am Duchess of Malfi still,"
was a line she pulled on me our first night in bed—not
bad, I thought, not bad, even if it was obviously something her actor husband had taught her. She had the
kind of crisp good looks that are associated with "dark
Irishmen"—only a little marred in her case by a lantern jaw—a lithe, wiry little body (the body of a tom-
boyish prepubescent, except for the sizable conical
breasts) and terrific energy and spirit. With her quick
movements and alert eyes, she was like one of nature's
undersized indefatigables, the bee or the hummingbird,
who are out working the flowers from sunup to sundown,
sipping from a million stamens in order to meet their
minimum daily nutritional requirements. She jocularly
boasted of having been the fastest runner, male or female, of her era in the Elmira, New York, grade-school
system, and that (of all she told me) may well have been
the truth. The night we met—at a poet's party uptown
—she had challenged me to a footrace from the Astor
Place subway station to my apartment two blocks
away on East Ninth: "Winner calls the shots!" she
cried, and off we went—I triumphed, but only by the
length of a brownstone, and at the apartment, breath-
less from the race she'd run me, I said, "Okay, the
spoils: take off your clothes," which she gladly (and

rapidly) proceeded to do in the hallway where we stood, panting. Hot stuff, this (thought I); very *interesting*. Oh yes, she was fast, that girl—but I was faster, was I not? . . . Also, I should mention here, Maureen had these scores to settle with my sex, and rather large delusions about her gifts, which she had come to believe lay somewhere, anywhere, in the arts.

At the age of sixteen, an eleventh-grader, she had run away from her family's home in Elmira—a runaway, that got me too. I'd never met a real one before. What did her father do? "Everything. Nothing. Handyman. Night watchman. Who remembers any more?" Her mother? "Kept house. Drank. Oh, Christ, Peter, I forgot them long ago. And they, me." She ran off from Elmira to become—of course, an actress . . . but of all places, to Rochester. "What did I know?" she said, dismissing her innocence with a wave of the hand; a dead issue, that innocence. In Rochester she met Mezik ("married the brute—and then met his buddy"), and after three years of frustration with the second-raters in the local avant-garde theater group, switched to art school to become—an abstract painter. Following her divorce, she gave up painting—and the painter whose mistress she had become during her separation from Mezik and who had broken his "promise" to help get her in with his dealer in Detroit—and took harpsichord lessons while waiting on tables in Cambridge, Massachusetts, a town she'd heard had fewer types like Mezik in residence. There, just twenty-one, she married Walker of the Brattle Theater; five long years followed, of him and his Harvard boys. By the time we met, she had already tried wood sculpture in Greenwich Village (her teacher's wife was fiercely jealous of her, so she dropped it) and was back "in the theater," temporarily "in the production end"—that is, taking tickets and ushering at an off-Broadway theater on Christopher Street.

As I say, I believed all these reversals and recoveries, all this *movement* of her, to be evidence of a game, audacious, and determined little spirit; and it was, it was.

So too did this mess of history argue for a certain instability and lack of focus in her life. On the other hand, there was so much focus to my own, and always had been, that Maureen's chaotic, daredevil background had a decidedly exotic and romantic appeal. She had been around—and around. I liked that idea; I hadn't been anywhere really, not quite yet.

She was also something of a rough customer, and that was new to me too. At the time I took up with Maureen, I had for nearly a year been having a passionate affair with a college girl named Dina Dornbusch, a senior at Sarah Lawrence and the daughter of a wealthy Jewish family from Long Island. She was an ambitious literature and language major, and we met when she came to my basement apartment, along with four other coeds and a *Mademoiselle* editor, to interview me about my work. I had just gotten out of the army, and my "work" at the time consisted only of the six short stories that had been published in the quarterlies while I had been stationed in Frankfurt; that they had been read by these awed young girls was very nice to know. I already knew of course that they had been read with interest by New York book publishers and literary agents, for their numerous letters of inquiry had reached me in Germany, and upon returning to the U.S. after my discharge, I had chosen an agent and subsequently signed a publisher's contract that provided me with a modest advance for the novel I was writing. But that I had, while serving as a draftee in Germany, achieved enough "fame" for these girls to settle on me as the young American writer they wished to interview for a feature in the magazine, well, needless to say, that opened up a fantasy or two in my head. To be sure, I talked to them about Flaubert, about Salinger, about Mann, about my experiences in Germany and how I thought I might put them to use in fiction, but nonetheless I was wondering throughout how to get the girl with the marvelous legs and the earnest questions to stay behind when the others left.

Oh, why did I forsake Dina Dornbusch—for Maureen! Shall I tell you? Because Dina was still in college writing papers on "the technical perfection" of "Lycidas." Because Dina listened to me so intently, was so much my student, taking my opinions for her own. Because Dina's father gave us front-row seats to Broadway musicals that we had to go to see for fear of offending him. Because—yes, this is true, too; incredible, but true—because when Dina came in to visit me from school, practically all we did, from the moment she stepped into the doorway, was fuck. In short, because she was rich, pretty, protected, smart, sexy, adoring, young, vibrant, clever, confident, ambitious—that's why I gave her up for Maureen! She was a girl still, who had just about everything. I, I decided at twenty-five, was beyond "that." I wanted something called "a woman."

At twenty-nine, with two unhappy marriages behind her, with no rich, doting father, no gorgeous clothes, and no future, Maureen seemed to me to have earned all that was implied by that noun; she was certainly the first person of her sex I had ever known intimately to be so completely adrift and on her own. "I've always been more or less in business for myself," she'd told me at the party where we'd met—straight, unsentimental talk, and I liked it. With Dina, everybody seemed always to be in business for her. Likewise with myself.

Prior to Maureen, the closest I had come to a girl who had known real upheaval in her life was Grete, the student nurse in Frankfurt, whose family had been driven from Pomerania by the advancing Russian army. I used to be fascinated by whatever she could tell me about her experience of the war, but that turned out to be next to nothing. Only a child of eight when the war ended, all she could remember of it was living in the country with her brothers and sisters and her mother, on a farm where they had eggs to eat, animals to play with, and spelling and arithmetic to learn in the village school. She remembered that when the family, in flight in the spring of '45, finally ran into the American army, a GI had given her an orange; and on the farm sometimes, when the children were being particularly noisy, her mother used to put her hands up to her ears and say, "Children, quiet, quiet, you sound like a bunch of Jews." But that was as much contact as she seemed to have had with the catastrophe of the century. This did not make it so simple for me as one might think, nor did I in turn make it easy for Grete. Our affair frequently bewildered her because of my moodiness, and when she then appeared to be innocent of what it was that had made me sullen or short-tempered, I became even more difficult. Of course, she *had* been only eight when the European war ended—nonetheless, I could never really believe that she was simply a big, sweet, good-natured, commonsensical eighteen-year-old girl who did not care very much that I was a dark Jew and she a blonde Aryan. This suspiciousness, and my self-conscious struggle with it, turned up in the affair between the two young lovers depicted in *A Jewish Father*.

What I liked, you see, was something taxing in my love affairs, something problematical and puzzling to keep the imagination going even while I was away from my books; I liked most being with young women who gave me something to think about, and not necessarily because we talked together about "ideas."

So, Maureen was a rough customer—I thought about that. I wondered if I was "up"—nice word—to someone with her history and determination. It would seem by the way I hung in there that I decided that I at least ought to be. I had been up to Grete and the problems she raised for me, had I not? Why back away from difficulties, or disorder, or even turbulence—what was there to be afraid of? I honestly didn't know.

Besides, for a very long time, the overwhelming difficulty—Maureen's helplessness—was largely obscured by the fight in her and by the way in which she cast herself as the victim always of charlatans and ingrates, rather than as a person who hadn't the faintest idea of the relationship of beginning, middle, and end. When she fought me, I was at first so busy fighting back I didn't have time to see her defiance as the measure of her ineptitude and desperation. Till Maureen I had

never even fought a man in anger—with my hands,
that is; but I was much more combative at twenty-five
than I am now and learned quickly enough how to
disarm her of her favorite weapon, the spike of a high-
heeled shoe. Eventually I came to realize that not even
a good shaking such as parents administer to recalcitrant children was sufficient to stop her once she was
on the warpath—it required a slap in the face to do that.
"Just like Mezik!" screamed Maureen, dropping dramatically to the floor to cower before my violence
(and pretending as best she could that it did not give
her pleasure to have uncovered the brute in the high-
minded young artist).

Of course by the time I got around to hitting her I
was already in over my head and looking around for a
way out of an affair that grew more distressing and bewildering—and frightening—practically by the hour.
It was not only the depths of acrimony between us
that had me reeling, but the shocking realization of
this helplessness of hers, that which *drove* her to the
episodes of wild and reckless rage. As the months
passed I had gradually come to see that nothing she
did ever worked—or, rather, I had finally come to
penetrate the obfuscating rhetoric of betrayal and victimization in order to see it *that way:* the Christopher
Street producer went back on his "promise" to lift
her from the ticket office into the cast; the acting teacher
in the West Forties who needed an assistant turned out
to be "a psychotic"; her boss at one job was "a slave
driver," at the next, "a fool," at the next, "a lecher,"
and invariably, whenever she quit in disgust or was
fired and came home in angry tears—whenever yet
another of those "promises" that people were forever
making to her had been broken—she would return to
my basement apartment in the middle of the day to
find me over the typewriter, pouring sweat—as happens
when I'm feeling fluent—and reeking through my
button-down oxford shirt like a man who'd been out
all day with the chain gang. At the sight of me working
away feverishly at what I wanted most to do, her rage

at the world of oppressors was further stoked by jealousy of me—even though, as it happened, she greatly admired my few published stories, defended them vehemently against all criticism, and enjoyed vicariously the small reputation that I was coming to have. But then vicariousness was her nemesis: what she got through men was all she got. No wonder she could neither forgive nor forget him who had wronged her by "forcing" her at sixteen into bed with his buddy, or him who preferred the flesh of Harvard freshmen to her own; and if she could not relinquish the bartender Mezik or the bit player Walker, imagine the meaning she must have found in one whose youthful earnestness and single-minded devotion to a high artistic calling might magically become her own if only she could partake forever of his flesh and blood.

Our affair was over (except that Maureen wouldn't move out, and I hadn't the sense, or the foresight, to bequeath to her my two rooms of secondhand furniture and take flight; having never before been defeated in my life in anything that mattered, I simply could not recognize defeat as a possibility for me, certainly not at the hands of someone seemingly so inept)—our affair was over, but for the shouting, when Maureen told me . . . Well, you can guess what she told me. Anybody could have seen it coming a mile away. Only I didn't. Why would a woman want to fool Peter Tarnopol? Why would a woman want to tell me a lie in order to get me to marry her? What chance for happiness in such a union? No, no, it just could not be. No one would be so silly and stupid as to do a thing like that *and certainly not to me*. I Had Just Turned Twenty-Six. I Was Writing A Serious Novel. I Had My Whole Life Ahead Of Me. No—the way *I* pictured it, I would tell Maureen that this affair of ours had obviously been a mistake from the beginning and by now had become nothing but a nightmare for both of us. "As much my fault as yours, Maureen"—I didn't believe it, but I would say it, for the sake of getting out without further altercation; the only sensible solution, I would say, was

for each now to go his own separate way. How could
we be anything but better off without all this useless
conflict and demeaning violence in our lives? "We just"
—I would tell her, in straight, unsentimental talk such
as she liked to use herself—"we just don't have any
business together any more." Yes, that's what I would
say, and she would listen and nod in acquiescence (she
would have to—I would be so decent about it, and so
sensible) and she would go, with me wishing her good
luck.

It didn't work out that way. Actually it was in the
midst of one of the ten or fifteen quarrels that we had
per day, now that she had decided to stay at home and
take up writing herself, that I told her to leave. The
argument, which began with her accusing me of trying
to prevent her from writing fiction because I was
"frightened" of competition from a woman, ended with
her sinking her teeth into my wrist—whereupon, with
my free hand, I bloodied her nose. "You and Mezik! No
difference *at all!*" The barkeeper, she claimed, used to
draw blood from her every single day during the last
year of their married life—he had turned her nose
"into a faucet." For me it was a first, however—and a
shock. Likewise her teeth in my flesh was like nothing
I had ever known before in my stable and unbloody
past. I had been raised to be fearful and contemptuous of violence as a means of settling disputes or venting
anger—my idea of manliness had little to do with
dishing out physical punishment or being able to absorb
it. Nor was I ashamed that I could do neither. To find
Maureen's blood on my hand was in fact *un*manning,
as disgraceful as her teeth marks on my wrist. "Go!" I
screamed, "Get out of here!" And because she had
never seen me in such a state before—I was so unhinged
by rage that while she packed her suitcase I stood over
her tearing the shirt off my own body—she left, borrowing my spare typewriter, however, so she could write a
story about "a heartless infantile son-of-a-bitch so-called
artist just like you!"

"Leave that typewriter where it is!" "But what will

I write on then?" "Are you kidding? Are you *crazy?* You're going to 'expose' me, and you want me to give you the weapon to do it with?" "But you have *two* of them! Oh, I'm going to tell the world, Peter, I'll tell them just what a selfish, self-important, egomaniacal baby you are!" "Just go, Maureen—and *I'll* tell them! But I won't have any more fucking screaming and arguing and *biting* around here when I am trying to do my work!" "Oh fuck your high and mighty work! What about *my life!*" "Fuck your life, it's not my affair any longer! Get out of here! Oh, take it—take it and just go!" Maybe she thought (now that my shirt was hanging off me in strips) that I might start in next tearing *her* to shreds—for all at once she backed off and was out of the apartment, taking with her, to be sure, the old gray Remington Royal portable that had been my parents' bar mitzvah present to the hotshot assistant sports editor of the *Yonkers High Broadcaster.*

Three days later she was back at the door, in blue duffel coat and knee socks, wan and scrappy looking as a street urchin. Because she could not face her top-floor room on Carmine Street alone, she had spent the three days with friends of hers, a Village couple in their early fifties whom I couldn't stand, who in turn considered me and my narratives "square." The husband (advertised by Maureen as "an old friend of Kenneth Patchen's") had been Maureen's teacher when she first came to New York and went into wood sculpture. Months back she had declared that she had been badly misled by these two "schizorenos," but never explained how.

As was her way the morning after even the most horrendous scenes, she laughed off the violent encounter of three days earlier, asking me (in wonderment at my naiveté) how I could take seriously anything she may have said or done in anger. One aspect of my squareness (according to those who worked in wood) was that I had no more tolerance for the irregular or the eccentric than George F. Babbitt of Zenith, Middle America. I was not open to experience in my basement apartment on East Ninth the way those middle-aged beatniks were in their Bleecker Street loft. I was a nice Jewish boy from Westchester who cared only about Success. I was their Dina Dornbusch.

"Lucky I am," I told her, "otherwise you'd be at the bottom of the East River." She was sitting in a chair, still in her duffel coat; I had given no sign that I had any intention of allowing her to move back in. When she had gone to peck me on the cheek in the doorway, I had—again, to her amusement—pulled my head away. "Where's the typewriter?" I asked, my way of saying that as far as I was concerned the only excuse Maureen could have to be visiting me was to return what she had borrowed. "You middle-class monster!" she cried. "You throw me out into the street. I have to go sleep on somebody's floor with sixteen cats lapping my face all night long—and all you can think about is your portable typewriter! Your *things*. It's a thing, Peter, *a thing*—and I'm a human being!" "You could have slept at your own place, Maureen." "I was *lonely*. You don't understand that because you have ice in your heart instead of feelings. And my own place isn't a 'place,' as you so blithely put it—it's a shithole of an attic and you know it! *You* wouldn't sleep there for half an hour." "Where's the typewriter?" "The typewriter is a *thing,* damn it, an inanimate object! What about *me?*" and leaping from the chair, she charged, swinging her pocketbook like a shillelagh. "CLIP ME WITH THAT, MAUREEN, AND I'LL KILL YOU!" "Do it!" was her reply. "Kill me! Some man's going to—why not a 'civilized' one like you! Why not a follower of Flaubert!" Here she collapsed against me, and with her arms around my neck, began to sob. "Oh, Peter, I don't have anything. Nothing at all. I'm really lost, baby. I didn't want to go to them—I *had* to. Please, don't make me go away again right now. I haven't even had a shower in three days. Let me just take a shower. Let me just calm down—and this time I'll go forever, I promise." She then explained that the loft on Bleecker Street had been burglarized one night when all except the cats were out eating spaghetti on Fourteenth Street;

my typewriter had been stolen, along with all of her friends' wood-carving tools, their recorders, and their Blatstein, which sounded to me like an automatic rifle but was a painting.

I didn't believe a word of it. She went off to the bathroom, and when I heard the shower running, I put my hand into the pocket of her duffel coat and after just a little fishing around in the crumpled Kleenex and the small change came up with a pawn ticket. If I hadn't been living half a block from the Bowery, I don't imagine it would have occurred to me that Maureen had taken the typewriter up the street for the cash. But I was learning—though not quite fast enough.

Now an even worldlier fellow than myself—George F. Babbitt, say, of Zenith—would have remembered the old business adage, "Cut your losses," and after finding the pawn ticket, would have dropped it back into her pocket and said nothing. Shower her, humor her, and get her the hell out, George F. Babbitt would have said to himself, and peace and quiet will reign once again. Instead I rushed into the bathroom—no Babbitt I— where we screamed at each other with such ferocity that the young married couple upstairs, whose life we made a misery during these months (the husband, an editor at a publishing house, cuts me to this day), began to pound on the floor above with a broom handle. "You petty little thief! You *crook!*" "But I did it for you!" "For me? You pawned my typewriter for *me?*" "Yes!" "What are you *talking* about?" Here, with the water still beating down on her, she slumped to the bottom of the bathtub, and sitting on her haunches, began actually to keen in her woe. Unclothed, she would sometimes make me think of an alley cat—quick, wary, at once scrawny and strong; now, as she rocked and moaned with grief under the full blast of the shower, something about the weight and pointiness of her large conical breasts, and her dark hair plastered to her head, made her look to me like some woman out of the bush, a primitive whose picture you might come upon in *National Geographic,* praying to the sun-god to roll back the waters. "Because—" she howled, "because I'm pregnant. Because—because I wasn't going to tell you. Because I was going to get the money however I could and get an abortion and never bother you again. Peter, I've been shoplifting too." "Stealing? Where?" "Altman's—a little from Klein's. I *had* to!" "But you *can't* be pregnant, Maureen—*we haven't slept together for weeks!*" "BUT I AM! TWO MONTHS PREGNANT!" "Two months?" "Yes! And I never said a word, because I didn't want to interfere with your ART!" "Well, you should have, goddam it, because I would have given you the money to go out and get an abortion!" "Oh, you are so generous—! But it's too late—I've taken enough from men like you in my life! You're going to marry me or I'm going to kill myself! And I will do it!" she cried, hammering defiantly on the rim of the tub with her two little fists. "This is no empty threat, Peter—I cannot take you people any more! You selfish, spoiled, immature, irresponsible Ivy League bastards, born with those spoons in your mouths!" The silver spoon was somewhat hyperbolic, and even she knew that much, but she was hysterical, and in hysteria, as she eventually made clear to me, anything goes. "With your big fat advance and your high Art—oh, you make me sick the way you hide from life behind that *Art* of yours! I hate you and I hate that fucking Flaubert, and you are going to marry me, Peter, because I have had enough! I'm not going to be another man's helpless victim! You are not going to dump me the way you dumped that girl!"

"That girl" was how she referred to Dina, toward whom she had never until that moment been anything but dismissive; now, all at once, she invoked in her own behalf not just Dina, but Grete *and* the Pembroke undergraduate who had been my girl friend during my senior year at Brown. All of them shared with Maureen the experience of being "discarded" when I had finished having my "way" with them. "But we are not leftovers, Peter; we're not trash or scum and we will not be treated that way! We are human beings, and we will not be thrown into a garbage pail by *you!*" "You're not pregnant, Maureen, and you know damn well you're not. That's what all this 'we' business is about," I said, suddenly, with perfect confidence. And with that, she all but collapsed—"We're not *talking* about me right now," she said, "we're talking about *you*. Don't you know *yet* why you got rid of your Pembroke pal? Or your German girl friend? Or that girl who had everything? Or why you're getting rid of me?" I said, "You're not pregnant, Maureen. That is a lie." "It is not—and listen to me! Do you have no idea at all why it is you are so afraid of marriage and children and a family and treat women the way that you do? Do you know what you really are, Peter, aside from being a heartless, selfish writing machine?" I said, "A fag." "That's right! And making light of it doesn't make it any less true!" "I would think it makes it more true." "It does! You are the most transparent latent homosexual I have ever run across in my life! Just like big brave Mezik who forced me to blow his buddy—*so that he could watch*. Because it's really what he wanted to do himself—but he didn't even have the guts for that!" "*Forced* you? Oh, come on, pal, you've got pointy teeth in that mouth of yours—I've felt your fangs. Why didn't you bite it off and teach them both a lesson, if you were being *forced* to?" "I should have! Don't you think I didn't think of it! Don't you think a woman doesn't think of it every time! And don't you worry, mister, if they weren't twelve inches taller than me, I would have bitten the thing off at the root! And spit on the bleeding stump—just like I spit on you, you high and mighty Artist, for throwing me two months pregnant out into the street!" But she was weeping so, that the spittle meant for me just rolled down her lips onto her chin.

She slept in the bed that night (first bed in three days, I was reminded) and I sat at my desk in the living room, thinking about running away—not because she continued to insist she had missed two periods in a row, but because she was so tenaciously hanging on to what I was certain was a lie. I could leave right then for any number of places. I had friends up in Providence, a young faculty couple who'd gladly put me up for a while. I had an army buddy in Boston, graduate-school colleagues still out in Chicago, there was my sister Joan in California. And of course brother Morris uptown, if I should require spiritual comfort and physical refuge near at hand. He would take me in for as long as was necessary, no questions asked. Since I'd settled in New York, I had been getting phone calls from Moe every couple of weeks checking to see if there was anything I needed and reminding me to come to dinner whenever I was in the mood. At his invitation I had even taken Maureen up to their apartment one Sunday morning for bagels and the smoked fish spread. To my surprise, she had appeared rather cowed by my brother's bearish manner (Moe is a great one to cross-examine strangers), and the general intensity of the family life seemed to make her morose; she did not have much to say after we left, except that Moe and I were very different people. I agreed; Moe was very much the public man (the university, the UN commissions, political meetings and organizations ever since high school) and very much the paterfamilias . . . She said, "I meant he's a brute." "A what?" "The way he treats that wife of his. It's unspeakable." "He's nuts about her, for Christ's sake." "Oh? Is that why he walks all over her? What a little sparrow *she* is! Has she ever had an idea of her own in her life? She just sits there, eating his crumbs. And that's her life." "Oh, that's not her life, Maureen." "Sorry, I don't like him—or her."

Moe didn't like Maureen either, but at the outset said nothing, assuming it was my affair not his, and that she was just the girl of the moment. As I had assumed myself. But when combat between Maureen and me stepped up dramatically, and I apparently began to look and sound as confused and embattled as I'd become, Moe tried on a couple of occasions to give me some brotherly advice; each time I shook him off. As I still couldn't imagine any long-range calamity befalling me, I objected strenuously to being "babied," as I thought of it—particularly by someone whose life, though admirable, was *grounded* in ways I was just too young to be concerned about. As I saw it, it was essential for me to be able to confront whatever troubles I'd made for myself without his, or anyone else's, assistance. In brief, I was as arrogant (and blind) as youth and luck and an aristocratic literary bent could make me, and so, when he invited me up to Columbia for lunch I told him, "I'll work it all out, don't worry." "But why should it be 'work'? Your *work* is your work, not this little Indian." "I take it that's some kind of euphemism. For the record, the mother's family was Irish, the father's German." "Yeah? She looks a little Apache to me, with those eyes and that hair. There's something savage there, Peppy. No? All right, don't answer. Sneer now, pay later. You weren't brought up for savagery, kid." "I know. Nice boy. Jewish." "What's so bad about that? You are a nice civilized Jewish boy, with some talent and some brains. How much remains to be seen. Why don't you attend to that and leave the lions to Hemingway." "What is that supposed to mean, Moey?" "You. You look like you've been sleeping in the jungle." "Nope. Just down on Ninth Street." "I thought girls were for fun, Pep. Not to scare the shit out of you." I was offended both by his low-mindedness and his meddling and refused to talk further about it. Afterward I looked in the mirror for the signs of fear—or doom. I saw nothing: still looked like Tarnopol the Triumphant to me.

The morning after Maureen had announced herself pregnant, I told her to take a specimen of urine to the pharmacy on Second and Ninth; that way, said I without hiding my skepticism, we could shortly learn just how pregnant she was. "In other words, you don't believe me. You want to close your eyes to the whole thing!" "Just take the urine and shut up." So she did as she was told: took a specimen of urine to the drugstore for the pregnancy test—only it wasn't her urine. I did not find this out until three years later, when she confessed to me (in the midst of a suicide attempt) that she had gone from my apartment to the drugstore by way of Tompkins Square Park, lately the hippie center of the East Village, but back in the fifties still a place for the neighborhood poor to congregate and take the sun. There she approached a pregnant Negro woman pushing a baby carriage and told her she represented a scientific organization willing to pay the woman for a sample of her urine. Negotiations ensued. Agreement reached, they retired to the hallway of a tenement building on Avenue B to complete the transaction. The pregnant woman pulled her underpants down to her knees, and squatting in a corner of the unsavory hallway—still heaped with rubbish (just as Maureen had described it) when I paid an unsentimental visit to the scene of the crime upon my return to New York only a few years later—delivered forth into Maureen's preserve jar the stream that sealed my fate. Here Maureen forked over two dollars and twenty-five cents. She drove a hard bargain, my wife.

During the four days that we had to wait—according to Maureen—for the result of the pregnancy test, she lay on my bed recalling scenes and conversations out of her wasted past: delirious (or feigning delirium—or both), she quarreled once again with Mezik, screamed her hatred at Mezik's buddy from the upholstery factory, and choked and wept with despair to discover Walker in their bathroom in Cambridge, dressed in her underwear, his own white sweat socks stuffed into the cups of the brassiere. She would not eat; she would not converse; she refused to let me telephone the psychiatrist who had once tried treating her for a couple of months; when I called her friends over on Bleecker Street, she refused to talk to them. I went ahead anyway and suggested to them that they might want to come over and see her—maybe they at least could get her to eat something—whereupon the wife grabbed the phone away from the husband and said, "We don't want to see that one again *ever*," and hung up. So, all was not well with the "schizorenos" on Bleecker Street either, after Maureen's brief visit . . . And I was afraid now to leave the apartment for fear that she would try to kill herself when I was gone. I had never lived through three such days before in my life, though I was to know a hundred more just as grim and frightening in the years to come.

The night before we were to learn the test results, Maureen abruptly stopped "hallucinating" and got up from bed to wash her face and drink some orange juice. At first she wouldn't speak directly to me, but for an hour sat perfectly still, calm and controlled, in a chair in the living room, wrapped in my bathrobe. Finally I told her that as she was up and around, I was going out to take a walk around the block. "Don't try anything," I said, "I'm just going to get some air." Her tone, in response, was mild and sardonic. "Air? Oh, where, I wonder?" "I'm taking a walk around the block." "You're about to leave me, Peter, I know that. Just the way you've left every girl you've ever known. Find 'em-fuck 'em-and-forget 'em Flaubert." "I'll be right back." When I unlatched the door to go out, she said, as though addressing a judge from the witness stand—prophetic bitch!—"And I never saw him again, Your Honor."

I went around to the drugstore and asked the pharmacist if by any chance the result of Mrs. Tarnopol's pregnancy test—so Maureen had identified herself, just a bit prematurely—due back tomorrow might have come in that night. He told me the result had come in that morning. Maureen had gotten it wrong—we hadn't to wait four days, only three. Was the error inadvertent? Just one of her "mistakes"? ("So I make mistakes!" she'd cry. "I'm not perfect, damn it! Why must everybody in this world be a perfect robot—a compulsive little middle-class success machine, like you! Some of us are *human*.") But if not a mistake, if intentional, why? Out of habit? An addiction to falsification? Or was this *her* art of fiction, "creativity" gone awry . . . ?

Harder to fathom was the result. How could Maureen be pregnant for two whole months and manage to keep it from me? It made no sense. Such restraint was beyond her—represented everything she was *not*. Why would she have let me throw her out that first time without striking back with this secret? It made no sense. *It could not be.*

Only it was. Two months pregnant, by me.

Only *how?* I could not even remember the last time we two had had intercourse. Yet she was pregnant, *somehow,* and if I didn't marry her, she would take her life rather than endure the humiliation of an abortion or an adoption or of abandoning a fatherless child. It went without saying that she, who could not hold a job for more than six months, was incapable of raising a child on her own. And it went without saying—to me, to me—that the father of this fatherless child-to-be was Peter Tarnopol. Never once did it occur to me that if indeed she were pregnant, someone other than I might have done it. Yes, I already knew what a liar she was, yet surely not so thoroughgoing as to want to deceive me about something as serious as fatherhood. *That* I couldn't believe. This woman was not a character out of a play by Strindberg or a novel by Hardy, but someone with whom I'd been living on the Lower East Side of Manhattan, sixty minutes by subway and bus from Yonkers, where I'd been born.

Now, unduly credulous as I may have been, I still needn't have married her; had I been so independent, so manly, so "up" to travail as I aspired to be in my middle twenties, she would never have become my wife, even if a laboratory test had "scientifically" proved that she was with child and even if I had been willing to accept on faith that mine was the penis responsible. I could still have said this: "You want to kill yourself, that's your business. You don't want an abortion, also up to you. But I'm not getting married to you, Maureen, under any circumstances. Marrying you would be insane."

But instead of going home to tell her just that, I walked from Ninth Street all the way up to Columbia and back, concluding on upper Broadway—only two blocks from Morris's building—that the truly manly way to face up to my predicament was to go back to the apartment, pretending that I still did not know the re-

sult of the pregnancy test, and deliver the following ora-
tion: "Maureen, what's been going on here for three
days makes no sense. I don't care if you're pregnant or
not. I want you to marry me, regardless of how the test
comes out tomorrow. I want you to be my wife." You
see, I just couldn't believe, given her behavior during
the past three days, that she was bluffing about doing
herself in; I was sure that if I walked out on her for
good, she would kill herself. And that was unthinkable
—I could not be the cause of another's death. Such a
suicide was murder. So I would marry her instead. And,
further, I would do my best to make it appear that in
marrying her I had acted out of choice rather than
necessity, for if our union were to be anything other
than a nightmare of recrimination and resentment, it
would have to appear to Maureen—and even, in a way,
to me—that I had married her because I had decided
that I wanted to, rather than because I had been black-
mailed, or threatened, or terrorized into it.

But why ever would I want to? The whole thing made
no sense—especially as we had not copulated in God
only knew how long! And I never wanted to again! I
hated her.

Yes, it was indeed one of those grim and unyielding
predicaments such as I had read about in fiction, such
as Thomas Mann might have had in mind when he
wrote in an autobiographical sketch the sentence that I
had already chosen as one of the two portentous epi-
graphs for *A Jewish Father*: "All actuality is deadly
earnest, and it is morality itself that, one with life, for-
bids us to be true to the guileless unrealism of our
youth."

It seemed then that I was making one of those moral
decisions that I had heard so much about in college
literature courses. But how different it all had been up
in the Ivy League, when it was happening to Lord Jim
and Kate Croy and Ivan Karamazov instead of to me.
Oh, what an authority on dilemmas I had been in the
senior honors seminar! Perhaps if I had not fallen so in
love with these complicated fictions of moral anguish, I

never would have taken that long anguished walk to the Upper West Side and back, and arrived at what seemed to me the only "honorable" decision for a young man as morally "serious" as myself. But then I do not mean to attribute my ignorance to my teachers, or my delusions to books. Teachers and books are still the best things that ever happened to me, and probably had I not been so grandiose about my honor, my integrity, and my manly duty, about "morality itself," I would never have been so susceptible to a literary education and its attendant pleasures to begin with. Nor would I have embarked upon a literary career. And it's too late now to say that I shouldn't have, that by becoming a writer I only exacerbated my debilitating obsession. Literature got me into this and literature is gonna have to get me out. My writing is all I've got now, and though it happens not to have made life easy for me either in the years since my auspicious debut, it is really all I trust.

My trouble in my middle twenties was that rich with confidence and success, I was not about to settle for complexity and depth in books alone. Stuffed to the gills with great fiction—entranced not by cheap romances, like Madame Bovary, but by *Madame Bovary* —I now expected to find in everyday experience that same sense of the difficult and the deadly earnest that informed the novels I admired most. My model of reality, deduced from reading the masters, had at its heart *intractability*. And here it was, a reality as obdurate and recalcitrant and (in addition) as awful as any I could have wished for in my most bookish dreams. You might even say that the ordeal that my daily life was shortly to become was only Dame Fortune smiling down on "the golden boy of American literature" (*New York Times Book Review,* September 1959) and dishing out to her precocious favorite whatever literary sensibility required. Want complexity? Difficulty? Intractability? Want the deadly earnest? Yours!

Of course what I also wanted was that my intractable existence should take place at an appropriately lofty moral altitude, an elevation somewhere, say, between

The Brothers Karamazov and *The Wings of the Dove*. But then not even the golden can expect to have everything: instead of the intractability of serious fiction, I got the intractability of soap opera. Resistant enough, but the wrong genre. Though maybe not, given the leading characters in the drama, of which Maureen, I admit, was only one.

I returned to Ninth Street a little after eleven; I had been gone nearly three hours. Maureen, to my surprise, was now completely dressed and sitting at my desk in her duffel coat.

"You didn't do it," she said, and lowering her face to the desk, began to cry.

"Where were you going, Maureen?" Probably back to her room; *I* assumed to the East River, to jump in.

"I thought you were on a plane to Frankfurt."

"What were you going to do, Maureen?"

"What's the difference . . ."

"Maureen! Look up at me."

"Oh, what's the difference any more, Peter. Go, go back to that Long Island girl, with her pleated skirts and her cashmere sweaters."

"Maureen, listen to me: I want to marry you. I don't care whether you're pregnant or not. I don't care what the test says tomorrow. I want to marry you." I sounded to myself about as convincing as the romantic lead in a high-school play. I think it may have been in that moment that my face became the piece of stone I was to carry around on my neck for years thereafter. "Let's get married," I said, as if saying it yet again, another way, would fool anyone about my real feelings.

Yet it fooled Maureen. I could have proposed in Pig Latin and fooled Maureen. She could of course carry on in the most bizarre and unpredictable ways, but in all those years of surprises, I would never be so stunned by her wildest demonstration of rage, her most reckless public ravings, as I was by the statement with which she greeted this proposal so obviously delivered without heart or hope.

She erupted, "Oh, darling, we'll be happy as kings!"

That was the word—"kings," plural—uttered wholly ingenuously. I don't think she was lying this time. She believed that to be so. We would be happy as kings. Maureen Johnson and Peter Tarnopol.

She threw her arms around me, as happy as I had ever seen her—and for the first time I realized that she *was* truly mad. I had just proposed marriage to a madwoman. In deadly earnest.

"Oh, I always knew it," she said joyously.

"Knew what?"

"That you loved me. That you couldn't hold out forever against that kind of love. Not even you."

She was crazy.

And what did that make of me? A "man"? *How?*

She went on and on about the paradise that lay before us. We could move to the country and save money by growing our own vegetables. Or continue to live in the city where she could become my agent (I had an agent, but no matter). Or she could just stay home and bake bread and type my manuscripts (I typed my own, but no matter) and get back to her wood sculpture.

"You'll have to stay at home anyway," I said. "The baby."

"Oh, lovey," she said. "I'll do it—for you. Because you *do* love me. You see, that's all I had to find out—that you loved me. That you weren't Mezik, that you weren't Walker. *That I could trust you.* Don't you understand? Now that I know, I'll do anything."

"Meaning?"

"Peter, stop being suspicious—you don't *have* to be any more. I'll have an abortion. If the test comes back tomorrow saying that I'm pregnant—and it will, I've never missed two periods before in my life, never—but don't worry, I'll go off and get an abortion. Whatever you want, I'll do it. I know of a doctor. In Coney Island. And I'll go to him, if you want me to."

I wanted her to, all right. I'd wanted her to right at the outset, and had she agreed then, I would never have made my "manly" proposal of marriage. But better now than not at all. And so the next day, after I phoned the drugstore and pretended to be hearing for the first time the lab report verifying Mrs. Tarnopol's pregnancy, I went to the bank and withdrew ten weeks' worth of advance and another twenty dollars for the round-trip taxi fare to Coney Island. And on Saturday morning, I put Maureen in a taxi and she went off to Coney Island by herself, which she said was the only way the abortionist would receive his patients. I stood out on Second Avenue watching the cab move south, and I thought: "Now get out. Take a plane to anywhere, but go while the going is good." But I didn't, because that isn't what a man like myself did. Or so I "reasoned."

Besides, in bed the night before, Maureen had wept in fearful anticipation of the illegal operation (had she had the abortion, it would actually have been her third, I eventually found out) and clinging to me, she begged, "You won't desert me, will you? You'll be here when I get home—won't you? Because I couldn't take it if you weren't . . ." "I'll be here," said I, manfully.

And there I was when she returned at four that afternoon, my fond lover, pale and wan (the strain of sitting six hours at the movies), wearing a Kotex between her legs to absorb the blood (said she), and still in pain from the abortion she had undergone (said she) without an anesthetic. She went immediately to bed to ward off the hemorrhage that she feared was coming on, and there she lay, on into the night, teeth chattering, limbs trembling, in an old, washed-out sweatshirt of mine and a pair of my pajamas. I piled blankets on top of her, but that still didn't stop her shaking. "He just stuck his knife up there," she said, "and wouldn't give me anything for the pain but a tennis ball to squeeze. He promised he would put me out, on the phone he promised me, and then when I was on the table and said, 'Where's the anesthetic?', he said, 'What do you think, girlie, I'm out of my mind?' I said, 'But you promised. How else can I possibly stand the pain?' And you know what he told me, that smelly old bastard? 'Look, you want to get up and go, fine with me. You want me to get rid of the baby, then squeeze the magic ball and shut up. You had your fun, now you're going to have to pay.' So I stayed, I stayed and I squeezed down on the ball, and I tried to think just about you and me, but it hurt, oh, he hurt me so much."

A horrifying tale of humiliation and suffering at the hands of yet another member of my sex, and a lie from beginning to end. Only it took me a while to find out. In actuality, she had pocketed the three hundred dollars (against the day I would leave her penniless) and after disembarking from the cab when it got to Houston Street, had gone back up to Times Square by subway to see Susan Hayward in *I Want to Live,* saw it three times over, the morbid melodrama of a cocktail waitress (if I remember correctly—I had already taken her to see it once myself) who gets the death penalty in California for a crime she didn't commit: right up Maureen's alley, that exemplary little tale. Then she'd donned a Kotex in the washroom and had come on home, weak in the knees and white around the gills. As who wouldn't be, after a day in a Times Square movie house?

All this she confessed three years later in Wisconsin.

The next morning I went alone to a booth—Maureen charging, as I left the apartment, that I was running away, leaving her bleeding and in pain while I disappeared forever with "that girl"—and telephoned my parents to tell them I was getting married.

"Why?" my father demanded to know.

"Because I want to." I was not about to tell my father, in whom I had not confided anything since I was ten, what I had been through in the past week. I had loved him dearly as a child, but he was only a small-time haberdasher, and I now wrote short stories published in the high-brow magazines and had a publisher's advance on a serious novel dense with moral ambiguity. So which of us could be expected to understand the principle involved? Which was what again? Something to do with my duty, my courage, my word.

"Peppy," my mother said, after having received the news in silence, "Peppy, I'm sorry, but I have to say it—there's something wrong with that woman. Isn't there?"

"She's over thirty years old," said my father.

"She's twenty-nine."

"And you're just twenty-six, you're a babe in the woods. Son, she's kicked around too long for my money. Your mother is right—something ain't right there with her."

My parents had met my intended just once, in my apartment; on the way home from a Wednesday matinee, they had stopped off to say hello, and there was Maureen, on my sofa, reading the script of a TV serial in which someone had "promised" her a part. Ten minutes of amiable, if self-conscious talk, and then they took the train back home. What they were saying about Maureen I assumed grew out of conversations with Morris and Lenore. I was wrong. Morris had never mentioned Maureen to them. They had figured her out on their own—after only ten minutes.

I tried acting lighthearted; laughing, I said, "She's not the girl across the street, if that's what you mean."

"What does she even do for a living? Anything?"

"She told you. She's an actress."

"Where?"

"She's looking for work."

"Son, listen to me: you're a college graduate. You're a summa cum laude. You had a four-year scholarship. The army is behind you. You've traveled in Europe. The world is before you, *and it's all yours.* You can have anything, *anything*—why are you settling for this? Peter, are you listening?"

"I'm listening."

"Peppy," asked my mother, "do you—love her?"

"Of course I do." And what did I want to shout into the phone at that very moment? *I'm coming home. Take me home. This isn't what I want to do. You're right, there's something wrong with her: the woman is mad. Only I gave my word!*

My father said, "Your voice don't sound right to me."

"Well, I didn't expect this kind of reaction, frankly, when I said I would be getting married."

"We want you to be happy, that's all," said my mother.

"This is going to make you happy, marrying her?" asked my father. "I'm not talking about that she's a Gentile. I'm not a narrow-minded dope, I never was. I don't live in a dead world. The German girl in Germany was something else, and her I never disliked personally, you know that. But that's water under the bridge."

"I know. I agree."

"I'm talking about happiness now, with another human being."

"Yes, I follow you."

"You don't sound right," he said, his own voice getting huskier with emotion. "You want me to come down to the city? I'll come in a minute—"

"No, don't be silly. Good Christ, no. I know what I'm doing. I'm doing what I want."

"But why so sudden?" my father asked, fishing. "Can you answer me that? I'm sixty-five years old, Peppy, I'm a grown man —you can talk to me, and the truth."

"What's 'sudden' about it? I've known her nearly a year. Please, don't fight me on this."

"Peter," said my mother, teary now, "we don't fight you on anything."

"I know, I know. I appreciate that. So let's not start now. I just called to tell you. A judge is marrying us on Wednesday at City Hall."

My mother's voice was weak now, almost a whisper, when she asked, "You want us to come?" It didn't sound as though she cared to be told yes. What a shock that was!

"No, there's no need for you to be there. It's just a formality. I'll call you afterwards."

"Peppy, are you still on the outs with your brother?"

"I'm not on the outs with him. He lives his life and I live mine."

"Peter, have you spoken to him about this? Peppy, your older brother is a brother boys dream about having. He adores you. Call him, at least."

"Look, it's not a point I want to debate with Moe. He's a great arguer—and I'm not. There's nothing to argue over."

"Maybe he wouldn't argue. Maybe at least he'd like to know, to come to whatever it is—the wedding ceremony."

"He won't want to come."

"And you won't talk to him, only for a few minutes? Or to Joan?"

"What does Joan know about my life? Dad, just let me get married, okay?"

"You make it sound like nothing, like marrying a person for the rest of your life is an everyday affair. It ain't."

"I'm summa cum laude. I know that."

"Don't joke. You left us when you were too young, that's the problem. You always had your way. The apple of your mother's eye—you could have anything. The last of her babies . . ."

"Look, look—"

"You thought you already knew everything at fifteen —remember? We should never have let you skip all those grades and get ahead of yourself—that was our first mistake."

On the edge of tears now, I said, "That may be. But I would have been out of grade school by now anyway. Look, I'm getting married. It'll be all right." And I hung up, before I lost control and told my father to come down and take back to his home his twenty-six-year-old baby boy.

4. Dr. Spielvogel

> We may incite [the patient] to jealousy or inflict
> upon him the pain of disappointed love, but no
> special technical design is necessary for that pur-
> pose. These things happen spontaneously in most
> analyses.

> —Freud, "Analysis Terminable and Interminable"

I first met Dr. Spielvogel the year Maureen and I were
married. We had moved out of my Lower East Side
basement apartment to a small house in the country
near New Milford, Connecticut, not far from where
Spielvogel and his family were summering at Candle-
wood Lake. Maureen was going to grow vegetables and
I was going to write the final chapters of *A Jewish
Father*. As it turned out, the seeds never got in the
ground (or the bread in the oven, or the preserves in
the jar), but because there was a twelve-by-twelve shack
at the edge of the woods back of the house *with a bolt
on the door,* somehow the book got finished. I saw
Spielvogel maybe three times that summer at parties
given by a New York magazine editor who was living
nearby. I don't remember that the doctor and I had
much to say to each other. He wore a yachting cap,
this New York analyst summering in rural Connecticut,
but otherwise he seemed at once dignified and without
airs—a tall, quiet, decorous man, growing stout in his
middle forties, with a mild German accent and that
anomalous yachting cap. I never even noticed which
woman was his wife; I discovered later that he had
noticed which was mine.

When, in June of '62, it became necessary, according to my brother, for me to remain in New York and
turn myself over to a psychiatrist, I came up with Spielvogel's name; friends in Connecticut that summer had
spoken well of him, and, if I remembered right, treating
"creative" people was supposed to be his specialty.
Not that that made much difference to me in the shape
I was in. Though I continued to write every day, I had

really stopped thinking of myself as capable of creating anything other than misery for myself. I was not a writer any longer, no matter how I filled the daylight hours—I was Maureen's husband, and I could not imagine how I could get to be anything else ever again.

His appearance, like mine, had changed for the worse in three years. While I had been battling with Maureen, Spielvogel had been up against cancer. *He* had survived, though the disease appeared to have shrunk him down some. I remembered him of course in the yachting cap and with a summer tan; in his office, he wore a drab suit bought to fit a man a size larger, and an unexpectedly bold striped shirt whose collar now swam around his neck. His skin was pasty, and the heavy black frames of the glasses he wore tended further to dramatize this shrinkage he had undergone—beneath them, behind them, his head looked like a skull. He also walked now with a slight dip, or list, to the left, the cancer having apparently damaged his hip or leg. In all, the doctor he reminded me of most was Dr. Roger Chillingworth in Hawthorne's *Scarlet Letter*. Appropriate enough, because I sat facing him as full of shameful secrets as the Reverend Arthur Dimmesdale.

Maureen and I had lived a year in western Connecticut, a year at the American Academy in Rome, and a year at the university in Madison, and as a result of all that moving around I had never been able to find anyone in whom I was willing to confide. By the end of three years I had convinced myself that it would be "disloyal," a "betrayal," to tell even the closest friends I had made in our wanderings what went on between Maureen and me in private, though I imagined they could guess plenty from what often took place right out on the street or in other people's houses. Mostly I didn't open up to anyone because I was so ashamed of my defenselessness before her wrath and frightened of what she might do either to herself or to me, or to the person in whom I'd confided, if she ever found out what I had said. Sitting in a chair immediately across from Spielvogel, looking in embarrassment

from his shrunken skull to the framed photograph of
the Acropolis that was the only picture on his cluttered desk, I realized that I still couldn't do it: indeed, to tell *this* stranger the whole sordid story of my
marriage seemed to me as reprehensible as committing
a serious crime.

"You remember Maureen?" I asked. "My wife?"

"I do. Quite well." His voice, in contrast to his appearance, was strong and vigorous, causing me to feel
even more puny and self-conscious . . . the little stool
pigeon about to sing. My impulse was to get up and
leave, my shame and humiliation (and my disaster)
still my own—and simultaneously to crawl into his lap.
"A small, pretty, dark-haired young woman," he said.
"Very determined looking."

"Very."

"A lot of spunk there, I would think."

"She's a lunatic, Doctor!" I began to cry. For fully
five minutes I sobbed into my hands—until Spielvogel
asked, "Are you finished?"

There are lines from my five years of psychoanalysis
as memorable to me as the opening sentence of *Anna
Karenina*—"Are you finished?" is one of them. The
perfect tone, the perfect tactic. I turned myself over to
him, then and there, for good or bad.

Yes, yes, I was finished. "All I do these days is collapse in tears . . ." I wiped my face with a Kleenex
from a box that he offered me and proceeded to "spill"
—though not about Maureen (I couldn't, right off) but
about Karen Oakes, the Wisconsin coed with whom I
had been maniacally in love during the winter and
early spring of that year. I had been watching her bicycle around the campus for months before she showed
up in my undergraduate writing section in the second
semester to become the smartest girl in the class. Good-
natured, gentle, a beguiling mix of assertive innocence
and shy adventurousness, Karen had a small lyrical
gift as a poet and wrote clever, somewhat magisterial
literary analyses of the fiction that we read in class;
her candor and lucidity, I told Spielvogel, were as much

a balm to me as her mild temperament, her slender
limbs, her pretty and composed American girl's face.
Oh, I went on and on about Ka-reen (the pet name
for the pillow talk), growing increasingly intoxicated,
as I spoke, with memories of our ardent "passion" and
brimming "love"—I did not mention that in all we
probably had not been alone with one another more
than forty-eight hours over the course of the three
months, and rarely for more than forty-five minutes at
a clip; we were together either in the classroom with
fifteen undergraduates for chaperones, or in her bed.
Nonetheless she was, I said, "the first good thing" to
happen in my private life since I'd been discharged
from the army and come to New York to write. I told
Spielvogel how she had called herself "Miss Demi-
Womanhood of 1962"; he did not appear to be one-
hundredth as charmed by the remark as I had been,
but then he had not just disrobed for the first time the
demi-woman who had said it. I recounted to him the
agonies of doubt and longing that I had experienced
before I went ahead, three weeks into the semester, and
wrote "See me" across the face of one of her A+ papers.
She came, as directed, to my office, and accepted my
courtly, professorial invitation to be seated. In the
first moments, courtliness was rampant, as a matter of
fact. "You wanted to see me?" "Yes, I did, Miss Oakes."
A silence ensued, long and opaquely eloquent enough
to satisfy Anton Chekhov. "Where do you come from,
Miss Oakes?" "Racine." "And what does your father
do?" "He's a physician." And then, as though hurling
myself off a bridge, I did it: reached forward and laid
a hand upon her straw-colored hair. Miss Oakes swallowed and said nothing. "I'm sorry," I told her, "I
couldn't help it." She said: "Professor Tarnopol, I'm
not a sophisticated person." Whereupon I proceeded
to apologize profusely. "Oh, please, don't worry," she
said, when I wouldn't stop, "a lot of teachers do it."
"Do they?" the award-winning novelist asked. "Every
semester so far," said she, nodding a little wearily; "and
usually it's English." "What happens then, usually?" "I

tell them I'm not a sophisticated person. Because I'm not." "And then?" "That's it, generally." "They get conscience-stricken and apologize profusely." "They have second thoughts, I suppose." "Just like me." "And me," she said, without blinking; "the doctrine of *in loco parentis* works both ways." "Look, look—" "Yes?" "Look, I'm *taken* with you. Terribly." "You don't even know me, Professor Tarnopol." "I don't and I do. I've read your papers. I've read your stories and poems." "I've read yours." Oh my God, Dr. Spielvogel, how can you sit there like an Indian? Don't you appreciate the *charm* of all this? Can't you see what a conversation like that meant to me in my despair? "Look, Miss Oakes, I want to see you—I *have* to see you!" "Okay." "*Where?*" "I have a room—" "I can't go into a dormitory, you know that." "I'm a senior. I don't live in the dorm any more. I moved out." "You did?" "I have my own room in town." "Can I come to talk to you there?" "Sure."

Sure! Oh, what a wonderful, charming, disarming, engaging little word that one is! I went around sibilating it to myself all through the rest of the day. "What are you so bouncy about?" asked Maureen. *Shoor. Shewer. Shur.* Now just how did that beautiful and clever and willing and healthy young girl say it anyway? *Sure!* Yes, like that—crisp and to the point. *Sure!* Oh yes, sure as sure is sure, Miss Oakes is going to have an adventure, and Professor Tarnopol is going to have a breakdown . . . How many hours before I decided that when the semester was over we would run off together? Not that many. The second time we were in bed I proposed the idea to Ka-reen. We would go to Italy in June— catch the Pan Am flight from Chicago (I'd checked on it by phone) the evening of the day she'd taken her last exam; I could send my final grades in from Rome. Wouldn't that be terrific? Oh, I would say to her, burying my face in her hair, I want to take you somewhere, Ka-reen, I want to go away with you! And she would murmur softly, "Mmmmmm, mmmmmm," which I interpreted as delicious acquiescence. I told her about all the lovely Italian piazzas in which Maureen and I had screamed bloody murder at one another: the Piazza San Marco in Venice, the Piazza della Signoria in Florence, the Piazza del Campo in Siena . . . Karen went home for spring vacation and never came back. That's how overbearing and frightening a character I had become. That murmuring was just the sound her good mind gave off as it gauged the dreadful consequences of having chosen this particular member of the conscience-stricken English faculty to begin sophisticated life with outside of a college dorm. It was one thing reading Tolstoy in class, another playing Anna and Vronsky with the professor.

After she failed to return from spring recess, I made desperate phone calls to Racine practically daily. When I call at lunchtime I am told she is "out." I refuse to believe it—where does she eat then? "Who is this, please?" I am asked. I mumble, "A friend from school . . . are you *sure* she isn't . . .?" "Would you care to leave your name?" "No." After dinner each night I last about ten minutes in the living room with Maureen before I begin to feel myself on the brink of cracking up; rising from my reading chair, I throw down my pencil and my book—as though I am Rudolph Hess, twenty years in Spandau Prison, I cry, "I have to take a walk! I have to see some faces! I'm suffocating in here!" Once out the door, I break into a sprint, and crossing back lawns and leaping low garden fences, I head for the dormitory nearest our apartment, where there is a telephone booth on the first floor. I will catch Karen at the dinner hour and beg her at least to come back to school for the rest of this semester, even if she will not run away in June to live in Trastevere with me. She says, "Hang on a sec—let me take it on another phone." A few moments later I hear her call, "Will you hang up the downstairs phone, please, Mom?" "Karen! Karen!" "Yes, I'm back." "Ka-reen, I can't bear it—I'll meet you somewhere in Racine! I'll hitch! I can be there by nine-thirty!" But she *was* the smartest girl in my class and had no intention of letting some overwrought creative writing teacher with a bad marriage and a stalled career ruin her life. She could not save me from my wife, she said, I would have to do that myself. She had told her family she had had an unhappy love affair, but, she assured me, she had not and would not tell them with whom. "But what about your degree?" I demanded, as though I were the dean of students. "That's not important right now," said Karen, speaking as calmly from her bedroom in Racine as she did in class. "But I love you! I want you!" I shouted at the slender girl who only the week before had bicycled in sneakers and a poplin skirt to English 312, her straw-colored hair in braids and her innards still awash with semen from our lunchtime assignation in her rented room. "You just can't leave, Karen! Not now! Not after how marvelous it's been!" "But I can't save you, Peter. I'm only twenty years old." In tears I cried, "I'm only twenty-nine!" "Peter, I should never have started up. I had no idea what was at stake. That's my fault. Forgive me. I'm as sorry as I can be." "Christ, don't be 'sorry'—*just come back!*" One night Maureen followed me out of the house and across the backyards to the dormitory, and after standing out of sight for a minute with her ear to the telephone booth, threw back the door while I was pleading with Karen yet again to change her mind and come with me to Europe on the Pan Am night flight from O'Hare. "Liar!" screamed Maureen, "whoremongering liar!" and ran back to the apartment to swallow a small handful of sleeping pills. Then, on hands and knees, she crawled into the living room in her underwear and knelt there on the floor with my Gillette razor in her hand, waiting patiently for me to finish talking with my undergraduate harlot and come on home so that she could get on with the job of almost killing herself.

I told Spielvogel what Maureen had confessed to me from the living-room floor. Because this had happened only two months earlier, I found with Spielvogel, as I had that morning with Moe in the taxi back from the airport, that I could not recount the story of the false urine specimen without becoming woozy and weak, as though once the story surfaced in my mind, it was only a matter of seconds before the fires of rage had raced through me, devouring all vitality and strength. It is not that easy for me to tell it today without at least a touch of vertigo. And I have never been able to introduce the story into a work of fiction, not that I haven't repeatedly tried and failed in the five years since I received Maureen's confession. I cannot seem to make it credible—probably because I still don't entirely believe it myself. How could she? To me! No matter how I may contrive to transform low actuality into high art, that is invariably what is emblazoned across the face of the narrative, in blood: HOW COULD SHE? TO ME!

"And then," I told Spielvogel, "do you know what she said next? She was on the floor with the blade of the razor right on her wrist. In her panties and bra. And I was just standing over her. Dumbstruck. *Dumbstruck.* I could have kicked her head in. I should have!"

"And what did she say?"

"Say? She said, 'If you forgive me for the urine, I'll forgive you for your mistress. I'll forgive you for deceiving me with that girl on the bicycle and begging her to run away with you to Rome.'"

"And what did you do?" asked Spielvogel.

"Did I kick her, you mean? No. No, no, no, no, no. I didn't do anything—to her. Just stood there for a while. I couldn't right off get over the *ingenuity* of it. The *relentlessness.* That she had thought of such a thing *and then gone ahead and done it.* I actually felt *admiration.* And pity, *pity!* That's true. I thought, 'Good Christ, what *are* you? To do this thing, *and then to keep it a secret for three years!*' And then I saw my chance to get out. As though it required this, you see, nothing less, for me to feel free to go. Not that I went. Oh, I *told* her I was going, all right. I said, I'm leaving, Maureen, I can't live any more with somebody who would do such a thing, and so on. But she was crying by then and she said, 'Leave me and I'll cut my wrists. I'm full of sleeping pills already.' And I said, and this is true, I said, 'Cut them, why should I care?' And so she pressed down with the razor—and blood came out. It turned out that she had only scratched herself, but what the hell did I know? She could have gone through to the bone. I started shouting, 'Don't—don't do that!' and I began wrestling with her for the razor. I was terrified that I was going to get my own veins slashed in the rolling around, but I kept trying to get it away, grabbing at the damn thing—and I was crying. That goes without saying. All I do now is cry, you know—and she was crying, of course, and finally I got the thing away from her and she said, 'Leave me, and I'll ruin that girl of yours! I'll have that pure little face in every paper in Wisconsin!' And then she began to scream about my 'deceiving' her and how I couldn't be trusted and she always knew it—and this is just three minutes after describing in detail to me buying the urine from that Negro woman on Avenue B!"

"And what did you do then?"

"Did I slit her throat from ear to ear? No. No! I fell apart. Completely. I went into a tantrum. The two of us were smeared with blood—my left palm had been cut, up by the thumb, and her wrist was dripping, and God only knows what we looked like—like a couple of Aztecs, fucking up the sacrificial rites. I mean, it's comical when you think about it. I am the Dagwood Bumstead of fear and trembling!"

"You had a tantrum."

"That's not the *half* of it. I got down on my knees —I *begged* her to let me go. I banged my head on the floor, Doctor. I began running from room to room. Then—then I did what she told me Walker used to do. Maybe Walker never even did it; that was probably a lie too. Anyway, *I* did it. At first I was just running around looking for some place to hide the razor from her. I remember unscrewing the head and dropping the blade into the toilet and flushing and flushing and the damn thing just lying there at the bottom of the bowl. Then I ran into our bedroom—I was screaming all this time, you see, 'Let me go! Let me go!' and sobbing, and so on. And all the while I was tearing my clothes off. I'd done that before, in a rage with her, but this time I actually tore everything off me. And I put on Maureen's underwear. I pulled open her dresser and I put on a pair of her underpants—I could just get them up over my prick. Then I tried to get into one of her brassieres. I put my arms through the shoulder loops, that is. And then I just stood there like that, crying—and bleeding. Finally she came into the room—no, she just got as far as the doorway and stood there, looking at me. And, you see, that's all she was wearing, too, her underwear. She saw me and she broke into sobs again, and she cried, 'Oh, sweetheart, no, no . . .' "

"Is that all she said?" asked Spielvogel. "Just called you 'sweetheart'?"

"No. She said, 'Take that off. I'll never tell anybody. Just take that off right now.' "

"That was two months ago," said Dr. Spielvogel, when it appeared that I had nothing more to say.

"Yes."

"And?"

"It's not been good, Doctor."

"What do you mean?"

"I've done some other strange things."

"Such as?"

"Such as staying with Maureen—that's the strangest thing of all! Three years of it, and now I know what I know, and I'm still living with her! And if I don't fly back tomorrow, she says she's going to tell the world 'everything.' That's what she told my brother to tell me on the phone. And she will. *She will do it.*"

"Any other 'strange things'?"

". . . with my sperm."

"I didn't hear you. Your sperm? What about your sperm?"

"My semen—I leave it places."

"Yes?"

"I smear it places. I go to people's houses and I leave it—places."

"You break into people's houses?"

"No, no," I said sharply—what did he think I was, a madman? "I'm invited. I go to the bathroom. I leave it somewhere . . . on the tap. In the soap dish. Just a few drops . . ."

"You masturbate in their bathrooms."

"Sometimes, yes. And leave . . ."

"Your signature."

"Tarnopol's silver bullet."

He smiled at my joke; I did not. I had still more to tell. "I've done it in the university library. Smeared it on the bindings of books."

"Of books? Which books?"

"Books! Any books! Whatever books are handy!"

"Anywhere else?"

I sighed.

"Speak up, please," said the doctor.

"I sealed an envelope with it," I said in a loud voice. "My bill to the telephone company."

Again Spielvogel smiled. "Now that is an original touch, Mr. Tarnopol."

And again I broke into sobs. "What does it mean!"

"Come now," said Dr. Spielvogel, "what do you think it 'means'? You don't require a soothsayer, as far as I can see."

"That I'm completely out of control!" I said, sobbing. "That I don't know what I'm doing any more!"

"That you're angry," he said, slapping the arm of his chair. "That you are furious. You are not *out* of control—you are *under* control. Maureen's control. You spurt the anger everywhere, except where it belongs. There you spurt tears."

"But she'll ruin Karen! She will! She knows who she is—she used to check out my students like a hawk! She'll destroy that lovely innocent girl!"

"Karen sounds as if she can take care of herself."

"But you don't know Maureen once she gets going. She could *murder* somebody. She used to grab the wheel of our VW in Italy and try to run us off the side of a mountain—because I hadn't opened a door for her leaving the hotel in Sorrento! She could carry a grudge like that for days—then she would erupt with it, in the car, weeks later! You can't imagine what it's like when she goes wild!"

"Well, then, Karen should be properly warned, if that is the case."

"It *is* the case! It's hair-raising! Grabbing the wheel from my hands and spinning it the other way when we're winding down a mountain road! You must believe what I've been through—I am not exaggerating! To the contrary, I'm leaving things *out!*"

Now, with my avenger dead and her ashes scattered from a plane into the Atlantic Ocean, now with all that rage *stilled,* it seems to me that I simply could not have been so extensively unmanned by Maureen Johnson Mezik Walker Tarnopol, dropout from Elmira High, as I indicated (and demonstrated) to Spielvogel during our first hour together. I was, after all, bigger than she was, more intelligent than she was, better educated than she was, and far more accomplished. What then (I asked the doctor) had made me such a willing, or will-less, victim? Why couldn't I find the strength, or just the simple survival mechanism, to leave her once it became obvious that it was no longer she who needed rescuing from her disasters, but I from mine? Even after she had confessed to committing the urine fraud, even *then* I couldn't get up and go! Now why? Why should someone who had battled so determinedly all his life to be independent—his own child, his own adolescent, his own man—why should someone with my devotion to "seriousness" and "maturity" knuckle under like a defenseless little boy to this cornball Clytemnestra?

Dr. Spielvogel invited me to look to the nursery for the answer. The question with which he began our second session was, "Does your wife remind you of your mother?"

My heart sank. Psychonanalytic reductivism was not going to save me from the IRT tracks, or worse, from returning to Wisconsin at the end of the week to resume hostilities with Maureen. In reply to the question I said, no, she did not. My wife reminded me of no one I had ever known before, anywhere. Nobody in my entire lifetime had ever dared to deceive, insult, threaten, or blackmail me the way she did—certainly no woman I had ever known. Nor had anyone ever hollered at me like that, except perhaps the basic training cadre at Fort Dix. I suggested to Spielvogel that it wasn't because she was like my mother that I couldn't deal with her, but, if anything, because she was so *unlike* her. My mother was not aggrieved, contentious, resentful, violent, helpless, or suicidal, and she did not ever want to see me humbled—far from it. Certainly, for our purposes, the most telling difference between the two was that my mother *adored* me, worshipped me across the board, and I had basked in that adoration. Indeed, it was her enormous belief in my perfection that had very likely helped to spawn and nourish whatever gifts I had. I supposed that it could be said that I had knuckled under to my mother when I was still a little boy—but in a little boy that is not knuckling under, is it? That is just common sense and a feel for family life: childhood realpolitik. One does not expect to be treated like a thirty-year-old at five. But at fifteen I certainly did expect deferential treatment of a kind, and from my mother I got it. As I remember it, I could sweet-talk that lady into just about anything during my high-school years, without too much effort get her to agree to the fundamental soundness of my position on just about every issue arising out of my blooming sense of prerogatives; in fact, it was with demonstrable delight (as I recalled it) that she acquiesced to the young prince whom she had been leading all these years toward the throne.

It was the supernumerary father I'd had to struggle with back then. He was anxious for me in my ambitiousness and cockiness. He had seen less of me as a child— off in the store all day, and in bad times selling roofing and siding for his brother-in-law door to door at night —and understandably he had some trouble when he

first discovered that the little bird's beak he'd been
feeding all those years had been transformed overnight
into a yapping adolescent mouth that could outtalk
him, outreason him, and generally outsmart him with
the aid of "logic," "analogy," and assorted techniques
of condescension. But then came my four-year scholarship to Brown, and that crown of crowns, straight As in
college, and gradually he too gave in and left off even
trying to tell me what to think and do. By my seventeenth year it was already pretty clear that I did not
mean to use my freedom from parental constraint and
guidance to become a bum, and so, to his credit, he did
the best an aggressive entrepreneur and indestructible
breadwinner and loving father could, to let me be.

Spielvogel wouldn't see it that way. He questioned
my "fairly happy childhood," suggesting that people
could of course delude themselves about the good old
days that had never been. There might be a harsher
side to it all that I was conveniently forgetting—the
threatening aspect of my mother's competence and vigor
and attentiveness, and the "castration anxiety," as he
called it, that it had fostered in her baby boy, the
last, and emotionally the most fragile, of her offspring.
From my descriptions of Morris's life and my few
vivid childhood recollections of him, Dr. Spielvogel concluded that my brother had been "constitutionally" a
much tougher specimen than I to begin with, and that
this biological endowment had been reinforced in his
formative years when he had virtually to raise himself
while my mother was off working most of each day in
the store with my father. As for Joan, it was Spielvogel's
educated guess that as the ugly duckling and the girl
in the family she had hardly been in danger of being
overwhelmed by my mother's attention; to the contrary,
she had probably felt herself at the periphery of the
family circle, neglected and useless as compared with
the hearty older brother and the clever younger one. If
so (he continued, writing his Tarnopol family history),
it would not be surprising to find her in her forties still so
avid to *have*—famous friends, modish beauty, exotic

travels, fancy and expensive clothes: to have, in a word, the admiration and envy of the crowd. He shocked me by asking if my sister also took lovers with such avidity. "Joannie? It never occurred to me." "Much hasn't," the doctor assured the patient.

Now I for one had never denied that my mother might have been less than perfect; of course I remembered times when she seemed to have scolded me too severely or needlessly wounded my pride or hurt my feelings; of course she had said and done her share of thoughtless things while bringing me up, and at times, in anger or uncertainty, had like any parent taken the tyrannical way out. But not until I came under the influence of Dr. Spielvogel could I possibly have imagined a child any more valued or loved than Mrs. Tarnopol's little boy. Any more, in fact, and I really *would* have been in trouble. My argument with this line the doctor began to take on my past was that if I had suffered anything serious from having had a mother like my own, it was because she had nourished in me a boundless belief in my ability to *win* whatever I wanted, an optimism and innocence about my charmed life that (now that I thought about it) could very well have left me less than fortified against the realities of setback and frustration. Yes, perhaps what made me so pathetic at dealing with Maureen in her wildest moments was that I simply could not believe that anybody like her could exist in the world that had been advertised to me as Peter's oyster. It wasn't the repetition of an ancient "trauma" that rendered me so helpless with my defiant wife—it was its uniqueness. I might as well have been dealing with a Martian, for all the familiarity I had with female rage and resentment.

I admitted readily to Dr. Spielvogel that of course I had been reduced in my marriage to a bewildered and defenseless little boy, but that, I contended, was because I had never been a *bewildered* little boy before. I did not see how we could account for my downfall in my late twenties without accounting simultaneously for all those years of success and good fortune that had pre-

ceded it. Wasn't it possible that in my "case," as I willingly called it, triumph *and* failure, conquest *and* defeat derived from an indestructible boyish devotion to a
woman as benefactress and celebrant, protectress and
guide? Could we not conjecture that what had made me
so available to the Bad Older Woman was the reawak-
ening in me of that habit of obedience that had stood
me in such good stead with the Good Older Woman of
my childhood? A small boy, yes, most assuredly, no
question about it—but not at all, I insisted, because
the protecting, attentive, and regulating mother of my
fairly happy memories had been Spielvogel's "phallic
threatening mother figure" to whom I submitted out of
fear and whom a part of me secretly loathed. To be
sure, whoever held absolute power over a child had inevitably to inspire hatred in him at times, but weren't
we standing the relationship on its head by emphasiz-
ing her fearsome aspect, real as it may have been, over
the lovingness and tenderness of the mother who dominated the recollections of my first ten years? And
weren't we drastically exaggerating my submissiveness
as well, when all available records seemed to indicate
that in fact I had been a striving, spirited little boy,
nicknamed Peppy, who hardly behaved in the world like
a whipped dog? Children, I told Spielvogel (who I assumed knew as much), had undergone far worse torment than I ever had for displeasing adults.

Spielvogel wouldn't buy it. It was hardly unusual,
he said, to have felt loved by the "threatening mother";
what was distressing was that at this late date I should
continue to depict her in this "idealized" manner. That
to him was a sign that I was still very much "under her
spell," unwilling so much as to utter a peep of protest
for fear *yet* of reprisal. As he saw it, it was my vulnerability as a sensitive little child to the pain such a mother
might so easily inflict that accounted for "the dominance
of narcissism" as my "primary defense." To protect myself against the "profound anxiety" engendered by my
mother—by the possibilities of rejection and separation, as well as the helplessness that I experienced in

her presence—I had cultivated a strong sense of superiority, with all the implications of "guilt" and "ambivalence" over being "special."

I argued that Dr. Spielvogel had it backwards. My sense of superiority—if he wanted to call it that—was not a "defense" against the threat of my mother, but rather my altogether willing acceptance of her estimation of me. I just agreed with her, that's all. As what little boy wouldn't? I was not pleading with Spielvogel to believe that I had ever in my life felt like an ordinary person or wished to be one; I was only trying to explain that it did not require "profound anxiety" for my mother's lastborn to come up with the idea that he was somebody to conjure with.

Now, when I say that I "argued" or "admitted," and Spielvogel "took issue," etc., I am drastically telescoping a dialectic that was hardly so neat and narrow, or so pointed, as it evolved from session to session. A summary like this tends to magnify considerably my own resistance to the archaeological reconstruction of my childhood that began to take shape over the first year or so of therapy, as well as to overdraw the subtle enough means by which the doctor communicated to me his hypotheses about the origin of my troubles. If I, in fact, had been less sophisticated about "resistance" —and he'd had less expertise—I might actually have been able to resist him more successfully. (On the basis of this paragraph, Dr. Spielvogel would undoubtedly say that my resistance, far from being overcome by my "sophistication," has triumphed over all in the end. For why do I assign to him, rather than myself, the characterization of my mother as "a phallic threatening figure," if not because I am *still* unwilling to be responsible for thinking such an unthinkable thought?) Also, had I been less desperate to be cured of whatever was ailing me, and ruining me, I probably could have held out somewhat longer—though being, as of old, the most willing of pupils, I would inevitably, I think, have seriously entertained his ideas just out of schoolboy habit. But as it was, because I so wanted to get a firm grip upon myself and to stop being so susceptible to Maureen, I found that once I got wind of Dr. Spielvogel's bias, I became increasingly willing to challenge my original version of my fairly happy childhood with rather Dickensian recollections of my mother as an overwhelming and frightening person. Sure enough, memories began to turn up of cruelty, injustice, and of offenses against my innocence and integrity, and as time passed, it was as though the anger that I felt toward Maureen had risen over its banks and was beginning to rush out across the terrain of my childhood. If I would never wholly relinquish my benign version of our past, I nonetheless so absorbed Spielvogel's that when, some ten months into analysis, I went up to Yonkers to have Passover dinner with my parents and Morris's family, I found myself crudely abrupt and cold with my mother, a performance almost as bewildering afterward to me as to this woman who so looked forward to each infrequent visit that I made to her dinner table. Peeved, and not about to hide it, my brother took me aside at one point in the meal and said, "Hey, what's going on here tonight?" I could not give him anything but a shrug for a reply. And try as I might, when I later kissed her goodbye at the door, I did not seem to have the wherewithal to feign even a little filial affection—as though my mother, who had been crestfallen the very first time she had laid eyes on Maureen, and afterward had put up with the fact of her solely to please me, was somehow an accomplice to Maureen's vindictive rage.

Somewhere along in my second year of therapy, when relations with my mother were at their coolest, it occurred to me that rather than resenting Spielvogel, as I sometimes did, for provoking this perplexing change in behavior and attitude toward her, I should see it rather as a strategy, harsh perhaps but necessary, designed to deplete the fund of maternal veneration on which Maureen had been able to draw with such phenomenal results. To be sure, it was no fault of my mother's that I had blindly transferred the allegiance she had inspired through the abundance of her love to someone who was in actuality my enemy; it could be taken, in fact, as a measure of just how gratifying a mother she had been, what a *genius* of a mother she had been, that a son of hers, decades later, had found himself unable to "wrong" a woman with whom his mother shared nothing except a common gender, and a woman whom actually he had come to *despise*. Nonetheless, if my future as a man required me to sever at long last the reverential bonds of childhood, then the brutal and bloody surgery on the emotions would have to proceed, and without blaming the physician in charge for whatever pain the operation might cause the blameless mother or for the disorientation it produced in the apron-strung idolatrous son . . . Thus did I try to rationalize the severity with which I was coming to judge my mother, and to justify and understand the rather patriarchal German-Jewish doctor, whose insistence on "the phallic threatening mother" I sometimes thought revealed more about some bête noire of his than of my own.

But that suspicion was not one that I cared, or dared, to pursue. I was far too much the needy patient to presume to be my doctor's doctor. I had to trust someone if I hoped ever to recover from my defeat, and I chose him.

I had, of course, no real idea what kind of man Dr. Spielvogel was outside of his office, or even in the office with other patients. Where exactly he had been born, raised, and educated, when and under what circumstances he had emigrated to America, what his wife was like, whether he had children—I knew no more about these simple facts of his life than I did about the man who sold me my morning paper; and I was too obedient to what I understood to be the rules of the game to ask, and too preoccupied with my own troubles to be anything more than sporadically curious about this stranger in whose presence I lay down on a couch in a dimly lit room for fifty minutes, three afternoons a week, and spoke as I had never spoken even to those who had proved themselves worthy of my trust. My attitude toward the doctor was very much like that of the first-grader who accepts on faith the wisdom, authority, and probity of his teacher, and is unable to grasp the idea that his teacher also lives in the ambiguous and uncertain world beyond the blackboard.

I had myself been just such a youngster, and experienced my first glimpse of my doctor riding a Fifth Avenue bus with the same stunned disbelief and embarrassment that I had felt at age eight when, in the company of my sister, I had passed the window of a neighborhood barbershop one day and saw the man who taught "shop" in my school getting a shine and a shave. I was four months into my analysis on the drizzly morning when I looked up from the bus stop in front of Doubleday's on Fifth Avenue and saw Spielvogel, in a rainhat and a raincoat, looking out from a seat near the front of the No. 5 bus and wearing a decidedly dismal expression on his face. Of course years before I had seen him in his yachting cap sipping a drink at a summer party, so I knew for a fact that he did not really cease to exist when he was not practicing psychoanalysis on me; I happened too to have been acquainted with several young training analysts during my year of graduate work at Chicago, people with whom I'd gotten along easily enough during evenings in the local student bar. But then Spielvogel was no casual beer-drinking acquaintance: he was the repository of my intimate history, he was to be the instrument of my psychic—my *spiritual*—recovery, and that a person entrusted with that responsibility should actually go out into the street and board a public vehicle such as carried the common herd from point A to point B—well, it was beyond my comprehension. How could I have been so stupid as to confide my darkest secrets to a person who went out in public and took a bus? How could I ever have believed that this gaunt, middle-aged man, looking so done in and defenseless beneath his olive-green rainhat, this unimpressive stranger on a *bus,* could possibly free me from my woes? And just what in God's name was I expected to do now—climb aboard, pay my fare, pro-

ceed down the aisle, tap him on the shoulder, and say
—say what? "Good day, Dr. Spielvogel, it's me—you
remember, the man in his wife's underwear."

I turned and walked rapidly away. When he saw me
move off, the bus driver, who had been waiting patiently for me to rise from my reverie and enter the
door he held open, called out, in a voice weary of
ministering to the citizenry of Manhattan, "*Another*
screwball," and drove off, bearing through an orange
light my shaman and savior, bound (I later learned, in-
credulously) for an appointment with his dentist.

It was in September of 1964, at the beginning of my
third year of analysis, that I had a serious falling out
with Dr. Spielvogel. I considered discontinuing the
therapy with him, and even after I decided to stay on,
found it impossible to invest in him and the process
anything like the belief and hope with which I had begun. I could never actually divest myself of the idea
that I had been ill-used by him, though I knew that the
worst thing I could do in my "condition" was nurse
feelings of victimization and betrayal. Six months ago,
when I left New York, it was largely because I was so
disheartened and confounded by what Susan had done;
but also it was because my dispute with Dr. Spielvogel,
which never really had been settled to my satisfaction,
had become again a volatile issue between us—revived,
to be sure, by Susan's suicide attempt, which I had been
fearing for years, but which Spielvogel had generally
contended was a fear having more to do with my
neurotic personality than with "reality." That I should
think that Susan might try to kill herself if and when I
should ever leave her, Spielvogel had chalked up to
narcissistic self-dramatization. So too did he explain my
demoralization after the fear had been substantiated by
fact.

"I am not a fortune-teller," he said, "and neither are
you. There was as much reason, if not more, to believe
she would not do it as that she would. You know your-

self—she knew *herself*—that this affair of yours was the most satisfying thing to happen to her in years. She had, literally, the time of her life. She began at last to become a full-grown woman. She *bloomed,* from all reports—correct? If when you left her, she did not have enough support from her doctor, from her family, from wherever, well, that is unfortunate. But what can *you* do? She did at least have what she had with you. And she could not have had it *without* you. To regret now having stayed with her all those years, because of this —well, that is not to look very carefully at the credit side of the ledger. Especially, Mr. Tarnopol, as she did not commit suicide. You act here, you know, as though that is what has happened, as though there has been a funeral, and so on. But she only *attempted* suicide, after all. And, I would think, with little intention of succeeding. The fact is that her cleaning woman was to arrive early the very next morning, and that the woman had a key with which to let herself into Susan's apartment. She knew then that she would be found in only a few hours. Correct? Of course, Susan took something of a risk to get what she wanted, but as we see, she pulled it off quite well. She did not die. You did come running. And you are running yet. Maybe only in circles, but that for her is still better than out of her life completely. It is you, you see, who is blowing this up out of all proportion. Your narcissism again, if I may say so. Much too much overestimation of—well, of practically everything. And to use this incident, which has not ended so tragically, you know—to use this incident to break off therapy and go off into isolation again, once more the defeated man, well, I think you are making a serious mistake."

If so, I went ahead and made it. I could not continue to confide in him or to take myself seriously as his patient, and I left. The last of my attachments had been severed: no more Susan, no more Spielvogel, no more Maureen. No longer in the path of love, hate, or measured professional concern—by accident or design, for good or bad, I am not there.

Note: A letter from Spielvogel arrived here at the
Colony just this week, expressing thanks for the copies
of "Salad Days" and "Courting Disaster" that I mailed
to him earlier in the month. I had written:

> For some time now I've been debating whether to send
> on to you these two (postanalytic) stories I wrote
> during my first months here in Vermont. I do now, not
> because I wish to open my case up to a renewed in-
> vestigation in your office (though I see how you might
> interpret these manuscripts in that way), but because of
> your interest in the processes of art (and because lately
> you have been on my mind). I know that your familiarity
> with the biographical and psychological data that fur-
> nished the raw material for such flights of fancy might
> give rise to theoretical speculation, and the theoretical
> speculation give rise in turn to the itch to communicate
> your findings to your fellows. Your eminent colleague
> Ernst Kris has noted that "the psychology of artistic
> style is unwritten," and my suspicion (aroused by past
> experience) is that you might be interested in taking a
> crack at it. Feel free to speculate all you want, of course,
> but please, nothing in print without my permission. Yes,
> that is still a sore subject, but not so sore (I've con-
> cluded) as to outweigh this considered impulse to pass
> on for your professional scrutiny these waking dreams
> whose "unconscious" origins (I must warn you) may not
> be so unconscious as a professional might like to con-
> clude at first glance. Yours, Peter Tarnopol.

Spielvogel's reply:

> It was thoughtful of you to send on to me your two new
> stories. I read them with great interest and enjoyment,
> and as ever, admiration for your skills and understand-
> ing. The two stories are so different and yet so expertly
> done, and to my mind balance each other perfectly. The
> scenes with Sharon in the first I found especially funny,
> and in the second the fastidious attention that the nar-
> rating voice pays to itself struck me as absolutely right,
> given his concerns (or "human concerns" as the Zucker-

man of "Salad Days" would have said in his undergraduate seminar). What a sad and painful story it is.
Moral, too, in the best, most serious way. You appear to
be doing very well. I wish you continued success with
your work. Sincerely, Otto Spielvogel.

This is the doctor whose ministrations I have re-
nounced? Even if the letter is just a contrivance to woo
me back onto his couch, what a lovely and clever contrivance! I wonder whom he has been seeing about his
prose style. Now why couldn't he write about *me* like
that? (Or wasn't that piece he wrote about me really as
bad as I thought? Or was it even worse? And did it
matter either way? Surely I know what it's like having
trouble writing up my case in English sentences. *I've*
been trying to do it now for years. Then, was ridding
myself of him wrong too? Or am I just succumbing—
like a narcissist! Oh, he knows his patient, this con-
jurer . . . Or *am* I being too suspicious?)

So: shall I go ahead now and confuse myself further
by sending copies of the stories to Susan? to my mother
and father? to Dina Dornbusch? to Maureen's Group?
How about to Maureen herself?

Dear Departed: It may cheer you up some to read the
enclosed. Little did you know how persuasive you were.
Actually had you played your cards right and been just a
little less nuts we'd be miserably married yet. Even as it is,
your widower thinks practically only of you. Do you
think of him in Heaven, or (as I fear) have you set
your sights on some big strapping neurotic angel ambiv-
alent about his sexual role? These two stories owe
much to your sense of things—you might have conceived of the self-intoxicated princeling of "Salad Days"
yourself and called him me; and, allowing for artistic
license of course, isn't Lydia pretty much how you saw
yourself (if, that is, you could have seen yourself as you
would have had others see you)? How is Eternity, by
the way? In the hope that these two stories help to pass
the time a little more quickly, I am, your bereaved,
Peter.

Out of the whirlwind, a reply:

> Dear Peter: I've read the stories and found them most
> amusing, particularly the one that isn't supposed to be.
> Your spiritual exertions (in your own behalf) are very
> touching. I took the liberty (I didn't imagine you would
> mind) of passing them on to the Lord. You will be
> pleased to know that "Courting Disaster" brought a
> smile to His lips as well. No wrath whatsoever, I'm
> happy to report, though He did remark (not without a
> touch of astonishment), "It *is* all vanity, isn't it?" The
> stories are currently making the rounds of the saints,
> who I'm sure will find your aspiration to their condition
> rather flattering. The rumor here among the holy mar-
> tyrs is that you've got a new work under way that you
> say is really going "to tell it like it is." If so, I expect that
> means Maureen again. How do you intend to portray me
> this time? Holding your head on a plate? I think a
> phallus would increase your sales. But of course you
> know best how to exploit my memory for high artistic
> purposes. Good luck with *My Martyrdom as a Man.*
> That *is* to be the title, is it not? All of us here in Heaven
> look forward to the amusement it is sure to afford those
> who know you from on high. Your beloved wife, Mau-
> reen. P.S. Eternity is fine. Just about long enough to for-
> give a son of a bitch like you.

And now, class, will you please hand in your papers,
and before turning to Dr. Spielvogel's useful fiction, let
us see what *you* have made of the legends here con-
trived:

English 312
M&F 1:00—2:30
(assignations by appointment)
Professor Tarnopol

THE USES OF THE USEFUL FICTIONS:
Or, Professor Tarnopol Withdraws
Somewhat from His Feelings

by Karen Oakes

Certainly I do not deny when I am reading
that the author may be impassioned, nor even

that he might have conceived the first plan of
his work under the sway of passion. But his
decision to write supposes that he withdraws
somewhat from his feelings. . . .

—Sartre, *What Is Literature?*

*On ne peut jamais se connaître,
mais seulement se raconter.*

—Simone de Beauvoir

"Salad Days," the shorter of the two Zuckerman stories
assigned for today, attempts by means of comic irony to
contrast the glories and triumphs of Nathan Zuckerman's golden youth with the "misfortune" of his twenties, to which the author suddenly alludes in the closing
lines. The author (Professor Tarnopol) does not eluci-
date in the story the details of that misfortune; indeed,
the point he makes is that, by him at least, it cannot be
done. "Unfortunately, the author of this story, having
himself experienced a similar misfortune at about the
same age, does not have it in him, even yet, midway
through his thirties, to tell it briefly or to find it funny.
'Unfortunate,' " concludes the fabricated Zuckerman,
speaking in behalf of the dissembling Tarnopol, "because he wonders if that isn't more the measure of the
man than of the misfortune."

In order to dilute the self-pity that (as I understand it)
had poisoned his imagination in numerous previous attempts to fictionalize his unhappy marriage, Professor
Tarnopol establishes at the outset here a tone of covert
(and, to some small degree, self-congratulatory) self-
mockery; this calculated attitude of comic detachment
he maintains right on down to the last paragraph, where
abruptly the shield of lightheartedness is all at once
pierced by the author's pronouncement that in his estimation the true story really isn't funny at all. All of which
could appear to suggest that if Professor Tarnopol has
managed in "Salad Days" to make an artful narrative
of his misery, he has done so largely by refusing directly
to confront it.

In contrast to "Salad Days," "Courting Disaster" is
marked throughout by a tone of sobriety and an air of
deep concern; here is all the heartfeltness that has been

suppressed in "Salad Days." A heroic quality adheres to the suffering of the major characters, and their lives are depicted as far too grave for comedy or satire. The author reports that he began this story intending that his hero should be tricked into marrying exactly as he himself had been. Why that bedeviling incident from Professor Tarnopol's personal history could not be absorbed into this fictional artifice is not difficult to understand: the Nathan Zuckerman imagined in "Courting Disaster" requires no shotgun held to his head for him to find in the needs and sorrows of Lydia Ketterer the altar upon which to offer up the sacrifice of his manhood. It is not compromising circumstances, but (in both senses) the *gravity* of his character, that determines his moral career; all the culpability is his.

In "Courting Disaster," then, Professor Tarnopol conceives of himself and Mrs. Tarnopol as characters in a struggle that, in its moral pathos, veers toward tragedy, rather than Gothic melodrama, or soap opera, or farce, which are the modes that generally obtain when Professor Tarnopol narrates the story of his marriage to me in bed. Likewise, Professor Tarnopol invents cruel misfortunes (i.e., Lydia's incestuous father, her sadistic husband, her mean little aunts, the illiterate Moonie) to validate and deepen Lydia's despair and to exacerbate Nathan's morbid sense of responsibility—this plenitude of heartache, supplying, as it were, "the objective correlative" for the emotions of shame, grief, and guilt that inform the narration.

And that informed Professor Tarnopol's marriage.

To put the matter altogether directly: if Mrs. Tarnopol had been such a Lydia, if Professor Tarnopol had been such a Nathan, and if I, Karen Oakes, had been a Moonie of a stepdaughter instead of just the star pupil of my sex in English 312 that semester, then, *then* his subsequent undoing would have made a certain poetic sense.

But as it is, he is who he is, she is who she is, and I am simply myself, the girl who would not go with him to Italy. And there is no more poetry, or tragedy, or for that matter, comedy to it than that.

Miss Oakes: As usual, A+. Prose overly magisterial in spots, but you understand the stories (and the author) remarkably well for one of your age and background. It is always something to come upon a beautiful young girl from a nice family with a theoretical turn of mind and a weakness for the grand style and the weighty epigraph. I remember you as an entirely beguiling person. On my deathbed I shall hear you calling from your room, "Will you hang up the downstairs phone, please, Mom?" That plain-spoken line spoke volumes to me too. Ka-reen, you were right not to run off to Italy with me. It wouldn't have been Moonie and Zuckerman, but it probably wouldn't have been any good. Still, you should know that whatever the "neurotic" reason, I was gone on you —let no man, lay or professional, say I wasn't, or ascribe my "hangup" over you simply to my having transgressed the unwritten law against copulating with those sort-of forbidden daughters known as one's students (though I admit: asking Miss Oakes, from behind my desk, to clarify further for the other students some clever answer she'd just given in class, only twenty minutes after having fallen to my knees in your room to play the supplicant beneath your belly, *was* a delicious sensation; cunnilingus aside, I don't think *teaching* has ever been so exciting, before or since, or that I've ever felt so tender or devoted to any class as I did to our English 312. Perhaps the authorities should reconsider, from a strictly pedagogical point of view, the existing taboo, being mindful of the benefits that may accrue to the class whose teacher has taken one of its members as his secret love; I'll write the AAUP about this, in good scholarly fashion of course outlining for them the tradition, from Socrates to Abelard to me—nor will I fail to mention the thanks we three received from the authorities for having thrown ourselves so conscientiously into our work. To think, I recounted to you on our very first "date" what they did to Abelard—yet, here I am still stunned at how I got mutilated by the state of New York). Ah, Miss Oakes, if only I hadn't been so overbearing! Memories of my behavior make me cringe. I told you about Isaac Babel and about my wife with the same veins popping. My insistence, my doggedness, and my tears. How it must have alarmed you to hear me sobbing over the phone—your esteemed professor! If only I had taken it a little easier and suggested a couple of weeks together in northern Wisconsin, some lake somewhere, rather than forever in tragic Europe, who knows, you might have been willing to start off that way. You were brave enough—it's just that I didn't have the wherewithal for a little at a time. At any rate, I have had enough Vivid Experience to last awhile, and am off in the bucolic woods writing my memoirs. Whether this will put the Vivid Experience to rest I don't know. Perhaps what I'll think when I'm done is that these pages add up to Maureen's final victory over Tarnopol the novelist, the culmination of my life as her man and no more. To be writing "in all candor" doesn't suggest that I've withdrawn that much from my feelings. But then why the hell should I? So maybe my animus is not wholly transformed—so maybe I am turning art into a chamberpot for hatred, as Flaubert says I shouldn't, into so much camouflage for self-vindication—so, if the other thing is what literature is, then this ain't. Ka-reen, I know I taught the class otherwise, but so what? I'll try a character like Henry Miller, or someone out-and-out bilious like Céline for my hero instead of Gustave Flaubert—and won't be such an Olympian writer as it was my ambition to be back in the days when nothing called personal experience stood between me and aesthetic detachment. Maybe it's time to revise my ideas about being an "artist," or "artiste" as my adversary's lawyer preferred to pronounce it. Maybe it was always time. Only one drawback: in that I am not a renegade bohemian or cutup of any kind (only a municipal judge could have taken me for that), I may not be well suited for the notoriety that attends the publication of an unabashed and unexpurgated history of one's erotic endeavors. As the history itself will testify, I happen to be no more immune to shame or built for public exposure than the next burgher with shades on his bedroom windows and a latch on the bathroom door—indeed, maybe what the whole history signifies is that I am sensitive to nothing in all the world as I am to my moral reputation. Not that I like being fleeced of my hard-earned dough either. Maybe I ought just to call this confession "The Case Against Leeches, by One Who Was Bled," and publish it as a political tract—go on Johnny Carson and angrily shake an empty billfold at America, the least I can do for all those husbands who've been robbed deaf, dumb, and blind by chorines and maureens

in the courts of law. Inveigh with an upraised fist against
"the system," instead of against my own stupidity for
falling into the first (the first!) trap life laid for me. Or
ought I to deposit these pages too into my abounding
liquor carton, and if I must embroil myself in the battle
yet again, go at it like an artist worthy of the name,
without myself as the "I," without the bawling and the
spleen, and whatever else unattractive that shows? What
do you think, shall I give this up and go back to Zucker-
manizing myself and Lydiafying Maureen and Moonie-
ing over you? If I do take the low road of candor (and
anger and so forth) and publish what I've got, will you
(or your family) sue for invasion of privacy and def-
amation of character? And if not you, won't Susan or
her family? Or will she go one better and, thoroughly
humiliated, do herself in? And how will *I* take it when
my photograph appears on the *Time* magazine book
page, captioned "Tarnopol: stripped to his panties and
bra." I can hear myself screaming already. And what
about the letter in the Sunday *Times* book review section, signed by members of Maureen's Group, challeng-
ing my malicious characterization of Maureen as a
pathological liar, calling *me* the liar and my *book* the
fraud. How will I like it when the counterattack is
launched by the opposition—will it strike me then that I
have exorcised the past, or rather that now I have wed
myself to it as irrevocably as ever I was wed to Maureen? How will I like reading reviews of my private life
in the Toledo *Blade* and the Sacramento *Bee*? And what
will *Commentary* make of this confession? I can't imagine it's good for the Jews. What about when the professional marital experts and authorities on love settle in
for a marathon discussion of my personality problems on
the "David Susskind Show"? Or is that just what I need
to straighten me out? Maybe the best treatment possible
for my excessive vulnerability and preoccupation generally with My Good Name (which is largely how I got
myself into this fix to begin with) is to go forth brazenly
crying, "Virtue! a fig! 'tis in ourselves that we are thus or
thus." Sure, quote Iago to them—tell them, "Oh, find me
self-addicted and self-deluded, find me self and nothing
more! Call me a crybaby, call me a misogynist, call me a
murderer, see if I care. 'Tis only in ourselves that we are
thus or thus—bra and panties notwithstanding. Your

names'll never harm me!" Only they do, Ka-reen, the names drive me wild, and always have. So where am I (to get back to literature): still too much "under the sway of passion" for Flaubertian transcendence, but too raw and touchy by far (or just too ordinary, a citizen like any other) to consider myself equal to what might, in the long run, do my sense of shame the greatest good: a full-scale unbuttoning, à la Henry Miller or Jean Genet . . . Though frankly (to use the adverb of the unbuttoned), Tarnopol, as he is called, is beginning to seem as imaginary as my Zuckermans anyway, or at least as detached from the memoirist—his revelations coming to seem like still another "useful fiction," and not because I am telling lies. I am trying to keep to the facts. Maybe all I'm saying is that words, being words, only approximate the real thing, and so no matter how close I come, I only come *close*. Or maybe I mean that as far as I can see there is no conquering or exorcising the past with words—words born either of imagination or forthrightness—as there seems to be (for me) no forgetting it. Maybe I am just learning what a past is. At any rate, all I can do with my story is tell it. And tell it. And tell it. And *that's* the truth. And you, what do you do to pass the time? And why do I care all of a sudden, and again? Perhaps because it occurs to me that you are now twenty-five, the age at which I passed out of Eden into the real unreal world—or perhaps it's just because I remember you being so uncrazy and so much your own person. Young, of course, but that to me made it all the more extraordinary. As did your face. Look, this sexual quarantine is not going to last forever, even I know that. So if you're ever passing through Vermont, give me a call. Maureen is dead (you might not have guessed from how I've gone on here) and another love affair ended recently with my friend (the Susan mentioned above) attempting to kill herself. So come on East and try your luck. See me. You always liked a little adventure. As did your esteemed professor of sublimation and high art, Peter T.

My dispute with Spielvogel arose over an article he had written for the *American Forum for Psychoanalytic Studies* and published in a special number focusing on

"The Riddle of Creativity." I happened to catch sight
of the magazine on his desk as I was leaving the office
one evening in the third year of my analysis—noticed
the symposium title on the cover and then his name
among the contributors listed below. I asked if I might
borrow it to read his paper. He answered, "Of course,"
though it seemed to me that before issuing gracious
consent, a look of distress, or alarm, had crossed his
face—as though anticipating (correctly) what my reaction to the piece would be . . . But if so, why had
the magazine been displayed so conspicuously on the
desk I passed every evening leaving his office? Since
he knew that like most literary people I as a matter
of course scan the titles of all printed matter lying
out in the open—by now he had surely observed that
reading-man's tic in me a hundred times—it would
seem that either he didn't care one way or another
whether I noticed the *Forum,* or that he actually wanted
me to see his name on the magazine's cover and read
his contribution. Why then the split second of alarm?
Or was I, as he was inevitably to suggest later, merely
"projecting" my own "anticipatory anxiety" onto him?

"Am I submitted in evidence?" I asked, speaking
in a mild, jesting tone, as though it was as unlikely as
it was likely and didn't matter to me either way. "Yes,"
answered Spielvogel. "Well," said I, and pretended to
be taken aback a little in order to hide just how surprised
I was. "I'll read it tonight." Spielvogel's polite smile
now obscured entirely whatever that might really mean
to him.

As was now my custom, after the six o'clock session
with Dr. Spielvogel, I walked from his office at Eighty-
ninth and Park down to Susan's apartment, ten blocks
to the south. It was a little more than a year since
Susan had become an undergraduate at City College,
and our life together had taken on a predictable and
pleasant orderliness—pleasant, for me, for being so
predictable. I wanted nothing more than day after day
without surprises; just the sort of repetitious experience

that drove other people wild with boredom was the
most gratifying thing I could imagine. I was high on
routine and habit.

During the day, while Susan was off at school, I went
home and wrote, as best I could, in my apartment on
West Twelfth Street. On Wednesdays I went off in the
morning to Long Island (driving my brother's car),
where I spent the day at Hofstra, teaching my two
classes and in between having conferences with my
writing students. Student stories were just beginning at
this time to turn heavily "psychedelic"—undergraduate
romantics of my own era had called their unpunctuated
pages of random associations "stream-of-consciousness"
writing—and to take "dope" smoking as their subject.
As I happened to be largely uninterested in drug-
inspired visions or the conversation that attended them,
and rather impatient with writing that depended for
its force upon unorthodox typographical arrangements
or marginal decorations in Magic Marker, I found
teaching creative writing even less rewarding than it
had been back in Wisconsin, where at least there had
been Karen Oakes. My other course, however, an
honors reading seminar in a dozen masterpieces of my
own choosing, had an unusually powerful hold on me,
and I taught the class with a zealousness and vehemence that left me limp at the end of my two hours.
I did not completely understand what inspired this
state of manic excitement or produced my molten vol-
ubility until the course had evolved over a couple of
semesters and I realized what the principle of selection
was that lay behind my reading list from the masters.
At the outset I had thought I was just assigning great
works of fiction that I admired and wanted my fifteen
senior literature students to read and admire too—
only in time did I realize that a course whose core had
come to be *The Brothers Karamazov, The Scarlet
Letter, The Trial, Death in Venice, Anna Karenina,*
and Kleist's *Michael Kohlhaas* derived of course from
the professor's steadily expanding extracurricular interest in the subject of transgression and punishment.

In the city at the end of my workday I would generally walk the seventy-odd blocks to Spielvogel's office—for exercise and to unwind after yet another session at the desk trying, with little success, to make art out of my disaster, but also in the vain attempt to get myself to feel like something other than a foreigner being held against his will in a hostile and alien country. A small-city boy to begin with (growing up in Yonkers in the thirties and forties, I probably had more in common with youngsters raised in Terre Haute or Altoona than in any of the big New York boroughs), I could not see a necessary or sufficient reason for my being a resident of the busiest, most congested spot on earth, especially since what I required above all for my kind of work were solitude and quiet. My brief tenure on the Lower East Side following my discharge from the service certainly evoked no nostalgia; when, shortly after my day in court with Maureen, I hiked crosstown one morning from West Twelfth Street to Tompkins Square Park, it was not to reawaken fond memories of the old neighborhood, but to search through the scruffy little park and the rundown streets nearby for the woman from whom Maureen had bought a specimen of urine some three and a half years earlier. In a morning of hunting around, I of course saw numerous Negro women of childbearing age out in the park and in the aisles of the local supermarket and climbing on and off buses on Avenues A and B, but I did not approach a single one of them to ask if perchance back in March of 1959 she had entered into negotiations with a short, dark-haired young woman from "a scientific organization," and if so, to ask if she would now (for a consideration) come along to my lawyer's office to sign an affidavit testifying that the urine submitted to the pharmacist as Mrs. Tarnopol's had in actuality been her own. Enraged and frustrated as I was by the outcome of the separation hearing, crazed enough to spend an entire morning on this hopeless and useless undercover operation, I was never *completely* possessed.

Or is that what I am now, living here and writing this?

My point is that by and large to me Manhattan was: one, the place to which I had come in 1958 as a confident young man starting out on a promising literary career, only to wind up deceived there into marriage with a woman for whom I had lost all affection and respect; and two, the place to which I had returned in 1962, in flight and seeking refuge, only to be prevented by the local judiciary from severing the marital bond that had all but destroyed my confidence and career. To others perhaps Fun City and Gotham and the Big Apple, the Great White Way of commerce and finance and art—to me the place where I paid through the nose. The number of people with whom I shared my life in this most populous of cities could be seated comfortably around a kitchen table, and the Manhattan square footage toward which I felt an intimate attachment and considered essential to my well-being and survival would have fit, with room to spare, into the Yonkers apartment in which I'd been raised. There was my own small apartment on West Twelfth Street —rather, the few square feet holding my desk and my wastebasket; on Seventy-ninth and Park, at Susan's, there was the dining table where we ate together, the two easy chairs across from one another where we read in her living room at night, and the double bed we shared; ten blocks north of Susan's there was a psychoanalyst's couch, rich with personal associations; and up on West 107th Street, Morris's cluttered little study, where I went once a month or so, as often willingly as not, to be big-brothered—that being the northernmost pin on this runaway husband's underground railway map of New York. The remaining acreage of this city of cities was just *there*—as were those multitudes of workers and traders and executives and clerks with whom I had no connection whatsoever—and no matter which "interesting" and lively route I took to Spielvogel's office at the end of each day, whether I wandered up through the garment district, or Times Square, or the diamond center, or by way of the old bookstores on Fourth Avenue, or through the zoo in

Central Park, I could never make a dent in my feeling of foreignness or alter my sense of myself as someone who had been *detained* here by the authorities, stopped in transit like that great paranoid victim and avenger of injustice in the Kleist novella that I taught with such passion out at Hofstra.

One anecdote to illustrate the dimensions of my cell and the thickness of the walls. Late one afternoon in the fall of '64, on my way up to Spielvogel's, I had stopped off at Schulte's secondhand bookstore on Fourth Avenue and descended to the vast basement where thousands of "used" novels are alphabetically arranged for sale in rows of bookshelves twelve feet high. Moving slowly through that fiction warehouse, I made my way eventually to the Ts. And there it was: my book. To one side Sterne, Styron, and Swift, to the other Thackeray, Thurber, and Trollope. In the middle (as I saw it) a secondhand copy of *A Jewish Father,* in its original blue and white jacket. I took it down and opened to the flyleaf. It had been given to "Paula" by "Jay" in April 1960. Wasn't that the very month that Maureen and I had it out amid the blooming azaleas on the Spanish Steps? I looked to see if there were markings on any of the pages, and then I placed the book back where I had found it, between *A Tale of a Tub* and *Henry Esmond.* To see out in the world, and in such company, this memento of my triumphant apprenticeship had set my emotions churning, the pride and hopelessness all at once. "That bitch!" said I, just as a teenage boy, cradling himself a dozen books in his arms, and wearing a washed-out gray cotton jacket, noiselessly approached me on his sneakers. An employee, I surmised, of Schulte's lower depths. "Yes?" "Excuse me," he said, "is your name Peter Tarnopol by any chance, sir?" I colored a little. "It is." "The novelist?" I nodded my head, and then *he* turned a very rich red himself. Uncertain clearly as to what to say next, he suddenly blurted, "I mean—what ever happened to you?" I shrugged. "I don't know," I told him, "I'm waiting to find out myself." The next instant I was out into the ferment and pressing north: skirting the office workers springing from the revolving doors and past me down into the subway stations, I plunged through the scrimmage set off by the traffic light at each intersection—down the field I charged, cutting left and right through the faceless counterforce, until at last I reached Eighty-ninth Street, and dropping onto the couch, delivered over to my confidant and coach what I had carried intact all the way from Schulte's crypt—the bookboy's heartfelt question that had been blurted out at me so sweetly, and my own bemused reply. That was all I had heard through the world-famous midtown din which travelers journey halfway round the globe to behold.

So then: after paying my call on the doctor, I would head on down to Susan's for dinner and to spend the evening, the two of us most nights reading in those easy chairs on either side of the fireplace, until at midnight we went to bed, and before sleep, regularly devoted ourselves for some fifteen or twenty minutes to our mutual effort at erotic rehabilitation. In the morning Susan was up and out by seven thirty—Dr. Golding's first patient of the day—and about an hour later I departed myself, book in hand, only occasionally now getting a look from one of the residents who thought that if the young widow McCall had fallen to a gentleman caller of the Israelite persuasion in baggy corduroy trousers and scuffed suede shoes, she might at least instruct him to enter and exit by way of the service elevator. Still, if not suitably haut bourgeois for Susan's stately co-op, I was in most ways leading the "regular and orderly" life that Flaubert had recommended for him who would be "violent and original" in his work.

And the work, I thought, was beginning to show it. At least there was beginning to *be* work that I did not feel I had to consign, because it was so bad, to the liquor carton at the bottom of my closet. In the previous year I had completed three short stories: one had been published in the *New Yorker,* one in the *Kenyon Review,* and the third was to appear in *Harper's*. They constituted the first fiction of mine in print

since the publication of *A Jewish Father* in 1959. The
three stories, simple though they were, demonstrated
a certain clarity and calm that had not been the hall-
mark of my writing over the previous years; inspired
largely by incidents from boyhood and adolescence that
I had recollected in analysis, they had nothing to do
with Maureen and the urine and the marriage. *That*
book, based upon my misadventures in manhood, I
still, of course, spent maddening hours on every day,
and I had some two thousand pages of manuscript in
the liquor carton to prove it. By now the various abandoned drafts had gotten so shuffled together and interwoven, the pages so defaced with Xs and arrows of
a hundred different intensities of pen and pencil, the
margins so tattooed with comments, reminders, with
schemes for pagination (Roman numerals, Arabic numerals, letters of the alphabet in complex combinations
that even I, the cryptographer, could no longer decode)
that what impressed one upon attempting to penetrate
that prose was not the imaginary world it depicted, but
the condition of the person who'd been doing the
imagining: the manuscript was the message, and the
message was Turmoil. I had, in fact, found a quo-
tation from Flaubert appropriate to my failure, and had
copied it out of my worn volume of his correspondence
(a book purchased during my army stint to help tide
me over to civilian life); I had Scotch-taped the quo-
tation to the carton bearing those five hundred thousand
words, not a one of them *juste*. It seemed to me it
might be a fitting epitaph to that effort, when and if
I was finally going to have to call it quits. Flaubert, to
his mistress Louise Colet, who had published a poem
maligning their contemporary, Alfred de Musset: "You
wrote with a personal emotion that distorted your outlook and made it impossible to keep before your eyes
the fundamental principles that must underlie any imaginative composition. It has no aesthetic. You have
turned art into an outlet for passion, a kind of chamberpot to catch an overflow. It smells bad; it smells of
hate!"

But if I could not leave off picking at the corpse and remove it from the autopsy room to the grave, it was because this genius, who had done so much to form my literary conscience as a student and an aspiring novelist, had also written—

Art, like the Jewish God, wallows in sacrifice.

And:

In Art . . . the creative impulse is essentially fanatic.

And:

. . . the excesses of the great masters! They pursue an idea to its furthermost limits.

These inspirational justifications for what Dr. Spielvogel might describe simply as "a fixation due to a severe traumatic experience" I also copied out on strips of paper and (with some self-irony, I must say) taped them too, like so many fortune-cookie ribbons, across the face of the box containing my novel-in-chaos.

On the evening that I arrived at Susan's with the *American Forum for Psychoanalytic Studies* in my hand, I called hello from the door, but instead of going to the kitchen, as was my habit—how I habituated myself during those years! how I coveted whatever orderliness I had been able to reestablish in my life!—to chat with her from a stool while she prepared our evening's delicacies, I went into the living room and sat on the edge of Jamey's flame-stitch ottoman, reading quickly through Spielvogel's article, entitled "Creativity: The Narcissism of the Artist." Somewhere in the middle of the piece I came upon what I'd been looking for—at least I *supposed* this was it: "A successful Italian-American poet in his forties entered into therapy because of anxiety states experienced as a result of his enormous ambivalence about leaving his wife. . . ." Up to this point in the article, the patients described by

Spielvogel had been "an actor," "a painter," and "a composer"—so this *had* to be me. Only I had not been in my forties when I first became Spielvogel's patient; I'd come to him at age twenty-nine, wrecked by a mistake I'd made at twenty-six. Surely between a man in his forties and a man in his twenties there are differences of experience, expectation, and character that cannot be brushed aside so easily as this . . . And "successful"? Does that word (in my mind, I immediately began addressing Spielvogel directly), does that word describe to you the tenor of my life at that time? A "successful" apprenticeship, absolutely, but when I came to you in 1962, at age twenty-nine, I had for three years been writing fiction I couldn't stand, and I could no longer even teach a class without fear of Maureen rushing in to "expose" me to my students. Successful? His forties? And surely it goes without saying that to disguise (in my brother's words) "a nice civilized Jewish boy" as something called "an Italian-American," well, that is to be somewhat dim-witted about matters of social and cultural background that might well impinge upon a person's psychology and values. And while we're at it, Dr. Spielvogel, a poet and a novelist have about as much in common as a jockey and a diesel driver. Somebody ought to tell you that, especially since "creativity" is your subject here. Poems and novels arise out of radically different sensibilities and resemble each other not at all, and you cannot begin to make sense about "creativity" or "the artist" or even "narcissism" if you are are going to be so insensitive to fundamental distinctions having to do with age, accomplishment, background, and vocation. And if I may, sir—his *self* is to many a novelist what his own physiognomy is to a painter of portraits: the closest subject at hand demanding scrutiny, a problem for his art to solve—given the enormous obstacles to truthfulness, *the* artistic problem. He is not simply looking into the mirror because he is transfixed by what he sees. Rather, the artist's success depends as much as anything on his powers of detachment, on *de*narcissizing himself. That's where the excitement comes in. That hard *conscious* work that makes it *art!* Freud, Dr. Spielvogel, studied his own dreams not because he was a "narcissist," but because he was a student of dreams. And whose were at once the least and most accessible of dreams, if not his own?

. . . And so it went, my chagrin renewed practically with each word. I could not read a sentence in which it did not seem to me that the observation was off, the point missed, the nuance blurred—in short, the evidence rather munificently distorted so as to support a narrow and unilluminating thesis at the expense of the ambiguous and perplexing actuality. In all there were only two pages of text on the "Italian-American poet," but so angered and disappointed was I by what seemed to me the unflagging wrongness of the description of my case, that it took me ten minutes to get from the top of page 85 to the bottom of 86. ". . . enormous ambivalence about leaving his wife. . . . It soon became clear that the poet's central problem here as elsewhere was his castration anxiety vis-à-vis a phallic mother figure. . . ." Not so! His central problem here as elsewhere derives from nothing of the sort. That will not serve to explain his "enormous ambivalence" about leaving his wife any more than it describes the prevailing emotional tone of his childhood years, which was one of intense *security*. "His father was a harassed man, ineffectual and submissive to his mother. . . ." What? Now where did you get that idea? My father was harassed, all right, but not by his wife—any child who lived in the same house with them knew that much. He was harassed by his own adamant refusal to allow his three children or his wife to do without: he was harassed by his own vigor, by his ambitions, by his business, by the times. By his overpowering commitment to the idea of Family and the religion he made of Doing A Man's Job! My "ineffectual" father happened to have worked twelve hours a day, six and seven days a week, often simultaneously at two exhausting jobs, with the result that not even when the store was as barren of customers as the Arctic tundra, did his loved ones lack for anything essential. Broke and overworked, no better off than a serf or an indentured servant in the America of the thirties, he did not take to drink, jump out of the window, or beat his wife and kids—and by the time he sold Tarnopol's Haberdashery and retired two years ago, he was making twenty thousand bucks a year. Good Christ, Spielvogel, from whose example did I come to associate virility with hard work and self-discipline, if not from my father's? Why did I like to go down to the store on Saturdays and spend all day in the stockroom arranging and stacking the boxes of goods? In order to hang around an ineffectual father? Why did I listen like Desdemona to Othello when he used to lecture the customers on Interwoven socks and Mc-Gregor shirts—because he was *bad* at it? Don't kid yourself—and the other psychiatrists. It was because I was so *proud* of his affiliation with those big brand names—because his pitch was so *convincing*. It wasn't his wife's hostility he had to struggle against, but the world's! And he did it, with splitting headaches to be sure, *but without giving in.* I've told you that a hundred times. Why don't you believe me? Why, to substantiate your "ideas," do you want to create this fiction about me and my family, when your gift obviously lies elsewhere. Let *me* make up stories—you make sense! ". . . in order to avoid a confrontation with his dependency needs toward his wife the poet acted out sexually with other women almost from the beginning of his marriage." But that just is not so! You must be thinking of some other poet. Look, is this supposed to be an amalgam of the ailing, or me alone? Who was there to "act out" with other than Karen? Doctor, I had a desperate *affair* with that girl—hopeless and ill-advised and adolescent, that may well be, but also passionate, also painful, also *warm-hearted,* which was what the whole thing was about to begin with: I was dying for some *humanness* in my life, *that's* why I reached out and touched her hair! And oh yes, I fucked a prostitute in Naples after a forty-eight hour fight with

Maureen in our hotel. And another in Venice, correct
—making two in all. Is that what you call "acting out"
with "other women almost from the beginning of his
marriage"? The marriage only lasted three years! It
was *all* "almost" the beginning. And why don't you
mention how it began? ". . . he once picked up a girl
at a party. . . ." But that was here in New York,
months and months *after* I had left Maureen in Wisconsin. The marriage was *over,* even if the state of New
York refused to allow that to be so! ". . . the poet
acted out his anger in his relationships with women, reducing all women to masturbatory sexual objects. . . ."
Now, do you really mean to say that? All women? Is
that what Karen Oakes was to me, "a masturbatory
sexual object"? Is that what Susan McCall is to me
now? Is that why I have encouraged and cajoled and
berated her into going back to finish her schooling, because she is "a masturbatory sexual object"? Is that
why I nearly give myself a stroke each night trying to
help her to come? Look, let's get down to the case of
cases: Maureen. Do you think that's what *she* was to
me, "a masturbatory sexual object"? Good God, what a
reading of my story *that* is! Rather than reducing that
lying, hysterical bitch to an object of any kind, I made
the grotesque mistake of *elevating* her to the status of a
human being toward whom I had a *moral responsibility.*
Nailed myself with my romantic morality to the cross of
her desperation! Or, if you prefer, caged myself in with
my cowardice! And don't tell me that was out of "guilt"
for having *already* made of her "a masturbatory sexual
object" because you just can't have it both ways! Had I
actually been able to treat her as some goddam "object," or simply to see her for what she was, I would
never have done my manly duty and married her! Did
it ever occur to you, Doctor, in the course of your
ruminations, that maybe *I* was the one who was made
into a sexual object? You've got it all backwards, Spielvogel—inside out! And how can that be? How can you,
who have done me so much good, have it all so wrong?
Now *there* is something to write an article about! *That*

is a subject for a symposium! Don't you see, it isn't that women mean too little to me—what's caused the trouble is that they mean so much. The testing ground, not for potency, but *virtue!* Believe me, if I'd listened to my prick instead of to my upper organs, I would never have gotten into this mess to begin with! I'd still be fucking Dina Dornbusch! And she'd have been my wife!

What I read next brought me up off the ottoman and to my feet, as though in a terrifying dream my name had finally been called—then I remembered that blessedly it was not a Jewish novelist in his late twenties or early thirties called Tarnopol, but a nameless Italian-American poet in his forties that Spielvogel claimed to be describing (and diagnosing) for his colleagues. ". . . leaving his semen on fixtures, towels, etc., so completely libidinized was his anger; on another occasion, he dressed himself in nothing but his wife's underpants, brassiere, and stockings. . . .?" Stockings? Oh, I didn't put on her stockings, damn it! Can't you get anything right? And it was not at all "another occasion"! One, she had just drawn blood from her wrist with my razor; two, she had just confessed (a) to perpetrating a fraud to get me to marry her and (b) to keeping it secret from me for three wretched years of married life; three, she had just threatened to put Karen's "pure little face" in every newspaper in Wisconsin—

Then came the worst of it, what made the protective disguise of the Italian-American poet so ludicrous . . . In the very next paragraph Spielvogel recounted an incident from my childhood that I had myself narrated somewhat more extensively in the autobiographical *New Yorker* story published above my name the previous month.

It had to do with a move we had made during the war, when Moe was off in the merchant marine. To make way for the landlord's newlywed daughter and her husband, we had been dispossessed from the second-floor apartment of the two-family house where we had been living ever since the family had moved to Yonkers from the Bronx nine years earlier, when I'd been born. My parents had been able to find a new apartment very like our old one, and fortunately only a little more expensive, some six blocks away in the same neighborhood; nonetheless, they had been infuriated by the high-handed treatment they had received from the landlord, particularly given the loving, proprietary care that my mother had taken of the building, and my father of the little yard, over the years. For me, being uprooted after a lifetime in the same house was utterly bewildering; to make matters even worse, the first night in our new apartment I had gone to bed with the room in a state of disarray that was wholly foreign to our former way of life. Would it be this way forevermore? Eviction? Confusion? Disorder? Were we on the skids? Would this somehow result in my brother's ship, off in the dangerous North Atlantic, being sunk by a German torpedo? The day after the move, when it came time to go home from school for lunch, instead of heading off for the new address, I "unthinkingly" returned to the house in which I had lived all my life in perfect safety with brother, sister, mother, and father. At the second-floor landing I was astonished to find the door to our apartment wide open and to hear men talking loudly inside. Yet standing in the hallway on that floor planed smooth over the years by my mother's scrub brush, I couldn't seem to get myself to remember that we had moved the day before and now lived elsewhere. "It's Nazis!" I thought. The Nazis had parachuted into Yonkers, made their way to our street, and taken everything away. *Taken my mother away.* So I suddenly perceived it. I was no braver than the ordinary nine-year-old, and no bigger, and so where I got the courage to peek inside I don't know. But when I did, I saw that "the Nazis" were only the housepainters sitting on a drop cloth on what used to be our living-room floor, eating their sandwiches out of wax-paper wrappings. I ran—down that old stairwell, the feel of the rubber treads on each stair as familiar to me as the teeth in my head, and through the neighborhood to our new family sanctum, and at the sight of my mother in her apron (unbeaten, unbloodied, unraped, though visibly distressed from imagining what might have happened to delay her punctual child on his way home from school), I collapsed into her arms in a fit of tears.

Now, as Spielvogel interpreted this incident, I cried in large part because of "guilt over the aggressive fantasies directed toward the mother." As I construed it—in the short story in journal form, entitled "The Diary of Anne Frank's Contemporary"—I cry with relief to find that my mother is alive and well, that the new apartment has been transformed during the morning I have been in school into a perfect replica of the old one —and that we are Jews who live in the haven of Westchester County, rather than in our ravaged, ancestral, Jew-hating Europe.

Susan finally came in from the kitchen to see what I was doing off by myself.

"Why are you standing there like that? Peter, what's happened?"

I held the journal in the air. "Spielvogel has written an article about something he calls 'creativity.' And I'm in it."

"By *name?*"

"No, but identifiably me. *Me* coming home to the wrong house when I was nine. He *knew* I was using it. I talked about that story to him, and still he goes ahead and has some fictitious Italian-American poet—!"

"Who? I can't follow you."

"Here!" I handed her the magazine. "Here! This straw fucking patient is supposed to be me! Read it! Read this thing!"

She sat down on the ottoman and began to read. "Oh, Peter."

"Keep going."

"It says . . ."

"What?"

"It says here—you put on Maureen's underwear and stockings. Oh, he's out of his mind."

"He's not—I did. Keep reading."

Her tear appeared. "You *did?*"

"Not the stockings, *no*—that's him, writing his banal fucking fiction! *He* makes it sound like I was dressing up for the drag-queen ball! All I was doing, Susan, was saying, 'Look, I wear the panties in this family and don't you forget it!' That's all it boils down to! Keep reading! He doesn't get *anything* right. It's all perfectly *off!*"

She read a little further, then put the magazine in her lap. "Oh, sweetheart."

"What? *What?*"

"It says . . ."

"My sperm?"

"Yes."

"*I did that too.* But I don't any more! Keep reading!"

"Well," said Susan, wiping away her tear with a fingertip, "don't shout at *me.* I think it's awful that he's written this and put it in print. It's unethical, it's reckless—and I can't even believe he would do such a thing. You tell me he's so smart. You make him sound so *wise.* But how could anybody wise do something so insensitive and uncaring as *this?*"

"Just read on. Read the whole hollow pretentious meaningless thing, right on down to the footnotes from Goethe and Baudelaire to prove a connection between 'narcissism' and 'art'! So what else is new? Oh, Jesus, what this man thinks of as *evidence!* 'As Sophocles has written,'—and that constitutes *evidence!* Oh, you ought to go through this thing, line by line, and watch the ground shift beneath you! Between every paragraph there's a hundred-foot drop!"

"What are you going to do?"

"What *can* I do? It's printed—it's out."

"Well, you just can't sit back and take it. He's betrayed your confidence!"

"I know that."

"Well, that's terrible."

"I know that!"

"Then *do* something!" she pleaded.

On the phone Spielvogel said that if I was as "distressed" as I sounded—"I am!" I assured him—he would stay after his last patient to see me for the second time that day. So, leaving Susan (who had much to be distressed about, too), I took a bus up Madison to his office and sat in the waiting room until seven thirty, constructing in my mind angry scenes that could only culminate in leaving Spielvogel forever.

The argument between us was angry, all right, and it went on unabated through my sessions for a week, but it was Spielvogel, not I, who finally suggested that I leave him. Even while reading his article, I hadn't been so shocked—so unwilling to believe in what he was doing—as when he suddenly rose from his chair (even as I continued my attack on him from the couch) and took a few listing steps around to where I could see him. Ordinarily I addressed myself to the bookcase in front of the couch, or to the ceiling overhead, or to the photograph of the Acropolis that I could see on the desk across the room. At the sight of him at my side, I sat straight up. "Look," he said, "this has gone far enough. I think either you will have now to forget this article of mine, or leave me. But we cannot proceed with treatment under these conditions."

"What kind of choice is that?" I asked, my heart beginning to beat wildly. He remained in the middle of the room, supporting himself now with a hand on the back of a chair. "I have been your patient for over two years. I have an investment here—of effort, of time, of hope, of money. I don't consider myself recovered. I don't consider myself able to go at my life alone just yet. And neither do you."

"But if as a result of what I have written about you, you find me so 'untrustworthy' and so 'unethical,' so absolutely 'wrong' and, as you put it, 'off' about relations between you and your family, then why would you want to stay on as a patient any longer? It is clear that I am too flawed to be your doctor."

"Come off it, please. Don't hit me over the head with the 'narcissism' again. You know why I want to stay on."

"Why?"

"Because I'm scared to be out there alone. But also because I *am* stronger—things in my life *are* better. Because staying with you, I was finally able to leave Maureen. That was no inconsequential matter for me, you know. If I hadn't left her, I'd be dead—dead or in jail. You may think that's an exaggeration, but I happen to know that it's true. What I'm saying is that on the practical side, on the subject of my everyday life, you have been a considerable help to me. You've been with me through some bad times. You've prevented me from doing some wild and foolish things. Obviously I haven't been coming here three times a week for two years for no reason. But all that doesn't mean that this article is something I can just forget."

"But there is really nothing more to be said about it. We have discussed it now for a week. We have been over it thoroughly. There is nothing new to add."

"You could add that you were wrong."

"I have answered the charge already and more than once. I don't find anything I did 'wrong.' "

"It was wrong, it was at the very least imprudent, for you to use that incident in your article, knowing as you did that I was using it in a story."

"We were writing simultaneously, I explained that to you."

"But I told you I was using it in the Anne Frank story."

"You are not remembering correctly. I did not know you had used it until I read the story last month in the *New Yorker*. By then the article was at the printer's."

"You could have changed it then—left that incident out. And I am not remembering incorrectly."

"First you complain that by disguising your identity I misrepresent you and badly distort the reality. You're a Jew, not an Italian-American. You're a novelist, not a poet. You came to me at twenty-nine, not at forty. Then in the next breath you complain that I fail to disguise your identity enough—rather, that I have *re-*

vealed your identity by using this particular incident.
This of course is your ambivalence again about your
'specialness.' "

"It is not of course my ambivalence again! You're
confusing the argument again. You're blurring important distinctions—just as you do in that piece! Let's at
least take up each issue in turn."

"We have taken up each issue in turn, three and
four times over."

"But you still refuse to get it. Even if your article
was at the printer, once you had read the Anne Frank
story you should have made every effort to protect my
privacy—and my trust in you!"

"It was impossible."

"You could have withdrawn the article."

"You are asking the impossible."

"What is more important, publishing your article or
keeping my trust?"

"Those were not my alternatives."

"But they *were*."

"That is the way you see it. Look here, we are clearly
at an impasse, and under these conditions treatment
cannot be continued. We can make no progress."

"But I did not just walk in off the street last week.
I am your patient."

"True. And I cannot be under attack from my patient
any longer."

"Tolerate it," I said bitterly—a phrase of his that had
helped me through some rough days. "Look, given that
you must certainly have had an *inkling* that I might be
using that incident in a piece of fiction, since you in
fact *knew* I was working on a story to which that incident was the conclusion, mightn't you at the very least
have thought to ask my permission, ask if it was all
right with me . . ."

"Do you ask permission of the people you write
about?"

"But I am not a psychoanalyst! The comparison
won't work. I write fiction—or did, once upon a time.
A Jewish Father was not 'about' my family, or about

Grete and me, as you certainly must realize. It may
have originated there, but it was finally a contrivance,
an artifice, a *rumination* on the real. A self-avowed
work of imagination, Doctor! I do not write 'about'
people in a strict factual or historical sense."

"But then you think," he said, with a hard look, "that
I don't either."

"Dr. Spielvogel, please, that is just not a good enough
answer. And you must know it. First off, you are bound
by ethical considerations that happen not to be the
ones that apply to my profession. Nobody comes to
me with confidences the way they do to you, and if
they tell me stories, it's not so that I can cure what ails
them. That's obvious enough. It's in the nature of
being a novelist to make private life public—that's a
part of what a novelist is up to. But certainly it is not
what I thought *you* were up to when I came here. I
thought your job was to treat me! And second, as to
accuracy—you are *supposed* to be accurate, after all,
even if you haven't been as accurate as I would want
you to be in this thing here."

"Mr. Tarnopol, 'this thing here' is a scientific paper.
None of us could write such papers, none of us could
share our findings with one another, if we had to rely
upon the permission or the approval of our patients
in order to publish. You are not the only patient who
would want to censor out the unpleasant facts or who
would find 'inaccurate' what he doesn't like to hear
about himself."

"Oh that won't wash, and you know it! I'm willing
to hear anything about myself—and always have been.
My problem, as I see it, isn't my impenetrability. As
a matter of fact, I tend to rise to the bait, Dr. Spielvogel,
as Maureen, for one, can testify."

"Oh, do you? Ironically, it is the narcissistic defenses
discussed here that prevent you from accepting the
article as something other than an assault upon your
dignity or an attempt to embarrass or belittle you. It
is precisely the blow to your narcissism that has swollen the issue out of all proportion for you. Simulta-

neously, you act as though it is about nothing *but* you, when actually, of the fifteen pages of text, your case takes up barely two. But then you do not like at all the idea of yourself suffering from 'castration anxiety.' You do not like the idea of your aggressive fantasies vis-à-vis your mother. You never have. You do not like me to describe your father, and by extension you, his son and heir, as 'ineffectual' and 'submissive,' though you don't like when I call you 'successful' either. Apparently that tends to dilute a little too much your comforting sense of victimized innocence."

"Look, I'm sure there are in New York City such people as you've just described. Only I ain't one of 'em! Either that's some model you've got in your head, some kind of patient for all seasons, or else it's some other patient of yours you're thinking about; I don't know what the hell to make of it, frankly. Maybe what it comes down to is a problem of self-expression; maybe it's that the writing isn't very precise."

"Oh, the writing is also a problem?"

"I don't like to say it, but maybe writing isn't your strong point."

He smiled. "Could it be, in your estimation? Could I be precise enough to please you? I think perhaps what so disturbs you about the incident in the Anne Frank story is not that by using it I may have disclosed your identity, but that in your opinion I plagiarized and abused your material. You are made so very angry by this piece of writing that I have dared to publish. But if I am such a weak and imprecise writer as you suggest, then you should not feel so threatened by my little foray into English prose."

"I don't feel 'threatened.' Oh, please, don't argue like Maureen, will you? That is just more of that language again, which doesn't at all express what you mean and doesn't get anyone anywhere."

"I assure you, unlike Maureen, I said 'threatened' because I meant 'threatened.'"

"But maybe writing *isn't* your strong point. Maybe that is an objective statement of fact and has nothing to do with whether I am a writer or a tightrope walker."

"But why should it matter so much to you?"

"Why? Why?" That he could seriously ask this question just took the heart out of me; I felt the tears welling up. "Because, among other things, I am the subject of that writing! I am the one your imprecise language has misrepresented! Because I come here each day and turn over the day's receipts, every last item out of my most personal life, and in return I expect an accurate accounting!" I had begun to cry. "You were my friend, and I told you the truth. I told you everything."

"Look, let me disabuse you of the idea that the whole world is waiting with bated breath for the newest issue of our little journal in which you claim you are misrepresented. I assure you that is not the case. It is not the *New Yorker* magazine, or even the *Kenyon Review*. If it is any comfort to you, most of my colleagues don't even bother to read it. But this is your narcissism again. Your sense that the whole world has nothing to look forward to but the latest information about the secret life of Peter Tarnopol."

The tears had stopped. "And that is your reductivism again, if I may say so, and your obfuscation. Spare me that word 'narcissism,' will you? You use it on me like a club."

"The word is purely descriptive and carries no valuation," said the doctor.

"Oh, is that so? Well, you be on the receiving end and see how little 'valuation' it carries! Look, can't we grant that there is a difference between self-esteem and vanity, between pride and megalomania? Can we grant that there actually is an ethical matter at stake here, and that my sensitivity to it, and your apparent indifference to it, cannot be explained away as a psychological abberation of *mine?* You've got a psychology too, you know. You do this with me all the time, Dr. Spielvogel. First you shrink the area of moral concern, you say that what I, for instance, call my responsibility toward Susan is so much camouflaged narcissism—and then if I consent to see it that way, and I leave off with the moral implications of my conduct, you tell me I'm a narcissist who thinks only about his own welfare. Maureen, you know, used to do something similar— only she worked the hog-tying game from the other way round. She made the kitchen *sink* into a moral issue! Everything in the whole wide world was a test of my decency and honor—and the moral ignoramus you're looking at believed her! If driving out of Rome for Frascati, I took a wrong turn, she had me pegged within half a mile as a felon, as a fiend up from Hell by way of Westchester and the Ivy League. And I believed her! . . . Look, look—let's *talk* about Maureen a minute, let's talk about the possible consequences of all this for me, 'narcissistic' as that must seem to you. Suppose Maureen were to get hold of this issue and read what you've written here. It's not unlike her, after all, to be on her toes where I'm concerned—where *alimony* is concerned. I mean it won't do, to go back a moment to what you just said—it won't do to say that nobody reads the magazine anyway. Because if you really believed that, then you wouldn't publish your paper there to begin with. What good are your findings published in a magazine that has no readers? The magazine is around, and it's read by somebody, surely here in New York it is—and if it somehow came to Maureen's attention . . . well, just imagine how happy she would be to read those pages about me to the judge in the courtroom. Just imagine a New York municipal judge taking that stuff in. Do you see what I'm saying?"

"Oh, I see very well what you're saying."

"Where you write, for instance, that I was 'acting out' sexually with other women 'almost from the beginning of the marriage.' First off, that is not accurate either. Stated like that, you make it seem as though I'm just another Italian-American who sneaks off after work each day for a quick bang on the way home from the poetry office. Do you follow me? You make me sound like somebody who is simply fucking around with women all the time. And that is not so. God knows what you write here is not a proper description of my affair with Karen. That was nothing if it wasn't earnest —and earnest in part because I was so *new* at it!"

"And the prostitutes?"

"Two prostitutes—in three years. That breaks down to about half a prostitute a year, which is probably, among miserably married men, a national record for *not* acting out. Have you forgotten? *I was miserable!* See the thing in context, will you? You seem to forget that the wife I was married to was Maureen. You seem to forget the circumstances under which we married. You seem to forget that we had an argument in every piazza, cathedral, museum, trattoria, pensione, and hotel on the Italian peninsula. Another man would have beaten her head in! My predecessor Mezik, the Yugoslav barkeep, would have 'acted out' with a right to the jaw. I am a literary person. I went forth and did the civilized thing—I laid a three-thousand-lire whore! Ah, and that's how you came up with 'Italian-American' for me, isn't it?"

He waved a hand to show what he thought of my *aperçu*—then said, "Another man might have confronted his wife more directly, that is true, rather than libidinizing his anger."

"But the only direct way to confront that woman was *to kill her!* And you yourself have told me that killing people is against the law, crazy wives included. I was not 'sexually acting out,' whatever that means—I was trying to stay alive in all that madness. Stay *me!* 'Let me shun that,' and so on!"

"And," he was saying, "you conveniently forget once again the wife of your young English department colleague in Wisconsin."

"Good Christ, who are you, Cotton Mather? Look, I may be childish and a weakling, I may even be the narcissist of your fondest professional dreams—*but I am not a slob!* I am not a bum or a lecher or a gigolo or some kind of walking penis. Why do you want to portray me that way? Why do you want to characterize me in your writing as some sort of heartless rapist manqué?

Surely, surely there is another way to describe my affair with Karen—"

"But I said nothing about Karen. I only reminded you of the wife of your colleague, whom you ran into that afternoon at the shopping center in Madison."

"You've got such a good memory, why don't you also remember that I didn't even fuck her! She blew me, in the car. So what? *So what?* I tell you, it was a surprise to the two of us. And what's it to you, anyway? I mean that! We were friends. She wasn't so happily married either. That, for Christ's sake, wasn't 'sexually acting out.' It was friendship! It was heartbrokenness! It was generosity! It was tenderness! It was despair! It was being adolescents together for ten secret minutes in the rear of a car before we both went nobly back into Adulthood! It was a sweet and harmless game of Let's Pretend! Smile, if you like, smile from your pulpit, but that's still closer to a proper description of what was going on there than what *you* call it. And we did not let it go any further, which was a possibility, you know; we let it remain a kind of happy, inconsequential accident and returned like good soldiers to the fucking front lines. Really, Your Holiness, really, Your Excellency, does that in your mind add up to 'acting out sexually with other women from the beginning of the marriage'?"

"Doesn't it?"

"Two street whores in Italy, a friend in a car in Madison . . . and Karen? No! I call it practically *monkish,* given the fact of my marriage. I call it pathetic, that's what! From the beginning of his marriage, the Italian-American poet had some crazy idea that now that he was a husband his mission in life was to be *faithful*—to whom never seemed to cross his mind. It was like *keeping his word* and *doing his duty*—what had gotten him married to this shrew in the first place! Once again the Italian-American poet did what he thought to be 'manly' and 'upright' and 'principled'— which, needless to say, was only what was cowardly and submissive. Pussywhipped, as my brother so suc-

cinctly puts it! As a matter of fact, Dr. Spielvogel,
those two Italian whores and my colleague's wife back
of the shopping center, and Karen, constituted the only
praiseworthy, the only manly, the only *moral* . . . oh,
the hell with it."

"I think at this point we are only saying the same
thing in our different vocabularies. Isn't that what you
just realized?"

"No, no, no, no, no. I just realized that you are
never going to admit to me that you could be mistaken
in any single particular of diction, or syntax, let alone
in the overriding idea of that paper. Talk about narcissism as a defense!"

He did not bristle at my tone, contemptuous as it
had become. His voice throughout had been strong
and even—a touch of sarcasm, some irony, but no
outrage, and certainly no tears. Which was as it should
be. What did he have to lose if I left?

"I am not a student any longer, Mr. Tarnopol. I do
not look to my patients for literary criticism. You would
prefer that I leave the professional writing to you, it
would seem, and confine my activities to this room. You
remember how distressed you were several years ago
to discover that I occasionally went out into the streets
to ride the bus."

"That was awe. Don't worry, I'm over it."

"Good. No reason for you to think I'm perfect."

"I don't."

"On the other hand, the alternative is not necessarily
to think I am another Maureen, out to betray and deceive you for my own sadistic and vengeful reasons."

"I didn't say you were."

"You may nonetheless think that I am."

"If you mean do I think that I have been misused by
you, the answer is yes. Maureen is not the issue—that
article is."

"All right, that is your judgment. Now you must decide what you are going to do about the treatment. If
you want to continue with your attack upon me, treatment will be impossible—it would be foolish even to

try. If you want to return to the business at hand, then of course I am prepared to go forward. Or perhaps there is a third alternative that you may wish to consider—perhaps you will choose to take up treatment with somebody else. This is for you to decide before the next session."

Susan was enraged by the decision I did reach. I never had heard her argue about anything as she did against Spielvogel's "brutal" handling of me, nor had she ever dared to criticize me so forthrightly either. Of course her objections were in large part supplied by Dr. Golding, who, she told me, had been "appalled" by the way Spielvogel had dealt with me in the article in the *Forum;* however, she would never even have begun to communicate Golding's position to me if it were not for startling changes that were taking place in her attitude toward herself. Now, maybe reading about me walking around in Maureen's underwear did something to boost her confidence with me, but whatever had triggered it, I found myself delighted by the emergence of the vibrant and emphatic side so long suppressed in her—at the same time that I was greatly troubled by the possibility that what she and her doctor were suggesting about my decision to stay with Spielvogel constituted more of the humbling truth. Certainly in my defense I offered up to Susan what sounded even to me like the feeblest of arguments.

"You should leave him," she said.

"I can't. Not at this late date. He's done me more good than harm."

"But he's got you all wrong. How could that do anybody any good?"

"I don't know—but it did me. Maybe he's a lousy analyst and a good therapist."

"That makes no sense, Peter."

"Look, I'm not getting into bed with my worst enemy any more, am I? I am out of that, am I not?"

"But any doctor would have helped you to leave her. Any doctor who was the least bit competent would have seen you through that."

"But he happens to be the one who did it."

"Does that mean he can just get away with anything as a result? His sense of what you are is all wrong. Publishing that article without consulting you about it first was all wrong. His attitude when you confronted him with what he had done, the way he said, 'Either shut up or go'—that was as wrong as wrong can be. And you know it! Dr. Golding said that was as reprehensible as anything he had ever heard of between a doctor and his patient. Even his writing stinks—you said it was just jargon and crap."

"Look, I'm staying with him. I don't want to talk about it any more."

"If *I* answered *you* like that, you'd hit the ceiling. You'd say, 'Stop backing away! Stand up for yourself, twerp!' Oh, I don't understand why you are acting like this, when the man has so clearly abused you. Why do you let people get away with such things?"

"Which people?"

"Which people? People like Maureen. People like Spielvogel. People who . . ."

"What?"

"Well, walk all over you like that."

"Susan, I cannot put in any more time thinking of myself as someone who gets walked over. It gets me nowhere."

"Then don't be one! Don't let them get away with it!"

"It doesn't seem to me that in this case anybody is getting away with anything."

"Oh, Lambchop, that isn't what Dr. Golding says."

Spielvogel simply shrugged off what Dr. Golding said, when I passed it on to him. "I don't know the man," he grunted, and that was that. Settled. As though if he did know him, he could tell me Golding's motives for taking such a position—otherwise, why bother? As for Susan's anger, and her uncharacteristic vehemence about my leaving him, well, I understood that, did I not? She hated Spielvogel for what Spielvogel had written about the Peter who was to *her* so inspira-

tional and instructive, the man she had come to adore
for the changes he was helping to bring about in her life.
Spielvogel had demythologized her Pygmalion—of
course Galatea was furious. Who expected otherwise?

I must say, his immunity to criticism *was* sort of
dazzling. Indeed, the imperviousness of this pallid
doctor with the limping gait seemed to me, in those days
of uncertainty and self-doubt, a condition to aspire to:
*I am right and you are wrong, and even if I'm not, I'll
just hold out and hold out and not give a single inch,
and that will make it so.* And maybe that's why I
stayed on with him—out of admiration for his armor,
in the hope that some of that impregnability would rub
off on me. Yes, I thought, he is teaching me by example,
the arrogant German son of a bitch. Only I won't give
him the satisfaction of telling him. Only who is to say
he doesn't know it? Only who is to say he does, other
than I?

As the weeks passed and Susan continued to grimace
at the mention of Spielvogel's name, I sometimes came
close to making what seemed to me the best possible
defense of him—and thereby of myself, for if it turned
out that I had been as deluded about Spielvogel as
about Maureen, it was going to be awfully hard ever to
believe in my judgment again. In order to substantiate
my own claim to sanity and intelligence, and to protect
my sense of trust from total collapse (or was it just to
perpetuate my childish illusions? to cherish and protect
my naiveté right on down to the last good drop?), I felt
I had to make as strong a case as I could for him. And
even if that meant accepting as valid his obfuscating
defense—even if it meant looking back myself with
psychoanalytic skepticism upon my own valid objections! "Look," I wanted to say to Susan, "if it weren't
for Spielvogel, I wouldn't even be here. If it weren't for
Spielvogel saying 'Why not stay?' every time I say
'Why not leave?' I would have been out of this affair
long ago. We have him to thank for whatever exists
between us—he's the one who was your advocate, not
me." But that it was largely because of Spielvogel's en-

couragement that I had continued to visit her almost nightly during that first year, when I was so out of sympathy with her way of living, was really not her business, even if she wouldn't let up about his "reprehensible" behavior; nor would it do her fragile sense of self-esteem any good to know that even now, several years into our affair—with me her Lambchop and her my Suzie Q., with all that tender lovers' playfulness between us—that it was Spielvogel who prevented me from leaving her whenever I became distressed about those burgeoning dreams of marriage and family that I did not share. "But she wants to have children—and now, before she gets any older." "But you don't want to." "Right. And I can't allow her to nurse these expectations. That just won't do." "Then tell her not to." "I *do*. I *have*. She can't bear hearing it any more. She says, 'I know, I know, you're not going to marry me—do you have to tell me that every *hour*?'" "Well, every hour is perhaps a little more frequent than necessary." "Oh, it isn't every hour—it just sounds that way to her. You see, because I tell her where things stand doesn't mean she takes it to heart." "Yes, but what more can you do?" "Go. I should." "I wouldn't think she thinks you should." "But if I stay . . ." "You might *really* fall in love with her. Does it ever occur to you that maybe this is what you are running away from? Not the children, not the marriage . . . but the love?" "Oh, Doctor, don't start practicing psychoanalysis. No, that doesn't occur to me. I don't think it should, because I don't think it's true." "No? But you are somewhat in love already—are you not? You tell me how sweet she is, how kind she is. How gentle. You tell me how beautiful she is when she sits there reading. You tell me what a touching person she is. Sometimes you are positively lyrical about her." "Am I?" "Yes, yes, and you know that." "But there is still too much that's wrong there, *you* know *that*." "Yes, well, this I could have warned you about at the outset." "Please, the husband of Maureen Tarnopol understands that the other gender is also imperfect." "Knowing this, the husband of Maureen Tarnopol should be grateful perhaps for a woman, who despite her imperfections, happens to be tender and appreciative and absolutely devoted to him. She is all these things, am I right?" "She is all these things. She also turns out to be smart and charming and funny." "And in love with you." "And in love with me." "And a cook—such a cook. You tell me about her dishes, you make my mouth water." "You're very hung up on the pleasure principle, Dr. Spielvogel." "And you? Tell me, where are you running again? To what? To whom? Why?" "To no one, to nothing—but '*why?*' I've told you why: suppose she tries to commit suicide!" "Still with the suicide?" "But what if she does it!" "Isn't that her responsibility? And Dr. Golding's? She is in therapy after all. Are you going to run for fear of this remote possibility?" "I can't take it hanging over my head. Not after all that's gone on. Not after Maureen." "Maybe you are too thin-skinned, you know? Maybe it is time at thirty to develop a thicker hide." "No doubt. I'm sure you rhinoceroses lead a better life. But my hide is my hide. I'm afraid you can shine a flashlight through it. So give me some other advice." "What other advice is there? The choice is yours. Stay or run." "This choice that is mine you structure oddly." "All right, *you* structure it." "The point, you see, is that if I do stay, she must realize that I am marrying no one unless and until *I want to do it*. And everything conspires to make me think that *I don't want to do it*." "Mr. Tarnopol, somehow I feel I can rely on you to put that proviso before her from time to time."

Why did I stay with Spielvogel? Let us not forget his Mosaic prohibitions and what they meant to a thin-skinned man at the edge of he knew not what intemperate act.

Thou shalt not covet thy wife's underwear.

Thou shalt not drop thy seed upon thy neighbor's bathroom floor or dab it upon the bindings of library books.

Thou shalt not be so stupid as to buy a Hoffritz hunting knife to slay your wife and her matrimonial lawyer.

"But why can't I? What's the difference any more? They're driving me crazy! They're ruining my life! First she tricked me into marrying her with that urine, now they're telling the judge I can write movies and make a fortune! She tells the court that I 'obstinately' refuse to go out to Hollywood and do an honest day's work! Which is true! I obstinately refuse! *Because that is not my work!* My work is writing fiction! And I can't even do *that* any more! Only when I say I can't, they say, right, so just get your ass out to Hollywood where you can earn yourself a thousand bucks a day! Look! Just look at this affidavit she filed! Look what she calls me here, Doctor—'a well-known seducer of college girls'! That's how she spells 'Karen'! Read this document, will you please? I brought it so you can see with your own eyes that I am not exaggerating! Just look at *this* version of me! 'A seducer of college girls'! They're trying to hold me up, Doctor Spielvogel—this is legalized extortion!" "To be sure," said my Moses, gently, "but still you cannot buy that knife and stick it in her heart. You must not buy a knife, Mr. Tarnopol." "WHY NOT? GIVE ME ONE GOOD REASON WHY NOT!" "Because killing is against the law." "FUCK THE LAW! THE LAW IS WHAT IS KILLING ME!" "Be that as it may, kill her and they will put you in jail." "So what!" "You wouldn't like it there." "I wouldn't care—she'd be dead. *Justice* would come into this world!" "Ah, but just as the world would become following her death, for you it still wouldn't be paradise. You did not even like the army that much, remember? Well, jail is worse. I don't believe you would be happy there." "I'm not exactly happy *here*." "I understand that. But there you would be even less happy."

So, with him to restrain me (or with him to pretend to restrain me, while I pretend to be unrestrained), I did not buy the knife in Hoffritz's Grand Central window (her lawyer's office was just across the street, twenty flights up). And a good thing too, for when I discovered that the reporter from the *Daily News* who sat in a black raincoat at the back of the courtroom throughout the separation proceedings had been alerted to the hearing by Maureen's lawyers, I lost all control of myself (no pretending now), and out in the corridor during the lunch recess, I took a swing at the dapper, white-haired attorney in his dark three-piece suit with the Phi Beta Kappa key dangling conspicuously from a chain. He was obviously a man of years (though in my state, I might even have attacked a somewhat younger man), but he was agile and easily blocked my wild blow with his briefcase. "Watch out, Egan, watch out for me!" It was pure playgroundese I shouted at him, language dating back to the arm's-length insolence of grade-school years; my eyes were running with rage, as of old, but before I could swing out at his briefcase again, my own lawyer had grabbed me around the middle and was dragging me backward down the corridor. "You jackass," said Egan coldly, "we'll fix your wagon." "You goddam thief! You publicity hound! What more can you do, you bastard!" "Wait and see," said Egan, unruffled, and even smiling at me now, as a small crowd gathered around us in the hall. "She tricked me," I said to him, "and you know it! With that urine!" "You've got quite an imagination, son. Why don't you put it to work for you?" Here my lawyer managed to turn me completely around, and running and pushing at me from behind, shoved me a few paces farther down the courthouse corridor and into the men's room.

Where we were promptly joined by the stout, black-coated Mr. Valducci of the *Daily News*. "Get out of here, you," I said, "leave me alone." "I just want to ask you some questions. I want to ask about your wife, that's all. I'm a reader of yours. I'm a real fan." "I'll bet." "Sure. *The Jewish Merchant*. My wife read it too. Terrific ending. Ought to be a movie." "Look, I've heard enough about the movies today!" "Take it easy, Pete—I just want to ask you, for instance, what did the missus do before you were married?" "The missus was a show girl! She was in the line at the Latin Quarter! Fuck off, will you!" "Whatever you say, whatever you say," and with a bow to my attorney, who had now interposed himself between the two of us, Valducci stepped back a ways and asked, deferentially, "You don't mind if I take a leak, do you? Since I'm already here?" While Valducci voided, we looked on in silence. "Just shut up," my lawyer whispered to me. "See you, Pete," said Valducci, after meticulously washing and drying his hands, "see you, Counselor."

The next morning, over Valducci's by-line, in the lower half of page five, ran this three-column head—

PRIZE-WINNING AUTHOR TURNS COURTROOM PRIZEFIGHTER

The story was illustrated with my book-jacket photo, dark-eyed, thin-faced innocence, circa 1959, and a photograph of Maureen taken the day before, her lantern jaw slicing the offending air as she strides down the courthouse steps on the arm of Attorney Dan P. Egan, who, the story noted (with relish) was seventy years old and formerly middleweight boxing champion at Fordham; in his heyday, I learned, he was known as "Red," and was still a prized toastmaster at Fordham alumni functions. The tears I had shed during my contretemps with Red did not go unreported. "Oh, I should never have listened to you about that knife. I could have killed Valducci too." "You are not satisfied with page five?" "I should have done it. And that judge too. Cut his self-righteous gizzard out, sitting there pitying poor Maureen!" "Please," said Spielvogel, laughing lightly, "the pleasure would have been momentary." "Oh, no, it wouldn't." "Oh, yes, believe me. Murder four people in a courtroom, and before you know it, it's over and you're behind bars. This way, you see, you have it always to imagine when your spirit needs a lift."

So I stayed on as Spielvogel's patient, at least so long as Maureen drew breath (and breathed fire), and

Susan McCall was my tender, appreciative, and devoted mistress.

5. FREE

Here lies my wife: here let her lie!
Now she's at rest, and so am I.

—John Dryden, "Epitaph Intended for His Wife"

It was three years later, in the spring of 1966, that Maureen telephoned to say she had to talk to me "personally" as soon as possible, and "alone," no lawyers present. We had seen each other only twice since that courtroom confrontation reported in the *Daily News*, at two subsequent hearings held at Maureen's request in order to determine if she could get any more than the hundred a week that Judge Rosenzweig had originally ordered the well-known seducer of college girls to pay in alimony to his abandoned wife. Both times a court-appointed referee had examined my latest tax return, my royalty statements and bank records, and concluded that no increase was warranted. I had pleaded that what was warranted was a reduction, since my income, rather than increasing, had fallen off by about thirty per cent since Judge Rosenzweig had first ordered me to pay Maureen five thousand dollars a year out of the ten I was then making. Rosenzweig's decision had been based on a tax return that showed me earning a salary of fifty-two hundred a year from the University of Wisconsin and another five thousand from my publisher (representing one quarter of the substantial advance I was getting for my second book). By 1964, however, the last of the publisher's four annual payments of five thousand dollars had been doled out to me, the book they had contracted with me for bore no resemblance to a finished novel, and I was broke. Out of each year's ten thousand in income, five thousand had gone to Maureen for alimony, three to Spielvogel for services rendered, leaving two for food, rent, etc. At the time of the separation there had been another sixty-eight hundred in a savings account—my paperback proceeds from *A Jewish Father*—but that too had been divided equally between the estranged couple by the judge, who then laid the plaintiff's legal fees on the defendant; by our third appearance at the courthouse, the remainder of those savings had been paid out to meet my own lawyer's bills. In '65 Hofstra raised me to sixty-five hundred a year for teaching my two seminars, but my income from writing consisted only of what I could bring in from the short stories I was beginning to publish. To meet expenses I cut down my sessions with Spielvogel from three to two a week, and began to borrow money from my brother to live on. Each time I came before the referee I explained to him that I was now giving my wife somewhere between sixty-five and seventy per cent of my income, which did not strike me as fair. Mr. Egan would then point out that if Mr. Tarnopol wished to "normalize" his income, or even "to improve his lot in life, as most young men strive to do," he had only to write fiction for *Esquire,* the *New Yorker, Harper's,* the *Atlantic Monthly,* or for *Playboy* magazine, whose editors would pay him—here, to read the phenomenal figure, he donned his tortoise-shell glasses—"three thousand dollars for a single short story." As evidence in support of his claim, he produced letters subpoenaed from my files, wherein the fiction editors of these magazines invited me to submit any work I had on hand or planned for the future. I explained to the referee (an attentive, gentlemanly, middle-aged Negro, who had announced, at the outset, that he was honored to meet the author of *A Jewish Father;* another admirer—God only knew what that meant) that every writer of any eminence at all receives such letters as a matter of course; they were not in the nature of bids, or bribes, or guarantees of purchase. When I finished writing a story, as I had recently, I turned it over to my agent, who, at my suggestion, submitted

it to one or another of the commercial magazines Mr.
Egan had named. There was nothing I could do to
make the magazine purchase it for publication; in
fact, over the previous few years three of these magazines, the most likely to publish my work, had repeatedly
rejected fiction of mine (letters of rejection submitted
here by my lawyer as proof of my plunging literary
reputation), despite those warm invitations for submis-
sion, which of course cost them nothing to send out.
Certainly, I said, I could not submit to them stories
that I had not written, and I could not write stories—
about here I generally lost my temper, though the
referee's equanimity remained serenely intact—*on demand!* "Oh, my," sighed Egan, turning to Maureen, "the
artiste bit again." "What? What did you say?" I threaten-
ingly inquired, though we sat around a conference table
in a small office in the courthouse, and I, like the
referee, had heard every word that Egan had whispered.
"I said, sir," replied Egan, "that I wish I was an artiste
and didn't have to work 'on demand' either." Here
we were brought gently to order by the referee, who,
if he did not give me my reduction, did not give Maureen her increase either.

I took no comfort in his "fairness," however. Money
was constantly on my mind: what was being extorted
from me by Maureen, in collusion (as I saw it) with the
state of New York, and what I was now borrowing from
Moe, who refused to take interest or to set a date for
repayment. "What do you want me to do, shylock
my own flesh and blood?" he said, laughing. "I hate this,
Moey." "So you hate it," was his reply.

My lawyer's opinion was that actually I ought to be
happy that the alimony now appeared to have been
"stabilized" at a hundred a week, regardless of fluctuation in my income. I said, "Regardless of fluctuation
down, you mean. What about fluctuation up?" "Well,
you'd be getting more that way, too, Peter," he reminded
me. "But then 'stabilized' doesn't mean stabilized at all,
does it, if I should ever start to bring in some cash?"
"Why don't we cross that bridge when we come to it?

For the time being, the situation looks as good to me as it can."

But it was only a few days after the last of our hearings that a letter arrived from Maureen; admittedly, I should have destroyed it unread. Instead I tore open the envelope as though it contained an unknown manuscript of Dostoevsky's. She wished to inform me that if I "drove" her to "a breakdown," I would be the one responsible for her upkeep in a mental hospital. And that would come to something more than "a measly" hundred dollars a week—it would come to *three* times that. She had no intention of obliging me by being carted off to Bellevue. It was clearly Payne Whitney she was shooting for. And this, she told me, was no idle threat—her psychiatrist had warned her (which is why she was warning me) that she might very well have to be institutionalized one day if I were to continue to refuse "to be a man." And being a man, as the letter went on to explain, meant either coming back to her to resume our married life, and with it "a civilized role in society," or failing that, going out to Hollywood where, she informed me, anybody with the Prix de Rome in his hip pocket could make a fortune. Instead I had chosen to take that "wholly unrealistic" job at Hofstra, working *one day a week,* so that I could spend the rest of my time writing a vindictive novel about *her.* "I'm not made of steel," the letter informed me, "no matter what it pleases you to tell people about me. Publish a book like that and you will regret the consequences till your dying day."

As I begin to approach the conclusion of my story, I should point out that all the while Maureen and I were locked in this bruising, painful combat—indeed, almost from the moment of our first separation hearing in January 1963, some six months after my arrival in New York—the newspapers and the nightly television news began to depict an increasingly chaotic America and to bring news of bitter struggles for freedom and power which made my personal difficulties with alimony payments and inflexible divorce laws appear by comparison to be inconsequential. Unfortunately, these highly visible dramas of social disorder and human misery did nothing whatsoever to mitigate my obsession; to the contrary, that the most vivid and momentous history since World War Two was being made in the streets around me, day by day, *hour by hour,* only caused me to feel even more isolated by my troubles from the world at large, more embittered by the narrow and guarded life I now felt called upon to live—or able to live—because of my brief, misguided foray into matrimony. For all that I may have been attuned to the consequences of this new social and political volatility, and like so many Americans moved to pity and fear by the images of violence flashing nightly across the television screen, and by the stories of brutality and lawlessness appearing each morning on page one of the *New York Times,* I simply could not stop thinking about Maureen and her hold over me, though, to be sure, my thinking about her hold over me was, as I well knew, the very means by which she continued to hold me. Yet I couldn't stop—no scene of turbulence or act of terror that I read about in the papers could get me to feel myself any less embattled or entrapped.

In the spring of 1963, for instance, when for nights on end I could not get to sleep because of my outrage over Judge Rosenzweig's alimony decision, police dogs were turned loose on the demonstrators in Birmingham; and just about the time I began to imagine myself plunging a Hoffritz hunting knife into Maureen's evil heart, Medgar Evers was shot to death in his driveway in Mississippi. In August 1963, my nephew Abner telephoned to ask me to accompany him and his family to the civil rights demonstration in Washington; the boy, then eleven, had recently read *A Jewish Father* and given a report on it in school, likening me, his uncle (in a strained, if touching conclusion), to "men like John Steinbeck and Albert Camus." So I drove down in their car to Washington with Morris, Lenore, and the two boys, and with Abner holding my hand, listened to Martin Luther King proclaim his "dream"—on the way home I said, "You think we can get him to speak when I go to alimony jail?" "Sure," said Moe, "also Sartre and Simone de Beauvoir. They'll assemble at City Hall and sing 'Tarnopol Shall Overcome' to the mayor." I laughed along with the kids, but wondered who *would* protest, if I defied the court order to continue to support Maureen for the rest of her natural days and said I'd go to jail instead, for the rest of mine if need be. No one would protest, I realized: enlightened people everywhere would *laugh,* as though we two squabbling mates were indeed Blondie and Dagwood, or Maggie and Jiggs . . . In September, Abner was student chairman of his school's memorial service to commemorate the death of the children killed in the Birmingham church bombing—I attended, again at his invitation, but halfway through a reading by a strapping black girl of a poem by Langston Hughes, slipped out from my seat beside my sister-in-law to race over to my lawyer's office and show him the subpoena that had been served on me earlier that morning while I sat getting my teeth cleaned in the dentist's office—I had been asked to show cause why the alimony shouldn't be raised now that I was "a full-time faculty member" of Hofstra College . . . In November President Kennedy was assassinated in Dallas. I made my walk to Spielvogel's office by what must have turned out to be a ten-mile route. I wandered uptown in the most roundabout fashion, stopping wherever and whenever I saw a group of strangers clustered together on a street corner; I stood with them, shrugged and nodded at whatever they said, and then moved on. And of course I wasn't the only unattached soul wandering around like that, that day. By the time I got to Spielvogel's the waiting-room door was locked and he had gone home. Which was just as well with me: I didn't feel like "analyzing" my incredulity and shock. Shortly after I arrived at Susan's I got a phone call from my father. "I'm sorry to bother you at your friend's," he said, somewhat

timidly, "I got the name and number from Morris."
"That's okay," I said, "I was going to call you." "Do
you remember when Roosevelt died?" I did indeed—
so too had the young protagonist of *A Jewish Father*.
Didn't my father remember the scene in my novel,
where the hero recalls his own father's grieving for
FDR? It had been drawn directly from life: Joannie and
I had gone down with him to the Yonkers train station
to pay our last respects as a family to the dead president,
and had listened in awe (and with some trepidation)
to our father's muffled, husky sobbing when the loco-
motive, draped in black bunting and carrying the body
of FDR, chugged slowly through the local station on its
way up the river to Hyde Park; that summer, when we
went for a week's vacation to a hotel in South Fallsburg,
we had stopped off at Hyde Park to visit the fallen
president's grave. "Truman should be such a friend to
the Jews," my mother had said at the graveside, and
the emotion that had welled up in me when she spoke
those words came forth in a stream of tears when my
father added, "He should rest in peace, he loved the
common man." This scene too had been recalled by
the young hero of *A Jewish Father,* as he lay in bed
with his German girl friend in Frankfurt, trying to
explain to her in his five-hundred-word German vocabulary who he was and where he came from and why
his father, a good and kindly man, hated her guts . . .
Nonetheless my father had asked me on the phone that
night, "Do you remember when Roosevelt died?"—for
whatever he read of mine he could never really associate with our real life; just as I on the other hand
could no longer have a real conversation with him that
did not seem to me to be a reading from my fiction. Indeed, what he then proceeded to say to me that night
struck me as something out of a book I had already
written. And likewise what little I said to him—for this
was a father-and-son routine that went way back and
whose spirit and substance was as familiar to me as a
dialogue by Abbott and Costello, . . . which isn't to
say that being a partner in the act ever left me unaf-

fected by our patter. "You're all right?" he asked, "I don't mean to interrupt you at your friend's. You understand that?" "That's okay." "But I just wanted to be sure you're all right." "I'm all right." "This is a terrible thing. I feel for the old man—he must be taking it hard. To lose another son—and like that. Thank God there's still Bobby and Ted." "That should help a little." "Ah, what can help," moaned my father, "but you're all right?" "I'm fine." "Okay, that's the most important thing. When are you going to court again?" he asked. "Next month sometime." "What does your lawyer say? What are the prospects? They can't sock you again, can they?" "We'll see." "You got enough cash?" he asked. "I'm all right." "Look, if you need cash—" "I'm fine. I don't need anything." "Okay. Stay in touch, will you, please? We're starting to feel like a couple of lepers up here, where you're concerned." "I will, I'll be in touch." "And let me know immediately how the court thing turns out. And if you need any cash." "Okay." "And don't worry about anything. I know he's a southerner, but I got great faith in Lyndon Johnson. If it was Humphrey I'd breathe easier about Israel—but what can we do? Anyway, look, he was close to Roosevelt all those years, he had to learn something. He's going to be all right. I don't think we got anything to worry about. Do you?" "No." "I hope you're right. This is awful. And you take care of yourself. I don't want you to be strapped, you understand?" "I'm fine."

Susan and I stayed up to watch television until Mrs. Kennedy had arrived back in Washington on Air Force One. As the widow stepped from the plane onto the elevator platform, her fingers grazed the coffin, and I said, "Oh, the heroic male fantasies being stirred up around the nation." "Yours too?" asked Susan. "I'm only human," I said. In bed, with the lights off, and clasped in one another's arms, we both started to cry. "I didn't even vote for him," Susan said. "You didn't?" "I could never tell you before. I voted for Nixon." "Jesus, but you were fucked up." "Oh, Lambchop,

Jackie Kennedy wouldn't have voted for him if she hadn't been his wife. It's the way we were raised."

In September 1964, the week after Spielvogel had published his findings on my case in the *American Forum for Psychoanalytic Studies,* the Warren Commission published theirs on the assassination. Lee Harvey Oswald, alone and on his own, was responsible for the murder of President Kennedy, the commission concluded; meanwhile Spielvogel had determined that because of my upbringing I suffered from "castration anxiety" and employed "narcissism" as my "primary defense." Not everyone agreed with the findings either of the eminent jurist or of the New York analyst: so, in the great world and in the small, debate raged about the evidence, about the conclusions, about the motives and the methods of the objective investigators . . . And so those eventful years passed, with reports of disaster and cataclysm continuously coming over the wire services to remind me that I was hardly the globe's most victimized inhabitant. I had only Maureen to contend with—what if I were of draft age, or Indochinese, and had to contend with LBJ? What was my Johnson beside theirs? I watched the footage from Selma and Saigon and Santo Domingo, I told myself that *that* was awful, suffering that could not be borne . . . all of which changed nothing between my wife and me. In October 1965, when Susan and I stood in the Sheep Meadow of Central Park, trying to make out what the Reverend Coffin was saying to the thousands assembled there to protest the war, who should I see no more than fifteen feet away, but Maureen. Wearing a button pinned to her coat: "Deliver Us Dr. Spock." She was standing on the toes of her high boots, trying to see above the crowd to the speaker's platform. The last word I'd had from her was that letter warning me about the deluxe nervous breakdown that I would soon be getting billed for because of my refusal "to be a man." How nice to see she was still ambulatory—I supposed it argued for my virility. Oh, how it burned me up to see her *here!* I tapped Susan. "Well, look who's against the war." "Who?" "Tokyo Rose over there. That's my wife, Suzie Q." "That one?" she whispered. "Right, with the big heartfelt button on her breast." "Why—she's pretty, actually." "In her driven satanic way, I suppose so. Come on, you can't hear anything anyway. Let's go." "She's shorter than I thought—from your stories." "She gets taller when she stands on your toes. The bitch. Eternal marriage at home and national liberation abroad. Look," I said, motioning up to the police helicopter circling in the air over the crowd, "they've counted heads for the papers—let's get out of here." "Oh, Peter, don't be a baby—" "Look, if anything could make me *for* bombing Hanoi, she's it. With that button yet. Deliver *me,* Dr. Spock—from *her!*"

That antiwar demonstration was to be my last contact with her until the spring of 1966, when she phoned my apartment, and in an even and matter-of-fact voice said to me, "I want to talk to you about a divorce, Peter. I am willing to talk sensibly about all the necessary arrangements, but I cannot do it through that lawyer of yours. The man is a moron and Dan simply cannot get through to him."

Could it be? Were things about to change? Was it about to be *over?*

"He is not a moron, he is a perfectly competent matrimonial lawyer."

"He *is* a moron, *and* a liar, but that isn't the point, and I'm not going to waste my time arguing about it. Do you or don't you want a divorce?"

"What kind of question is that? Of course I do."

"Then why don't the two of us sit down together and work it out?"

"I don't know that we two could, 'together.' "

"I repeat: do you or do you not want a divorce?"

"Look, Maureen—"

"If you do, then I will come to your apartment after my Group tonight and we can iron this thing out like adults. It's gone on long enough and, frankly, I'm quite sick of it. I have other things to do with my life."

"Well, that's good to hear, Maureen. But we surely can't meet to settle it in my apartment."

"Where then? The street?"

"We can meet on neutral ground. We can meet at the Algonquin."

"Really, what a baby you are. Little Lord Fauntleroy from Westchester—to this very day."

"The word 'Westchester' still gets you, doesn't it? Just like 'Ivy League.' All these years in the big city and still the night watchman's daughter from Elmira."

"Ho hum. Do you want to go on insulting me, or do you want to get on with the business at hand? Truly, I couldn't care less about you or your opinion of me at this point. I'm well over that. I have a life of my own. I have my flute."

"The flute now?"

"I have my flute," she went on, "I have Group. I'm going to the New School."

"Everything but a job," I said.

"My doctor doesn't feel I can hold a job right now. I need time to think."

"What is it you 'think' about?"

"Look, do you want to score points with your cleverness, or do you want a divorce?"

"You can't come to my apartment."

"Is that your final decision? I will not talk about a serious matter like this in the street or in some hotel bar. So if that is your final decision, I am hanging up. For God's sake, Peter, I'm *not* going to eat you up."

"Look," I said, "all right, come here, if that's all we're going to talk about."

"I assure you I have nothing else to converse about with a person like you. I'll come right from Group."

That word! "What time is 'Group' over?" I asked.

"I'll be at your place at ten," she said.

"I don't like it," said Spielvogel, when I phoned with the news of the rendezvous I'd arranged, all on my own.

"I don't either," I said. "But if she changes the sub-

ject, I'll throw her out. I'll have her go. But what else
could I say? Maybe she finally means it. I can't afford
to say no."

"Well, if you said yes, it's yes."

"I *could* still call her up and get out of it, of course."

"You want to do that?"

"I want to be *divorced,* that's what I want. That's
why I thought I had better grab hold of the opportunity
while I had it. If it means risking a scene with her, well,
I'll have to risk it."

"Yes? You are up to that? You won't collapse in
tears? You won't tear your clothes off your back?"

"No, no. That's over."

"Well, then," said Spielvogel, "good luck."

"Thanks."

Maureen arrived promptly at ten P.M. She was
dressed in a pretty red wool suit—a demure jacket
over a silk blouse, and a flared skirt—smarter than anything I'd ever seen her in before; and though drawn
and creased about the eyes and at the corners of the
mouth, her face was deeply tanned—nothing urchin-
like or "beat" about this wife of mine any longer. It
turned out that she had just come back from five days in
Puerto Rico, a vacation that her Group had insisted on
her taking. *On my money, you bloodsucker. And the
suit too. Who paid for that but putz-o here!*

Maureen made a careful survey of the living room
that Susan had helped me to furnish for a few hundred
dollars. It was simple enough, but through Susan's ef-
forts, cozy and comfortable: rush matting on the floor,
a round oak country table, some unpainted dining
chairs, a desk and a lamp, bookcases, a daybed covered
with an India print, a secondhand easy chair with a
navy-blue slipcover made by Susan, along with navy-
blue curtains she'd sewn together on her machine.
"Very quaint," said Maureen superciliously, eyeing the
basket of logs by the fireplace, "and very *House and
Garden,* your color scheme."

"It'll do."

From supercilious to envious in the twinkling of an

eye—"Oh, I would think it would do quite nicely. You ought to see what I live in. It's half this size."

"The proverbial shoe box. I might have known."

"Peter," she said, drawing a breath that seemed to catch a little in her chest, "I've come here to tell you something." She sat down in the easy chair, making herself right at home.

"To tell—?"

"I'm not going to divorce you. I'm never going to divorce you."

She paused and waited for my response; so did I.

"Get out," I said.

"I have a few more things to say to you."

"I told you to get out."

"I just got here. I have no intention of—"

"You lied. You lied *again*. You told me on the phone less than three hours ago that you wanted to talk—"

"I've written a story about you. I want to read it to you. I've brought it with me in my purse. I read it to my class at the New School. The instructor has promised to try to get it published, that's how good he thinks it is. I'm sure you won't agree—you have those high Flaubertian standards, of course—but I want you to hear it. I think you have a right to before I go ahead and put it in print."

"Maureen, either get up and go, under your own steam, or I am going to throw you out."

"Lay one finger on me and I will have you put in jail. Dan Egan knows I'm here. He knows you invited me here. He didn't want me to come. He's seen you in action, Peter. He said if you laid a finger on me I was to call him immediately. And in case you think it's on your lousy hundred dollars that I went to Puerto Rico, it wasn't. It was Dan who gave me the money, when the Group said I had to get away."

"Is that a 'Group' you go to or a travel agency?"

"Ha ha."

"And the chic outfit. Therapist buy you that, or did your fellow patients pass the cup?"

"No one 'bought' it for me. Mary Egan gave it to me —the suit used to be hers. She bought it in Ireland. Don't worry, I'm not exactly living the high life on the money you earn through the sweat of your brow four hours a week at Hofstra. The Egans are my friends, the best friends I've ever had."

"Fine. You need 'em. Now scram. *Get out.*"

"I want you to hear this story," she said, reaching into her purse for the manuscript. "I want you to know that you're not the only one who has tales to tell the world about that marriage. The story—" she said, removing the folded pages from a manila envelope— "the story is called 'Dressing Up in Mommy's Clothes.' "

"Look, I'm going to call the police and have *them* throw you out of here. How will that suit Mr. Egan?"

"You call the police and I'll call Sal Valducci."

"You won't call anybody."

"Why don't you telephone your Park Avenue millionairess, Peppy? Maybe she'll send her chauffeur around to rescue you from the clutches of your terrible wife. Oh, don't worry, I know all about the bee-yoo-tiful Mrs. McCall. A bee-yoo-tiful drip—a helpless, hopeless, rich little society drip! Oh, don't worry, I've had you followed, you bastard—I know what you're up to with women!"

"You've had me *what?*"

"Followed! Trailed! Damn right I have! And it cost me a fortune! But you're not getting away scot-free, you!"

"But I'll divorce you, you bitch, any day of the week! We don't *need* detectives, we don't *need*—"

"Oh, don't you tell me what I need, dealing with someone like you! I don't have a millionairess, you know, to buy me cuff links at Cartier's! I make my way in this world on my own!"

"Shit, so do we all! And what cuff links? What the hell are you talking about now?"

But she was off and running again, and the story of "the Cartier cuff links" she would carry with her to her grave. "Oh just your speed, she is! Poor little rich girls, or little teenage students all gaga over their artistical teacher, like our friend with the braids in Wisconsin. Or that Jewish princess girl from Long Island. And how about the big blonde German nurse you were fucking in the army? A nurse—just perfect for you! Just perfect for our big mamma's boy with the tearful brown eyes! A *real* woman, and you're in tears, Peter. A real woman and—"

"Look, who set you up in business as a *real* woman? Who appointed you the representative of womankind? Stop trying to shove your bloody Kotex down my throat, Maureen—you're not a real *anything, that's* your goddam trouble! Now get out. How *dare* you have me followed!"

She didn't budge.

"I'm telling you to *go*."

"When I'm finished saying what I came here to say I will leave—and then without your assistance. Right now I'm going to read this story, because I want you to understand in no uncertain terms that two can play this writing game, two can play at this kind of slander, if it's slandering me you have in your vindictive mind. Quid pro quo, pal."

"Get—out."

"It's a short story about a writer named Paul Natapov, who unknown to the readership that takes him so *seriously*, and the highbrow judges who give him *awards*, likes to relax around the house in his wife's underwear."

"You fucking lunatic!" I cried, and pulled her up from the chair by one arm. "Now out, out, out you psychopath! *There*—there's the only thing that's *real* about you, Maureen, *your psychopathology!* It isn't the woman that drives me to tears, it's the nut! Now *out!*"

"No! No! You're only after my story," she screamed —"but tear it to shreds—I still have a carbon in Dan Egan's safe!"

Here she flung herself to the floor, where she took hold of the legs of the chair and began kicking up at me, bicycle fashion, with her high-heeled shoes.

"Get up! Cut it out! Go! Go, Maureen—or I'm going to beat your crazy head in!"

"Just you try it, mister!"

With the first crack of my hand I bloodied her delicate nose.

"Oh, my God . . ." she moaned as the blood spurted from her nostrils and down onto the jacket of her handsome suit, blood a deeper red than the nubby wool.

"And that is only the beginning! That is only the start. I'm going to beat you to an unrecognizable *pulp!*"

"Go ahead! What do I care. The story's still in Dan's safe! Go ahead! Kill me, why don't you!"

"Okay, I *will*," and cuffed her head, first one side, then the other. "If that's what you want, I will!"

"Do it!"

"Now—" I said, striking at the back of her skull with the flat of my palm, "now—" I hit her again, same spot, "*now* when you go to court, you won't have to make it all up: now you'll have something *real* to cry about to the good Judge Rosenzweig! A real beating, Maureen! The real thing, at last!" I was on the floor, astraddle her, cuffing her head with my open hand. Her blood was smeared everywhere: over her face, my hands, the rush matting, all over the front of her suit, down her silk blouse, on her bare throat. And the pages of the story were strewn around us, most of them bloodied too. The real thing—and it was marvelous. I was loving it.

I, of course, had no intention of killing her right then and there, not so long as those jails that Spielvogel had warned me about still existed. I was not even really in a rage any longer. Just enjoying myself thoroughly. All that gave me pause—oddly—was that I was ruining the suit in which she'd looked so attractive. But overlook the suit, I managed to tell myself. "I'm going to kill you, my beloved wife, I'm going to end life for you here today at the age of thirty-six, but in my own sweet time. Oh, you should have agreed to the Algonquin, Maureen."

"Go ahead——" drooling now down her chin, "my life, my life is such shit, let me die already . . ."

"Soon, soon now, very soon now you're going to be nice and dead." I hadn't to wonder for very long where to assault her next. I rolled her onto her face and began to pound with a stiff palm at her behind. The skirt of the red suit and her half-slip were hiked up in the back, and there was her little alley cat's behind, encased in tight white underpants, perhaps the very pair about which her class at the New School had heard so much of late. I beat her ass. Ten, fifteen, twenty strokes—I counted them out for her, aloud—and then while she lay there sobbing, I stood up and went to the fireplace and picked up the black wrought-iron poker that Susan had bought for me in the Village. "And now," I announced, "I am going to kill you, as promised."

No word from the floor, just a whimper.

"I'm afraid they are going to have to publish your fiction posthumously, because I am about to beat your crazy, lying head in with this poker. I want to see your brains, Maureen. I want to see those brains of yours with my own eyes. I want to step in them with my shoes —and then I'll pass them along to Science. God only knows what they'll find. Get ready, Maureen, you're about to die horribly."

I could make out now the barely audible words she was whimpering: "Kill me," she was saying, "kill me kill me——" as oblivious as I was in the first few moments to the fact that she had begun to shit into her underwear. The smell had spread around us before I saw the turds swelling the seat of her panties. "Die me," she babbled deliriously—"die me good, die me long——"

"Oh, Christ."

All at once she screamed, *"Make me dead!"*

"Maureen. Get up, Maureen. Maureen, come on now."

She opened her eyes. I wondered if she had passed over at last into total madness. To be institutionalized forever—at my expense. Ten thousand bucks more a year! I was finished!

"Maureen! *Maureen!*"

She managed a bizarre smile.

"Look." I pointed between her legs. "Don't you see? Don't you know? Look, please. You've shit all over yourself. Do you hear me, do you understand me? *Answer me!*"

She answered. "You couldn't do it."

"What?"

"You couldn't do it. You coward."

"Oh, Jesus."

"Big brave man."

"Well, at least you're yourself, Maureen. Now get *up*. Use the bathroom!"

"A yellow coward."

"Wash yourself!"

She pushed up on her elbows and tried to bring herself to her feet, but with an agonized groan, slumped backward. "I—I have to use your phone."

"After," I said, reaching down with a hand to help lift her.

"I have to phone *now*."

I gagged and averted my head. "Later—!"

"You beat me"—as though the news had just that moment reached her. "Look at this blood! My blood! You beat me like some Harlem whore!"

I had now to step away from the odor she gave off. Oh, this was just too much madness, too much all around. The tears started rolling out of me.

"Where is your phone!"

"Look, who are you calling?"

"Whoever I want! You *beat* me! You filthy pig, *you beat me!*" She had made it now up onto her knees. One blow with the poker—still in my right hand, by the way—and she would phone no one.

I watched her stumbling over her own feet to the bedroom. One shoe on and one shoe off. "No, the *bath-room!*"

"I have to phone . . ."

"You're leaking your shit all over!"

"You beat me, you monster! Is that all you can think

of? The shit on your *House and Garden* rug? Oh, you middle-class bastard, I don't believe it!"

"WASH YOURSELF!"

"NO!"

From the bedroom came the sound of the casters rolling into the worn grooves in the wooden floor. She had collapsed onto the bed, as though dropping from the George Washington Bridge.

She was dialing—and sobbing.

"Hello? Mary? It's Maureen. He beat up on me, Mary—he—hello? No? *Hello?*" With an animalish whine of frustration, she hung up. Then she was dialing again, so slowly and fitfully she might have been falling off to sleep between every other digit. "Hello? Hello, is this the Egans? Is this 201-236-2890? Isn't this Egans? Hello?" She let out another whine and threw the receiver at the hook. "I want to talk to the Egans! I want the Egans!" she cried, banging the receiver up and down now in its cradle.

I stood in the doorway to the bedroom with my poker.

"What the hell are *you* crying about?" she said, looking up at me. "You wanted to beat me, and you beat me, *so stop crying.* Why can't you be a man for a change and *do* something, instead of being such a crybaby!"

"Do what? Do *what?*"

"You can dial the Egans! You broke my fingers! *I have no feeling in my fingers!*"

"I didn't touch your fingers!"

"Then why can't I dial! DIAL FOR ME! STOP CRYING FOR FIVE SECONDS AND DIAL THE RIGHT NUMBER!"

So I did it. She told me to do it, and I did it. 201-236-2890. Ding-a-ling. Ding-a-ling.

"Hello?" a woman said.

"Hello," said I, "is this Mary Egan?"

"Yes. Who is this, please?"

"Just a moment, Maureen Tarnopol wants to talk to you." I handed my wife the phone, gagging as her aroma reached me again.

"Mary?" Maureen said. "Oh Mary," and wretchedly, she was sobbing once again. "Is, is Dan home? I have to talk to Dan, oh Mary, he, he beat me, Peter, that was him, he beat up on me, bad—"

And I, fully armed, stood by and listened. Who was I to phone for her next, the police to come and arrest me, or Valducci to write it up in the *Daily News*?

I left her to herself in the bedroom, and with a sponge and a pan of water from the kitchen began to clean the blood and feces from the rush matting on the living room floor. I kept the poker by my side—now, ridiculously, for protection.

I was on my knees, the fifteenth or twentieth wad of paper toweling in my hand, when Maureen came out of the bedroom.

"Oh, what a good little boy," she said.

"Somebody has to clean up your shit."

"Well, you're in trouble now, Peter."

I imagined that she was right—my stomach felt all at once as though *I* were the one who had just evacuated in his pants—but I pretended otherwise. "Oh, am I?"

"When Dan Egan gets home, I wouldn't want to be in your shoes."

"That remains to be seen."

"You better run, my dear. Fast and far."

"*You* better wash yourself—and then go!"

"I want a drink."

"Oh, Maureen, please. You stink!"

"I NEED A DRINK! YOU TRIED TO MURDER ME!"

"YOU'RE TRACKING SHIT EVERYWHERE!"

"Oh, that's *typical* of you!"

"DO AS I SAY! WASH YOURSELF!"

"NO!"

I brought out a bottle of bourbon and poured each of us a big drink. She took the glass and before I could say "No!" sat right down on Susan's slipcover.

"Oh, you bitch."

"Fuck it," she said, hopelessly, and threw down the drink, barroom style.

"You call me the baby, Maureen, and sit there in

your diaperful, defying me. Why must you defy me like this? *Why?*"

"Why not," she said, shrugging. "What else is there to do." She held the glass out for another shot.

I closed my eyes, I didn't want to look at her. "Maureen," I pleaded, "get out of my life, will you? Will you *please?* I beg you. How much more time are we going to use up in this madness? Not only my time but *yours.*"

"You had your chance. You chickened out."

"Why must it end in *murder?*"

Coldly: "I'm only trying to make a man out of you, Peppy, that's all."

"Oh, give it up then, will you? It's a lost cause. You've won, Maureen, okay? *You're the winner.*"

"Bullshit I am! Oh, don't you pull that cheap bullshit on me."

"But what more do you want?"

"What I don't have. Isn't that what people want? *What's coming to me.*"

"But *nothing* is coming to you. Nothing is coming to *anyone.*"

"And that also includes you, golden boy!" And leaking through her underpants, she finally, fifteen minutes after the initial request, marched off to the bathroom— where she slammed and locked the door.

I ran up and hammered on it—"And don't you try to kill yourself in there! *Do you hear me?*"

"Oh, don't worry, mister—you ain't gettin' off that easy this time!"

It was nearly midnight when she decided on her own that she was ready to leave: I had to sit and watch her try to clean the blood from the pages of "Dressing Up in Mommy's Clothes" (by Maureen J. Tarnopol) with a damp sponge; I had to find her a large paper clip and a clean manila envelope for the manuscript; I had to give her two more drinks, and then listen to myself compared, not entirely to my advantage, with Messrs. Mezik and Walker. While I went about removing the odoriferous slipcovers and bedspread to the bathroom clothes hamper, I was berated at length for my class origins and allegiances, as she understood them; my virility she analyzed while I sprinkled the rush matting with Aqua Velva. Only when I threw all the windows open and stood there in the breeze, preferring to breathe fumes from outside rather than inside the apartment, did Maureen finally get up to go. "Am I now supposed to oblige you, Peter, by jumping?" "Just airing the place—but exit however you like." "I came in through the door and I will now go out through the door." "Always the lady." "Oh, you won't get away with this!" she said, breaking into tears as she departed.

I double-locked and chained the door behind her, and immediately telephoned Spielvogel at his home.

"Yes, Mr. Tarnopol. What can I do for you?"

"I'm sorry to wake you, Dr. Spielvogel. But I thought I'd better talk to you. Tell you what happened. She came."

"Yes?"

"And I beat her up."

"Badly?"

"She's still walking."

"Well, that's good to hear."

I began to laugh. "Literally beat the shit out of her. I'd bloodied her nose, you see, and spanked her ass, and then I told her I was going to kill her with the fireplace poker, and apparently the idea excited her so, she crapped all over the apartment."

"I see."

I couldn't stop laughing. "It's a longer story than that, but that's the gist of it. She just started to shit!"

Spielvogel said, after a moment, "Well, you sound as though you had a good time."

"I did. The place still stinks, but actually, it was terrific. In retrospect, one of the high points of my life! I thought, 'This is it, I'm going to do it. She wants a beating, I'll give it to her!' The minute she came in, you see, the minute she sat down, she virtually asked for it. Do you know what she told me? 'I'm not going to divorce you, ever.' "

"I expected as much."

"Yes? Then why didn't you say something?"

"You indicated to me it was worth the risk. You assured me you wouldn't collapse, however things went."

"Well, I didn't . . . did I?"

"Did you?"

"I don't know. Before she left—after the beating—she called her lawyer. I dialed the number for her."

"You did?"

"And I cried, I'm afraid. Not torrentially, but some. I tell you, though, it wasn't for me, Doctor—believe it or not, it was for her. You should have seen that performance."

"And now what?"

"Now?"

"Now you ought to call your lawyer, yes?"

"Of course!"

"You sound a little unstrung," said Spielvogel.

"I'm really all right. I feel fine, surprisingly enough."

"Then telephone the lawyer. If you want, call me back and tell me what he said. I'll be up."

What my lawyer said was that I was to leave town immediately and stay away until he told me to come back. He informed me that for what I had done I could be placed under arrest. In my euphoria, I had neglected to think of it that way.

I called Spielvogel back to give him the news and cancel my sessions for the coming week; I said that I assumed (please no haggling, I prayed) that I wouldn't have to pay for the hours that I missed—"likewise if I get ninety days for this." "If you are incarcerated," he assured me, "I will try my best to get someone to take over your hours." Then I telephoned Susan, who had been waiting by her phone all night to learn the outcome of my meeting with Maureen—was I getting divorced? No, we were getting out of town. Pack a bag. "At this hour? How? Where?" I picked her up in a taxi and for sixty dollars (it would have gone for three sessions with Spielvogel anyway, said I to comfort myself) the driver agreed to take us down the Garden State Parkway to Atlantic City, where I had once spent two idyllic weeks as a twelve-year-old in a seaside cottage with my cousins from Camden, my father's family. There, within the first twelve hours, I had fallen in love with Sugar Wasserstrom, a sprightly curly-haired girl from New Jersey, a schoolmate of my cousin's, prematurely fitted out with breasts just that spring (April, my cousin told me from his bed that night). That I came from New York made me something like a Frenchman in Sugar's eyes; sensing this, I told lengthy stories about riding the subway, till shortly she began to fall in love with me too. Then I let her have my Gene Kelly version of "Long Ago and Far Away," crooned it right into her ear as we snuggled down the boardwalk arm in arm, and with that, I believe, I finished her off. The girl was gone. I kissed her easily a thousand times in two weeks. Atlantic City, August 1945: my kingdom by the sea. World War Two ended with Sugar in my arms—I had an erection, which she tactfully ignored, and which I did my best not to bring to her attention. Doubled-up with the pain of my unfired round, I nonetheless kept on kissing. How could I let suffering stop me at a time like this? Thus the postwar era dawned, and, at twelve, my adventures with girls had begun.

I was to stay away as long as Dan Egan remained in Chicago on business. My lawyer was waiting for Egan to get back to be absolutely certain he wasn't going to press charges for assault with intent to kill—or to attempt to persuade him not to. In the meantime, I tried to show Susan a good time. We had breakfast in bed in our boardwalk hotel. I paid ten dollars to have her profile drawn in pastels. We ate big fried scallops and visited the Steel Pier. I recalled for her the night of V-J Day, when Sugar and I and my cousins and their friends had conga-ed up and down the boardwalk (with my aunt's permission) to celebrate Japan's defeat. Was I effusive! And free with the cash! But it's my money, isn't it? Not hers—mine! I still couldn't grow appropriately serious about the grave legal consequences of my brutality, or remorseful, quite yet, about having done so coldheartedly what, as a little Jewish boy, I had been taught to despise. A man beating a woman? What was more loathsome, except a man beating a child?

The first evening I checked in on the phone with Dr. Spielvogel at the hour I ordinarily would have been arriving at his office for my appointment. "I feel like the gangster hiding out with his moll," I told him. "It sounds like it suits you," he said. "All in all it was a rewarding experience. You should have told me about barbarism a long time ago." "You seem to have taken to it very nicely on your own."

In the late afternoon of our second full day, my lawyer phoned—no, Egan wasn't back from Chicago, but his wife had called to say that Maureen had been found unconscious in her apartment and taken by ambulance to Roosevelt Hospital. She had been out for two days and there was a chance she would die.

And covered with bruises, I thought. *From my hands.*

"After she left me, she went home and tried to kill herself."

"That's what it sounds like."

"I better get up there then."

"Why?" asked the lawyer.

"Better that I'm there than that I'm not." Even I wasn't quite sure what I meant.

"The police might come around," he told me.

Valducci might come around, I thought.

"You sure you want to do this?" he asked.

"I'd better."

"Okay. But if the cops are there, call me. I'll be home all night. Don't say anything to anyone. Just call me and I'll come over."

I told Susan what had happened and that we were going back to New York. She too asked why. "She's not your business any more, Peter. She is not your concern. She's trying to drive you crazy, and you're *letting* her."

"Look, if she dies I'd better be there."

"Why?"

"I ought to be, that's all."

"But why? Because you're her 'husband'? Peter, what if the police *are* there? What if they arrest you—and put you in jail! Do you see what you've done—you could go to jail now. Oh, Lambchop, you wouldn't last an *hour* in jail."

"They're not going to put me in jail," I said, my heart quaking.

"You beat her, which was stupid enough—but this is even *more* stupid. You keep trying to do the 'manly' thing, and all you ever do is act like a child."

"Oh, do I?"

"There *is* no 'manly' thing with her. Don't you see that yet? There are only crazy things. Crazier and crazier! But you're like a little boy in a Superman suit, with some little boy's ideas about being big and strong. Every time she throws down the glove, *you* pick it up! If she phones, you answer! If she writes letters, you go crazy. If she does nothing, you go home and work on your novel about her! You're like—like her puppet! She yanks—you jump! It's—it's *pathetic*."

"Oh, is it?"

"Oh," said Susan, brokenhearted, "why did you have to hit her? Why did you do that?"

"Actually, I thought it pleased you."

"Did you really? *Pleased* me? I hated it. I just haven't told you in so many words because you were so pleased with *yourself*. But why on earth did you do it? The woman is a psychopath, you tell me that yourself. What is gained by beating up someone who isn't even responsible for what she says? What is the good of it?"

"I couldn't take any more, that's the good of it! She may be a psychopath, but I am the psychopath's husband *and I can't take any more*."

"But what about your will? You're the one who is always telling me about using my will. You're the one who got me back to college, hitting me over the head with my *will*—and then you, you who hate violence, who are sweet and civilized, turn around and do something totally out of control like *that*. Why did you let her come to your apartment to begin with?"

"To get a divorce!"

"But that's what your *lawyer* is for!"

"But she won't cooperate with my lawyer."

"And who will she cooperate with instead? You?"

"Look, I am trying to get out of a *trap*. I stepped into it back when I was twenty-five, and now I'm thirty-three and I'm *still* in it—"

"But the trap is *you*. You're the trap. When she phoned you, why didn't you just hang up? When she said no to the Algonquin, why didn't you realize—"

"Because I thought I saw a way out! Because this alimony is bleeding me dry! Because going back and forth into court to have my income scrutinized and my check stubs checked is driving me mad! Because I am four thousand dollars in debt to my brother! Because I have nothing left of a twenty-thousand-dollar advance on a book that I cannot write! Because when little Judge Rosenzweig hears I teach only two classes a week, he's ready to send me to Sing Sing! He has to sit on his ass all day to earn his keep, while coed seducers like me are out there abandoning their wives left and right—and teaching only two classes! They want me to get a paper route, Susan! They wouldn't care if I sold Good Humors! Abandoned her? She's with me day and night! The woman is unabandonable!"

"By *you*."

"Not by me—by *them!*"

"Peter, you're going wild."

"I *am* wild! I've *gone!*"

"But Lambchop," she pleaded, "*I* have money. You could use *my* money."

"I could *not*."

"But it's not even mine. It's no one's, really. It's Jamey's. It's my grandfather's. And they're all dead, and there's tons of it, *and why not?* You can pay back your brother, you can pay back the publisher and forget that novel, and go on to something new. And you can pay her whatever the court says, and then just *forget her*—oh, do forget her, once and for all, before you ruin everything. If you haven't already!"

Oh, I thought, would that be something. Pay them all off, and start in clean. *Clean!* Go back to Rome and start again . . . live with Susan and our pots of geraniums and our bottles of Frascati and our walls of books in a white-washed apartment on the Janiculum . . . get a new VW and go off on all those trips again, up through the mountains in a car with nobody grabbing at the wheel . . . *gelati* in peace in the Piazza Navona . . . marketing in peace in the Campo dei Fiori . . . dinner with friends in Trastevere, *in peace:* no ranting, no raving, no tears . . . and writing about something other than Maureen . . . oh, just think of all there is to write about in this world that is not Maureen . . . Oh, what luxe!

"We could arrange with the bank," Susan was saying, "to send her a check every month. You wouldn't even have to think about it. And, Lambchop, that would be that. You could just wipe the whole thing out, like that."

"That wouldn't be that, and I couldn't wipe anything out like that, and *that* is that. Besides, she's going to die anyway."

"Not her," said Susan, bitterly.

"Pack your stuff. Let's go."

"But why will you let her crucify you with money when there's no need for it!"

"Susan, it is difficult enough borrowing from my big brother."

"But I'm not your brother. I'm your—*me*."

"Let's go."

"No!" And angrier than I could ever have imagined her, she marched off into the bathroom adjoining our room.

Sitting on the edge of the bed, I closed my eyes and tried to think *clearly*. My limbs weakened as I did so.

She's black and blue. Couldn't they say I killed her?
Couldn't they make the case that I stuffed the pills
down her throat and left her there to croak? Can they
find fingerprints on flesh? If so, they'll find mine!

Here I experienced a cold shock on the top of the
head.

Susan was standing over me, having just poured a
glass of water, drawn from the tap, on my head. Violence breeds violence, as they say—for Susan, it was
the most violent act she had ever dared to commit in
her life.

"I hate you," she said, stamping her foot.

And on that note we packed our bags and the box of
salt water taffy I had bought for Dr. Spielvogel, and in
a rented car we departed the seaside resort where many
and many a year ago I had first encountered romantic
love: Tarnopol Returns To Face The Music In New
York.

At the hospital, blessedly, no Valducci and no police
—no handcuffs, no squad car, no flashbulbs, no TV
cameras grinding away at the mug of the prize-winning
murderer . . . Paranoid fantasy, all that—grandiose delusions for the drive up the parkway, narcissismo, with
a capital N! Guilt and ambivalence over his specialness? Oh, Spielvogel, maybe you are right in ways you
do not even know—maybe this Maureen of mine is just
the Miss America of a narcissist's dreams. I wonder:
have I chosen this She-Wolf of a woman because I am,
as you say, such a Gargantua of Self-Love? Because
secretly I *sympathize* with the poor girl's plight, know it
is only *right* that she should lie, steal, deceive, risk her
very life to have the likes of me? Because she says with
every wild shriek and desperate scheme, "Peter Tarnopol, you are the cat's meow." Is that why I can't call it
quits with her, because I'm flattered so?

No, no, no, no more fancy self-lacerating reasons
for how I am being destroyed. I can walk away all
right—only let me!

I took the elevator to the intensive-care unit and
gave my name to the young nurse at the desk there.

"How," I asked softly, "is my wife?" She told me to take a seat and wait to talk to the doctor who was presently in with Mrs. Tarnopol. "She's alive," I said. "Oh, yes," the nurse answered, reaching out kindly to touch my elbow. "Good. Great," I replied; "and there's no chance of her—" The nurse said, "You'll have to ask the doctor, Mr. Tarnopol."

Good. Great. She may die yet. And I will finally be free!

And in jail!

But I didn't do it!

Someone was tapping me on the shoulder.

"Aren't you Peter?"

A short, chubby woman, with graying hair and a pert, lined face, and neatly attired in a simple dark-blue dress and "sensible" shoes, was looking at me rather shyly; as I would eventually learn, she was only a few years older than I and a fifth-grade teacher in a Manhattan parochial school (and, astonishingly, in therapy because of a recurrent drinking problem); she looked no more threatening than the helpful librarian out of my childhood, but there in that hospital waiting room all I saw looking up at me was an enemy, Maureen's avenger. I backed off a step.

"Aren't you Peter Tarnopol the writer?"

The kindly nurse had lied. Maureen was dead. I was being placed under arrest for first-degree murder. By this policewoman. "Yes," I said, "yes, I write."

"I'm Flossie."

"Who?"

"Flossie Koerner. From Maureen's Group. I've heard so much about you."

I allowed with a weak smile that that might be so.

"I'm so glad you got here," she said. "She'll want to see you as soon as she comes around . . . She has to come around, Peter—she has to!"

"Yes, yes, don't worry now . . ."

"She loves life so," said Flossie Koerner, clutching at one of my hands. I saw now that the eyes behind the spectacles were red from weeping. With a sigh, and a sweet, an endearing smile really, she said, "She loves you so."

"Yes, well . . . we'll just have to see now . . ."

We sat down beside one another to wait for the doctor.

"I feel I practically know you," said Flossie Koerner.

"Oh, yes?"

"When I hear Maureen talk about all those places you visited in Italy, it's all so vivid, she practically makes me feel I was there, with the two of you, having lunch that day in Siena—and remember that little pensione you stayed at in Florence?"

"In Florence?"

"Across from the Boboli Gardens. That that sweet little old lady owned, the one who looked like Isak Dinesen?"

"Oh, yes."

"And the little kitty with the spaghetti sauce on its face."

"I don't remember that . . ."

"By the Trevi Fountain. In Rome."

"Don't remember . . ."

"Oh, she's so proud of you, Peter. She boasts about you like a little girl. You should hear when someone dares to criticize the tiniest thing in your book. Oh, she's like a lioness protecting one of her cubs."

"She is, eh?"

"Oh, that's finally Maureen's trademark, isn't it? If I had to sum her up in one word, that would be it: loyalty."

"Fierce loyalty," I said.

"Yes, so fierce, so determined—so full of belief and passion. Everything means so *much* to her. Oh, Peter, you should have seen her up in Elmira, at her father's funeral. It was you of course that she wanted to come with her—but she was afraid you'd misunderstand, and then she's always been so ashamed of them with you, and so she never dared to call you. I went with her

instead. She said, 'Flossie, I can't go up there alone—
but I have to be there, I have to . . .' She had to be
there, Peter, to forgive him . . . for what he did."

"I don't know about any of this. Her father died?"

"Two months ago. He had a heart attack and died
right on a bus."

"And what had he done that she had to forgive?"

"I shouldn't say."

"He was a night watchman somewhere . . . wasn't
he? Some plant in Elmira . . ."

She had taken my hand again—"When Maureen
was eleven years old . . ."

"What happened?"

"I shouldn't be the one to tell it, to tell you."

"What happened?"

"Her father . . . forced her . . . but at the graveside, Peter, she forgave him. I heard her whisper the
words myself. You can't imagine what it was like—it
went right through me. 'I forgive you, Daddy,' she
said."

"Don't you think it's strange she never told me this
herself?"

Don't you think it might even be something she happened to read about in *Tender Is the Night*? Or Krafft-
Ebing? Or in the "Hundred Neediest Cases" in the
Christmas issue of the Sunday *Times*? Don't you think
that maybe she's just trying to outdo the rest of you
girls in the Group? Sounds to me, Flossie, like a Freudian horror story for those nights you all spend roasting
marshmallows around the therapist's campfire.

"Tell *you*?" said Flossie. "She was too humiliated to
tell *anyone,* her whole life long, until she found the
Group. All her life she was terrified people would find
out, she felt so—so polluted by it. Not even her mother
knew."

"You met her mother?"

"We stayed overnight at their house. Maureen's been
back twice to see her. They spend whole days talking
about the past. Oh, she's trying so hard to forgive her
too. To forgive, to forget."

"Forget what? Forgive what?"

"Mrs. Johnson wasn't much of a mother, Peter . . ."
Flossie volunteered no lurid details, nor did I ask.

"Maureen didn't want you, above all, ever to know
any of this. We would try so hard to tell her that they
weren't her fault. I mean intellectually of course she
understood that . . . but emotionally it was just em-
bedded in her from her earliest childhood, that shame.
It was really a classic case history."

"Sounds that way."

"Oh, I *told* her you would understand."

"I believe I do."

"How can she die? How can a person with her will
to live and to struggle against the past, someone who
battles for survival the way she does, and for a future—
how can she die! The last time she came down from
Elmira, oh, she was so torn up. That's why we all
thought Puerto Rico might lift her spirits. She's such a
wonderful dancer."

"Oh?"

"But all that dancing, and all that sun, and just
getting away—and then she got back and just took a
nose dive. And did *this*. She's so proud. Too proud
sometimes, I think. That's why she takes things so much
to heart. Where you're concerned, especially. Well, you
were everything to her, you know that. You see, intellectually she knows by now how sorry you are. She
knows that girl was just a tramp, and one of those things
men do. It's partly Mr. Egan—I shouldn't say it, but
it's being in his clutches. Every time you go plead with
her to come back to you, he turns around and says no,
you're not to be trusted. Maybe I'm telling tales out of
school—but we are talking about Maureen's *life*. But
you see, he's such a devout Catholic, Mr. Egan, and Mrs.
Egan even more so—and, Peter, being Jewish you may
not understand what it means to them when a husband
did what you did. My parents would react the same
way. I grew up in that kind of atmosphere, and I know
how strong it is. They don't know how the world has
changed—they don't know about girls like that Karen,

and they don't want to know. But I see those college girls today, the kinds of morals they have, and their disrespect for everything. I know what they're capable of. They get a beeline on an attractive man old enough to be their own father—"

The doctor appeared.

Tell me she is dead. I'll go to jail forever. Just let that filthy psychopathic liar be dead. The world will be a better place.

But the news was "good." Mr. Tarnopol could go in now to see his wife. She was out of danger—she had come around; the doctor had even gotten her to speak a few words, though she was so groggy she probably hadn't understood what either of them had said. Fortunately, the doctor explained, the whiskey she had taken with the pills had made her sick and she'd thrown up most of "the toxic material" that otherwise would have killed her. The doctor warned me that her face was bruised—"Yes? It is?"—as she had apparently been lying for a good deal of the time with her mouth and nose pushed into the mattress and her own vomit. But that too was fortunate, for if she had not been on her stomach while throwing up, she probably would have strangulated. There were also bruises on the buttocks and thighs. "There are?" Yes, indicating that she had spent a part of the two days on her back as well. All that movement, the doctor said, was what had kept her alive.

I was in the clear.

But so was Maureen.

"How did they find her?" I asked the doctor.

"I found her," Flossie said.

"We have Miss Koerner to thank for that," the doctor said.

"I was calling there for days," said Flossie, "and getting no answer. And then last night she missed Group. I got suspicious, even though she sometimes doesn't come, when she gets all wrapped up in her flute or something—but I just got very suspicious, because

I knew she was in this depression since coming back from Puerto Rico. And this afternoon I couldn't stand worrying any more, and I told Sister Mary Rose that I had to leave and in the middle of an arithmetic class I just got in a taxi and came over to Maureen's and knocked on the door. I just kept knocking and then I heard Delilah and I was *sure* something was up."

"Heard who?"

"The cat. She was meowing away, but there was still no answer. So I got down on my hands and knees in the corridor there, and there's a little space under the door, because it doesn't fit right, which I always told Maureen was dangerous, and I called to the pussy and then I saw Maureen's hand hanging down over the side of the bed. I could see her fingertips almost touching the carpet. And so I ran to a neighbor and phoned the police and they broke in the door, and there she was, just in her underwear, her bra too I mean, and all this . . . mess, like the doctor said."

I wanted to find out from Flossie if a suicide note had been found, but the doctor was still with us, and so all I said was, "May I go in to see her now?"

"I think so," he said. "Just for a few minutes."

In the darkened room, in one of the half dozen criblike beds, Maureen lay with her eyes closed, under a sheet, hooked up by tubes and wires to various jugs and bottles and machines. Her nose was swollen badly, as though she'd been in a street brawl. Which she had been.

I looked silently down at her, perhaps for as long as a minute, before I realized that I had neglected to call Spielvogel. I wanted all at once to talk over with him whether I really ought to be here or not. I would like to ask him his opinion. I would like to know my own. What *was* I doing here? Rampant narcissismo—or, as Susan diagnosed it, just me being a boy again? Coming when called by my master Maureen! Oh, if so, tell me how I stop! How do I ever get to be what is described in the literature as *a man?* I had so wanted to be one, too—why then is it always beyond me? Or—could it be?—is this boy's life a man's life after all? Is this *it?* Oh, could be, I thought, could very well be that I have been expecting much too much from "maturity." This quicksand is *it*—adult life!

Maureen opened her eyes. She had to work to bring me into focus. I gave her time. Then I leaned over the bed's side bars, and with my face looming over hers, said, "This is Hell, Maureen. You are in Hell. You have been consigned to Hell for all eternity."

I meant for her to believe every word.

But she began to smile. A sardonic smile for her husband, even in extremis. Faintly, she said, "Oh, delicious, if you're here too."

"This is Hell, and I am going to look down at you for all of Time and tell you what a lying bitch you are."

"Just like back in Life Itself."

I said, shaking a fist, "What if you had died!"

For a long time she didn't answer. Then she wet her lips and said, "Oh, you would have been in such hot water."

"But *you* would have been *dead.*"

That roused her anger, *that* brought her all the way around. Yep, she was alive now. "Please, don't bullshit me. Don't give me 'Life is Sacred.' It is not sacred when you are constantly in pain." She was weeping. "My life is just pain."

You're lying, you bitch. You're lying to me, like you lie to Flossie Koerner, like you lie to your Group, like you lie to everyone. Cry, but I won't cry with you!

So swore he who aspired to manhood; but the little boy who will not die began to go to pieces.

"The pain, Maureen,"—the tears from my face plopped onto the sheet that covered her—"the pain comes from all this *lying* that you do. Lying is the form your pain *takes*. If only you would make an effort, if only you would give it up—"

"Oh, how can you? Oh get out of here, you, with your crocodile tears. Doctor," she cried feebly, "help."

Her head began to thrash around on the pillow—

"Okay," I said, "calm down, calm yourself. *Stop*." I was holding her hand.

She squeezed my fingers, clutched them and wouldn't let go. It had been a while now since we'd held hands.

"How," she whimpered, "how . . ."

"Okay, just take it easy."

"—How can you be so heartless when you see me like this?"

"I'm sorry."

"I'm only alive two minutes . . . and you're over me calling me a liar. Oh, boy," she said, just like somebody's little sister.

"I'm only trying to suggest to you how to alleviate the pain. I'm trying to tell you . . ." ah, go on with it, go on, *the lying is the source of your self-loathing*."

"Bull*shit*," she sobbed, pulling her fingers from mine. "You're trying to get out of paying the alimony. I see right through you, Peter. Oh thank God I didn't die," she moaned. "I forgot all about the alimony. That's how mortified and miserable you left me!"

"Oh, Maureen, this *is* fucking hell."

"Who said no?" said she, and exhausted now, closed her eyes, though not for oblivion, not quite yet. Only to sleep, and rise in a rage one last time.

When I came back into the waiting room there was a man with Flossie Koerner, a large blond fellow in gleaming square-toed boots and wearing a beautifully cut suit in the latest mode. He was so powerfully good-looking—charismatic is the word these days—that I did not immediately separate out the tan from the general overall glow. I thought momentarily that he might be a detective, but the only detectives who look like him are in the movies.

I got it: he too must just be back from vacationing in Puerto Rico!

He extended a hand, big and bronzed, for me to shake. Soft wide French cuffs; gold cuff links cast in the form of little microphones; strange animalish tufts of golden hair on the knuckles . . . Why, just from the wrists to the fingernails he was something to conjure

with—now how in hell did she get *him*? Surely to
catch this one would require the piss of a pregnant con-
tessa. "I'm Bill Walker," he said. "I flew here as soon as
I got the news. How is she? Is she able to talk?"

It was my predecessor, it was Walker, who had
"promised" to give up boys after the marriage, and
then had gone back on his word. My, what a dazzler
he was! In my lean and hungry Ashkenazic way I am
not a bad-looking fellow, but this was *beauty*.

"She's out of danger," I told Walker. "Oh yes, she's
talking; don't worry, she's her old self."

He flashed a smile warmer and larger than the sarcasm warranted; he didn't even see it as sarcasm, I
realized. He was just plain overjoyed to hear she was
alive.

Flossie, also in seventh heaven, pointed apprecia-
tively to the two of us. "You can't say she doesn't know
how to pick 'em."

It was a moment before I understood that I was only
being placed alongside Walker in the category of Good-
Looking Six-Footers. My face flushed—not just at the
thought that she who had picked Walker had picked
me, but that both Walker and I had picked her.

"Look, maybe we ought to have a drink afterwards,
and a little chat," Walker suggested.

"I have to run," I replied, a line that Dr. Spielvogel
would have found amusing.

Here Walker removed a billfold from the side-vented
jacket that nipped his waist and swelled over his torso,
and handed me a business card. "If you get up to
Boston," he said, "or if for any reason you want to get
in touch about Maur."

Was a pass being made? Or did he actually care about
"Maur"? "Thanks," I said. I saw from the card that
he was with a television station up there.

"Mr. Walker," said Flossie, as he started for the
nurse's desk. She was still beaming with joy at the way
things had worked out. "Mr. Walker—would you?"
She handed him a piece of scratch paper she had drawn

hastily from her purse. "It's not for me—it's for my little nephew. He collects them."

"What's his name?"

"Oh, that's so kind. His name is Bobby."

Walker signed the paper and, smiling, handed it back to her.

"Peter, Peter." She was plainly chagrined and embarrassed, and touched my hand with her fingertips. "Would *you?* I couldn't ask earlier, not with Maureen still in danger . . . you understand . . . don't you? But, now, well, I'm just so elated . . . so relieved." With that she handed me a piece of paper. Perplexed, I signed my name to it. I thought: Now all she needs is Mezik's X and Bobby will have the set. What's going on with this signature business? A trap? Flossie and Walker in cahoots with—with whom? My signature to be used for *what?* Oh, please, relax. That's paranoid madness. More narcissismo.

Says who.

"By the way," Walker told me, "I admired *A Jewish Father* tremendously. Powerful stuff. I thought you really captured the moral dilemma of the modern American Jew. When can we expect another?"

"As soon as I can shake that bitch out of my life."

Flossie couldn't (and consequently wouldn't) believe her ears.

"She's not such a bad gal, you know," said Walker, in a low stern voice, impressive now for its restraint as well as its timbre. "She happens to be one of the gamest people I know, as a matter of fact. She's been through a lot, that girl, and survived it all."

"So have I been through it, pal. At her hands!" A film of perspiration had formed on my forehead and beneath my nose—I was greatly enraged by this tribute to Maureen's guts, particularly coming from this guy.

"Oh," he said icily, and swelling a little as he spoke, "I understand you know how to take care of yourself, all right. You've got hands too, from what I hear." He lifted one corner of his mouth, a contemptuous smile . . . tinged slightly (unless I was imagining things) with a coquettish invitation. "If you can't stand the heat, as they say——"

"Gladly. *Gladly*," I interrupted. "Just go in there and tell her to unlock the kitchen door!"

Flossie, a hand now on either of us, jumped in—— "He's just upset, Mr. Walker, from everything that's happened."

"I should hope so," said Walker. He took three long strides to the nurse's desk, where he announced, "I'm Bill Walker. I spoke earlier to Dr. Maas."

"Oh. Yes. You can see her now. But only for a few minutes."

"Thank you."

"Mr. Walker?" The nurse, a stout, pretty twenty-year-old, till then all tact and good sense, turned shy and awkward suddenly. Flushing, she said to him, "Would you mind? I'm going off duty. Would you, please?" And she too produced a piece of paper for him to sign.

"Of course." Walker leaned over the desk toward the nurse. "What's your name?" he asked.

"Oh, that doesn't matter," she said, going even a deeper scarlet. "Just say 'Jackie'—that'd be enough."

Walker signed the paper, slowly, with concentration, and then headed off into the intensive-care room.

"Who's he?" I asked Flossie.

My question confused her. "Why, Maureen's husband, between you and that Mr. Mezik."

"And that's why all the world wants his autograph?" I asked sourly.

"Don't—don't you really know?"

"Know what?"

"He's the Huntley-Brinkley of Boston. He's the anchorman of their six o'clock news. He was just on the cover of the last *TV Guide*. He's the one that used to be a Shakespearean actor."

"I see."

"Peter, I'm sure it's that Maureen just didn't want to make you jealous by mentioning him right now. He's just been helping her over the rough spots, that's really all there is to it."

"And he's the one who took her to Puerto Rico."

Flossie, out of her depth completely now, and not at all sure any longer what was to be said to smooth life over for this triumvirate with whose fate she was intimately involved, shrugged and nearly wilted. We, I realized, were her own private soap opera: she was the audience to our drama, our ode-singing chorus; this was the Fortinbras my Deep Seriousness had called forth. Fair enough, I thought—this Fortinbras for this farce!

Flossie said, "Well—"

"Well, what?"

"Well, I think so, that they were together there, yes. But, believe me, he's just somebody, well, that she could turn to . . . after you did . . . what you did . . . with Karen."

"I get it," I said, and pulled on my coat.

"Oh, *please* don't be jealous. It's a brother-sister relationship more than anything else—someone close, lending her a helping hand. She's over him, I swear to you. She knew long ago that with him it would always be career-career. He can propose from now till doomsday, she'd never go back to a man whose work and talent is his everything. That's true. Please don't jump to conclusions because of him, it's not fair. Peter, you must have faith—she *will* take you back, I'm sure of it."

I passed a phone booth on my way through the hospital lobby, but didn't stop to call anyone to ask if I was about to do the wrong thing again or the right thing at last—I saw a way out (I thought) and so I ran. This time to Maureen's apartment on West Seventy-eighth Street, only a few blocks from the hospital to which the ambulance had carried her some hours earlier. There had to be evidence against her *somewhere* in that apartment—in the diary she kept, some entry describing how she had laid this trap from which I still could not escape, a confession about the urine written

in her own hand—that we would submit in evidence to
the court, to Judge Milton Rosenzweig, whose mission
it was to prevent phallic havoc from being unleashed on
the innocent and defenseless abandoned women of the
county of New York of the state of New York. Oh,
little robed Rosenzweig, he would have kept the primal
horde in line! How he bent over backwards not to show
favoritism to his, the Herculean sex . . . Prior to my
own separation hearing there had been the case of
Kriegel v. Kriegel; it was still in session when I arrived
with my lawyer at the courthouse on Centre Street.
"Your Honor," pleaded Kriegel, a heavyset businessman of fifty, addressing himself (when we entered the
courtroom) directly to the judge; his attorney, standing
beside him, made sporadic attempts to quiet his client
down, but from Kriegel's posture and tone it was clear
that he had decided to Throw Himself Upon the Mercy
of the Court. "Your Honor," he said, "I understand full
well that she lives in a walk-up. But *I* didn't tell her to
get a walk-up. That was her choice. She could get an
elevator building on what I give her a week, I assure
you. But, Your Honor, *I cannot give her what I do not
have.*" Judge Rosenzweig, up by his bootstraps from
Hell's Kitchen to N.Y.U. Law, and still a burly little
battler for all his sixty-odd years, flicked continually
with one index finger at an earlobe as he listened—as
though over the decades he had found this the best
means to prevent the bullshit addressed to the bench
from passing down into the Eustachian tube and poison-
ing his system. His humorous bantering side and his
stern contemptuous side were all right there in that
gesture. He wore the gown of a magistrate, but the
manner (and the hide) was that of an old Marine
general who had spent a lifetime hitting the beaches in
defense of Hearth and Home. "Your Honor," said
Kriegel, "I'm in the feather business, as the court knows.
That's it, sir. I buy and I sell feathers. I'm not a million-
aire like she tells you." Judge Rosenzweig, obviously
pleased by the opportunity for light banter provided
him by Mr. Kriegel, said, "Still, that's a nice suit you

got on your back. That's a Hickey-Freeman suit. Unless my eyes deceive me, that's a two-hundred-dollar suit." "Your Honor—" said Kriegel, spreading his hands deferentially before the judge, as though he held in each palm the three or four feathers that he passed on to the pillow people in the course of a day, "Your Honor, please, I would not come to court in rags." "Thank you." "I mean it, Your Honor." "Look, Kriegel, I know you. You own more colored property in Harlem than Carter has little liver pills." "Me? No, not me, Your Honor. I beg to differ with Your Honor. That's my brother. That's *Louis* Kriegel. I'm Julius." "You're not in with your brother? Are you sure that's what you want to tell the court, Mr. Kriegel?" "*In* with him?" "In with him." "Well, if so, only on the side, Your Honor." Then me. I don't shilly-shally quite so long as Kriegel; no, no Judge Rosenzweig has to badger forever a man of my calling—*and* Thomas Mann's *and* Leo Tolstoy's —to get at the Truth! "What's it mean here, Mr. Tarnopol, 'a well-known seducer of college girls'? What's that mean?" "Your Honor, I think that's an exaggeration." "You mean you're not well-known for it, or you're not a seducer of college girls?" "I'm not a 'seducer' of anybody." "So what do they mean here, do you think?" "I don't know, sir." My lawyer nods approvingly at me from the defense table; I have done just as I was instructed to in the taxi down to the courthouse: ". . . just say you don't know and you have no idea . . . make no accusations . . . don't call her a liar . . . don't call her anything but Mrs. Tarnopol . . . Rosenzweig has a great feeling for abandoned women . . . he won't permit name-calling of abandoned women in his court . . . just shrug it off, Peter, and don't admit a thing—because he is a prick of the highest order under the best of circumstances. And this isn't the best of circumstances, a teacher fucking his students." "I didn't fuck my *students*." "Fine. Good. That's just what you tell him. The judge has a granddaughter at Barnard College, her picture, Peter, is all over his chambers. Friend, this old gent is the Stalin of Divorce Court Communism: 'From each according to his ability, to each according to her need.' And with a vengeance. So watch it, Peter, will you?" On the witness stand I unfortunately forgot to. "Are you telling me then," asked Rosenzweig, "that Mr. Egan, in his affidavit prepared for Mrs. Tarnopol, has lied to the court? Is this an outright lie—yes or no?" "As stated, it is, yes." "Well, how would you state it to make it true? Mr. Tarnopol, I'm asking you a question. Give me an answer, please, so we can get on here!" "Look, I have nothing to hide—I have nothing to feel guilty about—" "Your Honor," interrupted my lawyer, even as I told the judge, "I had a love affair." "Yes?" said Rosenzweig, smiling, his ear-flicking finger poised now at the side of his head—"How nice. With whom?" "A girl in my class—whom I loved, Your Honor—a young woman." And that of course helped the cause enormously, that qualification.

But now we would all find out just who the guilty party was, just who had committed a crime against whom! "Judge Rosenzweig, you may remember that the last time I appeared before you, I brought no charges against Mrs. Tarnopol. I was cautioned by my attorney, and rightly so, to say nothing whatsoever about a fraud that had been perpetrated on me by my wife, because at that time, Your Honor, we had nothing in the way of evidence to support so damning an accusation. And we realized that, understandably, His Honor would not take kindly to unsubstantiated charges being brought against an 'abandoned' woman, who was here only to seek the protection that the law rightfully provides her. But now, Your Honor, we have the proof, a confession written in the 'abandoned' woman's own hand, that on March 1, 1959, she purchased, for two dollars and twenty-five cents in cash, several ounces of urine from a pregnant Negro woman with whom she made contact in Tompkins Square Park, on the Lower East Side of Manhattan. We have proof that she did then take said urine to a drugstore at the corner of Second Avenue and Ninth Street, and that she submitted it, in the name of 'Mrs. Peter Tarnopol,' to the pharmacist for a pregnancy test. We further have proof . . ." No matter that my lawyer had already told me that it was much too late for evidence of a fraud to do me any good, if ever it would have. I had to get the goods on her! Find something to restrain her, something that would make her quit and go away! Because I could not take any longer playing the role of the Archenemy, Divorcing Husband as Hooligan, Moth in the Fabric of Society and Housewrecker in the Householder's State!

And luck (I thought) was with me! The door broken in by the police late that afternoon had not yet been repaired—the door (just as I'd been hoping and praying) was ajar, freedom a footstep away! Bless the mismanagement of this megalopolis!

A light was burning in the apartment. I knocked very gently. I did not want to rouse the neighbors in the other two apartments on the landing. But no one appeared to check out the door of their hospitalized neighbor—bless too this city's vast indifference! The only one I aroused was a fluffy black Persian cat who slithered up to greet me as I slipped into the empty apartment. The recent acquisition named Delilah. Nothing subtle there, Maureen. *I never said I was,* she answers as I push the door shut behind me. *You want subtlety, read* The Golden Bowl. *This is life, bozo, not high art.*

More luck! There, right out on the dining table, the three-ring school notebook in which Maureen used to scribble her "thoughts"—generally in the hours immediately following a quarrel. Keeping "a record," she once warned me, of who it was that "started" all our arguments, the proof of what "a madman" I was. When we were living together at the Academy in Rome and later in Wisconsin, she used to keep the diary carefully hidden away—it was "private property," she told me, and if I should ever try to "steal" it, she would not hesitate to call in the local constabulary, be it Italian or middle western. This, though she herself had no compunction about opening mail that came for me when I wasn't home: "I'm your wife, aren't I? Why shouldn't I? Do you have something to hide from your own wife?" I expected then that, when I did get my hands on it, the diary would contain much that she wanted to hide from her husband. I rushed to the dining table, anticipating a gold mine.

I turned to an entry dated "8/15/58," written in the early weeks of our "courtship." "It's hard to sketch my own personality really, since personality implies the effect one has on others, and it's difficult to know truly what that effect is. However, I think I can guess some of this effect correctly. I have a moderately compelling personality." And on in that vein, describing her moderately compelling personality as though she were a freshman back in high school in Elmira. "At best I can be quite witty and bright and I think at best I can be a winning person . . ."

The next entry was dated "Thursday, October 9, 1959." We were by then already married, living in the little rented house in the country outside New Milford. "It's almost a year—" actually it was over a year, unless she had removed a page, the one I was looking for, describing the purchase of the urine!

—since I've written here and my life is different in every way. It's a miracle how change of circumstances can truly change your essential self. I still have awful depressions, but I truly have a more optimistic outlook and only at the blackest moments do I feel hopeless. Strangely tho', I do think more often about suicide, it seems to grow as a possibility altho' I really wouldn't do it now, I'm certain. I feel P. needs me more than ever now, tho' that of course is something he would never admit to. If it weren't for me he'd still be hiding behind his Flaubert and wouldn't know what real life was like if he fell over it. What did he ever think he was going to write *about,* knowing and believing nothing but what he read in books? Oh, he can be such a self-important snob and fool! Why does he fight me like this? I could be his Muse, if only he'd let me. Instead he treats me like the enemy. When all I've ever really wanted is for him to be the best writer in the world. It's all too brutally ironic.

That missing page, *where was it?* Why was there no mention made of what she had done to get P. to need her so!

"Madison, May 24, 1962." A month after she had discovered me in the phone booth telephoning Karen; a month after she had taken the pills and the whiskey, put a razor to her wrist, and then confessed about the urine. An entry that caused a wave of nausea to come over me as I read it. I had been leaning over the table all this time, reading on my feet; now I sat down and read three times over her revelations of May 24, 1962: "Somehow"—somehow!—

P. has a deep hostile feeling for me and when face to face the emotion I sense now is hatred. Somehow I've finally become despairing and hopeless about it all and feel utterly cheerless most of the time. I love P. and our life together—or what our life *could* be if only he weren't so neurotic, but it seems impossible. It's so joyless. His emotional coldness grows in leaps and bounds. His inability to love is positively frightening. He simply does not touch, kiss, smile, etc., let alone make love, a most unsatisfying state for me. I felt fed up with everything this morning and ready to throw it all over. Yet I know I must not lose heart. Life is not easy—P.'s naive expectations to the contrary. However, I sometimes think that to think about and try to ferret out P.'s neurosis is fruitless, for accurate as I may be, even if he were analyzed it would take years and years with a case like his, and no doubt I'd be discarded in the process anyway, though he might at last see what a madman he is. The only satisfaction is that I know perfectly well that if he does give me up, he will inevitably marry next someone who has her own talent and ego to match, who will care for that instead of him. Would he be surprised then! I almost wish it for him except I don't wish it for myself. But he is killing my feeling so that if all this coldness from him should continue, finally my star will ascend and my heart will be stony instead of his. What a pity that would be, tho'.

"West 78th St., 3/22/66." The next-to-last entry, written just three weeks earlier. After our day in court with Judge Rosenzweig. After the two go-rounds with the court-appointed referee. After Valducci. After Egan. After alimony. Four years after I'd left her, seven years after the urine. The entry, in its entirety:

> Where have I been? Why haven't I realized this? Peter doesn't *care* for me. He never did! He married me only because he thought he *had* to. My God! It seems so plain now, how could I have been mistaken before? Is this insight a product of Group? I wish I could go away. It's so degrading. I wonder if I'll ever have the luck to be in love with someone who loves me, the real me, and not some cockeyed idea of me, à la the Meziks, Walkers, and Tarnopols of this world. That seems to me now nearly all I could want, though I now know how practical I really am—or how practical it's necessary to be to survive.

And the last entry. She *had* written a suicide note, but it would seem that no one had thought to look for it in her three-ring school notebook. The handwriting, and the prose, indicated that she was already under the influence of the pills, and/or the whiskey, when she began to write her final message to herself:

> Marilyn Monroe Marilyn Monroe Marilyn Monroe Marilyn Monroe why do they do these Marilyn Monroe why to use Marilyn why to use us Marilyn

That was it. Somehow she had then made it from the table back to the bed, nearly to die there like the famous movie star herself. Nearly!

A policeman had been watching me from the door for I didn't know how long. He had his pistol drawn.

"Don't shoot!" I cried.

"Why not?" he asked. "Get up, you."

"It's okay, Officer," I said. I rose on boneless legs. I rose on air. Without even being asked I put my hands over my head. The last time I'd done that I'd been eight, a holster around my sixteen-inch waist and a Lone Ranger gun, made in Japan and hollow as a chocolate bunny, poking me in the ribs—a weapon belonging to my little pal from next door, Barry Edelstein, wearing his chaps and his sombrero, and telling me, in the accent of the Cisco Kid, "Steeck 'em up, amigo." That, by and large, was my preparation for this dangerous life I now led.

"I'm Peter Tarnopol," I hurriedly explained. "I'm Maureen Tarnopol's husband. She's the one who lives here. We're separated. Legally, legally. I just came from the hospital. I came to get my wife's toothbrush and some things. She's my wife still, you see; she's in the hospital—"

"I know who's in the hospital."

"Yes, well, I'm her husband. The door was open. I thought I better stay here until I can get it fixed. Anybody could walk right in. I was sitting here. Reading. I was going to call a locksmith."

The cop just stood there, pointing his pistol. I should never have told him we were separated. I should never have told Rosenzweig I'd had "a love affair" with a student. I should never have gotten involved with Maureen. Yes, that was my biggest mistake.

I said some more words about a locksmith.

"He's on his way," the cop told me.

"Yes? He is? Good. Great. Look, if you still don't believe me, I have a driver's license."

"On you?"

"Yes, yes, in my wallet. May I reach for my wallet?"

"All right, never mind, it's okay . . . just got to be careful," he mumbled, and lowering his pistol, took a step into the room. "I just went down for a Coke. I seen she had her own, but I didn't want to take it. That ain't right."

"Oh," said I, as he dropped the pistol into his holster, "you should have."

"Fuckin' locksmith." He looked at his watch.

When he stepped all the way into the apartment I

saw how very young he was: a pug-nosed kid off the subway, with a gun and a badge and dressed up in a blue uniform. Not so unlike Barry Edelstein as I'd thought while the pistol was pointed at my head. Now he wouldn't engage my eyes directly, embarrassed it seemed for having drawn the gun, movie style, or for having spoken obscenely to an innocent man, or, most likely, for having been discovered by me away from his post. Yet another member of the sex, abashed to be revealed as unequal to his task.

"Well," I said, closing the three-ring notebook and tucking it under my arm, "I'll just get those things now, and be off—"

"Hey," he said, motioning to the bedroom, "don't worry about the mattress in there. I just couldn't take the stink no more, so I washed it out. That's how come it's wet like that. Ajax and a little Mr. Clean, and that did it. Don't worry—it won't leave no mark when it dries."

"Well, thank you. That was very nice of you."

He shrugged. "I put all the stuff back in the kitchen, under the sink there."

"Fine."

"That Mr. Clean is some stuff."

"I know. I've heard them say that. I'll just get a few things and go."

We were friends now. He asked, "What is the missus anyway? An actress?"

"Well . . . yes."

"On TV?"

"No, no, just around."

"What? Broadway?"

"No, no, not yet anyway."

"Well, that takes time, don't it? She shouldn't be discouraged."

I went into Maureen's bedroom, a tiny cell just big enough for a bed and a night table with a lamp on it. Because the closet door could only be opened halfway before it banged against the foot of the bed, I had to reach blindly around inside until I came up with a nightdress that was hanging on a hook. "Ah," I said, nice and loud, "*here* it is—right . . . where . . . she said!" To complete the charade, I decided to open and then shut loudly the drawer to the little night table.

A can opener. In the drawer there was a can opener. I did not immediately deduce its function. That is, I thought it must be there to open cans.

Let me describe the instrument. The can-opening device itself is screwed to a smooth, grainy-looking wooden handle, about two and a half inches around and some five inches long, tapering slightly to its blunt end. The opening device consists of a square aluminum case, approximately the size of a cigarette lighter, housing on its underside a small metal tooth and a little ridged gear; projecting upward from the top side of the case is an inch-long shaft to which is attached a smaller wooden handle, about three inches long. Placing the can opener horizontally over the edge of the can, you press the pointed metal tooth down into the rim, and proceed to open the can by holding the longer handle in one hand, and rotating the smaller handle with the other; this causes the tooth to travel around the rim until it has severed the top of the can from the cylinder. It is a type of can opener that you can buy in practically any hardware store for between a dollar and a dollar and a quarter. I have priced them since. They are manufactured by the Eglund Co., Inc., of Burlington, Vermont—their "No. 5 Junior" model. I have Maureen's here on my desk as I write.

"How ya' doin'?" the cop called.

"Oh, fine."

I slammed the drawer shut, having first deposited the No. 5 Junior in my pocket.

"So that's it," I said, coming back around into the living room, Delilah glued to my trouser cuff.

"Mattress look okay to you?"

"Great. Perfect. Thanks again. I'll be off, you know —I'll leave the locksmith to you then, right?"

I was one flight down and flying, when the young cop appeared at the landing over my head. "Hey!"

"What!"

"Toothbrush!"

"Oh!"

"Here!"

I caught it and kept going.

The taxi I flagged down to take me crosstown to Susan's was one of those fitted out like the prison cell of an enterprising convict or the den of an adolescent boy: framed family photographs lined up on the windshield, a large round alarm clock strapped atop the meter, and some ten or fifteen sharpened Eberhard pencils jammed upright in a white plastic cup fastened by a system of thick elastic bands to the grill separating the passenger in the back seat from the driver up front. The grill was itself festooned with blue-and-white tassels, and an arrangement of gold-headed upholstery tacks stuck into the roof above the driver's head spelled out "Gary, Tina & Roz"—most likely the names of the snappily dressed children smiling out from the family photographs of weddings and bar mitzvahs. The driver, an elderly man, must have been their grandfather.

Ordinarily I suppose I would have commented, like every other passenger, on the elaborate decor. But all I could look at and think about then was the Eglund Company's No. 5 Junior can opener. Holding the aluminum end in my left hand, I passed the larger handle through a circle formed out of the thumb and index finger of my right hand; then, wrapping the other three fingers loosely around it, I moved the handle slowly down the channel.

Next I placed the handle of the can opener between my thighs and crossed one leg over the other, locking it in place. Only the square metallic opening device, with its sharp little tooth facing up, poked out from between my legs.

The cab veered sharply over to the curb.

"Get out," the driver said.

"Do what?"

He was glaring at me through the grill, a little man, with dark pouches under his eyes and bushy gray eyebrows, wearing a heavy wool sweater under a suit. His voice quivered with rage—"Get the hell out! None of that stuff in my cab!"

"None of what? I'm not *doing* anything."

"Get out, I told you! Out, you, before I use the tire iron on your head!"

"What do you think I was doing, for Christ's sake!"

But by now I was on the sidewalk.

"You filthy son of a bitch!" he cried, and drove off.

Clutching the can opener in my pocket and holding the diary in my lap, I eventually made it to Susan's—though not without further incident. As soon as I had gotten settled in the back seat of a second cab, the driver, this one a young fellow with a wispy yellow beard, fixed me in the rearview mirror and said, "Hey, Peter Tarnopol." "What's that?" "You're Peter Tarnopol—right?" "Wrong." "You look like him." "Never heard of him." "Come on, you're putting me on, man. You're him. You're really him. Wow, man. What a coincidence. I just had Jimmy Baldwin in here last night." "Who's he?" "The writer, man. You're putting me on. You know who else I had in here?" I didn't answer. "Mailer. I get all you fuckin' guys. I had another guy in here, I swear to fuck he musta weighed eighty-two pounds. This tall string bean with a crew cut. I took him out to Kennedy. You know who it was?" "Who?" "Fuckin' Beckett. You know how I know it was him? I said to him, 'You're Samuel Beckett, man.' And you know what he said? He says, 'No, I'm Vladimir Nabokov.' What do you think of that?" "Maybe it *was* Vladimir Nabokov." "No, no, I never had Nabokov. Not yet. What are you writin' these days, Tarnopol?" "Checks." We had arrived at Susan's building. "Right here," I told him, "that awning." "Hey, you live all right, Tarnopol. You guys do okay, you know that?" I paid him, while he shook his head in wonderment; as I was leaving the taxi, he said, "Watch this, I'll turn the corner and pick up fuckin' Malamud. I wouldn't put it past me."

"Good evening, sir," said Susan's elevator man, appearing out of nowhere and startling me in the lobby, just as I had made it gravely past the doorman and was removing the can opener from my pocket . . . But once inside the apartment I pulled it from my pocket again and cried out, "Wait'll you see what *I* got!"

"She's alive?" asked Susan.

"And kicking."

"—the police?"

"Weren't there. Look—look at this!"

"It's a can opener."

"It's also what she masturbates with! Look! Look at this nice sharp metal tooth. How she must love that protruding out of her—how she must love to look down at that!"

"Oh, Peter, where ever did you—"

"From her apartment—next to her bed."

Out popped the tear.

"What are you crying about? It's perfect—don't you see? Just what she thinks a man is—a torture device. A surgical instrument!"

"But where—"

"I told you. From her bedside table!"

"You stole it, from her apartment?"

"Yes!"

I described to her then in detail my adventures at the hospital and after.

When I finished she turned and went off to the kitchen. I followed her and stood by the stove as she began to brew herself a cup of Ovaltine.

"Look, you yourself tell me I shouldn't be defenseless with her."

She would not speak to me.

"I am only doing what I have to do, Susan, to get sprung from this trap."

No reply.

"I am tired, you see, of being guilty of sex crimes in the eyes of every hypocrite, lunatic, and—"

"But the only one who thinks you're guilty of *anything* is *you.*"

"Yes? Is that why they've got me supporting her for the rest of my life, a woman I was married to for three years? A woman who bore me no children? Is that why they will not let me get divorced? Is that why I am being punished like this, Susan? Because *I* think I'm guilty? *I think I'm innocent!*"

"Then if you do, why do you need to steal something like *that*?"

"Because nobody believes me!"

"*I* believe you."

"But you are not the judge in this case! You are not the sovereign state of New York! I have got to get her fangs out of my neck! Before I drown in this rage!"

"But what good is a can opener? How do you even know it is what you say it is? You don't! Probably, Peter, she just uses it *to open cans*."

"In her bedroom?"

"Yes! People can open cans in bedrooms."

"And they can play with themselves in the kitchen, but usually it's the other way around. It's a dildo, Susan—whether you like that idea or not. Maureen's very own surrogate dick!"

"And so what if it is? What business is it of yours? It's not your affair!"

"Oh, isn't it? Then why is everything in my life *her* affair? And Judge Rosenzweig's affair! And the affair of her Group! And the affair of her class at the New School! I get caught with Karen and the judge has me down for Lucifer. She, on the other hand, fucks household utensils—"

"But you cannot bring this thing into court—they'd think you were crazy. It *is* crazy. Don't you see that? What do you think you would accomplish by waving it around in the judge's face? *What?*"

"But I have her diary, too!"

"But you told me you read it—you said there's nothing there."

"I haven't read it *all*."

"But if you do, it's only going to make you crazier than you are now!"

"I AM NOT THE ONE WHO'S CRAZY!"

Said Susan, "You *both* are. And I can't take it. Because I'll go mad too. I cannot drink any more Ovaltine in one day! Oh, Peter, I can't take you any more like this. I can't *stand* you this way. Look at you, with that thing. Oh, throw it away!"

"No! No! This way you can't stand me is the way that I am! This is the way that I am going to be—until I win!"

"Win *what?*"

"My balls back, Susan!"

"Oh, how can you use that cheap expression? Oh, Lambchop, you're a sensible, sweet, civilized, darling man. And I love you as you are!"

"But I don't."

"But you *should.* What possible use can those—"

"I don't know yet! Maybe none! Maybe some! But I'm going to find out! And if you don't like it, I'll leave. Is that what you want?"

She shrugged. ". . . if this is the way you're going to be—"

"This is the way I am going to be! And *have* to be! It's too rough out there, Susan, to be *darling!*"

". . . then I think you better."

"Leave?"

". . . Yes."

"Good! Fine!" I said, utterly astonished. "Then I'll go!"

To which she made no reply.

So I left, taking Maureen's can opener and diary with me.

I spent the rest of the night back in the bedroom of my own apartment—the living room faintly redolent still of Maureen's bowel movement—reading the diary, a dreary document, as it turned out, about as interesting on the subject of a woman's life as "Dixie Dugan." The sporadic entries rambled on without focus, or stopped abruptly in the midst of a sentence or a word, and the prose owed everything to the "Dear Diary" school, the pure expression of self-delusion and unknowingness. In one so cunning, how bizarre! But then writers are forever disappointing readers by being so "different" from their work, though not usually because the work fails to be as compelling as the person. I was mildly surprised —but only mildly—by the persistence with which Maureen had secretly nursed the idea of "a writing career," or at least tantalized herself with it in her semiconscious way, throughout the years of our marriage. Entries began: "I won't apologize this time for not writing for now I see that even V. Woolf let her journal go for months at a time." And: "I must set down my strange experience in New Milford this morning which I'm sure would make a good story, if one could write it in just the right way." And: "I realized today for the first time—how naive of me!—that if I were to write a story, or a novel, that was published, P. would have awful competitive feelings. Could I do that to him? No wonder I'm so reluctant to launch upon a writing career—it all has to do with sparing his ego."

Along the way there were a dozen or so newspaper clippings stapled or Scotch-taped to the loose-leaf pages, most of them about me and my work, dating back to the publication of my novel in the first year of our marriage. Pasted neatly on one page there was an article clipped from the *Times* when Faulkner died, a reprint of his windy Nobel Prize speech. Maureen had underlined the final grandiose paragraph: "The poet's voice need not merely be the record of man, it can be one of the props, the pillars to help him endure and prevail." Beside it she had penciled a bit of marginalia to make the head swim: "P. and me?"

To me the most intriguing entry recounted her visit two years earlier to Dr. Spielvogel's office. She had gone there to talk to him about "how to get Peter back," or so Spielvogel had reported it to me, following the call on him, which she had made unannounced at the end of the day. According to Spielvogel, he had told her that he did not think getting me back was possible any longer—to which she had, by his report, replied, "But I can do anything. I can play it weak or strong, whichever will work."

Maureen's version:

April 29, 1964

I must record my conversation with Spielvogel yesterday, for I don't want to forget any more than is inevitable. He said I had made one serious mistake: confessing to P. I realize that too. If I had not been so desolated by learning about him and that little student of his, I would never have made such an unforgivable error. If I had never told him we would still be together. That gave him just the sort of excuse he could use against me. Spielvogel agrees. Spielvogel said that he thinks he knows what course Peter would take if we were to come back together and remain married, and I understood him to mean that he would be constantly unfaithful to me with one student after another. S. has rather settled theories about the psyche and neuroses of the artist and it's hard to know whether he's right or not. He advised me very directly to "work through" my feelings for Peter and to find someone else. I told him I felt too old but he said not to think in terms of chronological age but how I look. He thinks I'm "charming and attractive" and "gaminlike." S.'s feeling is that it's impossible to be married to an actor or writer happily, that in other words, "they're all alike." He gave Lord Byron and Marlon Brando as examples, but is Peter really like that? I'm possessed today with these thoughts, I can hardly do anything. He emphasized that I wasn't facing the extreme narcissism of the writer, that he focuses such an enormous amount of attention on himself. I told him my own theory that I worked out in Group that P.'s unfaithfulness to me is the result of the fact that he felt me so high-powered that he felt it necessary to "practice" with his little student. That he could only really feel like a potent male with such an unthreatening nothing. S. seemed very interested in my theory. S. said that Peter goes back over and over again to the confession in order to rationalize his inability to love me, or to love anyone for that matter. S. indicates that this lovelessness is characteristic of the narcissistic type. I wonder if S. is fitting Peter into a preconceived mold, tho' it does make great sense when I think of how rejecting of me P. has been from the very beginning.

I thought, upon coming to the end of that entry, "What a thing—everybody in the world can write fiction about that marriage, except me! Oh, Maureen, you should never have spared my ego your writing career—better you should have written down everything in that head of yours and spared me all this reality! On the printed page, instead of on my hide! Oh, my one and only and eternal wife, is this what you really think? Believe? Do these words describe to you who and what you are? It's almost enough to make a person feel sorry for you. Some person, somewhere."

During the night I paused at times in reading Maureen to read Faulkner. "I believe that man will not merely endure: he will prevail. He is immortal, not because he alone among creatures has an inexhaustible voice, but because he has a soul, a spirit capable of compassion and sacrifice and endurance." I read that Nobel Prize speech from beginning to end, and I thought, "And what the hell are *you* talking about? How could you write *The Sound and the Fury,* how could you write *The Hamlet,* how could you write about Temple Drake and Popeye, and write *that?*"

Intermittently I examined the No. 5 Junior can opener, Maureen's corncob. At one point I examined my own corncob. Endure? Prevail? We are lucky, sir, that we can get our shoes on in the morning. That's what *I* would have said to those Swedes! (If they'd asked.)

Oh, there was bitterness in me that night! And much hatred. But what was I to do with it? Or with the can opener? Or with the diary confessing to a "confession"? What was *I* supposed to do to prevail? Not "man," but Tarnopol!

The answer was nothing. "Tolerate it," said Spielvogel. "Lambchop," said Susan, "forget it." "Face facts," my lawyer said, "you're the man and she's the woman." "Are you still sure of that?" I said. "Piss standing up and you're the man." "I'll sit down." "It's too late," he told me.

Six months later, on a Sunday morning, only minutes
after I had returned from breakfast and the *Times* at
Susan's and was settling down at my desk to work—the
liquor carton had just been dragged from the closet,
and I was stirring around in that dispiriting accumulation of disconnected beginnings, middles, and endings
—Flossie Koerner telephoned my apartment to tell me
that Maureen was dead.

I didn't believe her. I thought it was a ruse cooked
up by Maureen to get me to say something into the
telephone that could be tape-recorded and used to in-
criminate me in court. I thought, "She's going back in
again for more alimony—this is another trick." All I
had to say was, "Maureen dead? Great!" or anything
even *remotely* resembling that for Judge Rosenzweig or
one of his lieutenants to reason that I was an incorrigible
enemy of the social order still, my unbridled and bar-
baric male libido in need of yet stronger disciplinary
action.

"Dead?"'

"Yes. She was killed in Cambridge, Massachusetts.
At five in the morning."

"Who killed her?"

"The car hit a tree. Bill Walker was driving. Oh,
Peter," said Flossie, with a rasping sob, "she loved
life so."

"And she's dead . . . ?" I had begun to tremble.

"Instantly. At least she didn't suffer . . . Oh, why
didn't she have the seat belt on?"

"What happened to Walker?"

"Nothing bad. A cut. But his whole Porsche was
destroyed. Her head . . . her head . . ."

"Yes, what?"

"Hit the windshield. Oh, I knew she shouldn't go up
there. The Group tried to stop her, but she was just so
terribly hurt."

"By what? Over what?"

"What he did with the shirt."

"What shirt?"

"Oh . . . I hate to say it . . . given who he is . . . and I'm not accusing him . . ."

"What is it, Flossie?"

"Peter, Bill Walker is a bisexual person. Maureen herself didn't even know. She—" She broke down sobbing here. I meanwhile had to clamp my mouth shut to stop my teeth from chattering. "She—" said Flossie, starting in again, "she gave him this beautiful, expensive lisle shirt, you know for a present? And it didn't fit—or so he said afterward—and instead of returning it for a bigger size, he gave it to a man he knows. And she went up to tell him what she thought of that kind of behavior, to have a frank confrontation . . . And they must have been drinking late, or something. They had been to a party . . ."

"Yes?"

"I'm not blaming anyone," said Flossie. "I'm sure it was nobody's deliberate fault."

Was it true then? Dead? Really dead? Dead in the sense of nonexistent? Dead as the dead are dead? Dead as in death? Dead as in dead men tell no tales? Maureen is *dead*? *Dead* dead? Deceased? Extinct? Called to her eternal rest, the miserable bitch? Crossed the bar?

"Where's the body?" I asked.

"In Boston. In a morgue. I guess . . . I think . . . you'll have to go get her, Peter. And take her home to Elmira. Someone will have to call her mother . . . Oh, Peter, you'll have to deal with Mrs. Johnson—I couldn't."

Peter get her? Peter take her to Elmira? Peter deal with her mother? Why, if it's true, Flossie, if this isn't the most brilliant bit of dissimulation yet staged and directed by Maureen Tarnopol, if you are not the best supporting soap-opera actress of the Psychopathic Broadcasting Network, then Peter *leave* her. Why Peter even bother with her? Peter let her lie there and rot!

As I still didn't know for sure whether our conversation was being recorded for Judge Rosenzweig's edification, I said, "Of course I'll get her, Flossie. Do you want to come with me?"

"I'll do anything at all. I loved her so. And she loved you, more than you could ever know—" But here a noise came out of Flossie that struck me as indistinguishable from the wail of an animal over the carcass of its mate.

I knew then that I wasn't being had. Or probably wasn't.

I was on the phone with Flossie for five minutes more; as soon as I could get her to hang up—with the promise that I would be over at her apartment to make further plans within the hour—I telephoned my lawyer at his weekend place in the country.

"I take it that I am no longer married. Is that correct? Now tell me, is that right?"

"You are a widower, friend."

"And there's no two ways about it, is there? This is *it*."

"This is it. Dead is dead."

"In New York State?"

"In New York State."

Next I telephoned Susan, whom I had left only half an hour earlier.

"Do you want me to come down?" she asked, when she could ask anything.

"No. No. Stay where you are. I have to make some more phone calls, then I'll call you back. I have to go to Flossie Koerner's. I'll have to go up to Boston with her."

"Why?"

"To get Maureen."

"*Why?*"

"Look, I'll call you later."

"You sure you don't want me to come?"

"No, no, please. I'm fine. I'm shaking a little but aside from that everything's under control. I'm all right." But my teeth were chattering still, and there seemed nothing I could do to stop them.

Next, Spielvogel. Susan arrived in the middle of

the call: had she flown from Seventy-ninth Street? Or had I just gone blank there at my desk for ten minutes? "I had to come," she whispered, touching my cheek with her hand. "I'll just sit here."

"—Dr. Spielvogel, I'm sorry to bother you at home. But something has happened. At least I am assuming that it happened because somebody told me that it happened. This is not the product of imagination, at least not mine. Flossie Koerner called, Maureen's friend from group therapy. Maureen is dead. She was killed in Boston at five in the morning. In a car crash. She's dead."

Spielvogel's voice came back loud and clear. "My goodness."

"Driving with Walker. She went through the windshield. Killed instantly. Remember what I told you, how she used to carry on in the car in Italy? How she loved grabbing that wheel? You thought I was exaggerating when I said she used to actually try to kill us both, that she would *say* as much. But I wasn't! Christ! Oh, Christ! She could go wild, like a tiger—in that little VW! I told you how she almost killed us on that mountain when we were driving from Sorrento—do you remember? Well, she finally did it. *Only this time I wasn't there.*"

"Of course," Spielvogel reminded me, "you don't know all the details quite yet."

"No, no. Just that she's dead. Unless they're lying."

"Who would be lying?"

"I don't know any more. But things like this don't happen. This is as unlikely as the way I got into it. Now the whole *thing* doesn't make any sense."

"A violent woman, she died violently."

"Oh, look, a lot of people who aren't violent die violently and a lot of violent people live long, happy lives. Don't you see—it could be a ruse, some new little fiction of hers—"

"Designed to do what?"

"For the alimony. To catch me—off guard—*again!*"

"No, I wouldn't think so. Caught you are not. Released is the word you are looking for. You have been released."

"Free," I said.

"That I don't know about," said Spielvogel, "but certainly released."

Next I dialed my brother's number. Susan hadn't yet taken off her coat. She was sitting in a straight chair by the wall with her hands folded neatly in her lap like a kindergartener. At the sight of her in that posture an alarm went off in me, but too much else was happening to pay more than peripheral attention to its meaning. *Only why hasn't she taken off her coat?*

"Morris?"

"Yes."

"Maureen's dead."

"Good," my brother said.

Oh, they will get us for that—but who, who will get us?

I have been released.

Next I got her mother's number from Elmira information.

"Mrs. Charles Johnson?"

"That's right."

"This is Peter Tarnopol calling. I'm afraid I have some bad news. Maureen is dead. She was killed in a car crash."

"Well, that's what usually comes of runnin' around. I could have predicted it. When did this happen?"

"Early this morning."

"And how many'd she take with her?"

"None. Nobody. She was the only one killed."

"And what'd you say your name was?"

"Peter Tarnopol. I was her husband."

"Oh, is that so? Which are you? Number one, two, three, four, or five?"

"Three. There were only three."

"Well, generally in this family there is only one. Good of you to call, Mr. Tarnopol."

"—What about the funeral?"

But she'd hung up.

Finally I telephoned Yonkers. The man whose son I am began to choke with emotion when he heard the news—you would have thought it was somebody he had cared for. "What an ending," he said. "Oh, what an ending for that little person."

My mother listened in silence on the extension. Her first words were, "You're all right?"

"I'm doing all right, yes. I think so."

"When's the funeral?" asked my father, recovered now, and into his domain, the practical arrangements. "Do you want us to come?"

"The funeral—I tell you, I haven't had time to think through the funeral. I think she always wanted to be cremated. I don't know yet where . . ."

"Maybe he's not even going," my mother said to my father.

"You're not going?" my father asked. "You think that's a good idea, not going?" I could envision him reaching up to squeeze his temples with his free hand, a headache having all at once boiled up in his skull.

"Dad, I haven't thought it through yet. Okay? One thing at a time."

"Be smart," my father said. "Listen to me. You go. Wear a dark suit, put in an appearance, and that'll be that."

"Let him decide," my mother told him.

"He decided to marry her without my advice—it wouldn't hurt now if he listened when I told him how to stick her in the ground!"

"He says she wanted to be cremated anyway. They put the ashes in the ground, Peter?"

"They scatter them, they scatter them—I don't know what they do to them. I'm new to this, you know."

"That's why I'm telling you," my father said, "to *listen*. You're new to *everything*. I'm seventy-two and I'm *not*. You go to the funeral, Peter. That way nobody can ever call you pisher."

"I think they'll call me pisher either way, those disposed in that direction."

"But they can never say you weren't there. Listen

to me, Peter, please—I've lived a life. Stop being out
there on your own, *please*. You haven't listened to anybody since you were four-and-a-half years old and
went off to kindergarten to conquer the world. You
were four-and-a-half years old and you thought you
were the president of General Motors. What about the
day there was that terrible thunderstorm? Four-and-a-
half years old—"

"Look, Dad, not now—"

"Tell him," he said to my mother, "tell him how long
this has been going on with him."

"Oh, not now," said my mother, beginning to cry.

But he was fired up; miraculously, I was in the clear,
and so he could finally let me know just how angry he
was that I had squandered my familial inheritance of
industriousness and stamina and pragmatism—all those
lessons learned from him on Saturdays in the store,
why had I tossed them to the wind? "No, no," he would
say to me from atop the ladder in the stockroom, as I
handed up to him the boxes of Interwoven socks, "no,
not like that, Peppy—you're making it hard for yourself. Like this! Get it right! Always do a job right.
Doing it wrong, son, don't make sense at all!" All the
entrepreneurial good sense, all that training in manage-
ment and order, why hadn't I seen it for the wisdom that
it was? Why couldn't a haberdashery store be a source
of sacred knowledge too? Why, Peppy? Not profound
enough to suit you? All too banal and unmomentous?
Oh yes, what are Flagg Brothers shoes and Hickok
belts and Swank tie clasps to a unique artistic spirit
like yours!

"—it was a terrible thunderstorm," he was saying,
"there was thunder and everything, and you were in
school, Peter, in kindergarten. Four-and-a-half years
old and you wouldn't let anybody even take you, after
the first week, not even Joannie. No, *you* had to do it
alone. You don't remember this, huh?"

"No, no."

"Well, it was raining, I'll tell you. And so your
mother got your little raincoat, and your rainhat and

your rubbers, and she ran to the school at the end of the day so you shouldn't have to get soaked coming home. And you don't remember what you did?"

Well, at last I was crying too. "No, no, I guess I don't."

"You *balked*. You gave her a look that could have killed."

"I did?"

"Oh, you did! And told her off. 'Go home!' you told her. Four-and-a-half years old! And would not even so much as put on the *hat*. Walked out, right past her, and home in the storm, with her chasing after you. Everything you had to do by yourself, to show what a big shot you were—and look, Peppy, look what has come of it! At least now listen to your family *once*."

"Okay, I will," I said, hanging up.

Then, eyes leaking, teeth chattering, not at all the picture of a man whose nemesis has ceased to exist and who once again is his own lord and master, I turned to Susan, still sitting there huddled up in her coat, looking, to my abashment, as helpless as the day I had found her. Sitting there *waiting*. Oh, my God, I thought—now you. You being you! And *me!* This me who is me being me and none other!

ABOUT THE AUTHOR

PHILIP ROTH was born in New Jersey in 1933. He is the author of seven previous books: *Goodbye, Columbus* (1959), which won the National Book Award for Fiction; *Letting Go* (1962), *When She Was Good* (1967), *Portnoy's Complaint* (1969), *Our Gang* (1971), *The Breast* (1972) and *The Great American Novel* (1973). His shorter fiction has been widely reprinted in anthologies both in this country and abroad, and stories have been reprinted in Martha Foley's annual collection, *The Best American Short Stories,* and in the *O. Henry Prize Story* annuals. Mr. Roth has served as a visiting lecturer on the faculties of several American universities. In 1970 he was elected a member of the National Institute of Arts and Letters.

by Philip Roth

Winner of the National Book Award, creator of major bestsellers and recognized as one of America's foremost novelists, Philip Roth continues to dazzle readers with his amazing change of pace. Each book is unlike any other. Each book delves into another aspect of contemporary foibles. Yet all books reflect the exuberant human spirit that is distinctively Philip Roth.

Bantam Book Catalog

It lists over a thousand money-saving best-sellers originally priced from $3.75 to $15.00 —bestsellers that are yours now for as little as 50¢ to $2.95!

The catalog gives you a great opportunity to build your own private library at huge savings!

So don't delay any longer—send us your name and address and 10¢ (to help defray postage and handling costs).